WRITING PYNCHON

Also by Alec McHoul

TELLING HOW TEXTS TALK: Essays on Reading and Ethnomethodology
WITTGENSTEIN ON CERTAINTY AND THE PROBLEM OF RULE IN SOCIAL SCIENCE

Also by David Wills

SELF DE(CON)STRUCT: Writing and the Surrealist Text
SCREEN/PLAY: Derrida and Film Theory (*with Peter Brunette*)

Writing Pynchon
Strategies in Fictional Analysis

ALEC McHOUL
Senior Lecturer, Communication Studies,
Murdoch University, Western Australia

and

DAVID WILLS
Associate Professor, French and Italian,
Louisiana State University

© Alec McHoul and David Wills 1990

All rights reserved. No reproduction, copy or transmission of this publication may be made without written permission.

No paragraph of this publication may be reproduced, copied or transmitted save with written permission or in accordance with the provisions of the Copyright Act 1956 (as amended), or under the terms of any licence permitting limited copying issued by the Copyright Licensing Agency, 33–4 Alfred Place, London WC1E 7DP.

Any person who does any unauthorised act in relation to this publication may be liable to criminal prosecution and civil claims for damages.

First published 1990

Published by
THE MACMILLAN PRESS LTD
Houndmills, Basingstoke, Hampshire RG21 2XS
and London
Companies and representatives
throughout the world

Typeset by Footnote Graphics,
Warminster, Wilts

British Library Cataloguing-in-Publication Data
McHoul, A. W.
  Writing Pynchon: strategies in fictional analysis
  1. Fiction in English. American writers.
  Pynchon, Thomas – Critical studies
  I. Title. II. Wills, David
  813'.54
  ISBN 978-0-333-51509-9   ISBN 978-1-349-20674-2 (eBook)
  DOI 10.1007/978-1-349-20674-2

For Michele and Roberta

Contents

	Preface	viii
	Introduction Bookmatching, the end(s) of the book	1
1	*Gravity's Rainbow* and the post-rhetorical	23
2	PLS RECORD BOOK BID LOT 49 STOP J DERRIDA	67
3	Anti-Oedipa	86
4	Telegrammatology	108
5	Almost but not quite me...	131
6	V	163
7	A V	186
8	Fall out	211
	Bibliography	225
	Index	233

Preface

This work began in 1981 when we found ourselves and each other in new jobs in separate departments at James Cook University in Townsville, North Queensland. Neither of us, it must be said, were happy there all of the time and before long we were working with the slogan 'A new life in a new town'. That did eventuate some years later. In the meantime, we began to put some of our shared interests in Pynchon and literary theory into writing.

Before leaving James Cook, in 1985 and 1986, we had published versions of two of the chapters of this book. Special Research Grants from the University were generously provided for this purpose. The two chapters in question were a paper on *V.* – now revised as Chapter 6 – and an early version of *'Gravity's Rainbow* and the post-rhetorical', Chapter 1. These appeared in the Adelaide journal *Southern Review* in 1983 and 1986 respectively. We thank Ken Ruthven and Noel King as well as the present editors of the *Review* for their suggestions and ideas and for their permission to use material from those versions. The idea for Chapter 2 was suggested by Mark Deitch, to whom we are grateful, as well as to Anne Freadman for her comments on the text. We also owe a debt of gratitude to Lisha Kayrooz at the James Cook Computer Centre for his invaluable help during the process of transferring our wordprocessing files between systems and institutions.

The rest of the work has been completed by not-so-cute correspondence, a sort of telegrammatology in its own right. The difficulties involved have been partly overcome by research funding and other assistance from our present institutions, Louisiana State University (Baton Rouge) and Murdoch University (Perth). In particular, we are in the debt of Grant Stone at the Murdoch Library for his search and destroy missions in the Pynchon Zone. It would be a measure of our success if we could, on the basis of this book, persuade him to write his threatened paper on Pynchon's reception by SF fans.

Some earlier workings-out of the ethical-moral questions raised in our Chapter 3, 'Anti-Oedipa', have appeared in *Pynchon Notes* and *Philosophy Today*. While those versions have undergone major surgery and revision, we are extremely grateful to the editors of those journals for their support and encouragement then and now.

In particular John Krafft and Khachig Tölöyan at *Pynchon Notes* have shared their unique expertise and insights into Pynchon's writing and into the industry which has grown up around it. John Krafft lent particular assistance in tracking down copies of TRP's correspondence, his little-known preface to Richard Fariña's *Been Down So Long it Looks Like Up to Me*, and his journalism.

We thank these and other colleagues, both local and distant, for their comments and suggestions along the way, especially Tony Tanner, Frank Kermode, Lesley Stern and John Frow.

Extracts used in the text are taken with permission from the following sources:

V. by Thomas Pynchon, copyright © 1961, 1963 by Thomas Pynchon. Reprinted by permission of the Melanie Jackson Agency, Harper & Row, Publishers, Inc., and A. M. Heath & Co. Ltd.

The Crying of Lot 49 by Thomas Pynchon, copyright © 1965, 1966 by Thomas Pynchon. Reprinted by permission of the Melanie Jackson Agency, Harper & Row, Publishers, Inc., and A. M. Heath & Co. Ltd.

Gravity's Rainbow by Thomas Pynchon, copyright © 1973 by Thomas Pynchon. Reprinted by permission of the Melanie Jackson Agency, A. M. Heath & Co. Ltd., Jonathan Cape Ltd., and Viking Penguin Ltd.

Slow Learner by Thomas Pynchon, copyright © 1984 by Thomas Pynchon. Reprinted by permission of the Melanie Jackson Agency, Little, Brown and Company, Publishers, and Jonathan Cape Ltd.

Introduction
Bookmatching, the end(s) of the book

The idea of a book on Thomas Pynchon ends right here: with a bookend, the first of a pair – with the second, its matching half, coming naturally enough at the (other) end of the book. At least, that's how things ought to fall. But then there is always the risk, the hope even, that the leaves contained between the bookends will, in another sense, fall out, spill beyond their confines, arriving at unforeseeable destinations. More specifically, however, this bookend, this block supporting our book and the books it contains and matches, is also an end in the sense that something is, more or less, over.

What is over for us is the idea that we could write a unified, stepwise, single-argument book on the texts of Thomas Pynchon. In fact, to come closer to our primary concerns, the numerous attempts by literary critics to do just that are, we think, hopelessly inadequate. Our very real dissatisfaction with the Pynchon industry has been its inability to come to grips with Pynchon as, and in terms of, what we shall call a 'writing practice'. Almost any passage from any book by Pynchon ranged against almost any passage from any book or paper by his critics, sympathetic or otherwise, shows a simple *lack* of matching. At best, or at most, what Pynchon writings have given rise to is a certain informality, something of a modulation in the tone of academic address. Yet even when tone amounts to anti-academicism[1] it remains underscored by some of the most conservatively academic critical apparatuses. While Pynchon delights in the play of writing, the joke, the scholarly rip-off, the spurious derivation and the rest, his critics continue to expend great energy exercising what can only be called their 'exegetical drive'.[2] Into the play, the marked disunity of the perfectly fictional and imaginary Pynchon comes, time after time, the critical policeman, rulemaker and, above all, explainer of the 'actual', 'underlying', rationale for Pynchon's writing.

There is a further irony to this almost polarised but practically unnoticed opposition between Pynchon and the industry named after him. It goes like this. Those literary critics who have written on Pynchon tend to have ignored what may loosely be called *contemporary literary theory* (CLT) in favour of more traditional exegetical pastimes. Yet CLT itself, particularly under the names of Jacques Derrida and the later Roland Barthes, to name only two, has on the one hand tended to rework and recapture the works of the literary canon, and on the other, to display certain great philosophical works to be 'writing'. Normally, 'Pynchon' – to name a body of writings – would barely figure in that list. And this is perhaps because, as we try to show, Pynchon's fiction may be more contribution to CLT than 'object text' for it. Still it remains that the best theory lacks all conviction, when it comes to Pynchon, while the worst of Pynchon criticism is full of anti-theoretical intensity.

Thus Thomas Moore, for example, begins a very recent book on Pynchon this way:[3]

> Years of increasingly mysterious silence from the mysterious Thomas Pynchon have elapsed since the publication in 1973 of *Gravity's Rainbow*: the longest, most ambitious, and most vastly intimidating of his three novels. A co-winner of a National Book Award in 1973, and honoured in 1975 ... *Gravity's Rainbow* is among the most widely celebrated unread novels of the past thirty years...

And it goes on. The mysterious author is mentioned – while the category of author is left unproblematic. The greatness of the work is put on record, often by comparison with Joyce and Melville – while any theory of the text in general, let alone writing, is left untouched. The ratio of celebratory prose to critical insight is disturbingly unbalanced. The bookend, just quoted, and the book it begins, are far from atypical in the field. It is often difficult to tell the secondary works apart; and no pleasure to try. There is a constant wearying round ahead for anyone who ventures into this shelf of the library. They will encounter countless repetitions of the mysteriousness of the actual person called 'Thomas Ruggles Pynchon' if, that is, we are always told, there is such a person. This obsession with the person or its absence is often posed as a threat: as though the possible absence of an empirical author's life and character might spell the end of the critical project. (And in many of the cases which argue this, we wish it had.) The only positive mention of Pynchon's personal absence we have seen occurs in a recent undergraduate, or freshman, crammer on *Lot 49* where the absence:[4]

> may make the approach to the novels themselves more difficult [but] it also makes it more direct, and free from the distraction of thinking about their author or wondering why such a man came to write as he did.

We return to these questions of biographical author and narrative voice in more detail shortly.

The next compulsory item in the secondary literature, and one which concerns us much more, is the matter of Binary Pairs which supposedly provide the dynamism of the novels – such things as order vs. chaos, paranoia vs. anti-paranoia, the elect vs. the preterite, zero vs. one, and so on. In the words of one critic: '"Binarity" is one of Pynchon's favorite terms, and *Gravity's Rainbow* is really two giant molecule-chains of paired opposites'.[5] The pairs are trotted out almost as if there had never been a wave of poststructuralism to cast radical doubt on the benefits of working with the position/opposition binary.[6] Often acting in conjunction with the binary pairs is another favourite of the Pynchon critics, namely what we shall call the Grand Unifying Theme. For a while, and recently revived, the theme of entropy has bulked large on the scene, tying in to the wider theme of Pynchon as the novelist of the scientific imagination.[7] Or else history is invoked, with Pynchon being read as the one who has traced the complex lines of Modern America to its thematic roots earlier in the century and beyond its borders, particularly during and following the Second World War in Europe. This line tends to concentrate on 'the bomb' (nascent in the V-weapons), sexuality, race struggles, and so on to a more detailed catalogue of the contemporary social and political condition of that Amerika. Some of this literature, particularly that relating to the entropy theme, is taken up in a more detailed and piecemeal fashion in later chapters.

There are also more specialised works, including those which trace the 'factual' basis of Pynchon's 'fictional' detail.[8] This approach can be and has been called 'encyclopaedic' criticism. Its worst excesses produce writing of this sort:[9]

> Beams flashing the brightest in *Gravity's Rainbow* generate from Pynchon's own erudition. They cause us to blink and squint and

grope because he knows so many subjects we may know little about: quantum mechanics, the Beveridge Proposal, the five positions on the launching switch of an A-4 rocket. His reconditeness encompasses tarot cards, the Cabala, mandala, Qlippoth, the Wheel of Fortune, delta-t, double-integral, yin-yang, a mathematical equation for motion under yaw control. He dips into Orphic, Norse, and Teutonic myths and . . .

And . . . ? Well the list can certainly go on, as could our equally tedious typology of Pynchon criticism. But the ways of writing on Pynchon are quickly exhausted. And while we may often despair of making sense of these texts individually, let alone collectively, what appears to give them some sort of continuity – if anything – is their relatively constant faith in what might be called 'living presence', in the guises of history, science, myth, nature and so on, combined with an equally touching faith in the idea that someone, an actually existing person, an author, collects this presence together into fictional representations such that the critic's job is, as it were, the de-collecting of the same items, the recuperation of them 'from the novel' and 'back into (our) presence'. The ontology (theory of Being) is realist – and so is the implicit aesthetics that here passes for literary theory.

We can summarise as follows: *Pynchon has only been allowed to speak in certain ways and not in others.* Our complaint about this is twofold: not only are the possible ways of speaking thereby limited, they are also, only and always, precisely, ways of *speaking* – not of writing. The critical model of Pynchon-author as 'speaker' (that is 'pure representer') of the real world of living presence is limited in its logocentrism: its speech-centredness. We are obviously using shorthand here in order to refer to an important part of our own critical armature, some knowledge of which we assume on the part of the reader. What Derrida calls 'logocentrism' does not reduce to speech-centredness. He uses the term to refer, also in shorthand, to a system of constraints operating through numerous of the central fields of Western thought.[10] Constantly in Pynchon criticism we come across a kind of writing in which that author is presumed, or made, to speak. Clerc suggests that 'many of [*Gravity's Rainbow*'s] passages are so extraordinary that they ought to be read aloud'; that it is an 'author' who 'puts on an intellectual light show', that some person called Pynchon 'gets inside his characters . . . more so than other novelists'[11] and so on. We quote here from a single page of a single work, but this type of critical figure can be found with disturbing regularity.

As far as this type of approach is concerned, the writing should literally have been on the wall for it as early as 1973 when Kermode showed that *Lot 49* effectively defeats the earlier Barthes' structural analysis of narrative. What the Pynchon critics presumably did not see – though Kermode no doubt did – was that Pynchon's writing transgresses in a way prefiguring poststructuralist thinking rather than returning to prestructuralist aesthetics. Also running against the grain of the industry standard, Tony Tanner's work on Pynchon is always an exception to the rule of mere appreciationist logocentrism; particularly his booklength study, where he uses for his first bookend a tantalising quotation from Barthes on the death of the author. Our investigations have been, in part at least, motivated by a desire to follow through this type of connection to more radical conclusions.[12]

More recently, we have been heartened to read Brian McHale's work on Pynchon which has shown quite clearly that there is a gap in the field – a space for examining the relations not only between Pynchon's writings and those of Derrida, but also between Pynchon's writing and Derrida's retheorisation of the very concept of Writing. McHale's *Postmodernist Fiction* assembles Derrida and Pynchon in one text – but they are rarely put into direct association or confrontation there.[13] By and large they inhabit different parts of McHale's text, serving different functions. *Gravity's Rainbow* is held up as the paradigm case of postmodernist fiction; Derrida's *Glas* is mentioned for its use of columned typography and for its reforegrounding of the spacings between letters and words. To us, this indicates less of a 'solution' to the generally logocentric tendencies in Pynchon criticism and more of a job still to be undertaken. For McHale's book is hardly Derridean and it is only tangentially about Pynchon; and in any case, it is difficult for us to concur with McHale's very rigid divisions. He reads postmodernist texts as having centrally 'ontological' concerns with relations and collisions between different and distinct worlds. This, he writes, makes them opposite to modernist texts which are apparently 'epistemological' since they deal more with the problem of knowing 'this world'. It would be quite easy to show that this relates to other equally firm distinctions in McHale's theory and analysis: for example he seems to retain a distinction between fictions' 'literal worlds' and their hypertrophic transgressions of those worlds. To this extent his theory and analysis requires a positive affirmation of a distinction which, we argue, a text like *Gravity's Rainbow* makes utterly impossible. Thus, rather than further McHale's ontologistic analysis of that novel, we turn instead to concepts such as the 'post-rhetorical' and 'material typonymy' which we outline in Chapter 1. In that chapter, too, we give some reasons for suspecting that McHale's 'dream of a return', as he calls it at his own bookend (p. 235), is a dream of a return to an absolute signified. To do so, we look at the more detailed treatment he gives Pynchon in his paper entitled 'Modernist reading, postmodern text'.

Kermode, Tanner and possibly McHale may be exceptions to it, but by calling the more clearly mainstream work on Pynchon 'logocentric', as we have just done, we intend to point to its obsession with a simplistic literary model based on the primacy and purity of the voice (often of an actual historical author), gathering up, as it were, reality's own equally pure objects and depositing them in the listener's ear. What is forgotten is, quite simply, that this is Writing. Even when Pynchon is approached in terms of literary 'devices', these routinely boil down to concerns of the 'voice' and 'objective reality'. In fact it is very rare to encounter a reading of Pynchon's work which does not at some stage revert to a precritical notion of the author as not only integral consciousness but also identifiable historical person, and that in spite of the fact that the person is recognised as an enigma, and the 'author', in at least one of the novels, dissolves into an array of conflicting narrative voices. We are supposed to believe that it is Pynchon who says 'You will want cause and effect. All right.' on page 663 of *Gravity's Rainbow* although none of us has any idea who or what that Pynchon is. Speaking of *Gravity's Rainbow* Clerc calls the narrative voice 'extremely flexible ... of indeterminate gender, it stays detached to maintain an objective third-person point of view'; while Hite calls it 'Protean', matching a 'narrative strategy ... based on a tension essential to the novel as genre; not coincidentally, he [Pynchon] finds this tension essential to a modernist mode of being in the world'.[14] The whole framework of such a discussion seems to assume a certain kind of voluntarism – as if authors always spoke language, as if discourse, to broaden the frame, never *wrote* them. And even granting this, it would, we repeat, be a very peculiar thing to attach a narrative voice to an author. To cite all of the slippages we have found between concepts of author and narrator in the secondary literature would take up untellable space. Further examples are given in the chapters which follow.

And so: being allowed to speak only so narrowly (for all the Protean and Mercurial aspects of 'his' voice), Pynchon is barely allowed to write or to be writing. At the same time, to reinvoke our central irony, that – writing – is precisely what CLT has discovered with a vengeance in the most logocentric of classical texts, literary and otherwise. Again, we are thinking here especially of Derrida's considerations of Rousseau, Plato and Hegel; but also of his work on Genet, Blanchot and Ponge.[15] We can understand that philosophers would object to the idea that philosophy *is* a kind of writing over and above something else. We can understand that, for them, 'the philosophy they write treats writing as a means of expression which is at best irrelevant to the thought it expresses and at worst a barrier to that thought'.[16] While understanding it, we cannot of course sympathise with that view. On the other hand, what we fail to understand is why literary critics (at least those who have written extensively on Pynchon) would want to hold this view of writing – and almost everything they write, with the above exceptions noted, seems to us to attest to the fact that they do hold this view. What is so objectionable about reading Pynchon as, first and foremost, writing?

For CLT, at least of the Derridean or grammatological variety, writing is not simply a means of expression which, with varying degrees of success, merely maps on to something more important or *central* in the world – the real, for example. To view writing this way – as expression – is to be caught within the logocentrism of what Derrida calls 'the metaphysics of presence', which we have already seen operating in terms of the assumed voice-presence relation of much Pynchon criticism. Such a relation need not guide our readings and writings for all that it has underlain every Western philosophical tradition and for all, in our more marginal case, that it has informed the untheorised basis of the criticism in question here. A notion of writing which resists the logocentric impulse (while not simply stepping outside it) would hold that the meaning of an utterance – for example a sentence from *Gravity's Rainbow* – cannot simply be interpreted in terms of some structure of presence (say, in this case a researched historical fact about the Nazi V-weapons). Instead, it becomes clear that this 'meaning' is itself only available via certain other texts. We must do our historical research, in this case, on the basis of primary and secondary sources. Or perhaps we will consult the 'texts of experience' by interviewing those who were once rocket personnel at the firing sites. It makes no difference. In any case, the meaning, the actual presence to which we wish to attach the utterance, always slips back into being another utterance. Then the problem of the first utterance (from *Gravity's Rainbow*, in our hypothetical example) applies in turn to the second utterance (the primary document, history book, the reminiscence and so on). But at no point does presence *itself*, in some utterly pure form, arrive on the scene, divorced from writing. It is a heuristic of the particular discipline – here literary history – that we somehow agree that 'enough is enough'. It is always and only for certain practical purposes that we come to think of ourselves as having arrived at presence, that is to say at the meaning of the utterance behind the utterance. At the same time we know full well, in fact, that we can only do this precisely by *putting off* the arrival on the scene of presence itself. Real history, in this case, never quite arrives. And so writing works not despite but because it is always different from its assumed self-present meaning. Writing-in-general (as opposed, for example, to the mere writing down of speech) can, at the risk of an over-simplification, be *defined* as any practice which instantiates such a difference – what Derrida, in order to mark the peculiarity in the written but not the spoken form, calls differ*a*nce.

This notion of writing is, it seems to us, too 'Pynchonian' to ignore. But there is a more general connection between Pynchon and CLT, one which we would be hard-pressed to justify empirically, but which we believe to have nevertheless motivated our studies of Pynchon. We refer to what, for want of a better term, might be called an ambiance, a mentality perhaps, a loose assemblage of terms, concepts and attitudes which can *in no way* be reduced to the 'influences' we are told over and over that writers such as Henry Adams, Max Weber or T. S. Eliot have had on Pynchon.

First of all there is the tendency towards what Lévi-Strauss was first to call *bricolage* – borrowing, making do with whatever may be lying around rather than going out of one's way to get highly specific instruments for highly specific jobs. The *bricoleur* is the intellectual handyperson who will use a text or a passage from it by virtue of the fact that it comes to hand rather than because it has been specially unearthed for the occasion. As we shall see in Chapter 5, this borrowing can involve some risk for it may easily turn into 'plagiarism'. When the questions of authorship and ownership – in fact the very question of origins – are raised, however, the scholarly quotation and the fictional reworking can easily slide into each other unnoticed. Thus Derrida can create havoc with the 'actual texts' of Rousseau, and Pynchon can do a Willy Sutton on a Baedeker guide book. At the same time, in both sets of writings, the technique itself is never short of being theorised.[17]

This brings us to a second point of connection which has several names: quotation, citationality, the pick-up, eclecticism, synchretism. The fact that discourse can always be quoted or cited, put between quotation marks, moved between texts to make new effects from different material, all this shows that any text can always have indeterminate uses and meanings. A text or a fragment, no matter how small and apparently meaningless, can be given (or robbed of) significance and structure if located in the appropriate place. Thus Pynchon, in *V.*, can pipe the opening of Wittgenstein's *Tractatus* into an engineering experiment taking place in South-West Africa in 1922, thus making it appear, almost literally, a universal principle gathered from beyond the limits of the Earth and at the same time a complete nonsense:[18]

DIGEWOELDTIMSTEALALENSWTASNDEURFUALRLIKST

And Derrida can turn a seemingly trivial fragment of Nietzsche's, 'I have forgotten my umbrella', into a philosophical investigation that is a meditation on writing, woman, truth, the gesture of 'passing off' and the text as 'preservative'.[19]

Thirdly, in both Pynchon and CLT we can locate a penchant for play. Not only do we 'locate' it, we participate. But the play is not without its work-value. That is, while it is certainly the case, for example, that 'pop' music, fiction, film, art and so on have been valorised for some time at the expense of their 'serious' equivalents, that valorisation has not actually destabilised the difference between seriousness and play. At least not until the likes of Derrida and the later Barthes in 'theory' and Pynchon in 'fiction'. From the very first, Pynchon makes it impossible to treat jokes, philosophy, slapstick, death, tasteless movies, God, pornography, physics ... (one could go on) as forms of discourse bifurcated into the 'serious' and the 'frivolous'. A limerick stands in for a chemical formula; an elaborate plot-detour is made in order to perpetrate the

'My Word'-type extended pun 'For De Mille, young fur-henchmen can't be rowing!' and so forth.[20] Derrida has shown how 'play' can begin to unwrap the anal(ytical)ly tight seriousness of the structuralist enterprise in a way which has very serious consequences for social, literary and scientific modes of investigation.[21]

Finally then, the forms of writing we are addressing by means of the surrogates called 'Pynchon' and 'Contemporary Literary Theory', neither of which are particularly satisfactory, are forms in which the relations between 'writer' and critic have come unstuck. In some respects, the figure of the critic is, these days, one which can be as widely known and publicly celebrated as that of the poet or novelist. At least that distinction seems to be collapsing. If Rousseau's philosophical treatises can be read as fiction, we affirm here the right to read Pynchon as philosophy. Though that may only be an intermediate strategy in order to provoke the kind of levelling that we believe a concept like writing can achieve.

Hence the question which marks our approach to Pynchon is this: how can Pynchon be made to write? Or: how can Pynchon be read outside the logocentric tradition? The answer is the end of this book. The answer is to produce instances of, and strategies for, writing on/as Pynchon-as-writing. The instances do not cohere around a single and unified theme; instead they take up the differance of writing which is, necessarily, always indeterminate. They are not governed by a single opposition, but tend rather to explore the spacings between the many oppositions that can and have been worked into and through the texts of Pynchon. Neither, it should be made clear, do we speak through these instances with a single authorial voice. We have sought instead to profit from this collaborative project in order to multiply the devices of style or voice employed in the writing. The texts which constitute this book have been produced by various methods of individual and mutual composition, as well as cross-editing, and we intend that our approaches to writing be finally inseparable from approaches to the textual objects they examine. These 'techniques' – really exemplifications rather than the application of a method – we might call, not unaware of its paradoxicality, 'bookmatching'. Instead of 'writing a book', we have worked through a series of strategic exercises in which Pynchon is 'bookmatched' with and against other kinds of writing and in a variety of ways. For the most part, though not exclusively, these 'other kinds' are what could be called 'literary theory', and for the most part within that category, it is the work of Derrida which is most systematically invoked. We are most centrally interested in the spaces between Pynchon and CLT and – at the extreme – the space in which they could swap places. Accordingly at one stage in Chapter 4, 'Telegrammatology', we read Derrida's 'fictions' from the vantage of Pynchon's 'literary theory'.

The term 'bookmatching' could be thought of as an alternative title for the whole of our work here; yet it may seem a curious choice given that we have only just now rejected a position in which, for example, language is seen to work by mapping on to, or *matching* the world of living presence. But we intend this 'matching' in another sense. We are striking out of it its possible connotations of 'correspondence' – though in the somewhat perverse sense of the *postal* we would be happy to be called 'correspondence theorists'. Here we are referring to the later work of Derrida that comes up especially in Chapters 2–4, where the idea of communication is deconstructed by that of adestination – the possibility, or rather the structural necessity, that a message not arrive. For the match (in 'bookmatch') signifies the paradox by which something is mated and so has its own reproduction assured while, at the same time, it is designed to be set on fire and self-destruct. By removing its possible connotations of a correspondence theory of meaning and communication, we hope to avoid some of the kuter korrespondences to which Pynchon has been subjected in the name of criticism.

'Bookmatching' is a relatively esoteric term used by stringed instrument makers. The luthier, David Russell Young, describes it as follows:[22]

> Bookmatching is a way of cutting the pieces for the top and back. You take a single piece, and slice it into two sheets, each the same length and width as the original, but only half as thick. It's like opening a book at its center and laying out the two halves, which are now symmetrically grained. It looks very nice, and there are structural considerations as well. Most pieces of wood will 'work' or shrink a tiny bit, and bookmatching assures even, symmetrical seasoning.

By extension then, when we describe our practice as 'bookmatching', we mean to invoke an image whereby a series of writings is considered as a single piece, in the first instance, and then sliced through to reveal not so much the symmetry of their grain but new spaces between them.[23] A book opens like a V. The single 'book' for us is the agglomeration which is produced by treating the writings of Pynchon and CLT as, at least initially, uniform; that is, with no hierarchy governing 'text' and 'criticism' in either direction. Opening it up, for us, does not mean working back from its expression(s) to a real world of presence. It means displaying the space between the covers, between the bars of the V, between the bookends. To indicate such an overlooked space often means pulling up abruptly in the face of the text and saying 'Look here'. But, as we shall see, that space is always plural. We should always write, instead, 'spaces' or 'spacings'.

Before going on to examine some of these spacings, it is important to repeat what we hope to have already made clear; namely that our work here falls within a framework, that of CLT, which has well been recognised as having an important role to play inside and outside literary studies.[24] Indeed some would say that 'poststructuralism' comes close to dominating the domain even within the most conservative of academic institutions. While this may powerfully reinvest the discipline of literary studies which has been for so long a backwater sheltering novelists-, philosophers-, and sociologists-*manqués* from the storms of intellectual debate, it should not be taken as an invitation to regard the literary as holding some sort of magical privilege which comes from its supposed special insight. On the contrary, the very impetus of CLT, especially in the Derridean mode, is to break down the borders which constitute academic or artistic disciplines as sites of certain unexamined privileges. Gregory Ulmer's reading of Derrida, especially the first part of *Applied Grammatology*,[25] has admirably emphasised this, and our work to some extent is from the same mould.

Thus what might be read for some as an adversarial tone in our writing, we prefer to call the very necessary work of erasure that constitutes all writing. It is clear that we are disappointed with the lack of matching, in the normal sense, between CLT and Pynchon studies; and that similarly we find much of what has been written on Pynchon to be naïve forms of criticism. But our own matching is at the same time a putting together, a cross-sectioning, and a striking (out) of various sets of texts. We are at times disappointed with what Pynchon writes, too, and the advantage of our double interest in him and CLT – as well as the theoretical positions the

Introduction

latter implies concerning authorial intention and control – is that it allows us to 'match' his texts in more ways than one. And finally, the work of bookmatching as striking (out) or erasure invades in turn our own texts through the play of signatures – the simultaneous inscription and dissemination of our own meaning and intent – of which more in the pages which follow.

■ ■ ■ ■ ■ ■ ■

At the risk of overlabouring the introductory point, what surprises us is that such a theoretically 'advanced' figure as Pynchon should be treated, by and large, in such a theoretically retarded fashion. While the names of Derrida, Kristeva, Barthes, Cixous, Foucault, Irigaray, Lyotard, Deleuze and so forth are to be read in almost every literary domain, there is hardly a mention of them in the Pynchon industry. Plater, for example, relies on Wittgenstein for his grim phoen-ocentric reading of Pynchon, but he chooses the earlier logical atomism of Wittgenstein's *Tractatus* over the more adventurous and relativistic position of the *Investigations*, a text which has more than a few possible bookmatchings with CLT[26] and Pynchon for that matter.

Moving on, Derrida's *Speech and Phenomena* is listed in Hite's bibliography but never cited in the book. Instead, she touches, but leaves off at, the point where Derridean interests might begin. In her first chapter she states:[27] 'Within Pynchon's fictional worlds, language's hypothesized origin is this unifying presence, but language becomes language only when presence withdraws into the mythic past – into absence'. Later, picking up Hartman's note on Pynchon, she argues:[28]

> Pynchon outwits closure in his novel; indeed given the alternatives, it is difficult to see how Pynchon could have realized either possible conclusion [either 'absolute unity' or 'no connections']. *Lot 49* is so thoroughly apocalyptic in structure that the final revelation cannot occur. The conclusion is necessarily deferred.

Yet at the same time, Pynchon criticism has never failed to supply rewritings of that 'final revelation', its underlying significance, its connection with the American Imaginary, and so on. But Hite rarely, if at all, goes on with these noticings – acute as some of them are. She does nothing *with* the notion of deferral, either that of the origin or of the end. On the other hand, it is precisely from such points as these that we pick up the ball and try to run with it. Deferral may not be the most substantial of critical concepts to run with, but we prefer this difficulty and indeterminacy to Hite's mode of operating. She ends up dropping *Lot 49*'s differance and writes of *Gravity's Rainbow* that it is[29]

> a novel that affirms the nonsystematic, nontotalizing connections of a community based on making meanings. To understand the infinitely various ways in which human beings deal with their common fear by exfoliating networks of significance and language is to love the People....

This kind of recuperation of Pynchon for a conservative humanist tradition of belles-lettres is one of the procedures that our book-matching exercises work directly to counter – even if the cost (or benefit) is that we risk representing Pynchon in a 'bad' light morally. In fact, the risk of moral recuperations (ours as well as Pynchon's) becomes one of the central problematic issues of our third chapter, the 'Anti-Oedipa'.

In the context of previous, though rare, Pynchon–CLT connections, we should mention Bloom's halfhearted tinkerings, to be found in his identical introductions to two collections of 'the best criticism yet published' on Pynchon. If these volumes do indeed represent the best – such as the essay by Maureen Quilligan which we shall discuss shortly – they also contain some of the worst, and it is perhaps pertinent that the only essay, apart from his own, that Bloom prints in both volumes, is a most unabashed example of the moralistic humanism which has so dominated Pynchon studies.[30] Bloom's introduction makes some rather creative uses of crucial concepts like 'dissemination'. For example, of Slothrop, *Gravity's Rainbow*'s disappearing American abroad, Bloom writes:[31]

> When he is finally scattered, the book stops, and the apocalyptic rocket blasts off. Still, Slothrop is more than a Derridean dissemination, if only because he does enable Pynchon to gather together seven hundred and sixty pages. Nor is *Gravity's Rainbow* what is now called 'a text'. It is a novel....

Not only does Bloom use 'dissemination' in a rather odd way (as a noun describing a character) but he is factually incorrect about the connection between Slothrop's disappearance and the timing of any one of several rocket launchings. Besides, we would argue strongly that Slothrop as much enables Pynchon to scatter seven hundred and sixty pages as he enables him to gather those pages together; and that it is precisely such practices which do make *Gravity's Rainbow* a text, and a very *writerly* one at that, to use Barthes' term.[32] We do not see what is to be gained, other than the comfort of domestication, in rescuing Pynchon for the Eurocentric literary canon, via the story of Byron the Bulb, as Bloom attempts to do here.

Given the dead-ends that most encounters between CLT and Pynchon have led to up until now – again Kermode, Tanner and bits of McHale excluded – we would prefer to follow a different intertextual trail in order to create the spacing necessary for our own bookmatching exercise. In discussing Derrida's well-known penchant for wordplay, Ulmer ties it back to Freud's concern with slips and errors which is at once highly analytic and derived from 'personal experience'.[33]

> Freud's attention to word play may be seen in this context as a revival of the operation characterizing all allegory 'from Spenser to Pynchon'. Allegory, Quilligan argues, oscillates between the metaphorical and literal understanding of words....

Hence our *pre*textualisation goes like this: since Derrida, if not quite literally, authorises *Applied Grammatology* (at least he read it 'with recognition and admiration'), and since that text quotes Quilligan's allegoricising of Pynchon with approval, one could legitimately imagine that Quilligan would be an improvement on the usual critical fare served up in Pynchon's name. To some extent this is what we find, as does Brian McHale in his reading of Quilligan; and we are disappointed to find also that this form of authorisation is no guarantee. Yet this does not surprise us, for a linear genealogy of textual meaning might, in the light of our discussion, reasonably be expected to involve a recuperation of writing effects. Thus even before a glance at Quilligan, the idea of allegory – unless it be in de Man's sense[34] – would seem suspect *vis-à-vis* writing. When all else fails, the allegorical – as we discuss in the next chapter – is the mode of writing or reading in which one thing stands for another – where the literary figure, for example, stands for some (usually intangible) presence such as love, pity or hope. This use of allegory – in the sense of the personification or figuration of spiritual ineffables – is not ruled out by Quilligan, though for us it would be a mainstay of the presence of the metaphysics of presence in literary analysis. Her second, and more important, sense of the term stems from the first. If allegory is traditionally the figure of substitution (in general? in particular?), it can work in texts which substitute signs not for 'life but the life of the psyche'. To do this, 'the author' needs 'that system of signs which retrieves for us the process of intellection itself'. By making a traditional, if highly problematic, substitution of 'language' for this 'process of intellection', Quilligan then comes up with her formula of allegory as the doubling of language upon itself:[35]

> When language itself becomes the focus of his attention rather than the action language describes, the author may be said to write allegory.

But this doubling is not the abyss of language's referential function that it might at first glance seem to be. We are right back to the metaphysics of presence. What language normally does, for Quilligan, is to describe action: linguistic signs map on to actional presences. But in the allegorical 'mode' it maps firstly on to ineffable spirit, then, by a strange transformation, on to intellection, then, finally, by an even stranger transformation, on to itself alone. It takes the place of both the linguistic sign and the living presence which that sign supposedly represents. And it does this, moreover, via the conscious strategy of 'the author'.

While we would want to share Quilligan's interest in language's doubling upon itself, even though we would hardly call this 'allegory', or even the more technically correct 'metalepsis', we are less certain that this doubling derives its significance from a comparison with a more 'normal' use of language.[36] As CLT has often repeated, if (any) language refers, it refers to itself.[37] And this is *only if* it can be said to refer at all, if its meaning is not always already deferred beyond the reach of reference. Quilligan has no such qualms. The literary is marked by the allegorical, which is marked by its 'doubling' and thus by its disjuncture from 'normal' use. Her reference to Derrida in the context of *Gravity's Rainbow*'s section on the New Turkic alphabet shows the extent to which she fails to comprehend either the import or the impetus of Derrida's critique of linguistic operations:[38]

Pynchon is concerned with what happens to language when it gets written down; through alphabetization, the means of human communication get bureaucratized and language loses (at the same time it gains) magic power ... Language, in so far as it is just another bureaucratic system, is another instrument by which 'they' stop true human communication.

The unquestioned assumption is that *Gravity's Rainbow* itself can be read as conflating language with speech, and writing with written-down-speech. Moreover, it puts the novel into the position of accepting, on the basis of this, a positive moral thesis: one according to which the writing down of speech involves a regrettable loss of something as unspecific and metaphysical as 'magic' and/or 'human communication'. We have little doubt that *Gravity's Rainbow* contains a strong satire on bureaucratisation; but we do not see why it should therefore be read as a pro-logocentric fiction or as a homage to magic humanism. On the contrary, from our first chapter we work through a concept of the 'post-rhetorical' precisely in order to show how Pynchon, like Derrida (and for want of a better word) *deconstructs* the difference between positivities (such as humanism) and their opposites (in this case nihilism?) without, in so doing, rendering them identical.

Against Quilligan's logocentric reading – and we stress again that we think this is among the best readings of Pynchon to date[39] – and therefore *a fortiori* against a Pynchon industry obsessed with binary oppositions, an industry which has practically made an industry out of choosing between twofold options, we would argue that Pynchon can be read with something more of the indeterminacy that Derrida risks, and extensively theorises, in his 'Double Session'.[40] Our work on Pynchon, our bookmatch, simply asks, and tries to show, what can be done with, in the face of, this inevitable undecidability – one which we find in CLT, particularly in Derrida, and certainly in Pynchon, but equally one which cannot easily be recuperated as mere 'literary ambiguity' though it must always run that risk. So to talk of any possible victory or defeat will, ipso facto, be nonsensical. But there are other risks we are prepared to run: not the least that our bookmatch will turn around into a matchbook and, in igniting, self-ignite, or ignite an apocalypse.[41]

Notes

1. Cf. Molly Hite: 'I was astonished to learn ... that Pynchon is frequently criticized for being the academic's academic, the writer whose books are intended to be taught, not read. For a long time, the most ardent Pynchon fans that I knew were a weight lifter, a short-order cook, and a pizza deliveryman'. *Ideas of Order in the Novels of Thomas Pynchon* (Columbus: Ohio State University Press, 1983), p. *ix*.
2. 'Exegetical drive' is a concept we owe to Lesley Stern (personal communication). She uses it to describe the paradox of the journal *Screen*. While *Screen* was a major organ for the introduction of French structuralism and psychoanalysis into English-speaking countries, it seemed to ignore the pedagogic strategies of those very movements, preferring to explain, to categorise, to map the field in quite traditional Anglo-Saxon ways. Just as we attempt in the present work to counter the exegetical drive we find to be current in Pynchon criticism, so we are also concerned to resist the simple 'importation' that theory (such as that of Derrida) has usually been subjected to in Anglo-American scholarship.
3. T. Moore, *The Style of Connectedness: 'Gravity's Rainbow' and Thomas Pynchon* (Columbia: University of Missouri Press, 1987), p. 1.
4. C. E. Nicholson and R. W. Stevenson, *Notes on Pynchon's 'The Crying of Lot 49'* (Beirut: Longman/York Press, 1981), p. 7.
5. D. Fowler, *A Reader's Guide to 'Gravity's Rainbow'* (Ann Arbor: Ardis Publishers, 1980), p. 47.
6. Plater writes in his preface the most honest refusal to cope with obstacles of this degree of difficulty: 'Conspicuously absent are a number of hermeneutic, new textual, or structuralist critics, in addition to Barthes and Moles, whose strategies offer a great deal for the analysis of Pynchon's fiction'. From that point on Barthes, in any of his guises, is conspicuously absent and, from what we can tell, Moles is a minor American information theorist. See W. M. Plater, *The Grim Phoenix: Reconstructing Thomas Pynchon* (Bloomington: Indiana University Press, 1978), p. *x*.
7. A paradigm case of this sub-genre of Pynchon criticism is the fourth chapter ('Pynchon's Cosmos') in P. L. Cooper, *Signs and Symptoms: Thomas Pynchon and the Contemporary World* (Berkeley: University of California Press, 1983), pp. 110–30.
8. D. Cowart, *Thomas Pynchon: The Art of Allusion* (Carbondale: Southern Illinois University Press, 1980) is an exceptionally high-quality example of this genre. Although we have not been able to consult it before this work goes to press, we imagine Steven Weisenburger's *A 'Gravity's Rainbow' Companion* (Athens: University of Georgia Press, 1988) to be similarly well-informed. Another example is Fowler's *Reader's Guide* (see note 5).
9. C. Clerc (ed.), *Approaches to 'Gravity's Rainbow'* (Columbus: Ohio State University Press, 1983), p. 20.
10. Derrida has summed up his analysis as a series of devices designed

Introduction 19

to 'detect not only in the history of philosophy and in the related socio-historical totality, but also in what are alleged to be sciences and in so-called post-philosophical discourses that figure among the most modern (in linguistics, in anthropology, in psychoanalysis), to detect in these an evaluation of writing, or, to tell the truth, rather a devaluation of writing whose insistent, repetitive, even obscurely compulsive character was the sign of a whole set of long-standing constraints'. See J. Derrida, 'The time of a thesis: punctuations', in A. Montefiore (ed.), *Philosophy in France Today* (Cambridge: Cambridge University Press, 1983), pp. 34–50. This quotation, p. 40.

11. Clerc, p. 12.
12. F. Kermode, 'The use of codes', in S. Chatman (ed.), *Approaches to Poetics* (New York: Columbia University Press, 1973), pp. 51–79; T. Tanner, *Thomas Pynchon* (London: Methuen, 1982).
13. B. McHale, *Postmodernist Fiction* (Methuen: New York, 1987). The exception is where McHale reads the character, Slothrop, from *Gravity's Rainbow*, as the model of a character 'under erasure', p. 105.
14. Clerc, p. 17; Hite, p. 21.
15. See J. Derrida, *Of Grammatology*, trans. G. C. Spivak (Baltimore: The Johns Hopkins University Press, 1976), on Rousseau; 'White mythology', in his *Margins of Philosophy*, trans. A. Bass (Chicago: University of Chicago Press, 1982), pp. 207–71, on Plato; *Glas*, trans. J. P. Leavey and R. Rand (Lincoln: University of Nebraska Press, 1986), on Genet and Hegel; *Parages* (Paris: Galilée, 1986), on Blanchot; and *Signéponge/Signsponge*, trans. R. Rand (New York: Columbia University Press, 1984), on Ponge.
16. J. Culler, *On Deconstruction: Theory and Criticism after Structuralism* (Ithaca: Cornell University Press, 1982), p. 90.
17. See *Of Grammatology*, again on Rousseau; and Pynchon's *Slow Learner* (Boston: Little Brown, 1984), p. 17, on Baedeker and Sutton. Derrida discusses the concept of iteration in 'Signature event context', in *Margins of Philosophy*, pp. 307–30. Pynchon reflects on the same concept under the rubric 'a strategy of transfer' in the text called 'Introduction' in *Slow Learner*. We take this matter up in Chapter 5.
18. *V.* (New York: Bantam Books, 1964), p. 258.
19. J. Derrida, *Spurs/Eperons*, trans. B. Harlow (Chicago: University of Chicago Press, 1979), pp. 122ff.
20. *Gravity's Rainbow* (New York: Viking, 1973), p. 559.
21. See for example, 'Structure sign and play in the discourse of the human sciences', in his *Writing and Difference*, trans. A. Bass (Chicago: University of Chicago Press, 1978), pp. 278–93. Any number of later texts by Derrida take the idea of play further than this essay, but as always, the play takes place within a carefully constructed set of reading strategies. Derrida is very wary of 'unlimited play' or play for its own sake, and uses the term more in the sense of the 'give' in a machine. See his informal comments in C. V. McDonald (ed.), *The Ear of the Other* (New York: Schocken Books, 1985), pp. 67–9.

22. D. R. Young, 'Acoustic guitar construction', in T. Wheeler (ed.), *The Guitar Book* (New York: Harper & Row, 1974), pp. 46–53. This quote, p. 46.
23. Alice Jardine nicely captures some of the components of bookmatching with her four-term expression, 'Intersections – Interfacings – Intertexts – Interferences'. See A. Jardine, *Gynesis: Configurations of Woman and Modernity* (Ithaca: Cornell University Press, 1985). Interference with Pynchon's novel *V.* is bookmatched with another form of contemporary feminist literary theory in our Chapter 7, 'A V'.
24. An interesting example of the extension of grammatology into adjacent social science fields is J. Clifford and G. Marcus (eds), *Writing Culture: The Poetics and Politics of Ethnography* (Berkeley: University of California Press, 1986).
25. G. Ulmer, *Applied Grammatology: Post(e)-pedagogy from Jacques Derrida to Joseph Beuys* (Baltimore: The Johns Hopkins University Press, 1985).
26. See Plater, *Grim Phoenix*; L. Wittgenstein, *Tractatus Logico-Philosophicus* (London: Routledge & Kegan Paul, 1961); and his *Philosophical Investigations* (Oxford: Blackwell, 1968). For a commentary on Wittgenstein and his contribution to contemporary debates about textual interpretation, see A. McHoul, *Wittgenstein On Certainty and the Problem of Rule in Social Science* (Toronto: Toronto Semiotic Circle, 1986).
27. Hite, *Ideas of Order*, p. 35.
28. Hite, p. 69. She refers to G. Hartman, *The Fate of Reading and Other Essays* (Chicago: University of Chicago Press, 1975), p. 211.
29. Hite, p. 156.
30. See C. H. Werner, 'Recognizing reality, realizing responsibility' in H. Bloom (ed.), *Thomas Pynchon* (New York: Chelsea House, 1986), pp. 191–202; also in Bloom's *Thomas Pynchon's 'Gravity's Rainbow'* (New York: Chelsea House, 1986) pp. 85–96.
31. Bloom (both volumes), p. 3. A further incongruous and undeveloped mention of Derrida is made by Schwab in Bloom's *Gravity's Rainbow* collection: 'Heisenburg's quantum theory, and Derrida's critique of Western metaphysics are invoked to introduce Pynchon's hobbyhorse – entropy – the key concept that informs the narrative structure, style, and implicit philosophy of *Gravity's Rainbow*'. See Schwab's 'Creative paranoia and frost patterns of white words', p. 109 in Bloom.
32. See R. Barthes, *S/Z* (London: Cape, 1975).
33. Ulmer, p. 89; and the attribution to Derrida, in parentheses following the quote, is from Ulmer's blurb. The point about the duality of Freudian discourse is made well by Barbour who writes that it is 'confessional/symptomatic of romance/fantasy, but analytic/controlling in its publications'. See J. Barbour, 'Oedipa and the Scottish Demon', in T. Threadgold (ed.), *SASSC Working Papers, Vol. 2* (Sydney: Sydney Association for Studies in Society and Culture, 1988), pp. 55–63. This quote, p. 55. Also highly pertinent in

this respect is Derrida's 'To Speculate – on "Freud"' in his *The Post Card*, trans. A. Bass (Chicago: University of Chicago Press, 1987).
34. See P. de Man, *Allegories of Reading: Figural Language in Rousseau, Nietzsche, Rilke, and Proust* (New Haven: Yale University Press, 1979).
35. M. Quilligan, '["Thomas Pynchon and the language of allegory"]' in R. Pearce (ed.), *Critical Essays on Thomas Pynchon* (Boston: G. K. Hall, 1981), pp. 187–212. All quotes so far from p. 187.
36. One of the main sources for Quilligan's theory (that 'Literature . . .', not just allegory, then, '. . . is language which "arises for its own sake"') is Foucault's *The Order of Things*. While we have some sympathy with her reading, we find it constantly dogged by her failure to read Pynchon and Foucault in a wider framework that would have to include, most pertinently, Foucault's own 'What is an author?' See M. Foucault, *The Order of Things* (London: Tavistock, 1970); and 'What is an author?', in his *Language, Countermemory, Practice*, trans. D. Bouchard (Oxford: Blackwell, 1977) pp. 113–38.
37. Our formulation is taken from D. Silverman and B. Torode, *The Material Word: Some Theories of Language and its Limits* (London: Routledge & Kegan Paul, 1980).
38. Quilligan, pp. 191–2.
39. For example, the following sentence from Quilligan – in conjunction with a Derridean interest – could well have led her along a postal route similar to that which became our second chapter, PLS RECORD BOOK BID: 'We learn that the mysterious bidder at the final auction [in *Lot 49*] is initially a "book bidder", that is, one who sends in bids by mail which, in the context of the Trystero stamps, is suspicious' (p. 200). In another sense, this passage would probably have made a better bookmatch with the section of our first chapter which contains a reading of the 'language theme' in *Gravity's Rainbow* – a reading which we ended up rejecting for a number of reasons raised in that chapter.
40. J. Derrida, 'The Double Session' in his *Dissemination*, trans. B. Johnson (Chicago: University of Chicago Press, 1981). We take up some of the ideas discussed in that essay in our seventh chapter, 'A V'.
41. At least one of us has encountered this before. See D. Wills, 'Post/Card/Match/Book/*Envois*/Derrida', *SubStance*, 43 (1984), pp. 19–38.

1
Gravity's Rainbow and the post-rhetorical

Now everybody – we too, started reading *Gravity's Rainbow* in 1973. We haven't spoken to hitch-hikers in Arizona, like Siegel,[1] but we've met a few who never got past the first hundred pages, like Leverenz.[2] A Sydney film critic and feminist friend thought it was pretentious to be seen with a tattered copy at an academic conference and was surprised to meet someone who had not only actually read it but was almost through a second time. We thought the novel merited at least two readings, being perhaps the most important work of fiction of the second half of the century. And yet most literary-critical responses we read failed to do justice to its importance. Certainly they sang its praises but this amounted finally to little more than a dry and repetitive litany. They failed, it seemed to us, to provide the analytic framework that might delineate the novel's difference.

Hoping eventually to arrive at such an analysis, we decided to rehearse some types of reading for ourselves. We came up with some ideas of our own which other critics seemed not to have gone into; but, being afraid as ever of the reproach that theorists over-generalise without textual substantiation, we decided to do some spade-work. Besides, with Brecht, we wanted to admit that any attempt at what might be called an 'immediately theoretical reading' would amount to forgetting the production process necessitated by the organisation of such a large, and ever-increasing, body of writing – *Gravity's Rainbow* and the texts it has spawned. And besides, with everybody, we really did want to know what happens to Slothrop; kept searching back through the pages to remind ourselves who Dodson-Truck was; tried to keep track of the various possible components of the S-gerät, and so on.

Like others entering the labyrinth, we began by noting points of reference, producing a page-by-page sketch map which came under constant revision, still has a lot of loose ends and often leads nowhere. Even at this level, the nearest we got to degree-zero of interpretation, it proved impossible to avoid double readings, to separate commentary and paraphrase; we inevitably made either intelligent or far-fetched guesses and what turned out later to be very obvious mistakes; sometimes there was nothing at all to say about a passage, an obvious privileging of certain themes, or the operation of arbitrary selection and exclusion criteria.

Working from the map, we set out to produce our readings. In the first instance this took the form of a summary of the narrative based on a finite set of characters and which involved trying to relate a limited set of events to each; a very traditional approach but we admitted it to be one which we would have at some stage indulged in anyway. Given the obvious amount of overlap, we thought that by starting from a number of different characters, we would come up with a set of data (or *capta*) which could be given to a hitch-hiker in Arizona who asked what *Gravity's Rainbow* was about; or to one's mother who wanted to know the story but didn't get past the first hundred pages because of (*sotto voce*) 'the sex'; or for that matter a feminist friend in a similar situation – after all, it is a pretty blatantly sexist book.[3] So we are still reading *Gravity's Rainbow*, like this:

> The first character mentioned by name in the book is Captain Geoffrey ('Pirate') Prentice. He works for Special Operations Executive, the Firm having been informed of his talent for dreaming other people's dreams for them. He dreams at least the first couple of pages of the novel. Such experiences are said to cease after V-E day but he remains haunted by Frans van der Groov, Katje Borgesius' ancestor who helped exterminate the Mauritian dodo, and whose cosmic windmill is reminiscent of the rocket symbol and the Zone-Hereros' mandala. Slothrop finds one of the latter and later gives it to the Schwarzkommando in return for the mantra which Enzian had taught him at their second meeting.
>
> Enzian (Oberst Enzian of Bleicheröde, whence Blicero also takes his name) and the Schwarzkommando are some of the survivors of a Nazi plan to set up puppet governments in British and French colonies in Africa. As it happens a similar unit is invented by British intelligence as a propaganda exercise, using mock-up films, after SOE learns of the existence of a Black rocket corps. After the war they live in abandoned mineshafts in the mountains around Nordhausen.

There are a number of factions among these Zone-Hereros or Erdschweinhöhle, including the Otukungurua who advocate racial suicide by refusing to procreate, as a means of preventing a repetition of the situation where an uprising in Africa was repressed by von Trotha at the expense of 60 000 Herero lives, or 60 per cent of the race, perhaps the century's first genocide. To the end Enzian has an uneasy relationship with the Otukungurua led by Josef Ombindi and they may be responsible for his undoing.

Prentice shares a Chelsea maisonette, famous for its home-grown banana breakfasts, with, among others, Osbie Feel and Teddy Bloat. He has privileged access to incoming mail (rockets) and uses his ejaculate to render legible a Kryptosam message found in the cone of one which falls at Greenwich, as a result of which he goes to Holland to bring out Katje who is his Dutch operative. She stays in the maisonette and she and Pirate form some sort of attachment. She never talks much about her experiences in Holland. He arranges for her to work at The White Visitation but doesn't know exactly what Pointsman has her doing there. Prentice's nosing around later leads Pointsman to suspect that they are in love. In fact she trains with Pointsman's octopus Grigori, to which end Osbie Feel makes films of her, for the 'attack' from which Slothrop will rescue her in the south of France. She and Slothrop have a short intense affair before her cover is blown by Sir Stephen Dodson-Truck and Slothrop begins his search for the rocket.

In Holland, Katje has been spying for the British at the rocket site near The Hague where, along with the young soldier Gottfried, she becomes the third member of Blicero's sado-masochistic trio, often acting out Hansel and Gretel fantasies involving the threat of the oven. Dominus Blicero, Master (of the White) Death, is the SS code name for Weissmann, captain of rocket launch control units at various firing sites. He likes Rilke's *Duino Elegies*, transvestism, and sadism, and has spent some time in South West Africa where he met Enzian. He brought his Herero favourite back to Germany and they worked together on the rocket program until parting company at the time of the move from Peenemünde to the Mittelwerke (Nordhausen). Blicero secretly builds the 00000 rocket, with its mysterious Schwarzgerät apparatus, thanks to the cooperation of Franz Pökler and Klaus Närrisch. Pökler, a plastics chemist and former student of Jamf, inventor of Imipolex G and Kryptosam, among other things, is brought to the rocket project by Kurt Mondaugen, a fellow student, whom Pökler runs into one night when he is out sticking up posters for Erdmann/von Göll/Schlepzig films. Mondaugen had known Weissmann in South West Africa, as recounted in *V*. The latter manipulates Pökler by controlling visits by Pökler's daughter Ilse to her father, during the time she is imprisoned with her mother in Dora. As a result of this indirect blackmail, Pökler is responsible for developing the plastic fairing for the S-gerät.

Blicero never forgives Katje for escaping, although she seems not to betray the actual location of the firing site to the British, either to protect Gottfried, or out of some feeling for Blicero. After Holland, Blicero retreats to Germany and to the Lüneberg Heath where his 'final madness' occurs. It is there that the firing of the 00000 is supposed to have taken place, with Gottfried dressed in white lace and accommodated in the specially designed S-gerät, an Imipolex G shroud, located in the tail section of the rocket. When Slothrop meets up with Enzian's Schwarzkommando in the Zone after the War they are attempting to assemble a rocket on the model of the 00000, to be called the 00001. They build an A4 piece by piece, find the Jamf Ölfabriken Werke AG in working order, and by the time of their disappearance from the narrative the Schwarzkommando have gained all the information they need about the 00000, and have transported their disassembled A4, and necessary parts for the 00001, to its firing site where its reassembly is said to occur 'in a geographical way'. The firing which occurs at the end of the book makes sense as that of the 00000, but in terms of narrative sequentiality it could be that of the 00001. For the Schwarzkommando and for Enzian, a high priest of the rocket, the latter has come to be the godhead of a mythology which combines tribal beliefs and technological fetishism.

The plan to bring Katje and Slothrop together as a prelude to setting him loose in search of the 00000, has been contrived mainly by Kevin Spectro and Pointsman. Mr Edward W. A. Pointsman FRCS is an extreme behaviourist with a position of some importance in PISCES. He has Katje indulge Brigadier Pudding's coprophilic and masochistic fantasies there. He works with dogs to begin with but seems to know a lot about Slothrop – his conditioning to Imipolex by Laszlo Jamf when his father 'sold' him as a guinea-pig in return for a Harvard education for the boy; his subsequent before-the-fact erection responses to the dropping of V2s on London. He places Slothrop under sodium amytal at The White Visitation and learns something of his fear of Black cock. Pointsman seems to have sexual hang-ups of his own, gets lonely at night and a blow-job at a Christmas party in 1944.

Working with Pointsman, unhappily, is Prentice's friend Roger Mexico, an amorous statistician. He is plotting the fall of the rockets according to a Poisson distribution and his map corresponds exactly with that Slothrop has made of his London sexual conquests, each of which prefigures a strike by an average of four and a half days. Teddy Bloat has microfilmed this map and Prentice passes it on to Mexico. Mexico is in love with Jessica Swanlake, a liaison which reminds Prentice of a relationship he had with Scorpia Mossmoon. Mexico and Swanlake often go for drives and one Christmas they end up at a Church service somewhere in Kent. On Boxing Day 1944 they visit Jessica's sister and children. After the war Jessica goes back to Jeremy, to whom she was forsworn, to Cuxhaven where they are to fire disused rockets out to sea.

Mexico dislikes his colleagues at The White Visitation for being mystics, psychologists, and ESP freaks, and has a view of science diametrically opposed to that of Pointsman. There is a work called The Book, probably connected with Pavlov, that circulates there among its seven owners. Mexico eventually discovers that he is being manipulated by Pointsman who has planted Jessica with him, and that Pointsman knew about Slothrop from well before the war through his ICI/IG Farben connections. But Slothrop gets out of Pointsman's reach after the Riviera episode until his men catch up with him at Cuxhaven and try to neutralise him by castration but perform the operation on Major Marvy instead. Pointsman had already gone pathological at a post-war seaside holiday and after the castration incident he falls into official disgrace and has his activities curtailed. He goes back to working with dogs.

The Old Firm Convention sees a bittersweet reunion between Prentice and Katje. Then Prentice, Mexico, and Katje set out separately into the Zone to try to reach Slothrop. Katje hears of him from Enzian, who knows her as the 'Golden Bitch of Blicero's last letters'. Mexico gets sidetracked to take revenge on Jessica and Jeremy and at the Gross Suckling Conference he and Seaman Bodine do their alliterative shit-food number. Mexico has already at least imagined pissing all over Pointsman's corporate friends. Pirate Prentice hijacks a plane to Berlin and is last heard of flying over the top of Slothrop asleep in a field before he runs out of fuel.

Castration victim Major Marvy is a bigoted American whom Slothrop meets on a train when he first arrives in the Zone, before the Major is thrown overboard by Enzian who gets angry at his racist talk. After that Marvy has it in for Slothrop and chases him in more than one scene. He teams up with the Russian Tchitcherine, who is Enzian's half-brother. Tchitcherine's father had gone AWOL in the Südwest in 1904, en route to the Pacific to relieve the Russian fleet during the war with Japan, and in the course of things fathered Enzian. Tchitcherine develops a private obsession to eradicate Enzian and his Schwarzkommando. He had had an association with Wimpe, from a subsidiary of IG Farben, the company responsible for the development of plastics research in Germany before the War, and possibly for shadowing Slothrop since his conditioning by Jamf. Later, and Tchitcherine thinks it is because of this association, he is assigned to work on the New Turkic Alphabet in Central Asia, where he sees the Kirghiz Light, before coming to the Zone to hunt Enzian. He catches up with Slothrop at Potsdam and puts him under sodium amytal. Slothrop has been sleeping with Geli Tripping, one of Tchitcherine's lovers in the Zone, and has stolen his boots. He will later steal his whole uniform at Peenemünde, and inform Enzian of an impending raid by the Russians. Tchitcherine fears his superiors will catch up with him before he gets to Enzian and they may well do, but he and Enzian meet in passing and exchange a few words in broken German without recognising one another.

When Slothrop comes round after the sodium amytal session he is in a disused movie studio near Potsdam that Tchitcherine has commandeered. Former actress Margherita Erdmann has come to reminisce and she and Slothrop begin a sado-masochistic relationship there and then using the torture chamber set from old von Göll movies in which she had

Gravity's Rainbow *and the post-rhetorical* 29

starred. Margherita is a Lombard and her entry into the narrative has been prefigured through the Saüre Bummer Potsdam dope deal. She is described as Slothrop's 'Lisaura', existing less than the film images of her. She has been, or still is, in love with former co-star Max Schlepzig, whose identity card Slothrop used to enter Potsdam. She thinks Schlepzig is the father of her daughter Bianca, conceived profilmicly during the shooting of *Alpdrücken*, although Stefania Procalowska, wife of the owner of the ship *Anubis*, will claim it could have been any one of the jackal men playing in the pack-rape scene in footage which only survives in Goebbels' private collection.

Margherita played in a number of S&M movies directed by von Göll, who used a special emulsion invented by Jamf for developing. It is von Göll who makes films for the British Schwarzkommando project before returning to the Zone as Der Springer, a marketeer ostensibly raising money for future films. He is said to have the S-gerät for sale, and Slothrop tracks him down at Swinemünde, in the company of Klaus Närrisch who worked on the apparatus with Franz Pökler. Der Springer gets captured by Tchitcherine and is sprung by Närrisch and Slothrop, which is when Slothrop steals the Russian's uniform, but this is at the expense of Närrisch whom Tchitcherine drugs and so learns important details about the 00000. Närrisch worked on guidance and modified weight specifications and reveals that there was a one-way ground-to-rocket radio in the S-gerät and an oxygen line running to it.

It is after a screening of *Alpdrücken* that Franz Pökler comes home horny to his wife Leni, as a result of which Ilse is supposed to have been conceived. Leni leaves Franz when the child is still young, after he switches from paint to rocketry. She has perhaps been a prostitute since World War I times and is involved with Peter Sachsa, a medium at séances on behalf of corporate Nazi chemists. She is also close to a group of leftist intellectuals and draws Sachsa into anti-Nazi activities. He is killed in a street action, receiving it would seem the truncheon blow meant for Franz who happens to be standing beside him. Leni is interned with Ilse at Dora, near Nordhausen, and thinks her relations with the SS secure some freedom for her daughter. Slothrop will meet Leni at Cuxhaven where she is the prostitute Solange, and so avoid being castrated. When they sleep, Slothrop dreams of Margherita's daughter Bianca on the ferris wheel at Zwölfkinder (where Franz and Ilse often went during her visits), and Leni dreams of Ilse riding a freight train through the Zone.

Slothrop and Erdmann stay together for a while in an old house near the Spree and he becomes less motivated to solve the rocket mystery. But Greta's agoraphobia and masochism create an increasingly unliveable situation and they set out for Swinemünde – she to find Bianca, he after the S-gerät, acting on information from Geli Tripping. Erdmann is called the White Woman but dresses in black, and is frightened by a woman in black they meet on the street at Bad Karma. According to Ensign Morituri's story, this would have reminded her of herself when, before the war, addicted to Oneirine (an IG Farben/Jamf product) and other things, having returned from an unsuccessful spell in Hollywood, she began to imagine she was part Jewish, and perpetrated ritual killings of Jewish children. Morituri, a native of Hiroshima, tells Slothrop this story on board the *Anubis* where Greta is reunited with husband Miklos Thanatz and daughter Bianca. There are a number of suggestions that Thanatz and Bianca have a sexual history together, just as Margherita has a long history of masochism. She tells Slothrop how Thanatz used to read her scars and lashes like a gypsy the palm of a hand, as well as the story of their involvement with Blicero when they were touring camps and rocket sites to entertain the SS. Blicero called Greta 'Katje' and in an orgy which took place in a petrochemical plant called the Castle, she dressed in an Imipolex G suit open at the crotch. Thanatz seems to have fallen for young Gottfried who, for both him and Greta, is another Bianca, and stays on to witness the firing of the 00000 on the Heath. Enzian claims in conversation with Katje that that is as far as Blicero got, but Thanatz hears of him later as the chosen absolute leader of a group of homosexuals liberated from Dora, who have resettled in the Russian zone. Blicero's identity or status here is never confirmed, though Thanatz asserts that, whether alive or dead, myth or just name, he is 'real'. Erdmann's story convinces Slothrop that he will keep being reminded of the rocket no matter how much he tries to ignore it, but after the Peenemünde episode, when he and Närrisch are said to approach a holy Center, he begins to fade from the narrative, although he does tell the Schwarzkommando all he has heard from Margherita.

Still on board the *Anubis*, Slothrop sees Margherita, on the urging of the other passengers, beat Bianca as the climax to an orgy. Then, after hearing Morituri's story, and subsequent to having frenzied sex with the girl himself, he begins to fear for her safety as her mother slips into a delirium in which Slothrop comes to be seen as the reincarnation of Margherita's sacrificial victims. He looks for Bianca but only finds a fragment of her clothing in the engine room, and can get no sense out of Margherita. There are glimpses of her after that and it may be Bianca who mugs Slothrop when he boards the *Anubis* again later, that is if she hasn't hanged herself.

That is not how the book ends, and it is no doubt more than one needs to tell Mother. There is obviously no minimal narrative summary one can make; one is immediately in the business of anticipating the host of questions posed by the listener, making mnemonic repetitions, and indulging one's own narrative pleasure. On the other hand, in spite of trying, at any given point in the summary, to provide readers with sufficient information for them to know who was who and what was what up to that point, we inevitably repeated some of the irregularities of the narrative order,[4] the ellipsis and anachrony with which the text is constructed.

The fate of Bianca highlights the problem with reading *Gravity's Rainbow* even at this level. One will never know just what does happen to her. The episode after Margherita's story about the Imipolex G suit orgy has a storm and Slothrop is swept over the side of the *Anubis* when he thinks he catches sight of Bianca again, slipping herself 'on the slimy deck... under the chalky lifelines and gone' (491).[5] But even that is ambiguous, and hinges on how one reads the syntax: '... Slothrop will think he sees her, think he has found Bianca again ... he will see her lose her footing on the slimy deck ... he will lunge after her without thinking much, slip himself as she vanishes under the chalky lifelines and gone', which could either mean 'slip himself ... under the chalky lifelines', or 'she vanishes under the chalky lifelines'. He is rescued by Frau Gnahb and taken to Swinemünde. During the voyage he sleeps for a few hours in the pilot house, and 'Bianca comes to snuggle in under his blanket with him' (492). She talks to him. Did she not then drown? A little later Der Springer will reassure a still anxious Slothrop that 'Bianca's a clever child, and her mother is hardly a destroying goddess' (494). Did Slothrop imagine having her in his bed again the previous night? Whoever mugs Slothrop back in the engine room of the *Anubis* kicks his head in with what feels like 'the pointed toe of a dancing-pump' (530), and at the end of the ordeal, getting up in a stupor, he touches 'stiff taffeta ... slippery satin ... hooks and eyes ... something hanging from the overhead. Icy little thighs in wet silk ... long wet hair ... cold nipples ... the deep cleft of her buttocks, perfume and shit and ...' (531)

And so we resort to the longhand of citing and encounter two associated problems. Firstly, the above narrative summary was already a type of citation, at least a paraphrase that took its terms as closely as possible from the text whenever there was doubt about an event. Secondly, there is no simple opposition between the said and the unsaid in *Gravity's Rainbow*. What does it mean to say that Katje never says much to Pirate about 'her experiences in Holland'? The text, more precisely, says: 'Pirate is having second thoughts. . . . He keeps recalling that Katje now avoids all mention of the house in the forest. She has glanced into it, and out, but the truth's crystal sheets have diffracted all her audible words – often to tears – and he can't quite make sense of what's spoken, much less infer to the radiant crystal itself. Indeed why did she leave Schußstelle 3? *We are never told why*' (107, italics ours). So although Katje, through Prentice, never tells us much about her experiences in Holland, Katje, through the text, and the text through itself, says a great deal about those experiences. And similarly, it may be that Katje had already told Prentice all we know before she started avoiding all mention of the house.

In every case we face indeterminacies of this kind. The narrative refuses to be stitched together as whole cloth out of the wefts and warps of the characters. Most of the critical readings one encounters make that very clear, but they often go on to make surprising assumptions about events or characters, or to develop interpretations of the novel which rely on an assumed determinacy behind it all. Slothrop of course, is the paradigmatic case of the vanishing hero. After Peenemünde he turns up only infrequently and as a minor figure in other people's accounts. Not that his appearances weren't always somewhat infrequent and aleatory. By the 'end' he becomes a legend in his own novel. It seems to us that even a narrative summary that recounted the tale from the point of view of Slothrop as protagonist would be occluding that indeterminacy. But the same goes for any other character. Prentice is literally left up in the air. One cannot be sure whether Gottfried really is the pilot/cargo of the 00000, whether it is actually fired by Blicero on the Lüneberg Heath and whether he meets his end this way. The Schwarzkommando, after beginning on film, then coming into focus, or reality, express doubts about their own existence (361–2).

A further problem with a 'characterological' reading is that the characters cannot be kept separate as persons in any obvious way. They are often paired: Slothrop with Pökler, for example, through the rocket and through their respective paternal relations to Ilse and Bianca (who also go proxy for each other at certain points). Enzian and Tchitcherine are another obvious pair, and Enzian can also be paired with Gottfried; as can Katje, his 'sister' in the Grimm fantasy; as can Bianca with Erdmann and Thanatz. Erdmann herself is called 'Katje' by Blicero, and so on. And furthermore, if characters are not based on the idea of separate and unique biological, psychological, or social personages, then one could easily make a case for recounting the narrative from the point of view of, say, Imipolex G, as much a node in the grid, or a thread in the weave, of the story as 'someone' like its creator Jamf. Not to mention the rocket.

Seeing the idea of a narrative structured through the trajectories of characters put in jeopardy, we were led to look elsewhere for a reading of *Gravity's Rainbow*, albeit in the form of another traditional approach common in literary studies in general, and, to our surprise given the look of the novel, to Pynchon studies in particular. Critics return to the book in terms of its themes. The 'entropy' theme, relevant to a number of Pynchon's texts, has been worked to death[6]; but many other 'themes' present themselves in *Gravity's Rainbow*: death itself, sex, science, religion, art, music. Perhaps as devotees of semiosis or grammatology, perhaps because the choice hardly matters, we decided to pursue *inter alia* the idea or the theme of the word, the alphabet, the book, the sign, or the linguistic mark in *Gravity's Rainbow*. Thus we continued to read, like this:

> The word, sometimes the 'Word', has a large number of material configurations in *Gravity's Rainbow*. There are four sizes of standard typeface if one includes the section titles; two sets of italics, one in the text proper, another for references to

epigraphs; two sets of lower case capitals whose function sometimes doubles for that of the italics; two sets of mixed lower and upper case capitals, one of which is used most notably for the (inter)titles which become frequent in the last eighty pages of the book; and a set of upper case capitals, occasionally italicised, used in the main for acronyms and onomatopoeic neologisms. A small number of phonetic characters is used. There are diacritical subscriptings in technical discussions along with delta, integral, and other mathematical symbols. A mandala, the rocket symbol, and a finger are other instances of graphic representation. Runes, on the other hand, are described without typographical intervention.

Onomatopoeic neologisms range from 'hunh' (405) to 'KRUPPALOOMA' (690) and beyond, but are far from being the only concrete linguistic interventions to be found in the book. Instances such as 'A-and' (65) and a consistent 'sez' (64, 200, 201), the seemingly random capitalisation of words in passages like that which recounts Katje's time with Blicero (95–7), a fondness for alliteration ('Kute Korrespondences', 590) and an arcane lexicon ('ctenophile', 123, 'crwth', 639), similarly foreground the written word. Much of the emphasis here is on vocalisation of written language through phonetic rendition of accents ('Getcher ass offa dat fire', 641), or the use of hyphens for unusual intonation patterns ('shape-less *blob* of ex*per*-ience', 81). Mention of film actors like Cary Grant (240) or Bela Lugosi (557) is a shorthand for typifying accents. Argotic usages also carry over into the narrative prose ('but def', 128, 'natch', 653). When Hilary Bounce talks to an increasingly paranoid Slothrop on the Riviera, two of his words occur between quotation marks which Slothrop is said to be able to hear (241). Placenames referred to by Katje, Slothrop and later Bianca, are prefixed by the demonstrative adjective 'that' (193, 195, 493) in their direct speech as well as in the narrative proper (198).[7]

Further intralinguistic play includes the series of puns on the Kenosha Kid sentence (60ff); a play on the expression 'unto thee I pledge my trough' (576); Mexico's literalisation of Rózsavölgyi's 'I say' (634); and a cryptic reference to the Hiroshima headline (693). Just as common are interferences relating to interlinguistic functions such as the mistranslation of a Morse message (515), Michele's misunderstanding about

Gravity's Rainbow *and the post-rhetorical*

getting fixed up with a big oilman (243), the narrator's play on Geli Tripping's sub-enunciated 'warum' (331), and the discussions concerning 'ass-backwards' and 'shit 'n' shinola' (683–8). Languages in use include English, French, German, Italian, Spanish, Latin, Russian (not Cyrillic), Herero, and Japanese (not characters).

Mastery of the spoken word is related on more than one occasion to life and death situations. The Dodoes are exterminated because they can't speak, except in Frans van der Groov's fantasy conversion miracle (110–11), and Germans have to be taught to correctly pronounce words of surrender (230). For the Kirghiz who have the New Turkic Alphabet imposed upon them, the written word represents a destruction of cultural values, incapable in any case of translating their silences (338–41). The alphabetisation program is given over to bureaucratic infighting aimed at reducing the diversity of oral utterance and which rides roughshod over political and religious sensibilities (352–6).

The idealisation of unmediated communication implied in Tchitcherine's Kirghiz experience is more explicitly referred to in a case where an intralinguistic misunderstanding occurs without the humour that normally characterises such instances. During a discussion with the Schwarzkommando that marks the final mention of her, Katje asks why anyone would want to fight for a desert. The preposition is corrected to 'in' and the narrator notes that it 'Saves trouble later if you can get the Texts straight soon as they're spoken' (729). The Schwarzkommando with their rocket mystique and Enzian with his Illumination, perhaps come closest to this type of idealised communication, but the séance cultists may well be another such example.

On the other hand the Word that is the Rocket, 'the one Word that rips apart the day' (25), like the word 'death' the most frequent utterance during séances (32),[8] is an instance of direct communication. Thus it stands at the centre of the Zone-Hereros' new religion as the vehicle of the true message for a people whose history is one of lost messages (322), although Enzian will later opine that the rocket is only apocryphal to the real Text (520). When Slothrop and Närrisch approach the holy Center at Peenemünde there is a reference to words being only delta-t from what they stand for, such words being contrasted with the Operational Word (510). The delta-t gap is echoed in the fall of the Rocket in the book's penultimate paragraph, reinforcing the idea that what the rocket communicates, so directly as to *perform* (contact) before it *utters* (sound), is death. The rocket is also referred to as the Torah (727) and incoming mail (6).

The Word exists along with shit and money as one of the American truths which the Slothrop family industry embraces in producing paper for newspapers, toilet tissue, and banknotes (28). Other types of text range from the orthodox – quotations, songs, limericks, poems, epitaphs, proverbs, graffiti, the Tarot, a mantra; to the less so – human palimpsests (50), Teddy Bloat (188), the day (204), joint papers (442), whipped bodies (484), shivers (641), Blicero's eye (670), a photograph (693), Slothrop who is only a pretext (738), and the screen seen as a page (760). There is also the Book to do with Pavlov which circulates at The White Visitation and has a reducing membership (47, 139).

In Herero the holy Text of the rocket is called 'orururumo orunene', except that the second word, meaning 'the great one', is being modified to 'omunene', the eldest brother (520). The Empty Ones make their own linguistic change to take the name 'Otukungurua' with its prefix referring to the inanimate. The act of naming is given prominence in Herero. The name 'Enzian' is used as a chant (321), the name of God is the same as the word for fucking (100), and they have many words for shit (325). Saüre Bummer revives the ritual of naming when he christens Slothrop the 'Raketemensch' (366). The narrator refers to the German habit of naming (probably that language's use of compound nouns), which seems to be adopted by Slothrop under Tchitcherine's sodium amytal, as an analytical mania for dividing the Creation finer and finer, setting namer apart from named, building words like molecular structures (391). This sort of naming presumably contrasts with that practised by the Hereros. But Slothrop has been naming since the days of his London map (cf. 271), and the book's characters not only have strange proper names of their own, but many nicknames and pseudonyms. Besides, there is some confusion of characters' names such as when Blicero calls Greta 'Katje'. The relationship between naming of characters and neologism in general is highlighted when Slothrop takes on the name and role of Plechazunga for a day, that name being repeated as the onomatopoeia 'PLECCCHHAZUNNGGA!' (569) when the fireworks begin. *Gravity's Rainbow*'s most obvious neologisms apart from names and vocal transcriptions are proper nouns like 'Oneirine', 'Imipolex', and 'Schwarzgerät', which exist as words needing to have meaning ascribed to them. More than that, being written without being spoken, these words remain strictly speaking unpronounceable. A first ordering of such words during Slothrop's second meeting with Enzian provides the basis for the twin possibilities of random events or organised conspiracy (363).

What proceeds, however naïvely or ingenuously, as a simple presentation of data (*capta*) collected along thematic lines, is obviously less able to contain itself and prescribe its limits than that which relied on the notion of integral characters. The word here concludes by abutting on to a theme as broad and as commonly referred to as entropy in Pynchon studies, namely the plot/conspiracy vs. chaos/randomness relation. From there it is but a short distance to questions of ethics and recipes for living, and thereupon a host of political questions arise: black/white, men/women, force/counterforce, right/left, humane/inhumane, and so on. Thus a modernist reading of *Gravity's Rainbow* is also in jeopardy. How can a novel of ideas, especially one whose philosophers and technocrats are so close to the surface of the text, slip and slide around so much? For if our characterological reading overlooked but was forced to confront the problem of narrative time in the novel, what thematic studies must deal with, and will never solve, are the matters of narrative mood and voice.[9] These are plural in *Gravity's Rainbow*, so much so as to preclude the organisation of thematic material into anything resembling a coherent set of ideas which might be called the 'philosophy' of the novel. And we are leaving aside the enormous associated problems of authorship on the one hand, and, pardon the shorthand, logocentrism on the other, that is to say the underlying notion(s) that the signifiers of the novel can ultimately be returned or reduced to a coherent whole, be it an author or a philosophy. Nevertheless many of the commentators we have read are happy not only to overlook the plurality of narrative voices in the novel, but also to unconsciously perform the enormous ellipsis which assimilates the narrator(s) to someone called Thomas Pynchon.[10]

Thus our comments on the word were not as naïve or as ingenuous as they might have first appeared. They go too far, inevitably, and are already in the business of making interpretations which fail to examine the assumptions upon which they depend; but from the point of view we adopted there, that is one which is directed towards some final ideological or philosophical coherence, such a study of the novel can hardly go further than a taxonomy of instances and still retain its own critical integrity. Many readings we have encountered illustrate this dilemma.

Accordingly we wanted to undertake a reading which worked not from just a different theme or idea, but a whole new order or conception of textuality. Such an order has been the source for much of that commentary which considers Pynchon as a postmodernist – with its overtones of intertextuality and the encroachment of the non-literary.[11] Cinema might be such an order, it seemed to us, already instanced by Cowart, Clerc and Simmon, although not on our terms.[12] In our reading of cinema we deliberately abandon the ideal of a 'degree-zero' reading; by letting a certain degree of free-play emerge in, or as, the reading; by letting reference lead to reference in a looser or less structured way than is normally practised in either traditional or modernist readings. However, it should be remembered that this is still an empiricist reading. It still works close to the text; it still cites instances of the text as its evidence; it still works through the text in a very particularistic and piecemeal fashion, even though it re-uses the material (*data*? *capta*?) it obtains there in a less constrained manner than previously. Thus we continued reading *Gravity's Rainbow*, like this:

> Cinema, like Pirate Prentice, has the ability to dream other people's dreams for them. Since the novel begins with one of Pirate's dreams, it may be read as one whole dream or one whole film. To write about cinema in *Gravity's Rainbow* then would be to begin with 'A screaming comes across the sky . . . ' and to proceed from there to the final falling of the rocket (which precedes the screaming) upon the picture theatre where the readership sits watching the trajectories of the bouncing ball from word to word, at the end of the rainbow, now . . . everybody . . . It's not that life imitates cinema, or vice versa. The two are indistinguishable here, or related in some yet to be defined manner.

Katje first appears only as the film image of herself in the 14th sub-section of Part One, right after the line of seven sprocket holes or frames. (Who put them there does not seem to us to be an important question – why should we believe publishers who are under express instructions to cover over the 'real' Thomas Ruggles?[13] and if we were to believe it was Ruggles himself, what would that tell us when we hardly know who he is?) The film she is in, made by Osbie Feel, is probably one of those used to train Grigori, 'the biggest fucking octopus Slothrop has ever seen outside of the movies, Jackson' (186). But the film soon gives way to some supposedly non-filmic details of Katje's life with no clear boundaries separating the two. At the end of the section, the whole film plays again: 'The camera follows as she moves deliberately nowhere...' (92, 113). It loops around perhaps. And later still in the novel (553ff) Katje, or another image of her, watches this film of herself, 'the same unfolding' (29). *Gravity's Rainbow* is full of the same unfolding difference. Science, death, sex, parabolas, literature, the word, language, psychology, plot, history, ESP, theatre, music, religion, and Angels are played as films. The curve, the geometrical rainbow, the arc, the parabola, the rocket's trajectory are essentially projected. Ballistics and optics, missile and *camera obscura*, both had a common ancestry in Leonardo's monocular perspective long before Kekulé and Rathenau.

Most of all the war is played as a movie containing, as Cowart points out, action, scenarios, bombing, shooting and theatres.[14] 'Yes, it is a movie! Another World War II situation comedy...' (691–2). Early on, Pointsman directs, but only on Their behalf: 'you are trapped inside Their frame with your wastes piling up, ass hanging out all over Their Movieola viewer, waiting for Their editorial blade' (694). Mexico, for example, finds one 'bad cinema spring' (628) that his 'love' for Jessica was no more than a fiction dreamed up by Pointsman in order to keep camera-like surveillance on him, the deviant statistician, lost man of science in a ghost movie. For another example, let's not mention again the (dis)appearance of the Black rocket corps. In this connection though, it is worth noting that even someone as distantly removed from Hollywood as the Herero Enzian, gobbles Pervertins 'like popcorn at the movies' (522); he's 'just as smooth as that Cary Grant'

(661), and his fellow Schwarzkommando, Pavel, on a massive sniffing binge, sees, inter alia, 'Bing Crosby in a baseball cap' (523).

Von Göll's other major film project in the novel concerns a group of Argentinian U-boat sailors with heavy nationalist tendencies. Their idea is to make a film of the great gaucho epic *Martín Fierro*. One of their number, Squalidozzi, is first encountered hiding in a cinema in Bavaria where 'the filmlight flickered blue' (385). On the U-boat there are stock puns like 'Gaucho Marx'. The proposed film is never made but sections of it survive in *filmprose* on the pages of *Gravity's Rainbow* (for instance, 386–7). Von Göll is driven to believe that his film can make the Argentinians' political dreams come true, for 'since discovering that Schwarzkommando are really in the Zone, leading real, paracinematic lives that have nothing to do with him or the phony Schwarzkommando footage he shot last winter in England for Operation Black Wing, Springer has been zooming [!] around in a controlled ecstasy of megalomania' (388). Later (612–13), though the film is yet to be made, the Argentinians are inhabiting a set of real buildings which will remain unstruck, a type of statehood thus realised, and Felipe explains his weird notion of the intellect of rocks in terms of cinematic discontinuity – 'We're talking frames per century ... per millennium!' (612). In this war/movie where the sets have more 'reality' than historic materialities like the Reichstag building – 'is that King Kong, or some creature closely allied, squatting down, evidently just taking a shit' (368) – who can delineate the cinematic from the real?

No wonder the War drives Slothrop to paranoia, of the type learned in cinemas – 'there's always someone behind him being careful not to talk, rattle paper, laugh too loud: Slothrop's been to enough movies that he can pick up an anomaly like that right away' (114). In the theatre, in the film: cinema combines the two. And many a manipulation can be produced or directed in the space in between. But as we have already seen, the film is not only out to shoot Slothrop, no one escapes it. Not even the director, Pointsman, can stay out of camera range, appearing 'in a medium shot, himself backlit, alone at the high window' (142). Not even the critic, Mitchell Prettyplace (who might be called 'Sprocketman' because he picks technical holes in film), for all his scholarship including eight volumes on *King Kong*, can anticipate that the film ape will give birth to the Schwarzkommando.

The War film, of course, extends to the Axis powers. Leni Pökler, like Erdmann, conceives thanks to film, and she dreams of flight while the film/novel projects its own cinematic theory: 'real flight and dreams of flight go together. Both are part of the same movement. Not A before B, but all together' (159), that 'all together' prefiguring the final words. Later 'film and calculus, both pornographies of flight' (567) will set up another parallel between forms of representation, modes of abstraction. Husband Franz sticks bills for Ufa movies. He sees, among other films, Lang's *Die Frau im Mond* for which the countdown is said to have been conceived (753), and nods off to sleep occasionally. As a rocket engineer he watches 'the daily rushes' taken of the rocket's flight, its fall 'photographed by Askania cinetheodolite rings on the ground' (407). When his daughter Ilse makes her annual visits she will appear so different each time that he will wonder whether it is her or an actress playing the part. Film has made the child and 'Isn't that what they made of my child, a film? . . . the moving image of a daughter, flashing him only these summertime frames of her, leaving him to build the illusion of a single child' (398, 422). Strangely enough, their last visit to Zwölfkinder, where rear-projection creates an Antarctic panorama (420), occasions the mention of an Ilse who persists 'beyond her cinema mother, beyond film's end', in the context of a Double Light that 'was always there, outside all film', seemingly the shadows of shadows of Cain and Abel (429). We don't know what that might mean after all this, for an outside of/to representation seems a slim hope given the net of interconnected or overlayered mediations that the novel throws out.

Film, especially in war, works as propaganda, as a way of making a certain political version of the world seem natural. In *Gravity's Rainbow* it works by being indistinguishable from real tyranny and freedom – real oppression and flight – and so on. But the material of film is also a political matter, of political substance. The many chemicals in the book centre around international capital deals and conspiracies and co-incidences of ownership, especially among ICI, IG Farben and their subsidiaries. Von Göll's special developing emulsion which makes the skin transparent (like a literal dissolve) is a case in point. Pirate's Kryptosam which makes messages legible only when doused in semen is another. But IG Farben also own General Aniline and Film and Spottbilligfilm AG, a manufacturer of cheap film connected with the dye market and with the emerging polymer research that leads to the production of the quasi-organic Imipolex G. Cine film is taken as the distant relative of this living chemical, the 'plastic film' activated by, inter alia, projection of an '"image" analogous to a motion picture' (700). One could go on into Erdmann's addiction to Oneirine, her bathing in Imipolex like Gottfried in his shroud in the final frames of the film, moving 'image to image' (721); for the film, like the rocket, exists as a series of delta discontinuities run together to produce a semblance of smooth flight, and like the rocket it needs to be forced to get going until at a certain point, its *Brennschluss*, it gathers its own, gravity's, or history's momentum, and we are in its grip.

Some sort of reference to cinema underwrites much of what happens in *Gravity's Rainbow*, so much so that one could well ask whether narrative prose is still possible without such reference. But here there is no need to look any further than the explicit. The casino where Slothrop and Katje get involved is like one huge set, where they are trying to get their lines right, where her wardrobe is 'mostly props' (195), and Slothrop begins his series of costume changes: US Army uniform to an English one; a fake moustache with its own cinematic history (210), and a zoot suit; a Rocketman costume and a tuxedo. Once the series is established in the context of a cinema set, and even if it hadn't been – his borrowing of Tchitcherine's boots and later his whole uniform, his pig costume, to final 'fade-out' ('letting his hair and beard grow, wearing a dungaree shirt and trousers Bodine liberated for him from the laundry of the *John E. Badass*', then spending 'whole days naked' (623)) – all such changes obey a metonymy which is cinematic through and through, right up to the Fay Wray costume in the transvestites' toilet (688), although we would refrain from placing that (or any other) episode chronologically. Slothrop's only definite ID, registered on paper, is that of the film actor Max Schlepzig. He fakes a Russian accent thanks to Bela Lugosi (557, 561), resorts to Fred Astaire wistfully searching for a lost Ginger when completely at a loose end (561), and after kicking a would-be attacker in the balls, lets out his own version of hiyo Silver – 'Fickt nicht mit der Raketemensch!' (435). Chase scenes begin in the Casino. The infamous They have planted the props, right down to an American Seltzer bottle and Slothrop anticipates the cream pies to complete the slapstick (197), although the cream pies will come later when Major Marvy comes at him for the second time (333ff). There is more chasing when Der Springer/von Göll falls into the Russians' hands and is rescued by Slothrop and Närrisch. Here it is pure slapstick complete with chimps, trombones and vodka bottles (503–4); then 'sneaky-Peteing like two cats in a cartoon' (508), a hold-up, chase, chorus girls (511–14), and Närrisch's imminent fate written under the sign of Dillinger/Clark Gable and further film allusions (516–17). Dillinger, we are later reminded, was shot outside a movie theatre – 'subdebs just out the movies with the sweat still cold on their thighs ... everybody was there ... [trying to] soak up some of John Dillinger's blood' (741).

Just as no one escapes from the movies, neither does any place. Even the Seven Rivers country visited by Tchitcherine in the early Stalin days is 'like a Wild West movie' (338). The world is essentially seen through a Hollywood lens no matter how culturally un-American the scene. The movies are imperialist: Nazis are cinema Nazis, even the feelings are cinema Nazi feelings – Slothrop sick in the British sector of the Zone, 'with the sovereign Nazi movie-villain fist clamping in his bowels ja – you vill *shit* now, ja?' (360). And the 'comic Nazi routine' Roger does with Miss Müller-Hochleben (633) should be mentioned here too. Even a gun, 'the racy 8mm French Hotchkiss' is as 'nasal and debonair as a movie star' (697). The Nazi movie-villain routine, like the King Kong Reichstag, makes the movie/shit connection, movies being locales for two other types of shit – bullshit (talk) and dope. At Neubabelsberg, the aptly named 'old movie capital of Germany' (371), Slothrop goes to get Saüre's stash. Before setting off, he inspects the morning streets of Berlin but can't recognise it as the city he 'used to see back in those newsreels' (372). The people in the street are 'extras' (374) involved in this cine-plot. Talking to Saüre about the rocket turns to talk about the movies (as does a later conversation with Pökler (578ff)). In the course of the talk it turns out Tchitcherine is setting up his HQ in the old Potsdam movie studios and it is as the film character of Rocketman that Slothrop must carry out his dope-quest (376). At Potsdam he gets entangled in a smart party with 'colonels' ladies in Garbo fedoras ... a strange collection of those showbiz types' (380), for the peace conference is no more nor less than another film with special mention going to Oliver Hardy, Don Ameche, and Errol Flynn, and above all a guest appearance by none other than Mickey Rooney who steps out on to the terrace for some fresh air just after Slothrop finds the dope – 'well, this may sound odd, but it's Mickey Rooney ... Mickey Rooney stares at Rocketman holding a bag of hashish, a wet apparition in helmet and cape ... He *knows* he is seeing Mickey Rooney, though Mickey Rooney, wherever he may go, will repress the fact that he ever saw Slothrop. It is an extraordinary moment' (382). For Slothrop, for Mickey Rooney, and for narrative prose.

Once Margherita Erdmann comes on the scene cinematic references abound – and remember, she waits for nearly thirty pages after her first mention, in a form 'less [real?] than the images of herself' (364) until meeting with Slothrop in the Potsdam studios – will she be more real thereafter? The 'Anti-Dietrich' (394), she hears explosions as 'cue calls for the titanic sets of her dreams' (446). Aboard the *Anubis*, where 'filthy movies are showing in the boiler room' (490), Greta materialises in the form of 'a shy fade-in, as Gerhardt von Göll must have brought her on a time or two' (459). Stefania Procalowska believes Greta and her daughter are aboard only because of the cinematic possibilities, for one Karel is also there posing as a film producer 'this month' (460). The orgy is stimulated to its wildest excesses following Bianca's Shirley Temple routine, while the inscrutable Ensign Morituri, who used to 'sit most of the day watching Allied footage for what could be pulled out and worked into newsreels to make the Axis look good' (473), but also knows Greta's dark past when she wore 'yellow sunglasses and Garbo hats' (476) and men had their 'faces shaven very smooth, film-star polished' (477), plays the part of the perfect spectator-voyeur, '[n]ot masturbating or anything' (467).

Greta fades back into her movie connection when Slothrop meets von Göll who says that she is supposed to be dead, to which Slothrop replies: 'W-well you're supposed to be a movie director'. And from von Göll: 'Same thing, same problems of control. But more intense' (494). Here too the cinematic creeps into the mundane aspects of people's lives as Der Springer and Slothrop stroll along the promenade and little Otto 'goes chasing seagulls, hands out in front of him movie style' (495), and Springer's latest batch of black-market valuables happens to contain three reels of *Lucky Pierre Runs Amok* (497). And so on, through one of the final sections entitled 'Chase Music' (751) to Richard M. Zhlubb's Orpheus Theatre and midnight showings (754–5), the repeating 'CATCH' of the Ascent (759) to the 'screen a dim page' of the final show (760). Just as the novel opens with a Prentice dream-movie, so its last section is an odd movie scene, perhaps a Slothrop dream (within a continuing dream or fantasy of Prentice's?). In it Bette Davis and Margaret Dumont get mixed up with the Marx Brothers. The characters of the novel, except perhaps Gottfried, have faded rather than made dramatic Hollywoodian exits. They project their vision of the future and perhaps our present. Blicero, for instance, in his final speech to Gottfried, speaks of a colony on the Moon where a 'handful of men have a frosty appearance, hardly solid, no more alive than memories, nothing to touch . . . only their remote images, black and white film-images, grained, broken . . .' (723). Film now less like life than death. With that muddled schema for the relations between forms and representations of reality we are back to the bouncing ball, the words of a song, within the ultimate delta-t where it is the turn of everybody, a set of words to follow and little time to dwell on the subtleties of register and inflexion, caught in the space of a final ellipsis, a dash to represent a film run out or caught in the gate, a wipe, fade, or jump cut, a pulled plug, the possibilities run on and on.

It is almost impossible to resist the distinction between the cinematic and the real. However, this form of distinction is a virtually impossible one to make in the case of *Gravity's Rainbow*, although it hasn't prevented a number of critical readings from trying. In fact it's possible to argue that all critical readings are based on assumptions about what constitutes the 'real' (as opposed to, say, the dreamed, the fantasised, the cinematic, the fictive and so on). Mrs Quoad is a case in point. McHale works through a reading in which the Mrs Quoad of the Disgusting English Candy Drill (114–20) is quite different from the Mrs Quoad whom

Pointsman's agents, Speed and Perdoo, uncover in their attempt to verify Slothrop's map (271). The former, on McHale's reading, emerges in 'Slothrop's fantasy life', whereas the latter has authentic status and must therefore be part of 'our reconstructed world.'[15]

Given that the real/fantasy distinction arises from the contrast of two third-person narratives, on what grounds could we give priority to one over the other? For example, if the rockets do fall where Slothrop fucks, then presumably the first, quite real Mrs Quoad, is dead, and the sophomoric spies have found an equally real somebody else. Two Mrs Quoads does not mean that one is mere fantasy. Similarly, if Slothrop is making it all up, then even a cursory reading should remain sufficiently doubtful about Speed and Perdoo's integrity as to allow them to be equally capable of creative invention:

> ... they went off practically *skipping*, obsessive as munchkins ... the two gumshoes become so infected with the prevailing fondness out here for mindless pleasures that they presently are passing whole afternoons sitting out in restaurant gardens dawdling over chrysanthemum salads and mutton casseroles, or larking at the fruitmongers ... (270, italics his).

The duo's propensity for *skipping* may well refer to more than just their ambulatory activities and point in the direction of omissions. McHale, it must be said, does recognise the unreliability of Speed and Perdoo, and concludes that 'we are left with elements whose ontological status is unstable, flickering, indeterminable',[16] but as long as he retains the notion of (presumably sovereign) consciousnesses being represented in the text, then verification of the ontological status of each datum is an assumed possibility. But we cannot be that sure.

When a decision as to the real is based only on a comparison of text with more-text – and we have demonstrated that traditional hierarchisations of textual material, such as those which place a narrative or authorial voice at the top, clearly collapse in *Gravity's Rainbow* – there can be no intratextual justification. Explicit decisions (such as in McHale's proposed reading) or implicit assumptions (such as Cowart's decision that V. is Stencil's mother[17]) concerning what is veridical in *Gravity's Rainbow* may not be in point at all, and yet we know of no critical reading which can do without one or the other (present company included).

But if the problem with Mrs Quoad involves an intratextual distinction between 'real' and 'imagined', similar problems apply where so-called extratextual material, such as the historical real, is brought into play. Cowart has been very astute to identify the Hannomag Storm motorcar which Gretel (Greta? Margherita?) and Thanatz come across in the forest at the end of their time with Blicero (485), as that in which Werner von Braun crashed and broke his arm, when driving from Bleicheröde to Berlin on 16 March 1945.[18] Both the car and the arm have previous mentions in the novel. The arm is one of a number of historical events including the arrival of spring, Lloyd George's imminent death and the month of March (237), which set the scene for the section which follows Brigadier Pudding's just dessert. It becomes a reference point for Slothrop and Katje's tryst at the Casino Hermann Goering. The(?) automobile is pluralised and lost in the forest in Slothrop's dreaming about Margherita (447). And when it turns up as the Hannomag Storm it is in one of Margherita's accounts of her history to Slothrop, where again the distinctions between real and fantasy are not preserved. For all its astuteness, Cowart's assertion about von Braun's car is no more or less apropos than Mendelson's decision that The White Visitation's Book *is* Pavlov's, Weisenburger's determination that Slothrop 'pores over the [...] same pages' as those found by Polish underground agents in the latrines of a test site in Blizna in September 1944.[19]

When historical phenomena are cited in fictional texts, corroboration can usually be had from extratextual sources (the texts we call history), cf. *War and Peace*. But as we can see from the treatment of von Braun/Blicero (again with the inevitable question mark about their identity), paralleling the question of Mrs Quoad/Mrs Quoad, no such corroboration can be had. In the case of *Gravity's Rainbow*, that corroboration is only possible if one can ascribe to a third-person narrative (or authorial voice?) priority over Slothrop's dreams or Greta Erdmann's paranoid delusions and/or recountings. The intratextual distinctions – between pieces of the text – and the intratextual/extratextual distinctions all fail in *Gravity's Rainbow*.

Where this leaves us then is essentially with the problem of different ways of sorting texts. While some may claim 'if the narrative says it, it's real', we could equally claim 'if the film says it, it's real' and so on for dream, hallucination, stoned rave, etc. In this case, a narrative voice has no real privilege over or against what we might call, say, a cinematic voice and to this we could add, for example, the voices of science, technology, history and so on. We have already seen how, at the quite simple levels of character, event and theme, it is pushing the bounds of plausibility to make categorical assertions about *Gravity's Rainbow*. If this basis fails us then we must ask the question 'what actually governs the relations of difference in *Gravity's Rainbow*?'; for without difference, it could have no meaning and quite 'senseless' readings could be generated. Quite plainly, not just any reading will do.

But we have no idea what the criteria of acceptability are any more. For instance, is the following reading acceptable? We think it is, but many critics would not; but then we would want to know the grounds on which such a reading should be excluded. It is far from senseless, and we doubt whether it contradicts any of the empirical data of the text:

> Slothrop wants to get laid for free, like Benny Profane in *V.*, and other aimless types we could mention. His work with ACHTUNG has brought him into contact with many others with their own expense accounts and he dreams of being a big star foreign agent like Pirate Prentice. Knowing how paranoid the Firm is, if Pointsman is anything to go by, he need only leave something like a map of London lying around and their suspicions will be aroused. To this end... Next thing he is being well fucked and fed on the Riviera, travelling free through the Zone, answerable to no one, getting to indulge his transvestism, having an extraordinary variety of sexual experiences, still perhaps ending with an honourable discharge. It is the authorities who are paranoid in this reading and Slothrop who has a firm grasp on reality and as a result connives to get out of London where rockets are falling on his head. It is normal that he is a little nervous about getting found out.

Given this indeterminacy regarding the parameters of acceptability of empirical readings, whether they be traditional, modernist or postmodernist, it would be as well to look outside the question of narratorial authority and thereby outside the problematic of real/non-real separations for the relations of difference upon which *Gravity's Rainbow*'s sense turns. The question which now faces us is that of alternatives to real/non-real or true/fictional distinctions and the ways in which the novel articulates such alternatives.

To this extent, we hope at least to be able to show how empirical readings (of whatever kind – see the partial list above) can be resisted. In our final offering/reading, then, the question of textual verification must cease to arise. Bits of *Gravity's Rainbow*, then, should be treated as bits of other text rather than as privileged 'quotations' or points of determinate verification of the reading.

((One further problem: the upcoming reading is unsure as to how to situate itself with respect to the typographical format so far employed. While the *readings* we have quoted (from ourselves) are indented as 'displayed extracts', our *commentary* on those readings is flush to the left margin. A similar problem exists with respect to the current paragraph – and indeed the very distinction is quite unfortunate given what we have been saying about the relations between text and commentary, or data and analysis, in *Gravity's Rainbow*. Still the problem remains and by way of acknowledging it, what follows appears with an indentation somewhere between the two.))

■ ■ ■ ■ ■ ■ ■

McHale's hang-up with readers having to reconstruct what 'really' happened from what a character dreamed, hallucinated, etc..., is nicely summed up in Tony Tanner's phrase. With *Gravity's Rainbow*, he says, we cannot tell 'whether we are in a bombed-out building or a bombed-out mind'.[20] This also shows where McHale goes wrong and how we can begin to get another reading of the text. Because: what's the difference? That is, we can argue that the mind is no more and no less real than the building. 'In the building' and 'in the mind' are equivalent as mere *sites* for the playing out of discursive operations.

Indeed, in the latter part of his article, McHale discusses the operations which a reader, narrator or author performs in order to make shifts in a text coherent. He works more in terms of intertextual relations at this point than in terms of consciousness (mind) and object (building). On the other hand, his analysis remains bound to a concept of consciousness as transcendent even though, as we have tried to argue, none of the categories (be they character, event, and so on) were ever sufficiently fixed as to give such a concept much sense. For example, in his analysis of the connection between Sachsa and Eventyr, McHale assumes that relatively fixed texts (such as thoughts) can transfer between relatively fixed identities (such as minds).[21] This begs the question of the reading of *Gravity's Rainbow* we are in the process of making. For: can these narratorial mind-merging measures be said to take place when neither mind nor message are fixed in any recognisable sense? McHale's reading of the passage (218–20) as *mise en abyme* – though he does not use the term – might therefore be dubious, which he himself suggests by moving to more complex cases. He is, however, left at the end with 'the demoralising prospect of free and all-but-unmanageable analogical patterning'.[22] This prefigures what we are about to indicate as the 'post-rhetorical' character of *Gravity's Rainbow* but rather than, perhaps, being aghast at its demoralising prospects we would instead wish to exploit the capabilities of this 'negativity'.

For these reasons, it would be best to over-write what is a crucial separation for McHale (that between the mental and the real), for we can now see that there would be no need for a reader to make such a separation in order to make sense of the novel. Instead, the reader might be attuned to the 'orders of discourse'[23] played out in mind, building, on screen or wherever and however the novel articulates these so as, perhaps, to make some point about perennial problems of discourse and the human subject, about moral and political dilemmas in a world of discourse, about plots and plans and knowledge of them when there are only arbitrary signifiers and no definite or independently available signifieds to match them up with.

Any analysis of relations between bits of text, before being discussed in terms of, for instance, the rhetorical, must rely on the structure of the relations between signifier and signified. We take that relation to be one of arbitrariness. In point of fact, and to return briefly to the concerns of our Introduction, a whole body of Pynchon criticism seems to have noticed the arbitrariness of the signifier in *Gravity's Rainbow* and, to put it mildly, panicked, sensing in its aestheticist way the absence of order, anarchy, disharmony, threats to traditional canons of literary organisation and a challenge to routine, clear and beautiful renditions of 'reality'.[24] What to do in the face of this? Answers to the question have practically exhausted the pantheon of *Gravity's Rainbow* criticism – the remainder being taken up with 'technical' explanations of rocketry, entropy and so on. Sanders says, for example, that 'God is the original conspiracy theory';[25] but we prefer to maintain that it is rather the death of God that makes conspiracy theories proliferate. Once the honest-to-God signifier is found to be arbitrary, one is necessarily paranoid until one accepts this state of affairs. A more extreme form of this exasperation is the 'Please beat me again, Thomas' school of criticism, exemplified by Leverenz who finally has 'enough clarity to refuse the guilt and self-hatred that *Gravity's Rainbow* required of [him]', although his final response to the insecurity is to find a Pynchon (nb. not a Pynchon text – though this is a common transposition) who creates 'the most powerfully aching language for natural descriptions in our literature'.[26]

A certain amount of Pynchon criticism almost realises (but stops short of interrogating) the fact that a problematic of reading such as that posed by *Gravity's Rainbow* implies also a problematic of writing. There are indeed close structural similarities between Leverenz's picaresque commentary and our own various revisions of the strategy of reading.[27] Our work in general experiments with the bits of text at our disposal in ways which could be construed as congruent with McHale's invitation to read Pynchon with 'negative capability'. However, what is all the more surprising is McHale's implication that experimentation with reading/writing strategies represents a completely uncharted territory. After all, Barthes did not wait upon the invitation of something like *Gravity's Rainbow* to explore a more radical form of intervention into the text on the part of the reader.[28] He wrote about a classic realist text. Further: Derrida finds his targets anywhere on the line from Plato to Sollers.

In deference to the predominance of classicist and romanticist readings of Pynchon which seem stunned by the apparent abyss of *Gravity's Rainbow*, we would accept that whereas the much earlier novel *V.* works mostly with the problematic of the arbitrariness of the signifier, *Gravity's Rainbow* goes further or elsewhere. It is certainly not just more of the same. We would argue that there can be a reading of *Gravity's Rainbow* in which the arbitrariness of the signifier is accepted for what it is and is no longer a cause for sustained humanist angst. Instead, such a reading would point to the novel's working with rhetorical strategies and devices. It would point to its status as game, design, practice, play, inscription or diagram rather than, say, its status as representation of some confused – but really existing – universe.

To see how *Gravity's Rainbow* plays with rhetorical strategies,[29] then, is not to examine merely its 'language' in some stylistic or other technicist way, leaving for another reader the matter of 'to what that language refers'. It is in fact to learn our lesson and put aside completely the matter of linguistic reference and ontic referent, acknowledging that if there is a reality here it is only ever and always already a discursive/rhetorical one. Though, as we shall see, even what this means can be subject to doubt in *Gravity's Rainbow*.

Instead of continuing with McHale's distinction between

(1) definite/indefinite

or

(2) real/non-real

as the basis for a reading of difference and, therefore, of sense in *Gravity's Rainbow*, we might turn to a more obviously rhetorical distinction, that between

(3) use/mention

As this distinction is raised in formal logic, it applies to the difference between a sign's employment as such in a proposition and a reference to its capacity as a sign. Thus 'Slothrop's not alone' may be a perfectly ordinary use of the term 'Slothrop', whereas '"Slothrop" contains eight letters' would constitute a mention of the term itself. The reader could no doubt separate the uses from the mentions in the sentence preceding this one, and that separation would no doubt lead to problematic terms like 'mentions of use' and 'uses of mention' and so forth. At a purely textual level, *Gravity's Rainbow* plays with the use/mention distinction:

> "Oh – where've you *been*, gate?"
> "'Here'."
> "'"Here"'?"
> "Yes, like that, you've got it – once or twice removed like that . . ." (552)

Exactly how one is supposed to utter marks of citation (associated with mention) remains to be established (notwithstanding Slothrop's ability to hear them (241)) – but *Gravity's Rainbow* or its narrator is shown to be taking the distinction as one which is less than clear; one in which the two terms slide into one another. Again:

Gravity's Rainbow and the post-rhetorical 53

"You say *what*," Roger has been screaming for a while.
"I-*say*," sez Rózsavölgyi, again.
"You say, 'I say'? Is that it? Then you should have said, 'I say, "I say."'"
"I did."
"No, no – you said, 'I say,' *once*, is what you – "
"A-*ha*! But I *said* it *again*. I-*said* it . . . *twice*."
"But that was after I asked you the question – you can't tell me the two 'I say's were both part of the same statement," unless, "that's asking me to be unreasonably," unless it's really true that, "credulous, and around *you* that's a form of," that we're the *same person*, and that the whole exchange was ONE SINGLE THOUGHT yaaaggghhh and that means, "insanity, Rózsavölgyi – " (634)

Notice here how the narrator's 'own' speech-quote marks are dropped and interrupted, threatening the very separation between speakers, and between them and the narrator. The whole distinction between 'my prose' and 'what I cite' is crumbling away here and with it the idea of subject separation. The distinction between use and mention is in jeopardy, as Derrida shows in his critique of Searle[30] – the text, as it were, is becoming *flat* as the levels of use and mention, serious and parasitic, normal and citational disappear. There are now, perhaps, only material marks on the page. A material equivalence between the signifiers replaces a rhetorical difference between them. This equivalence we should like to call *material typonomy*. The term carries the senses of *homogeneity* (L. *typus*: model, symbol), *printing, leaving an impression* (Gr. *tupos*: mark, imprint, writing character), and *naming* (Nat. Hist. *typonym*: name based on type or specimen).

But we can consider another instance of use and mention in *Gravity's Rainbow*. This involves the use, as against the mention, of cinema (though other text-domains or themes could also be instances here). In this case we could notice, following our 'cinematic' reading of *Gravity's Rainbow*, that the text in places makes direct reference to filmic texts, actors, scenes and so on while, in others, it appears to use the very techniques of the cinema itself without such mentions, relying as it does on slapstick, camera shots and angles, frames and so on. The first case is clearly a mention of the cinematic and the latter is closer to being a use. However, the two often blur into one another to the point where use and mention become materially identical. For example:

> And if he could find a few triangular scraps of leather, figure a way to sew them on to Tchitcherine's boots ... yeah a-and on the back of the cape put a big, scarlet, capital R— It is as pregnant a moment as when Tonto, after the legendary ambush, attempts to— (366)

Here it becomes impossible to distinguish cinematic use from cinematic mention. What remains is a levelling of the distinction, a flattening that we are calling *material typonomy*:

(4) use/mention // *material typonomy*

Below, we want to explore further this way in which *Gravity's Rainbow* handles or plays with dualistic differences such that they are overcome by making any dilemma's dual aspects appear identical, these then producing, conjointly, a new 'first' term for a further, and qualitatively distinct, duality. However, in each case, it should be noted that the new right hand term routinely indicates 'materiality', 'substance' or 'being'.

We should note that rhetorical devices classically work around playing off one side of a dualism with its opposite (e.g., literal/metaphorical). In *Gravity's Rainbow*, insofar as this postmodernist rhetoric is reworked (we are loath to say 'transcended'), it could be claimed that the novel is post-rhetorical. By coining this phrase we do not wish simply to add to the proliferation of posts – 'postmodern', 'poststructuralist', and so on – that is already rife in critical discourse, nor to imply that there is an accessible outside or after for rhetoric. 'Post' may as well be read here as the sign of an event which does and does not arrive, in the Derridean sense of (a)destination, a central theme in the chapters to follow.

By contrast with such a notion of the post-rhetorical, the sign in classical semiology is taken to have a dual aspect of recto and verso.[31] Thus:

(5) recto/verso
      sign

In *Gravity's Rainbow*, however, the entire recto/verso doublet is taken as a single side of the signifying relation. It becomes a token, one which *betokens* a typonymic object. Thus:

(6) recto/verso // object
       token

To make this point, we could compare *Gravity's Rainbow* with *V*. In the latter, as we show in Chapter 6, there is an insistent dialectic between the animate and the inanimate, an incessant 'debate' about the degree to which one has become suffused with the other through humankind's inhumanity, through prosthesis, through the effect of an historical telos. Characteristically, there is no 'resolution' of this conflict. The text, *V*., does not come down on the side of soft human nature or hard synthetic machine. At times it does try to display a possible middle way, as we shall see. In *Gravity's Rainbow*, however, the debate cannot arise in this way. The recto and verso of (in)animation, to continue with this particular sign, are over-ridden by the existence, the *textual* existence – for there is no other kind – of certain phenomena such as Imipolex G, the living chemical, or Byron the Bulb, the living element, the light of life. Thus:

(7) animate/inanimate // *Byron the Bulb*

Others on the list of possible candidates here would be some persons such as the Kamikazis who have their own counter-rocket, the Hotchkiss machine-gun, the Adenoid and so on. (Could one prototype here be the speaking soap from *Ulysses*?)

The post-rhetorical process also works at the level of events. In the modernist and postmodernist novel, two events may be juxtaposed against one another such that their relation is metaphorical. In Proust, for example, the same/difference relations between Marcel's adult tasting of a madeleine and his tasting of them in childhood become the basis for, or the device for, the recovery of 'lost time'. The explicandum and explanans (each of which is a madeleine), although temporally separated, are analogically connected. Thus points of time may be connected, metaphorically. In *Ulysses*, of course, the metaphorical relations between classical heroism (the *Odyssey*) and the mundaneity of Irish no-hopers, provide the fundamental difference and sameness which sets the novel in train – at least on one very standard reading. For example:

(8) Ulysses escapes the Cyclops throwing boulders by sailing out to sea / Bloom escapes the one-eyed man throwing biscuit tins by jumping on a passing milk-cart.

The relation is essentially metaphorical/analogical. To take one further example, in a Robbe-Grillet text like *La Jalousie*, a number of accounts of a character's arrival in a truck are repeated throughout the novel and, on Genette's account, represent a paradigmatic series (a number of choices as to what might have happened) which has been syntagmatised (deployed linearly through the text, instead of a simple selection being made).[32] Inasmuch as Jakobson defines the poetic function in terms of a transgression of principles which govern those two linguistic planes (paradigmatic and syntagmatic),[33] Robbe-Grillet's writing might be said to fall within the ambit of rhetorical operations, although we would hesitate to describe the precise figure employed. Lodge's description of the realist/modernist/postmodernist distinctions as discussed by Bennett would seem to be in the same line.[34]

A common 'finding' about *Gravity's Rainbow* is that it reverses standard narrative sequentiality. The sight of the V2 falling precedes the sound of its arrival. Slothrop's erection precedes the mysterious stimulus (perhaps). Many readings are motivated, that is, by an odd reversal of what Barthes calls 'the post hoc ergo propter hoc' fallacy.[35] To this extent *Gravity's Rainbow* has been taken as a sometime reversal of standard narrative syntax. But, and this is the rub, nothing comes of the reversed chain. There can be no outcome; it is literally impossible to reach back before the Zero or forward into the indefinite Void. No future or past history, no definite origin or destination can be guaranteed. The telos has been cancelled. In its place there are only possibilities which occasionally coalesce into material typonyms – Jamf, the Rocket, Imipolex and so on.

However, it could be a matter of speculation as to whether *Gravity's Rainbow*'s use of typonyms, insofar as they constitute *third* terms, marks a new form of narrative syntagm (three items in a chain being the minimal requirement for syntagma). While this is quite different from Jakobson's 'poetic function' it nevertheless appears to us to be an interesting play on syntagmatic/paradigmatic relations. It is for these reasons that we are dubious about readings of *Gravity's Rainbow* which rely on standard rhetorical figures.

A good number of critical readings of Pynchon do resort to types of rhetorical figure in order to describe the relations between textual material, and it remains that any attempt to pinpoint the operations involved is in its conception far from misguided. The history of writing has produced something of a taxonomy of the spaces within language or between (bits of) texts. In the case of *Gravity's Rainbow*, Seidel refers to satire, whereas McHale refers to 'Pynchon's outrageous and subversive manipulation of analogies'.[36] The above-mentioned article by Bennett sums up some of these readings of postmodernist fiction in general, finding them to remain within Poirier's conception of self-parody; and, as Bennett is right to point out, such readings have been used to conclude with an idea of indeterminacy, and hence interpretative autonomy, which 'may be a reworking in the discourse of literary criticism of a bourgeois individualist ideology'.[37] We have encountered plenty of that, with or without any 'theoretical overlay'.

In our judgment, however, neither parody, satire, nor analogy is sufficient to describe textual relations in *Gravity's Rainbow*, though the reader will certainly find examples of each. Such figures, modelled on the literal/metaphoric paradigm, deal only with dual relationships, that is to say with an assumed relationship between an original and a copy, though the copies may be plural in number. On the other hand, what we have found repeatedly, is a relationship of duality which is undercut/ rewritten/overruled by another term, which as a result sets up a *second duality* (the words are uttered 'under erasure') between it and the first two terms. One well-known but non-pertinent model for this type of operation involves transcendence, as for instance in Barthes' description of connotation or metalanguage.[38] But what distinguishes what we now call the postrhetorical from that model is the fact that the order of the third term in no way transcends or embraces the order of the first two terms; it may well be a counter-rhetorical operation, again something we call *material typonomy*.

A further model for this sort of switch exists in poststructuralist rhetoric, and that is *mise en abyme*. Although based on the idea of the mirror within the mirror, the image within the image, it is an operation which must be performed rather than shown. However, it is probably not oversimplifying too much to say that *mise en abyme* relies on a type of second level subdivision of a duality. For example,

(9) same / other
   difference
      /   <<<<< Here, the standard parameter
   deferral   for preserving the first-order
                difference (same/other), is
                subverted by its own internal
                difference or disunity.

Though the *mise en abyme* model effects a sort of collapsing of the dualism, which is poles apart from the transcendence of the 'meta-' model, it still does not fit the operation we are trying to describe here with respect to *Gravity's Rainbow*.

What we have called here *mise en abyme* is the 'rhetorical' operation practised by Derrida through terms such as *differance, supplement, pharmakon*, and so on.[39] It is designed to exceed classic rhetorical operations and comes close to being 'post-rhetorical' in the sense we are developing. However, there is another set of devices that Derrida employs and which overlap more obviously with the *material typonym* we find in *Gravity's Rainbow*. We refer here to 'conceptual objects' such as the matchbox, postcard and umbrella which might be seen on one level as metaphors for a set of ideas such as, in the case of the umbrella, Nietzsche's conflicting pronouncements concerning woman and truth.[40] But as Gregory Ulmer makes clear, for Derrida such simple material objects are part of a wider design to deconstruct the operations of classical and hierarchical conceptual thinking which favours form over matter, and represent 'the expansion out of bounds, the abounding, of a commonplace ... item, image, or thing into a theoretical model or models of the invention process itself'.[41] The object thus cancels the form/matter, idea/object distinction by means of an object which functions like a (new type of) idea. These deconstructive devices remain closely parallel to the sort of rhetorical levelling found in Pynchon.

To return to the specific case at hand, let us resume the set of dualistic rhetorical operations – analogy, parody, satire, metaphor – within the notion of the parable. It is on first sight a less apposite figure than those above, rather restricted in its usage, being largely superseded, if in name only, by allegory. On the other hand, as its prefix (*para* – beside, instead of, etc.) suggests, its etymology does provide sufficient imprecision to allow for any dualistic relationship between a model and a copy, a literal and a *para*literal. Furthermore, it seems that readings based on the idea of either a satirical, analogical, or parodic relationship between bits of text, do in the final analysis resort to the allegorical. Pynchon's free-form analogies are treated as allegories for the absence of any centring force in the modern world, of its entropy, and Slothrop's paranoia is a satire on 'the pathology of the modern individual'; out of the force/ counterforce, or System/Zone duality comes a reading of the banana breakfasts as an allegorical representation of the 're-generative powers of the "Earth"'.[42]

The parable, and hence the choice of word, is also the parabolic; in French for instance, the two senses reside within the same word (*la parabole*). It joins that set of geometrical/ rhetorical figures which includes hyperbole and ellipsis. But the switch here is not simply a case of etymological licence. The parabola is the model therefore for any plotting of dualisms, and implies the emergence or contouring of a path between the two axes. Besides, the parabola is particularly generous in its range of possibilities, allowing for any 'curve' from the asymptotic to the symmetrical. Thus in spite of the precise sense given to the parable since the Gospels, and in spite of the very controlled type of analogical operation that it is supposed to describe, it, like the other figures which we have made to fall within it, finally begs the question of the exact rhetorical operation which it involves. The parable is thus undermined (*mise en abyme*) by the parabola, by its own internal imprecision. Unless there be an equation for it, unless satire, analogy, and parody are superseded by their presumed meanings, the relationship between bits of text cannot be defined in terms of those figures.

In other words, readings which refer to parodic, analogical, or satiric relations between bits of the text of *Gravity's Rainbow* inevitably depend in practice on an assumed rhetorical relationship between the text and a sense which resides in the world, usually the human. For the intertextual relations themselves are not sufficiently clear for the name of a single existing figure to be ascribed to them. Such readings are therefore parabolic; on the one hand designed to both embellish and disappear in favour of a sense that was always present to itself; on the other hand, unable to define their terms more precisely than to say that they involve a type of supplement.

So *Gravity's Rainbow* does involve or invite the *mise en abyme* of rhetorical relations, subdividing those relations with their own terms of reference. Either by having the assumed relation between the inside and outside of the text undercut by the variety of intratextual relations; or by having the particularity of one set of intratextual relations subverted by another set, such as seems to occur in McHale's description of 'mapping'.[43] That operation might be resumed thus: the notion of the spiritual world, or the material/spiritual opposition (surely governed by some sort of rhetorical operation) is exploited to allow the narrative to pass from The White Visitation séance to Peter Sachsa's in Weimar Germany. But then there is another transition which relies on an occult type of mapping, a relation which is foreign to, and contradicts, the operations of the material world; the material opens a space between it and the spiritual which the spiritual exploits to ruin the coherence of the material.

However, if parable and parabolic operate as rhetorical relations in *Gravity's Rainbow*, we are overlooking the fact that the parabola also exists, in the form of the flight of the rocket, as perhaps the most important *material typonym* in the novel. Not the rocket itself, for that object is as if subordinate to the trajectory it must follow, and its design, manufacture, propulsion and so on remain obedient to, all point towards, the path of its flight. Such a parabola is gravity's rainbow. So first: much of *Gravity's Rainbow* is a parable of such a parabola, allowing for rhetorical operations which stretch all the way from the simple metonymy of the book's title, to the explicited metaphoric sense of the characters' actions:

> But it is a curve each of them feels, unmistakably. It is the parabola. They must have guessed, once or twice – guessed and refused to believe – that everything, always, collectively, had been moving toward that purified shape latent in the sky, that shape of no surprise, no second chances, no return. (209)
>
> Katje has understood the great airless arc as a clear allusion to certain secret lusts that drive the planet and herself . . . (223)

And second: across from that set of rhetorical dualities, there is the fact of the parabola that is the rocket's flight, material phenomenon of the simplest order. Hence:

(10) parable/parabola // *rocket trajectory*

Gravity's Rainbow *and the post-rhetorical* 61

A representation of the general form of this relation might be as follows:[44]

(11) a/b // *substance*

Other examples of it might be:

(12) rocket/penis // *Jamf*
(13) penis/polymer // *Imipolex*
(14) reality/fantasy // *cinema*
(15) us/Them // *Slothrop*

The post-rhetorical is constituted by the form of these cases. The form can only be instantiated, not defined – shown, not said. In the above cases the form is realised thusly: the left-hand side, itself constituted as a dualism, is over-ridden on the right-hand side by an object or person (at least something of material substance, no matter how mysterious). Substance, that is, supplants rhetoric – though all this, need we stress, is accomplished within and *as* the play of signs, in themselves, of course, nothing but material points.

One interesting thing we can notice about this formula (11) is that it differs from the use of dualisms in Pynchon's other two novels. For example, in *V.*, the character McClintic Sphere is introduced to the flip/flop mechanism which underpins the binary workings of computational devices. He sees this, as Tanner has pointed out, as a moral dilemma.[45] Flop represents our current denial of humanity while flip represents a challenge to that inhuman world, an acknowledgement of passions, feelings and inner life that may end up, quite randomly itself, as love or war among fellow human beings. Both flip and flop are dangerous options. Sphere decides on a narrow middle way and his motto is 'Keep cool but care'.[46] Trite as this may be ethically, it shows *V.* to be searching for the crevice, the fold, between the two left-hand terms. As it were, *V.* is formed in the oblique strokes between the dualities. It seeks a middle way.

The next novel, *Lot 49*, also devolves around the possibility of re-including excluded middles – this is in fact an explicit theme in the text itself.[47] But it seeks to erase the oblique stroke, as it were, between opposing terms – especially moral terms – and to replace it with a new space, a breathing space perhaps. This space may be between the literal and the metaphorical (for example, the space Oedipa must traverse between 'real' and 'imaginary' postal organisations); or it may be between more obviously moral alternatives such as over-imagining patterns in events (paranoia) and under-imagining them (hebephrenia). In each case, Oedipa explores the possibility of re-including excluded middles. This is shown in (17) below as a form of cancellation which is not quite the form of post-rhetorical supplanting we find in *Gravity's Rainbow*. thus, if *V.* can be represented Thus:

(16) a/b   look here

then, *Lot 49* looks like:

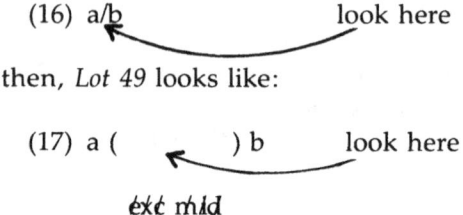

(17) a (   ) b   look here

       exc mid

Already in *Lot 49* there are a couple of cases of awkward problematisations of rhetorical relations. One is Maxwell's Demon, for its regulation of a relation between thermodynamics and information flow; the other is that between delta-t and delirium tremens. The narrator will refer to metaphor to describe and resolve those relations, but not without some ambiguity.[48]

Gravity's Rainbow, on the other hand, tries to over-ride the whole idea of *solutions* to dualisms, moral, logical or rhetorical by treating them as aspects of a single side of another dualism which has the moral, logical or rhetorical dilemma on one side, and the material on the other. A number of critics have insisted that Pynchon's work returns the human subject and subjectivity to the novel.[49] They argue that his work captures a new essence for humanity in a world fraught with objects. Such humanist readings now appear quite untenable. Whatever we may say of the first two novels, and there is no reason to expect consistency between all three, the last novel, *Gravity's Rainbow*, points towards the *dissolution* of this type of debate or dilemma – along with a number of others we have mentioned. In fact both the humanist and the technologistic critics of Pynchon may be getting the debate quite wrong.[50] There may be no (re)solution to/of their readings and counter-readings. For this would assume that *Gravity's Rainbow* works at a specific rhetorical level, as parody, as meta-fiction and so on. None of these things can hold up, the divisions are erased, flattened. The search for rhetorical stitches fails and we are left only with surplus yarns. Pynchon's texts do not work at or on 'levels' in order to allow such readings

– or rather to allow them and their opposites. Thus, for *Gravity's Rainbow*

(18) a/b //   ⬅_____   look here

■ ■ ■ ■ ■ ■ ■

What next?
Perhaps Pynchon's fourth novel has appeared – is already somewhere but not in the form of a book or in words. It could be anything. Preferably material. Something like a hot air balloon?

Notes

1. M. Siegel, *Pynchon: Creative Paranoia in Gravity's Rainbow* (Port Washington: Kennikat Press, 1978), p. vii.
2. D. Leverenz, 'On trying to read *Gravity's Rainbow*', in G. Levine and D. Leverenz (eds), *Mindful Pleasures: Essays on Thomas Pynchon* (Boston: Little Brown, 1976), pp. 229–49.
3. Cf. M. Kaufman, 'Brünnhilde and the chemists: women in *Gravity's Rainbow*', in Levine and Leverenz, pp. 197–227. A particularly egregious case of sexism among Pynchon enthusiasts occurs when Paul Fussell concludes that the Katje/Pudding scene is 'disgusting, *ennobling*, and touching, all at once' (our italics). Such an ennobling occurs simply by transferring the disgust on to Katje, 'a literal filthy slut ... and the incarnation of the spirit of military memory'. See 'The ritual of military memory' in H. Bloom (ed.), *Thomas Pynchon's 'Gravity's Rainbow'* (New York: Chelsea House, 1986), pp. 21–8; this passage, p. 27.
4. Cf. G. Genette, *Narrative Discourse* (Oxford: Blackwell, 1980).
5. References to pages of the Viking/Cape edition of *Gravity's Rainbow* (1973) are given henceforth in parentheses in the text.
6. For example: J. W. Slade, *Thomas Pynchon* (New York: Warner Communications, 1974); P. L. Abernethy, 'Entropy in Pynchon's *The Crying of Lot 49*', *Critique*, 14, 2 (1972) pp. 18–33; W. M. Plater, *The Grim Phoenix: Reconstructing Thomas Pynchon* (Bloomington: Indiana University Press, 1978), pp. 1–63; A. Mangel, 'Maxwell's demon, entropy, information: *The Crying of Lot 49*', in Levine and Leverenz, pp. 87–100; R. O. Richardson, 'The absurd animate in Thomas Pynchon's *V.*', *Studies in the Twentieth Century*, 9 (1972), pp. 35–58; D. Seed, 'Order in Thomas Pynchon's "Entropy"', *Journal of Narrative Technique*, 11 (1981), pp. 135–53; D. Simberloff, 'Entropy, information and life: biophysics in the novels of Thomas Pynchon', *Perspectives in Biology and Medicine*, 21 (1978), pp. 617–25.
7. Lakoff notes the linguistic oddities of Slothrop's use of the demonstrative 'that'. Beside the fact that other characters do use it, we

would see some limitations in explaining this usage in terms of the 'isolation' of a unitary 'character'. In view of the variety of linguistic licence in *Gravity's Rainbow*, it is difficult to see by what criteria this usage is to be judged 'extraordinary'. See R. Lakoff, 'Remarks on this and that', in M. W. Galy et al. (eds), *Papers from the Tenth Regional Meeting of the Chicago Linguistic Society* (Chicago: Chicago Linguistic Society, 1979), pp. 345–56.

8. Although we have not tested it empirically, we would hypothesise that, excepting routine words like 'the', 'a', etc., 'death' is the most frequently used word in *Gravity's Rainbow*.
9. Genette, *Narrative Discourse*.
10. A particularly glaring example of this occurs in Kaufman's article: '"Of all her putative fathers," intones *Pynchon* . . . ' (italics ours). We accept that the shorthand of referring to the narrator by the name of the author is a recognised practice, and often convenient, but ellipses such as that above require comment in view of the difficulty of establishing a single narrator in *Gravity's Rainbow*. The fact that Kaufman converts this piece of text into Pynchon's direct speech renders explicit the general habit of assuming that narrated material belongs to an author's scarcely mediated 'world-view'. Leverenz's discussion is fraught with that assumption. See Kaufman, 'Brünnhilde', p. 215 and Leverenz, 'On trying to read'.
11. B. McHale, 'Modernist reading, postmodern text: the case of *Gravity's Rainbow*', *Poetics Today*, 1, 1/2 (1979), pp. 85–110.
12. D. Cowart, *Thomas Pynchon: The Art of Allusion* (Carbondale: Southern Illinois University Press, 1980), pp. 31–62; C. Clerc, 'Film in *Gravity's Rainbow*', in C. Clerc (ed.), *Approaches to 'Gravity's Rainbow'* (Columbus: Ohio State University Press, 1983), pp. 103–51; and S. Simmon, 'Beyond the theatre of war: *Gravity's Rainbow* as film', in Pearce, pp. 124–39. Simmon's view of 'this novel-as-film' (p. 138) is closer to ours than Cowart's purely thematic approach. Clerc takes the analogy even further, such that *Gravity's Rainbow* 'illustrates . . . the workings of an "auteur" theory of fiction' (p. 150). We doubt, however, whether that represents an advance for Pynchon criticism.
13. See E. Mendelson, 'Introduction', in E. Mendelson (ed.), *Pynchon: A Collection of Critical Essays* (Englewood Cliffs: Prentice-Hall, 1978), p. 15. For similar information, see Siegel, *Creative Paranoia*, pp. 126, 127.
14. Cowart, p. 35.
15. McHale, p. 95.
16. McHale, p. 95.
17. Cowart, p. 67.
18. Cowart, p. 139.
19. E. Mendelson, 'Gravity's encyclopedia', in Levine and Leverenz, p. 182; S. Weisenburger, 'The end of history?: Thomas Pynchon and the uses of the past', in Pearce, pp. 140–56.
20. T. Tanner, 'V. and V-2', in Mendelson, p. 51.
21. McHale, pp. 102–4.
22. McHale, p. 106.

23. M. Foucault, 'Orders of discourse', *Social Science Information*, 10, 2 (1971), pp. 7–30.
24. Examples are: Leverenz, 'On trying to read'; G. Levine, 'Risking the moment: anarchy and possibility in Pynchon's fiction', in Levine and Leverenz, pp. 229–49; W. T. Lhamon, 'Pentecost, promiscuity, and Pynchon's *V.*: from the Scaffold to the Impulsive', in Levine and Leverenz, pp. 69–86.
25. S. Sanders, 'Pynchon's paranoid history', in Levine and Leverenz, pp. 139–59.
26. Leverenz, 'On trying to read', pp. 242, 248.
27. We would maintain privately, however, that we wrote our commentary as a parody of Leverenz, even though we read his after we first wrote ours. Perhaps we knew what it would contain, perhaps we knew things like this would happen with regard to a novel in which effect precedes cause and response stimulus. A further parallel which occurs to us after the event is that between our series of readings and the connotative codes established by Barthes' reading of *Sarrasine*. See R. Barthes, *S/Z* (London: Cape, 1975).
28. Barthes, *S/Z*.
29. We see rhetorical strategies as a subset of discursive orders (*à la* Foucault) generally.
30. See J. Derrida, 'Signature event context', *Glyph*, 1 (1977), pp. 172–97; J. Derrida, 'Limited inc.: abc ...', *Glyph*, 2 (1978), pp. 162–254; J. R. Searle, 'Re-iterating the differences: a reply to Derrida', *Glyph*, 1 (1977), pp. 198–208.
31. F. de Saussure, *Course in General Linguistics* (London: Fontana, 1974).
32. See: A. Robbe-Grillet, *Jealousy* (=*La Jalousie*) (London: Calder, 1965); G. Genette, *Figures I* (Paris: Seuil, 1966). Some interesting parallels can be noted here. If *La Jalousie* marks the space of the postmodern more clearly than many a novel, *Gravity's Rainbow* marks the space of the post-rhetorical equally clearly. Both novels have near, or at, their start, a description of a banana plantation – indeed Tanner sees the banana as *Gravity's Rainbow*'s main symbol, and it surely is the most haunting theme of *La Jalousie*. Robbe-Grillet's bananas are, however, laid out in a precise structuralist grid and induce paranoia in the narrator. Pynchon's bananas, by contrast grow in a random collection of soils and composts. They are unpredictable and, while they have a certain commercial function (as Robbe-Grillet's no doubt also do), they are more readily used for play and pun, even though they are as scarce as Robbe-Grillet's are plentiful. We write this extended commentary suspecting ourselves to be the only Pynchon scholars with direct experience of cultivating bananas. See T. Tanner, *Thomas Pynchon* (London: Methuen, 1982), p. 89.
33. R. Jakobson, 'Linguistics and poetics', in his *Selected Writings Vol. III* (The Hague: Mouton, 1981), pp. 18–51.
34. D. Bennett, 'Parody, postmodernism, and the politics of reading', *Critical Quarterly*, 27, 4 (1985), pp. 27–43. This reference, p. 36.
35. R. Barthes, 'Towards a structural analysis of narrative', in S. Sontag (ed.), *A Barthes Reader* (London: Cape, 1982), pp. 251–95.

36. M. Seidel, 'The satiric plots of *Gravity's Rainbow*', in Mendelson, pp. 193–212; McHale, p. 106.
37. Bennett, 'Parody', pp. 40–1. Evidently he has in mind R. Poirier's 'The politics of self-parody', *Partisan Review*, 35, 3 (1968), pp. 339–53 which he refers to more specifically on pp. 30–3.
38. R. Barthes, *Elements of Semiology* (London: Cape, 1967).
39. J. Derrida, *Of Grammatology*, trans. G. C. Spivak (Baltimore: The Johns Hopkins University Press, 1976), pp. 141–57; *Dissemination*, trans. B. Johnson (Chicago: University of Chicago Press, 1981), pp. 61–171.
40. J. Derrida, *Spurs/Eperons*, trans. B. Harlow (Chicago: University of Chicago Press, 1979).
41. G. Ulmer, *Applied Grammatology: Post(e)-pedagogy from Jacques Derrida to Joseph Beuys* (Baltimore: The Johns Hopkins University Press, 1985), p. 114. At this level, the concept-object can be found in a number of postmodernist fictions. For example Don DeLillo's, *White Noise* (New York: Viking/Penguin, 1984), p. 103: 'I watched the coffee bubble up through the center tube and perforated basket into the small pale globe. A marvellous and sad invention, so roundabout, ingenious, human. It was like a philosophical argument rendered in terms of the things of the world – water, metal, brown beans. I had never looked at coffee before.'
42. Seidel, 'Satiric plots', p. 208; Tanner, *Pynchon*, p. 88.
43. McHale, pp. 103–5.
44. Read as follows: 'a' and 'b' (sides of a given duality); '/' (the difference separating a from b); '//' (marks which could signify the cancellation of a and b respectively); and the italicised third term (the typonym).
45. Tanner, *Pynchon*, pp. 49–50.
46. See the 1964 Cape/Bantam edition of *V.*, pp. 342–3.
47. See the 1967 Cape/Bantam edition of *Lot 49*, especially the text bounded by the following: 'She had heard all about excluded middles ... full circle into some paranoia' (pp. 136–7).
48. *Lot 49*, pp. 77–8 and 95–6. Metaphor's ambiguous position in *Lot 49* is discussed in our next chapter, PLS RECORD BOOK BID.
49. Cowart, *Art of Allusion*; Mendelson, 'Introduction'; C. Clerc, 'Introduction', in Clerc, C. (ed.), *Approaches to 'Gravity's Rainbow'* (Columbus: Ohio State University Press, 1983), pp. 3–30; T. Moore, 'Introduction', in his *The Style of Connectedness: 'Gravity's Rainbow' and Thomas Pynchon* (Columbia: University of Missouri Press, 1987), pp. 1–29.
50. Respective examples of each would be: J. O. Stark, *Thomas Pynchon and the Literature of Information* (Athens: Ohio University Press, 1980); and Mangel, 'Maxwell's demon'.

2
PLS RECORD BOOK BID LOT 49 STOP J DERRIDA

What next? If the dualities in *Gravity's Rainbow* match – link and annul – along the lines of the equations or relations we have just been describing, what might be the terms of a critical rhetoric that addresses the texts of Pynchon? That is to say, given the model of *Gravity's Rainbow*, how might we proceed to write about the ways the dualities are deployed in his other books? – or indeed about any relation between two or more texts, or pieces of text? And every piece of text by our reckoning is always at least dual – for, as long as we are writing, that relation will fall within the context of a rhetorical, or post-rhetorical one.

In this chapter we work from the premise that *The Crying of Lot 49* and Derrida's 'Envois' (in *The Post Card*)[1] have something in common.

Perhaps, a lot.

In *Lot 49*, Oedipa Maas, appointed executrix to the estate of a former lover Pierce Inverarity, stumbles, or is led, on to what seems to be an underground postal system, and a long and involved story of sex, politics, and death. The answer, if any, to the enigma into which she is drawn, or at least its next episode, the end of the book, begins at the auction of Pierce's stamp collection, at Lot 49, containing a series of forged stamps which have been issued and postmarked by the mysterious Tristero, an organisation waging a guerrilla campaign against postal monopoly.

By the end of the text, Oedipa is said to have uncovered not just a system through which 'God knew how many citizens, deliberately chose not to communicate by U.S. Mail . . . a calculated withdrawal, from the life of the Republic, from its machinery' (92), but a legacy that was America (134). Every stone she turns in her search suggests a relation to an organised and coherent whole. But every stone she turns in her search, right up to her waiting for the new and mysterious bidder to reveal his identity as Lot 49 is cried, suggests that she is further than ever from being in a position to plot out the system which organises that assumed whole. *The Crying of Lot 49* becomes thus the story of the hermeneutic bind, when the will to know comes up against the manoeuvres of a permanently assumed, yet ceaselessly deferred, truth. In Pynchon, at least in *V.* and *Lot 49*, that bind is underscored on the one hand by a sort of nostalgia for resolution of the enigma (in terms *other* than those of an interminable sorting of the contagion that is meaning); and on the other hand, by the paranoia that such a daunting task inevitably evokes.

Since Derrida's writing, since Derrida's *writing*, the crisis in, or with respect to truth, the possibility that it will not hold together the differences which come to be inscribed within its ambit, is no longer a function of disintegration in the teleological sense, a falling away of animate into inanimate, or a confederation of the lost. Rather, there are always already such differences; the smallest conceivable event depends on the idea of displacement and deferral. In 'Envois', as has been detailed elsewhere,[2] such ideas are reworked through the notion of adestination, through the possibility that a letter can not arrive, and the structure of the letter as communication of a message, of a truth, within a closed circuit between sender and addressee, is undermined by that of the postcard and the play between public and private address.

But to return to *Lot 49*, what we described above as its treatment of the hermeneutic bind, is interestingly interwoven with at least one sub-plot (the term is inaccurate) which raises the question of the textual in terms which have much in common with Derrida. We refer to *The Courier's Tragedy*, in French *la tragédie du courrier* no doubt, the play published on Shattuck Avenue, Berkeley, which Oedipa goes to see after she has been told that its plot resembles a story she is hearing about Inverarity's involvement in a scheme to market the bones of dead GIs for the development of a new Beaconsfield charcoal filter. In the aforementioned Jacobean revenge play, the villain uses the bones of his massacred messengers to produce the ink with which he writes a letter of negotiation addressed to the commander of the army which is advancing upon him. The fact that the messengers were massacred at the same lake as the GIs, and that the letter the villain addresses is intercepted and totally rewritten: these are not for us the most interesting corollaries between *The Courier's Tragedy* of *Lot 49* and *la tragédie du courrier*, that is 'Envois' – in which, by the way, the postwoman comes to be called 'Nemesis'. They are no doubt very interesting corollaries, but they threaten to intercept and totally rewrite this chapter.

To continue with the revenge play, it is in its fourth act, its last word, that the name 'Trystero' is uttered and the murderers of the rightful heir Niccolo, the purloiners and perverters of the letter, are so identified. And Oedipa Maas subsequently learns that the word 'Trystero' exists only in one of a number of variants for that final couplet of Act IV. In her post-performance conversation with producer-actor Driblette, the pronouncer of the word, the terms of the hermeneutic operation are very much couched in those of the textual.

> 'You came to talk about the play', he [Driblette] said. 'Let me discourage you. It was written to entertain people. Like horror movies. It isn't literature, it doesn't mean anything'. . . .
> 'Why', Driblette said at last, 'is everybody so interested in texts?' . . .
> 'You don't understand', getting mad. 'You guys, you're like Puritans are about the Bible. So hung up with words, words. You know where that play exists, not in that file cabinet, not in any paperback you're looking for, but – ' a hand emerged from the veil of shower steam to indicate his suspended head – 'in here. That's what I'm for. To give the spirit flesh. The words, who cares? They're rote noises to hold line bashes with, to get past the bone barriers around an actor's memory, right? But the reality is in *this* head' . . . .
> 'If I were to dissolve in here', speculated the voice out of the drifting steam, 'be washed down the drain and into the Pacific, what you saw tonight would vanish too. . . . The only residue in fact would be things Wharfinger didn't lie about. Perhaps Squamuglia and Faggio, if they ever existed. Perhaps the Thurn and Taxis mail system. Stamp collectors tell me it did exist. Perhaps the other, also. The Adversary. But they would be traces, fossils. Dead, mineral, without value or potential'. (55–6)

According to Driblette's rationale, blatant in its own contradictions, there is a truth, a living truth to which the text of *The Courier's Tragedy* reduces, and it is able to disappear, washed down the drain and into the Pacific, while at the same time remain. On the other hand, what does remain, the traces, the text in all its variants and performances, is given only the status of residue, 'without value or potential'. But Oedipa will not be so easily fooled, in spite of her inability to reply to Driblette's *voice which speculates* in the prospect of its own disappearance, *out of the drifting steam*. And while it is true that her quest will henceforth concentrate on discovering the meaning of the Word, now that it has been pronounced (which means that she still subscribes to Driblette's idea of a logos remaining present to itself throughout the functioning of its infinite differences), what happens in the event is that she begins to trace those differences through a system which is more and more that of the text and that of the letter.

In fact this tendency for the problematics of hermeneutics to be described in textual terms, has an earlier and simpler explicitation in *Lot 49*. When Oedipa first meets Pierce's lawyer, Metzger, it is in the course of an evening's entertainment involving a television rerun of a movie in which the young Metzger starred as Baby Igor, set in the Dardanelles in the First World War. She and Metzger indulge in a game of 'strip Botticelli' (21–2) to establish the outcome of the narrative, a trivial yes/no pursuit – but in the course of the proceedings not only does the television station get the reels mixed up, thus altering the order of events, but a hairspray can runs amok during the battle scene, as Oedipa and Metzger copulate to the accompaniment of New Zealanders and Turks bayonetting one another, so that she is forced once again to confront her conception of a complicated but overseen system of order, with the eventualities of chance and accident.

Whereas *Lot 49* provides explicit textual material for its own deconstruction, 'Envois' to some extent resembles a parody of the theoretical basis of Derrida's other texts. 'To some extent' because the matter is more complicated than that. However, it remains that 'Envois' at least *posits* a site other than that of textual play, inhabited by the lover who is *addressed* in the singular in these letters – our italics serving to remind that as long as all forms of pose including address are the very question of 'Envois', our formulation of the mechanism involved remains very tentative. It is said that sender and addressee will remain, if only to attend an auction or a bonfire, after the fact of the public disclosure of the letters, although once again the precise delineation and order of those events is ill-defined. This, to some extent this confusion, will be their beginning:

> Everything that from near or far touches on the post card (this one, in which one sees Socrates reading us, or writing all the

others, and every post card in general), all of this we would keep, or finally would doom to loss by publishing it, we would hand it over to the antiques dealer or the auctioneer. The rest, if there is any that remains, is us, is for us, who do not belong to the card. We are the card, if you will, and as such, accountable, but they will seek in vain, they will never find us in it . . . . Like me, I exclude you absolutely from the marketplace. You are the excluded one, the kept one, the absolute non-addressee of whatever would still remain legible. Since it is to you my love that I say I love you and that I love you cannot be posted (176–7, 238).

The reading of 'Envois' though, does not allow an addressee to be constituted in the ideal terms in which she seems to be posited above, even if those terms are returned to with great insistence. She changes gender, is never identified, is partitioned by the reader as other addressee. Similarly the sender suggests that he is talking to himself, that in fact nothing has been left out in spite of the blanks in the text, that the ideal space of love is simply a lure for those who would love to catch Derrida in flagrant self-contradiction. One could even be so perverse as to suggest that this 'she' of the 'Envois' is truth itself, Lacan himself, the psychoanalytic institution being flirted with, and so on. For all such sites are addressed; all fall within the scope of the postcard, little if anything falls outside it.

At a certain point therefore, Derrida's difficulty in sorting the letters to decide what relates to his discussion of the postcard and will therefore be published, or burned (which may or may not be one and the same thing), and what on the other hand relates to him and her, and so will remain in another form, is not unlike Oedipa Maas' attempt to map out the operations of silent Tristero's empire within the grand legacy that is America. Here is Derrida:

> the necessity of everything [*du tout*] announces itself terribly, the fatality of saving everything from destruction: what is there, rigorously in our letters that does not derive from the *fort:da*, from the vocabulary of going-coming, of the step, of the way or the away, of the near and the far, of all the frameworks in *tele-*, of the adestination, of the address and the maladdress, of everything that is passed and comes to pass between Socrates and Plato, Freud and Heidegger, of the 'truth', of the *facteur*, '*du*

tout', of the transference, of the inheritance and of the genealogy, of the paradoxes of nomination, of the king, of the queen and of their ministers, of the magister and of the ministries, of the private or public detectives? Is there a word, a letter, an atom of a message that rigorously speaking *should* not be withdrawn from the burning with the aim of publication? (222)

Given this extreme proliferation of the postal, which is not the same as the reduction of everything to the postal, for the postal does not reduce to a single simple concept, it is not surprising that much of what is discussed in 'Envois' is the subject, the subjects, of *Lot 49*.

Firstly: an indisputable nexus which ties in the matter of postage with that of inheritance. When the letter issues from a dead author, by virtue of the fact that writing is designed, or destined, to function in the absence of its author or sender, then we must say that it is also destined for partition, for division among a number of beneficiaries. Plato and Socrates, as the postcard shows, conceived of a plot whereby that structural necessity was concealed for a few thousand years, and as Derrida sees it (191), Freud and Heidegger were responsible for breaking that unwritten contract. The plot involved invention of the dialogue, to be published after Socrates' death, but in such a form as to have that death forgotten. Plato thus tried to take over the whole estate without even paying death duties, let alone including any other rightful heirs. Socrates' truth would be made available to third parties only upon receipt of a stamped self-addressed envelope. In the meantime, Socrates and Plato had instituted the postage stamp and taken out a patent on it (97–101). It was not until the end of the nineteenth century, the age of Freud and Heidegger, the establishment of the penny post and of the postcard, that their age-old manoeuvre could be denounced. Once what had existed in theory for so long came into practice, its internal contradictions became visible.

The postage stamp, as method of prepayment, admits adestination, at least as a possibility, and therefore seeks to ensure against that eventuality. In the event that the addressee is absent, whatever shape or form that absence may take, prepayment ensures that the service is accounted for. Now you may say that prepayment in the form of a postage stamp exists because the sender might address messages which are unsolicited, junk mail, and for which an unwilling addressee would refuse to be charged. But that is tantamount to saying the same thing, to admitting adestination. For the unwillingness of addressees to accept the message destined for them surely amounts to a form of misaddress.

The other peculiarity of the postage stamp is, as Derrida notes (141–2), the fact that payment is assessed according to a naïve conception of *weight*, a failure to correlate weight and import, so that one word may cost as much as the most secret affairs of state, a greeting as much as a desperate avowal of love. We might say therefore, that on the one hand the postage stamp conceals the truth of the letter's message, the truth that the message purports to be. On the other hand it vindicates Derrida's conception of the text, whose level of intricacy seems almost to be in inverse proportion to its length, and it concentrates the matter of partition with respect to the letter, existing as a tiny rectangle within the rectangle of the envelope, placing the system of address *en abyme*. And finally, it exists only in order to be obliterated; its franking or enfranchisement is also its destruction.

Following on from the problematic of inheritance, the fact of its involving division and partition, a crack – or at least a nick – in the solidity of the name of the father, there will exist an extreme case of dispossession involving an auction. And henceforth every act of inheritance will be threatened with the possibility of the auction, mercenary, hazardous, and competitive: that is to say, in every way political. The question of value is up for total reassessment as a result of that sort of vulgarisation. So we have Oedipa Maas scrutinising napes of necks as the lots are disposed of one by one, up to the number that is seven times seven, and Derrida a phantom bidder for a series of postcards that are already charred with the prospect of their burning so that what is being disputed here is the price of an apocalypse, a holocaust.

The other obvious similarity between *Lot 49* and 'Envois', perhaps more obvious than the first – and in any case part of the same nexus into which they are drawn – is a problem with the matter of naming, a corruption of naming with the structure of citationality. The two-year period which is embraced by the letters which constitute 'Envois' relates more or less to two visits Derrida paid to Oxford, the first involving the discovery of the postcard with *p*lato and Socrates, the second for a verification of the original in Matthew Paris' fortune-telling book. But that period might also be said to embrace Derrida's introduction into English-speaking scholarship on a grand scale, an introduction which occurred very much through, firstly the debate with Searle and speech-act theory, and secondly, that with Lacan. If the latter debate can be seen to relate to truth and its partition, and hence to what we have just discussed as common ground, a plot (like that one arranged in the name of plato), or a lot, between Pynchon and Derrida, then naming in the context of use, mention, and iterability, becomes the background to this other similarity. The unnamed addressee of the postcards concentrates the matter of linguistic ambiguity as it were at the level of the constitution of the utterance, there where she is called but not named:

> and when I call you my love, my love, is it you I am calling or my love? You, my love, is it you I thereby name, is it to you that I address myself ... when I call you my love, is it that I am calling you, yourself, or is it that I am telling my love? and when I tell you my love is it that I am declaring my love to you or indeed that I am telling *you*, yourself, my love, and that you are my love (8).

Meanwhile every single message of the letters gets repeated through the system of double address that the postcards depend upon, with the result that every single addressee, and they are legion, from Socrates to Lacan, to you and us, is simultaneously used, sorely, and mentioned, discussed and called in the presence or (over-)hearing of all the others.

As we suggested, *The Crying of Lot 49* is constructed (and perhaps deconstructed) on the possibility of there being a single name, the Word. Once there is the event of Pierce Inverarity's death, and thereby an enigma, the assumption is, to Oedipa's mind, that there exists a single word to dispel that questioning. And so she traces through to the Tristero, through its acronyms and chance anagrams, through all those deferrals, hoping at the end, at Lot 49, to find the unnameable, or at least a further index thereof. By the end of the story she has not only discovered the Other, but realised it to be everywhere, yet she continues to hope for some magic reconciliation of the differences which constitute her legacy:

> If only she'd looked.... She remembered drifters she had listened to, Americans speaking their language carefully, scholarly, as if they were in exile from somewhere else invisible

yet congruent with the cheered land she lived in; and walkers along the roads at night, zooming in and out of your headlights without looking up, too far from any town to have a real destination. And the voices before and after the dead man's that had phoned at random during the darkest slowest hours, searching ceaseless among the dial's ten million possibilities for that magical Other who would reveal herself out of the roar of relays, monotone litanies of insult, filth, fantasy, love whose brute repetition must someday call into being the trigger for the unnamable act, the recognition, the Word. (135–6)

So despite the traces and erasures of writing Oedipa has encountered, despite the fact that naming, especially such an important naming, is accompanied by the operation of deferrals, as she is informed during *The Courier's Tragedy* when, prior to the mention of the Trystero, 'things get really peculiar, and a gentle chill, an ambiguity, begins to creep in among the words ... a new mode of expression takes over' (49–50); despite all that, Oedipa finds herself at the end in the bind of the digital, the binary of the either/or, all or nothing:

She had heard all about excluded middles; they were bad shit, to be avoided; and how had it ever happened here, with the chances once so good for diversity? For it was now like walking among matrices of a giant digital computer, the zeroes and ones twinned above, hanging like mobiles right and left, ahead thick, maybe endless. Behind the hieroglyphic streets there would either be a transcendent meaning, or only the earth .... Another mode of meaning behind the obvious, or none. Either Oedipa in the orbiting ecstasy of a true paranoia, or a real Tristero. For there either was some Tristero behind the appearance of the legacy America, or there was just America.... (136–7)

The problem here, now that sufficient information has been collected, is, as Oedipa all but realised back at *The Courier's Tragedy*, a problem of reading. A problem of reading that has been concerning us here for a couple of decades as criticism has tried to treat the myriad signifiers it is presented with as elements in a system, and if so what system, or as more random signs. It seems to us that Derrida's writing, and his *writing*, aims at rethinking the possibilities outside of a dualism of appropriation and exclusion.

We can turn back to *Lot 49* for a model of reading which Oedipa tries out, and thinks she fails at, and which contains a number of the elements reminiscent of, or developed from, the Derridean schema. It is a model we shall call, or name, again, the *prosthetic*,[3] and it is staged in the novel when Oedipa seeks to test her sensitivity with respect to Maxwell's Demon. The Demon, postulated by scientist Clerk Maxwell, was a tiny intelligence that could

> sit in a box among air molecules that were moving at all different random speeds, and sort out the fast molecules from the slow ones. Fast molecules have more energy than slow ones. Concentrate enough of them in one place and you have a region of high temperature. You can then use the difference in temperature between this hot region of the box and any cooler region, to drive a heat engine. Since the Demon only sat and sorted, you wouldn't have put any real work into the system. So you would be violating the Second Law of Thermodynamics, getting something for nothing, causing perpetual motion.
>
> 'Sorting isn't work?' Oedipa said. 'Tell them down at the post office' . . . (62)

Indeed. As it happens, the machine John Nefastis has invented, said to contain such a demon, requires the cooperation of a human 'sensitive' in order to function. As he explains when Oedipa offers herself:

> 'Communication is the key', cried Nefastis. 'The Demon passes his data on to the sensitive, and the sensitive must reply in kind. There are untold billions of molecules in that box. The Demon collects data on each and every one . . . . The sensitive must receive that staggering set of energies, and feed back something like the same quantity of information' . . . .
>
> 'Entropy is a figure of speech, then', sighed Nefastis, 'a metaphor. It connects the world of thermodynamics to the world of information flow. The Machine uses both. The Demon makes the metaphor not only verbally graceful, but also objectively true'.
>
> 'But what', she felt like some kind of heretic, 'if the Demon exists only because the two equations look alike? Because of the metaphor?' (77–8)

Oedipa tries to be a sensitive and considers she has failed. But what appears as her naïve questioning about the theoretical and practical standpoints she is being asked to subscribe to, in fact provides the description of a *prosthetic* function that radically shifts the terms of the argument. For John Nefastis, the machine works because the Demon and the sensitive communicate on some 'deep psychic level' (77). What the Demon puts out is reshuffled but returned to him intact. And so Oedipa's inability to make the machine work parallels her inability to carry out what she sees as her duty with respect to Pierce's inheritance:

> If it was really Pierce's attempt to leave an organized something behind after his own annihilation, then it was part of her duty, wasn't it, to bestow life on what had persisted, to try to be what Driblette was, the dark machine in the centre of the planetarium, to bring the estate into pulsing stelliferous Meaning.... (58)

But as we just said, and as no doubt her experiences with the postal have led her to surmise, the matter can be posed in other terms, those raised by her questions. The sensitive becomes pointsman or -woman, instrument of digital relay which functions across the twin communicative possibilities whereby the message may be either forwarded or diverted, destined or adestined, preserved or wasted. Such a function cannot be considered work in the normal sense, for its system of production involves operations that would normally be called counterproductive. The task is not to preserve an order, or a priority, of man over machine, the natural over the artificial, but to serve as that transferential interface over which or through which the event occurs; and we can think of two important events, particularly strategic events that are occurring in Oedipa's case, those of reading and being a woman.

Oedipa's second question, that posed to John Nefastis just before she tries out as a sensitive, suggests a reluctance to subscribe to his logocentric conception of language, that which views metaphor as an aberration from the literal, so that the beauty of the machine for him is its ability to return the metaphoric *to* the literal. His reply to Oedipa's question as to whether the demon exists because of the metaphor, is that the demon existed for Clerk Maxwell 'long before the days of the metaphor' (78). Whenever that was. But once again, the sensitive, whom we shall henceforth call the 'reader', if she is involved in the business of information flow, so-called, or communication, exists as an interface of language, or languages, for any transfer which occurs in language, just like an inheritance, involves partition, a division of the singular coherence of language. There cannot be, within that operation, a pure literal which is prior to an aberrant metaphoric. So the Demon remains both metaphor and literality, just as the reader, through her relationship with the demon, remains in and out of the machine.

Being what we have called a 'transferential interface' of/across languages, does not reduce merely to handling the relationship between the dualities, for the relationship of duality is exceeded at the same time as it is put into operation, and the exact rhetorical function which is in play is difficult to determine. This becomes clearer in another case, another metaphor so-called, where a prosthetic reading presents itself as alternately a trembling delirium and an exercise in differential calculus. Let us enlarge on that.

Oedipa walks through the night, falling upon a whole series of muted post-horns, then stumbles on an alcoholic sailor who asks her to post a letter for him using the W.A.S.T.E. system. It is thanks to his addiction, she surmises, that he has been able to change tracks and switch on to the alternative that Tristero represents. It is explained in terms of a metaphor of ploughing: 'Cammed each night out of that safe furrow the bulk of this city's waking each sunrise again set virtuously to plowing, what rich soils had he turned, what concentric planets uncovered?' (93). The drunk comes to be seen as another type of sensitive who, trained in the processing of unusual experience, has gained expertise in the economics of mental functions:

> She knew, because she had held him, that he suffered DT's. Behind the initials was a metaphor, a delirium tremens, a trembling unfurrowing of the mind's plowshare. The saint whose water can light lamps, the clairvoyant whose lapse in recall is the breath of God, the true paranoid for whom all is organized in spheres joyful or threatening about the central pulse of himself, the dreamer whose puns probe ancient fetid shafts and tunnels of truth all act in the same special relevance to the word, or whatever it is the word is there, buffering, to protect us from. (95)

The activity called here 'metaphor' and explained metaphorically with the ploughing image again, is promoted as a short-(cir)cu(i)t giving more direct access to the truth. Similarly, W.A.S.T.E.

although a parody of America Post, is presented as a less cluttered, less institutionalised, more free, means of communication; a bypass which is a short-cut. In fact what we have here with DT's is anything but an uncluttered rhetorical space: literal shakes, synecdochical initials signifying a shift of register, and metaphoric unfurrowing which falls *en abyme* as that unfurrowing becomes the metaphor of metaphor. Conceived of according to a logocentric model the sensitive and the drunk are involved in preserving intact the circulation of the signifier, or accounting for its vagaries in terms of notions which smack of the mystical.

However, both this reading and Pynchon's description (seek to) exceed that model. In the case of DT's an already overloaded rhetorical figure under the agency of the drunk, takes another turn when Oedipa herself slips sidewise, 'trembling', 'unfurrowed', and connects DT's with *dt* to gain enlightenment concerning change and difference:

> Trembling, unfurrowed, she slipped sidewise, screeching back across grooves of years, to ... freshman calculus; 'dt', God help this old tattooed man, meant also a time differential, a vanishingly small instant in which change had to be confronted at last for what it was, where it could no longer disguise itself as something innocuous like an average rate; where velocity dwelled in the projectile though the projectile be frozen in midflight, where death dwelled in the cell though the cell be looked in on at its most quick. She knew that the sailor had seen worlds no other man had seen if only because there was that high magic to low puns, because DT's must give access to dt's of spectra beyond the known sun.... (95–6)

Let us not be baffled by this rhetorical overdetermining: *dt* is itself but another convention, a differential consisting of the sum of imperceptibly small units of change, each approaching zero. It has no more literality than the shakes, and the metaphoric switch has only led to a further rhetorical configuration. However much more the language of the text seems to lean towards the mystical, it continues to provide the terms of a different reading, notions of *différance*, signs of death in the generation of meaning, validation of word-play, all of which could be followed up at this or another time, with or without warning, literally or metaphorically or as rhetorically excessive as language allows.

So what is our point here? Firstly, that the notion of metaphor as a departure from a more direct literal merely repeats the most naïve conception of the operation of language itself, assumed as a fall away from unmediated perception. Secondly, as we saw in our discussion of *Gravity's Rainbow*, Pynchon's fiction puts into effect relations which are called metaphor but whose rhetorical operations are in fact more complicated than that – 'entropy' in the case of the relationship between thermodynamics and information flow, an 'unfurrowing of the mind's plowshare' in the case of that between DT's and *dt*.

To the extent that *dt* is a non-apposite repetition of DT's, or vice versa, one might be tempted to call the relationship between them one of parody, especially in view of the importance given to parody in discussion of postmodernist fiction;[4] in view of our earlier suggestion that 'Envois' is in part a parody of Derridean theory as expounded in other texts over the same signature; and in view of a certain rhetorical looseness that has come to mark the term 'prosthesis' in its attachment here and there to a wooden leg. But, to come back then to prosthesis, like all the relationships just described by the DT's/*dt* relation, parody alone does not account for it, no more than does 'high magic', metaphor, or delirium. Parody, like metaphor, can too easily be used as a term to neutralise the effect of a whole range of rhetorical effects. Prosthesis, in its concentrated yet inadequate sorting of information, in its short-circuiting of levels of discourse, would both call for and operate an as yet undetermined and unclassified repartition of the rhetorical domain.

At least part of the problem (and we mean a rhetorical problem) with the terms in which demon and delirium are conceived in *Lot 49*, lies with the idea, expressed by Oedipa earlier on, that excluded middles are 'bad shit', that they imply the opposite of diversity; which means that the digital represents the threat of the mechanistic, the denial of the human, and must be compensated for by some kind of reaffirmation – the psychic in the case of the demon, something very akin to that, and to a romantic notion of creative inspiration, in the case of DT's/*dt*. On the other hand, if one resists that discursive overlay, what is most common to prosthesis and to a sort of DT's/*dt* shift, is the possibility that digital relay provides the very diversity that exists in information flow; that a constant switching between the direct and the *détourné*, between communication and dissemination, between destination and adestination, is the means by which its resource is best developed. Pending a rewriting of the binary mechanism, one is left with the same set of opposite terms, but one can work at establishing that the relationship between them no longer be necessarily preconceived or pre-empted by the same threat of a reduction to a lifeless zero which the binary seemed to imply, for the zero comes to be a condition of possibility for any relationship, for any operation of partition. To go a step further it might be suggested that that threat of reduction to the zero is in fact intrinsic to a logocentric conception which, more than anything else, is permanently in the business of such reductions, constantly resolving difference by appropriation to the singular or exclusion to an opposite other.

Thus prosthesis aims to offset the traditional conception of meaning as fulness within the text which successive readings come to disturb; of reading as the inadequate supplement to the text rather than a necessity already inscribed within the writing. Within that classic conception of natural/artificial relations based on notions of disintegration and ideals of retrieval or restoration which conceal the contrivances they entail, the prosthetic would merely be interpreted as the recognition of a failure, the regretful admission of loss. Here is Oedipa, towards the end of *Lot 49*, faced with the disappearance of a number of characters who seem to her vital links in the chain of meaning of the Tristero:

> Oedipa sat on the earth, ass getting cold, wondering whether, as Driblette had suggested that night from the shower, some version of herself hadn't vanished with him. Perhaps her mind would go on flexing psychic muscles that no longer existed; would be betrayed and mocked by a phantom self as the amputee is by a phantom limb. Someday she might replace whatever of her had gone away by some prosthetic device, a dress of a certain colour, a phrase in a letter, another lover. (121)

On the other hand, if the prosthetic were to be conceived, or at least imagined in cybernetic or post-humanist terms, as a necessity rather than a regretful eventuality, then we could imagine a number of significant changes in reading strategy. Whereas a more traditional reading might work at recovery to compensate loss, the prosthetic might profit from detachability, reversibility, redundance, and replacement, to stimulate further production. Whereas the humanist might strive for integrality, the prosthetic might encourage radical intervention and radical detour; might oppose to decay the advantages of artificiality and contrivance; rework the idea of the impasse with the activity of delay and transfer. As a result the text in its prosthetic function might lend itself more readily to analyses of its systems, and the world Oedipa sets out to read might come to be viewed as the network of circuitry she evokes early in the book:

> She looked down on a vast slope, needing to squint for the sunlight, onto a vast sprawl of houses ... and she thought of the time she'd opened a transistor radio to replace a battery and seen her first printed circuit ... Though she knew even less about radios than Southern Californians, there were to both outward patterns a hieroglyphic sense of concealed meaning, of an intent to communicate. There'd seemed no limit to what the printed circuit could have told her ... (13)

Strip away the now familiar hermeneutic overtones from that description and what one has is an infinite number of passages and detours depending on the multiple operations of a digital system. And reading then becomes an activity of sorting, of intervention at the points of articulation to follow along or push along the byways of the text, not with the prospect of codifying all those detours according to some presumed main current, for there is no end to textual detour which would take the reader outside to a point from which such an overview would be possible; rather reading, to refer back to the Demon, will involve a sort of perpetual motion between sensitivity and diabolism in which animate connects with inanimate to produce, or constitute sense. Or a perpetual switching between delirium and differential. The flip-flops of prosthesis will never be simple repetitions or diversions that work from the possibility of an ultimate return, but transferences through a network designed along the simplest of lines multiplied by a coefficient that only the size of a text will determine.

■ ■ ■ ■ ■ ■ ■

Oedipa Maas is called upon to interpret and execute the will of Pierce Inverarity, and finds herself trying to read the text of America, if not of the world. One will always come back to problems of writing and of the text in the development of the notion of prosthesis, for it is with respect to the text that man and machine, natural and artificial, can be observed in one of their most classic relationships. For writers, in the act of writing, are usually seen to be at their most human, on the one hand doing something a mere machine could not do, while on the other hand setting in motion something which will continue to function beyond their control, yet whose dispensability cannot be doubted. So a prosthetic articulation of difference comes to be applicable not only to the relationship between reader and text, but for instance, in this case, to that between one text and another, to the operation of comparative literature that concerns us here. How then does *The Crying of Lot 49* fit into Derrida's 'Envois', or vice versa, how is the matter of partition to be treated between a forged postage stamp postmarked with a gold-knotted horn, or the acronym W.A.S.T.E. seemingly neatly positioned in the top right-hand corner of a postcard sent from Plato and Socrates to Freud and Heidegger and beyond as the lots are cried in the auction of sense? It is only a simple digital operation that is required, the yes/no of the raising or lowering of a trembling hand, to up the stakes, or to defer. The voices get louder, the words come fast, uniform acceleration to burn-out, are accompanied with the static of a professional jargon, and you gear yourself to slip into a mode of flip-flop within the stringent limits allowed for reflection before the moment is lost and the matter abandoned to other bidders, tempted by the partial anonymity of this ritual to make your own gesture and so participate in the game, mindful of what you could be left with should your bid be the last, for there is any number of lots up for grabs here, leftover from any number of wills read or unread in this conjunction of fictions, these 'Envois' with that *Lot 49*, Plato and Socrates come to be supplemented to a post-industrial southern Californian delirium, this pS addendum to an orderly division of the field, literary and theoretical, that presents itself here, just when a resolution or at least a finishing seemed near, the postscript of the letter adjoined to the integrity of the domain inviting the anagrammatical twist by which 'lot' gives 'plotS' and whereby the materiality of the signifier echoes the etymological drift that embraces this whole discussion, that drift, or shift, like movement of a fault that opens the ground over which language is constructed; we mean once again that movement from the origin, accident and misconstruing are all envisaged by it, conceived within it, so that this is our lot, our inheritance, this is the intrigue bequeathed to us, this is the field whose ownership remains open to dispute, this is potentially the field bought for a meagre sum, the price of a passion or at least a kiss, in which some will erect a potence for their own destruction now that the master is dead, and others will raise their stakes in order to contain the cacophony that threatens to erupt once the word is uttered, no swords turned to ploughshares this field is cut-throat we are all in it together and our intervention a single stake, a frail 'I', perhaps a wooden leg at other times or in other circumstances sufficient to denounce the postmaster as plotsmaster, and our excuse, our pretext, this Derrida who will materialise as soon as and wherever Lot 49 is called, and if Tristero appears to Oedipa riddled by the textual, riven by writing, then look again at that inkwell into which Socrates dips his quill and tell us if it doesn't resemble the gold-knotted horn, and look again at *The Courier's Tragedy*, at bad guy Angelo's cryptic remarks about ink made from the remains of drowned messengers:

> This pitchy brew in France is 'encre' hight;
> In this might dire Squamuglia ape the Gaul,
> For 'anchor' it has ris'n, from deeps untold (49)

look there on page 49 and try to tell us that a Francophone with a Pynchon or a penchant for playing on words hasn't got in on this act, Act IV of *The Courier's Tragedy*, Lot 49 of *la tragédie du courrier*, and tell us what isn't playing on words in the functioning of language, tell us how, having contracted to participate by your presence here, dear Reader, whether it was fate that befell you, or reception of a testament, your naming as beneficiary or not, tell us how, now that you are here, reading like a demon prosthetic to this text, how do you plan to put down or close this script without having your gesture read by an astute auctioneer as the signature of your bidding, how then after all do you plan to close the play without copping this lot?

Notes

1. *The Crying of Lot 49* (New York/London: Bantam Books/Jonathan Cape, 1967). J. Derrida, *The Post Card*, trans. A. Bass (Chicago: University of Chicago Press, 1987). Page references appearing in parentheses in this chapter are from these editions.
2. See D. Wills' 'Post/Card/Match/Book/*Envois*/Derrida', *SubStance*, 43 (1984), pp. 19–38.
3. See D. Wills, 'Prosthesis: an introduction to textual artifice', *Southern Review*, 17, 1 (1984), pp. 59–67; and 'Post(e(s)', in E. Grosz *et al.* (eds), *Futur*Fall: Excursions into Postmodernity* (Sydney: Power Institute Publications, 1986), pp. 146–58. In these articles, the text of theory and criticism is called upon to treat with the interventions of a story of a father's wooden leg. Prosthesis will be the subject of a future study by David Wills.
4. David Bennett makes some important observations concerning the use of the term 'parody' to characterise readings of the (post)modern novel. The discussion which follows owes much to those observations. See D. Bennett, 'Parody, postmodernism, and the politics of reading', *Critical Quarterly*, 27, 4 (1985), pp. 27–43. Parody and its relations to postmodernism are also treated – we think less successfully – by McHale and Quilligan. See B. McHale, *Postmodernist Fiction* (New York: Methuen, 1987), pp. 144–5; and M. Quilligan, *The Language of Allegory: Defining the Genre* (Ithaca: Cornell University Press, 1979).

3
Anti-Oedipa

> ... are not the goddesses of Destiny also the goddesses of the human Lot, of allotment – the Moirai, the last of whom is the Silent One, Death?
>
> (Roland Barthes, *Lover's Discourse*[1])

Absolutely as a heuristic only, as a way of marking this chapter's attempt to shift positions in the field of Pynchon criticism, we could begin with the fiction of there being a 'standard reading'. By invoking a 'standard reading', we are pointing to what we see as a tendency of Pynchon criticism as a whole, namely a type of metaphysical reductionism. This is to be found in the criticism on all three novels, but particularly on *Lot 49* where critics have considered the metaphysical dilemmas to be very explicitly narrated. That is, in *Gravity's Rainbow* they are supposedly more elliptically treated and in *V.* the crasser 'solutions' such as 'Keep cool but care' are more likely to be quoted. To put it crudely (and so risking a charge of reductionism against the present text) this critical reductionism entails asking whether the fictions – and 'Pynchon himself', inevitably – are positive or negative in terms of their ultimate prognostications for 'humanity' considered in terms of some kind of undifferentiated global mass, even though the dilemma which this mass faces can mean splits and fissures. The 'elect vs. preterite' division is a particular favourite in this case.[2] The point of the 'standard reading', as we read it, is to reassert some solution, global truth, or human condition in the face of global problems dualistically conceived. The 'standard reading' is most clearly represented by those works, such as Hite's,[3] which try to deal explicitly with such matters as 'order vs. chaos'; or Moore's book which borrows Kolodny and Peters' replacement of 'either/or' readings by 'both/and' readings.[4] And we mention these texts in particular because while 'standard' on this account, they do attempt to work with the dualisms as reasonably problematic matters, and not as simply clear-cut 'choices'.

Yet even in apparently 'specialist' informational readings of

Pynchon, such as Friedman and Pütz's paper on science metaphors,[5] the critics do not fail to make dualistic demarcations between Pointsman's science on the one hand (cause-and-effect, universal rules) and Mexico's on the other (probability, statistical randomness). And these are methodological demarcations which are said to result in, or stem from, a moral dilemma between the advocacy of paranoia or its opposite (anti-paranoia) as ways of coping with 'nature', itself riven between order and chaos.

Much of the mass of secondary literature on *The Crying of Lot 49*, including the works we have referenced, but also many others,[6] turns upon the apparently ethical-moral dilemma of Oedipa Maas which is read as stemming, in turn, from her reading of the metaphysical conditions of possibility. This is how the critics' stories go, if a short parody may be excused – and as in Chapter 1 we make use of indentation to mark our trial readings and writings:

> Oedipa, the mass of America, is left with four possibilities: 'Those symmetrical four. She didn't like any of them, but hoped she was mentally ill; that that's all it was' (128).[7] Mentally ill, then, that's one. The other three: (1) a true network of Americans, really communicating, a real community, (2) she is hallucinating, (3) there is a plot, most likely set up by Inverarity, to place post-horns and such like in her path. The four finally dwindle, over the last few pages of the book, down to two: a real Other, a Word (136) behind the obvious; or else only that latter itself, the humdrum empirical bits and pieces of everyday life. The essential or the contingent. The Platonic form or the in-essence of its mere filling-in. And this real, if it exists, is a community, a real America behind its 'crust and mantle' (133), behind its mere 'name'. Oedipa's question, put bluntly, is: is the Word behind the 'word'? A hideous excluded middle, Word vs. 'word', and Oedipa knew excluded middles to be 'bad shit, to be avoided' (136).

> To find anything behind the name, the inscription, is to be paranoid – in America all the more so because it means community, and we all know how the first six or seven letters of that word can be used. It fractures the American dream of independence, of atomisation, of self-security, of what the Germans called, in reference both to writing and the development of the independent self, *bildung*: 'they'd call her names, proclaim her through all Orange County as a redistributionist and pinko . . .'

(136). Not much choice here, you crack up inside or else lose all possibility of a real outside. If the world is together, I'm mad; I am only sane if it is fragmented. And so we are (or it is) left, awaiting the crying.

In Chapter 1 we diagrammatised this relation between poles and middles as follows:

a (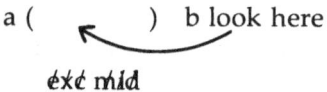) b look here

exc mid

Yet, by describing things in this way, we have already moved slightly apart from the 'standard account' of *Lot 49*'s moral-ethical dilemma, because our formulation allows *a* and *b* to be a number of things or signs, not simply the sides of a strictly metaphysical dualism. For example, we could say that Oedipa has to exist uncertainly between signifier and signified, between, for example, the signifying post-horns and their meaning, the Tristero. If she veers too closely to the signifier alone, she is left with a meaningless array of figures. On the other hand, to veer the other way – towards meaning – induces paranoia. She lives in a world where there is no longer any clear correspondence between Sr and Sd – and so she can't take the option of bringing the two together; it's not there for the taking.

Again, *a* and *b* might be literal and metaphorical forms of signification. In this case, Oedipa cannot veer too closely towards a literal reading of what she sees and hears – and neither can 'the reader'. Nor can she get lost in the abyss of metaphoric connections because that would lead nowhere but to her own insanity. We could probably also plunder a number of other valencies for *a* and *b*, other dualisms in which *Lot 49* abounds: the real and fake postal systems, the undefinable left and right of Mike Fallopian's odd politics (63–4), the animate and the inanimate, the humane and the mechanical, the 'transcendent meaning' or 'only the earth' behind the 'hieroglyphic streets' (136):

> For it was now like walking among matrices of a great digital computer, the zeroes and ones twinned above, hanging like balanced mobiles right and left, ahead, thick, maybe endless. (136)

As a matter of fact, *Lot 49* does not tell us if or how Oedipa 'resolves' all this – she is simply left to await the crying of the lot, of the mass perhaps, the not-too-critical mass. But plainly, the extremes are not recommended. The excluded middle, somehow (but how?), has itself to be excluded, cancelled, and a space opened (if you'll excuse the syntax) parenthetically up. The novel says 'look here' – but won't tell us where 'here' is and what can be found there.

At such a point of interpretation as this, it is difficult to distinguish the supposedly pure, almost linguistic problem of signifying practice and a whole range of moral/ethical problems. In the same way, a purely logical paradox becomes a practical double-bind when it ceases to be a mere proposition in a textbook and becomes instead an order or command. For example, the army barber is *ordered* to shave all the men except those who shave themselves and is on a charge whether or not he shaves himself. The matter could perhaps be put this way: whereas moral philosophy asks 'Who am I?' and ethics 'What is the good?' – both disciplines supposing in spite of their questions that there is an 'I' and a 'good' to be found (somewhere) and identified – the semiotic tradition we are working in here does not allow 'I' or 'the good' to correspond to such transcendental signifieds. Thus on the one hand signifying practice implicates itself in the questions of morality and ethics inasmuch as notions of identity and good are always, perhaps primarily, problems of signification and representation. And on the other hand our implicit and explicit reference to the work of Derrida throughout this discussion means that problems of representation and signification are reformulated as problems of writing, where 'writing' refers to those functions by which both classical models of signification (the one-to-one relation of words to things) and their counterparts in structuralism (the transcendental relation of the operations of the signifier) are exceeded by effects of the system itself.

Such is our reading of Pynchon, where not only is a stable morality or ethics continually interrupted by various flip-flops, as countless critics have been at pains to establish, but more than this, which most critics have failed to take fully into account, the very problems of representation and signification that we have just held to be inseparable from those problems of ethics and morality, are similarly called into question. The radical problematisation of representation in Pynchon is a question so analogous to the equally radical problematisation of moral prescription that they can be treated as one and the same question.

Thus the semiotic becomes ethical at the point where we ask: how to live in a world where the side of the signifier and the side of the signified cannot be conjoined and where neither alone is to be trusted, neither pure materiality (Sr) nor absent or continually deferred meaning/spirit (Sd), neither substance nor phantom? The questions we want to open up in the remainder of this chapter then are, appropriately, twofold. (1) What is Oedipa's problem formulated 'semio-ethically'? – where, by this term, we put on record a desire to move in some measure against, or elsewhere than, the standard dualistic account while acknowledging its massive historical presence in the Pynchon industry. (2) What form of moral/ethical position could we formulate for the postmodern world which *Lot 49*, at the very least, anticipates? Or to anticipate ourselves a little, can there be an ethics-without-a-thesis, an athetical ethics? And here we have to acknowledge that as a form of resistance against the standard reading's hold on the text, we are encouraged to relinquish the traditional unity of the text in our attempt to deal with the very question it opens up. That is, we may have to risk losing the stocks-in-trade of literary criticism, the tight textual connection, the apposite quote, and so on. We may have to risk some labyrinthine detours and some modes of resisting the authorised version of *Lot 49*.

We could resume, then, with Oedipa's semio-ethical problem. While 'the middle' is, in some sense, officially perhaps, excluded, Oedipa finds herself in a middle of some sorts.[8] At the very least, she is *in media res*. She is caught between Origin (being) and Destination (purpose), between 'because' and 'in order to'.[9] She is caught in *destinerrance* like a dead letter, WASTEd communication, left in trash-can rather than postbox. She is – or is manipulated into being – exactly where no binary system will allow anyone to be. And so we must reformulate the idea of her being in a position of choice, exactly.

For example, she is in much more than a double-bind in the classical sense analysed by Bateson, Laing and others.[10] For in the double-bind proper, neither term can operate. It is prevented by the other term. Someone who is doubly-bound cannot, for example, be said to be *either* loved or unloved by their mother and, equally, they cannot be said to be *both*. In excluding (while requiring) *a* and *b*, the double-bind's logic excludes both of the

Anti-Oedipa

propositions 'both *a* and *b*' and 'either *a* or *b*'.[11] There is, after all, something definite, literal, logical, or non-modal, about the double-bind as we know and love it. No doubt that is why Bateson thought it could be resolved by 'metacommunications'.

On the other hand, for Oedipa, both terms can, at least potentially, at least in principle, be operative at once. The trouble is that she can't tell if, and if so which, or if both. If Origin points to Truth and if mere presence (experience) is paranoid, then Oedipa is prevented from finding a further truth, namely the truth of the relation between Truth and experience – or Origin and presence. That truth would tell her 'what-to-do'. It would signal destination, somewhere to go and something to be. Thereby even the metaphysical conception of Truth (as Origin) is displaced for Oedipa. (While, for the one who is merely doubly-bound, two overarching, terribly obvious, and contradictory truths run amok.) Something has to be sought. But this truth lies in a relation between two terms, one of which is, itself, Truth and that is, by definition, unavailable. If our end is indeed our beginning (and *Lot 49* it should be remembered, does end with 'lot 49'), then there is no comfort when the beginning is just as obscure(d) as the end. Oedipa is if anything doubly-unbound. She is in a double-bind. By comparison with Oedipa's position, there may be something comforting in that which is binding, in the legal sense, because one can know where one is with it. But such comfort is unavailable to her. Even the binding contract of the will seems indifferent to her.

Moving now on to the much more labour-intensive question, (2), we can see that given (a) the relation between ethics/morality and signification/representation and (b) its rewriting in *Lot 49* – that rewriting being situated in a context of questions of twin possibilities and excluded middles, these in turn becoming a question of beginnings and ends – it will be important to consider that there is always a double direction to be followed when it comes to beginnings and ends. Our premise as always is that these two directions are a function of the same impulse, namely that which relates ethics to signification. And so immediately below we take up question (2) – the idea of beginning and end as moral/ethical terms or termini, while in the next chapter, 'Telegrammatology', we take the other pathway and discuss the same idea of beginnings and ends in terms of textual points or *puncta*. Thus we are involved now in the problem of Origin/Destination that Oedipa faces and the ways in which a deconstruction of that opposition might yield what we call an *athetical ethics* – a way of dealing with, though not necessarily 'solving', Oedipa's dilemma. It is here, then, that we enter Labyrinths.

■ ■ ■ ■ ■ ■ ■

In our previous chapter, PLS RECORD BOOK BID, we refused some of the possibilities which other readers of *Lot 49* have taken to be positive ways for *avoiding* binaries, for example the psychic insights of the old sailor's dt's or the sensitivity of conspiring with Maxwell's Demon, to mention only two obvious ones.[12] But somewhat in their place, there is a turn towards 'the flip-flops of prosthesis', 'a perpetual switching', 'perpetual motion between sensitivity and diabolism'.[13] Prosthesis, then, separates a space between *a* and *b*, an indefinite series of delta-t discontinuities. It prizes apart signifier and signified so that neither one seems to be satisfied. And in the spectrum or rainbow which the two terms make, what we are and what we make of ourselves, now has a field of indefinite play rather than being fixed to the two terms (Sr/Sd) themselves. This makes BOOK BID related to, and also different from, some readings of *Gravity's Rainbow* in which the straight-laced lines of gravity (seriousness) are split through a prism into play (unseriousness) creating an infinitely expanding bandwidth.[14] *Gravity's Rainbow*, then, would not be unlike 'Limited inc...', having infinite ways of being spilled on the page.[15]

On the other hand, in and through these labyrinths, we want to suggest some other ways – not necessarily incommensurate with the prosthetic elements of BOOK BID/Pynchon/Derrida. These ways explore a new theme, however, in relation to the semio-ethical dualisms represented by *a/b*, that of refusal rather than splitting. Each has its own voice or writing position. And so here is a slightly different, self-appointed, guide through the labyrinths, though its trustworthiness *vis-à-vis* the athetical must remain a matter of conjecture. It speaks in the first person and it says:[16]

> What are we all looking for? – the religious, the theoretician, the person (like Oedipa so often) in the street? For want of yet another metaphor, it can be said that what we are looking for is origins, that the search for an answer, a truth, a centre, a cause – especially for what we are, since we cannot but think of ourselves in progressive or teleological terms – can be summarised

as a search for the origin. Perhaps this is especially so also for those of us in the New World(s) where, ultimately, past a certain point, history is always elsewhere. It is as if the finding of origins were the method we could all agree on as the correct means of self-knowledge. If, we think, we know from whence we derive, we will know ourselves. The two terms – who we are, where we come from – are now almost synonymous, so firm is the grip of the discourse on origins among us. The theorist of human nature, with all her stories of primeval humanity, and the man in the office of the Registrar of Births, Marriages and Deaths, looking up family history, or else Oedipa on the trail of Pierce's will, all are on the same quest, the 'plot which has no name' to invoke the conceit of Herbert Stencil in *V*..

One problem with this will to origin is that we do not know where to stop. Because everything seems to derive from what we call origins, so too does this knowledge of where to stop. Only when we have found our origins, only, that is, when we have learned how to stop, will we know, among other things, how to stop searching. The process is obviously self-defeating and makes postmodern societies seem backward by comparison with those that have strong origin myths and, so the story goes, non-linear conceptions of both historical and conceptual time.

In its potential for endlessness, the search for origins is like a labyrinth. Except that in thinking of labyrinths we are apt to imagine the wrong form of it. Most of the mazes we are familiar with have definite starting and ending points. The starting point is 'here', on the outside. The ending point is 'there', usually in some as-yet-unknown-but-projected centre. And this indeed shows the strong connections between our notions of origin and centre. But anyone who has ever got to the centre of, for example, a large garden maze will know that the centre contains nothing special. It is an almost arbitrary point in the general landscape. Its hedges, seats, pathways and personnel and so forth are pretty much identical with the hedges, seats, pathways and personnel to be found in any other byway of the labyrinth. Centres, then, are arbitrary and are simply places we imbue with special significance.

Another version of the labyrinth is Oedipa's view of the streets of Southern California, well laid-out, mainlining to the heart (14). As we suggested previously, reading might do well to pursue the interminable series of moves to be made around a text taken as such a maze of circuits and lines, once the idea of a centre is removed from it, since such a circuit cannot be said to have a suitable centre. Mythically, however, we have tended to view labyrinths as having centres and to populate those maze-centres. Usually with monsters or treasure. That is, we imagine our origins as being either hideously natural or corruptingly cultural. And, as we follow mazes, it is certainly a motivating force if we can clearly imagine things of this kind. Trepidation or fortune are certainly more attractive than aimlessness – yoyoing perhaps. The monsters to be killed and the gold to be won keep us on our track to the empty, arbitrary centre. We know, though we rarely think of it, that the centre is no centre. The goods there are no good.

So, if we chance upon some possible centre, we feel always as if we have reached nothing. And then we want to return to our exploring because that at least gives us a sense of purpose, and defers the terrible point of arriving precisely nowhere. So the search continues, even if we have discovered the centre to be empty. But now there is a continual feeling of having been let down. It's the same feeling we get on the journey home. It always passes quicker than the outward journey. The freshness, the newness of the scene, the hope of an end in sight have all been removed. Hence whether we feel pleasure or anguish, our search for origins is still unsatisfiable. It is no more and no less than an addiction – much like the old sailor's addiction in *Lot 49*. Like all addictions, it has no purpose except for the satisfaction of the addiction itself. (Though of course you can't tell the addict that – the addict always feels like some extra-addictional thing is to be filled, some unnameable that sends him to the cigarette packet, the needle, the bottle. . . .) The way in and the way out are equally baffling. They provide the same kind of puzzle. And so every point along the way becomes a potential centre – and end.

From this point of view then, our problem is not 'too few origins'. It is not scarcity, rather it is 'too many origins', overabundance. War, love, god, self, man, wealth, nature, truth. . . . We can't see 'the' point because there are too many points, not too few. The will to origin and its pluralism constitute a central contradiction in our lives – and so we live in an eternal chasm between dogma and aimlessness, uneasily, and even though tending to one side, still carving a 'middle way' through, aided by various tools with such titles as 'religion', 'ideology', 'belief' and so on. We feel sometimes that we can never reach the, or a, goal. But what we get wrong in all of this is the idea of a goal.[17] Goals perhaps, are more like goals scored in football, where there can always be another one, later, quite different in character, scored in a different way. There is no ultimate goal, only perhaps the goal of the month. If so, then it makes no more sense to say we *can't* reach it than it does to say we can. And the myth of 'the' goal is, for us and perversely, the origin. We have turned our ends into mythical beginnings, willed them to be so.

Here is the mistake again: we want to stop, but we think that stopping means reaching for the origin/end while, in fact, stopping means stopping either to search or to feel hopeless in the absence of anything to search for. What I want to posit here is a morality which refuses both. An athetical ethics. For the two sides of the mistake are sides of the same coin – and the coinage as a whole is debased. We should continue *to want to stop* – but in another sense entirely. This different sense of stopping means refraining from the hope for a definite origin and refraining equally from the hopelessness of an absent origin. The labyrinthine search for official origins can, after all, be a way of deferring crucial moral questions. In *Gravity's Rainbow*, Franz Pökler is able temporarily to defer questions of morality – specifically the fact that the Nordhausen rocket-site is worked by prisoners from the neighbouring Dora camp (which briefly holds Leni, his wife). This deferral is the 'gift of Daedalus that allowed him to put as much labyrinth as required between himself and the inconveniences of caring' (428). Refusing the labyrinth, then, may curiously enough be a way of actually caring – no matter how 'inconvenient'. To see this, we could engage in a speculation about what would happen were the origin actually to return.

If, by some miracle, this were to happen, then it would happen without our aid, without our going out and looking for it. But like some lost souls deserted by their mothers or their spouses, we go searching in the night through all the likely, and some of the unlikely, places. What we don't see is that our quest, if it does anything at all, actually prevents any return. Refraining will not guarantee it either but, unlike the search, it won't prevent it. That is the odd paradox, there is most hope in abstention from hope. But this is as far as something called 'hope' can be allowed to go, mindful that this is one pole of the 'hope vs. hopelessness' dualism of the standard reading.

This writing position is already, we can see, putting itself under erasure in a peculiarly self-referential way. That is, it seeks to put the ethical itself under erasure. It seeks to be that which erases, like a teacher at a blackboard or the teacher's sponge.[18] Yet at the same time it cannot but posit direct ethical theses in order to achieve this. And in so doing it self-erases its athetical position. The sponger is sponged! And so we might try a further writing position which picks up the Ariadne thread in a more conceptual way.

> The positive search for an origin is associated with the concept of 'same'. It demands that all things have not just an origin but the *same* origin and the return of the origin is conceived of as a return to a state of singularity prior to the fall into difference. A life lived on the concept of sameness (despite the empirical plurality of candidate origins) is a life which valorises 'mystique' in Péguy's sense.[19] To believe, on the contrary, that the origin cannot be attained, is to live a life on the concept of difference – the bases of life, in the absence of an origin, one believes, must be plural, fragmented, differentiated, one for each of us, or each group of us. Here the origin is, too, deferred, continually put off. Such a life, again in Péguy's sense, valorises 'politique'. Here the origin is absent and condemns us to this world, to politique. While, with the former course, the positive origin is *never* of this world – hence mystique.
>
> But 'same and different', 'mystique and politique', in themselves, constitute merely another dualism, or order of difference. The division between them is, therefore, on the side of politique. We need to see *this* difference-of-a-different-order as the difference which mobilises the refrain or abstention (from the search for origins and also from fears of the goal being absent). The mystical dogmatist sees only a uniform world in which even the unbeliever has her origins in one central and primordial form. The unbeliever sees a multitude of worlds, among them the mistaken beliefs of the mystic. But difference-of-a-different-order projects a world that is uniform and plural and, at the same time, neither; for its essential energy derives from *relations between* dualisms such as same and different, mystique and politique, uniformity and plurality. Similarly, physical energy comes neither from a single indivisible sub-atomic particle, nor from the plurality of such particles but instead from the relations

Anti-Oedipa 97

between them. That much was clear in the Demon machine, in relations between hot and cold, fast and slow.

The mistake is to go looking in the properties of objects (e.g., the will, the Tristero, etc.) instead of cancelling the object domain and focusing instead on the domain of relations. Within the model of a/b, this means treating it as a triple term, one in which the slash has more than the simple status of, say, marking a relation of opposition. And saying 'look here' would entail drawing attention to that fact while at the same time asking that the relation not be simply read as one of exclusion. In physics, relations can be represented mathematically – as relatively pure writing. In the 'human' domain we have no exact equivalent of this although, granted, we should not see the human and the mathematical as representing a simple opposition. The sorts of relations that apply in ethics and morality, in questions of living, one might say, are more susceptible to being shown than represented. That is, they require to be lived. Yet inasmuch as this living is another form of representation, a means of putting into effect the differences which give rise to the experiences of living – as 'politique' rather than 'mystique' – living becomes a form of writing(-living). Attempts at representation of the relations – in sociology, anthropology, philosophy and so on – are problematic because they over-value the analogue with physics and seek a higher order representation. They are, for all their protestations, positivistic, in the sense that they hold life to be representable in some form other than life. The difference which gives human life meaning(s) is different from the difference which creates physical energy. And so the attempt which Oedipa makes at contact with the Demon, through the representation of Maxwell on the box cover, is always doomed. The two differences cannot be treated as the same, there is no equivalent of a mathematics to which we can turn.[20]

Now this position moves towards a self-destruction similar to the previous one. It tries to construct a set of binaries and meta-binaries (difference, difference-of-a-different-order) and to disassemble them in the name of the athetical at the same time. While it wants to refuse the ethical as representation and take it up instead in terms of what it calls 'living', it can still only achieve this by invoking, and then cancelling certain 'thetical' positions in philosophy and science. Suppose now another athetical position were instituted, one which attempted to tackle the question of the ethical more crudely, more 'head on'?

> The goal of the ethical, the good, cannot eventuate as long as we insist on treating the good as synonymous with an attainable origin (the ultimately 'same') *or* an unattainable origin (the ultimately 'different'). Still, in a postmodern context of rocket-culture and apocalypse, it is probably easiest to take the latter option – 'No Future', 'God/Man is Dead', etc.[21] In such circumstances, it's very easy to distrust the route of sameness (or positive origin) which served well for our pre-nuclear ancestors. Yet there is still little evidence of any other position except that which would replace this with its antithesis, its inverted image. The point would then be to remove either image and not to mistake the removal of the first with a popular ideology of mere difference and hopelessness.
>
> One beginning was the search for *secular* forms of 'same' and 'origin' – and some have made this move under the rubric of 'humanism'.[22] That may be an important initial corrective – and it shows the historical importance of movements such as existentialism – yet it is only on a par with adolescent impersonations of adulthood. The modernist age of humanism is effectively over. But we have mistaken the new impersonality for nihilism instead of seeing it as a possible freedom – albeit a freedom within the vestigial constraints of same and different.
>
> So it may be true that one does not know any, let alone 'the', way ahead. But it is as important as ever to find out what its limits are. All of the beliefs we have relied on in the past were either beliefs to get us into the labyrinth or beliefs to get us out. What we need, then, are counter-beliefs which will prevent us from entering at all. But this is like saying 'Stop crying!' to one who is interminably disturbed. It is no good simply saying 'Don't enter!' We have to find not only reasons but also motivations for not entering.
>
> I'm talking here like a child who has had enough of the maze game. But I have no idea how I can persuade anyone that there are other games, including games of refusal, to move on to.[23] Maybe I simply have to complain loudly and long enough. I'm not sure. But one thing is obvious, there's no going it alone. *We* have to give up together for it to make sense, even if a new game is not well formulated in anyone's mind. I cannot give anything

like rational reasons for wanting to cease and to begin in a new way.

Now too the athetical begins to flounder, for it is manifestly against the policy of refusing ethical theses that one should 'persuade' or 'motivate', that one should generate positive 'counter-beliefs' and so on even though, or especially because, they cannot be enunciated as 'rational reasons'. Another strategy, common to the domain of the moral, is storytelling. Traditionally stories, after all, have had their 'ends', their 'morals'. And so another guide to the athetical might invoke this allegorical strategy. Thus:

> Once upon a time we used to tell stories of morality in which there were quests. Chrétien de Troyes almost single-handedly invented the Grail legends. The Bible tells us nothing of it. In de Troyes' story and in many quest stories up to Tolkien, Pynchon and beyond, a young man is born, the last of a noble line. He is kept sheltered from the world of chivalry, often by his mother, in a country (or a country retreat) far from civilisation. But one day, by accident, he wanders and meets a knight on the road – or hears/reads of rumours of knights. Torn between his seemingly lowly origins and chivalry, he chooses the latter and goes off on his quest – unsure of his, or its, authenticity. Often the Grail, or its equivalent, elude him at a crucial moment. For example, he may fail to ask or answer a simple question properly.
> His lowly origins extend to common insecurities about language in formal situations. We simply go wrong, against our own better judgment and capacities – as the common phenomenon of *esprit de l'escalier* shows. The young man does, however, despite this and other failings, turn into a great king or leader in some new zone. But he is always insecure about his 'natural' ability. His success seems to him more a matter of luck than of ability in any true or ultimate sense. This is especially so in the light of his failure in the face of the Question. But he makes wise laws, keeps in touch with the people and often dies or disappears, childless. But he does return from time to time – shadowy and not quite material. Sometimes this is in the prefigurement of other legends. Sometimes it is in later stories. And sometimes it is in the works we call 'scholarship', 'criticism', or 'mythology' (in the disciplinary sense). The scholar's quest for the hero is often just like the hero's own quest – like all

literature it doubles itself.[24] And of course the hero – or the Grail – can turn out to be a monster or a treasure.

And now, if this allegory were to have an explicit moral appended to it, it might read as follows:

> There is a peculiar sense in which, for all our contemporary will to origin, the quester as a possible self-image has become unpopular. We see no point in constructing ourselves as searchers. Nothing seems to be worth it, to have any value to us either in terms of the destruction of evil nature (the monster) or in terms of the value of goods (treasure). Essentially we have lost what used to be called a 'model of man', a conception of human nature. But the denial of the quest, the refusal of a metaphysics of human nature, is an ethos in itself. The absence of a 'model of man' assumes a 'model of man' from whom the model is absent. We think we have gone without (in the sense of 'lack' and/or in the sense of 'beyond') – but the pull of the origin, one would like to say, the *form* of the origin-quest, for all its inversion, holds us still, whatever our anguish, aimlessness or despair.
>
> The one who goes on a quest – Oedipa, Quixote, Parsifal – is like the paranoid. The 'model of man' for the quester is paranoia; for the paranoid can see pattern and purpose in absolutely everything. The hand of God is visible in the configuration of cigarette butts/ends around the library steps. The windmills are giants. Whatever John, Paul and George may say, the sect are after Ringo's ring.[25] Old milk bottle tops are (real) gold and silver. Ring-pulls among the litter are rings which guarantee invisibility. But the anti-quester is simply the anti-paranoid. She is, to use Bateson's term for the patternless, hebephrenic.[26] The hebephrenic can make no sense of the most significant events or objects (data, experiences, etc.). The quester is relation-ful and the anti-quester is relation-less.

It's very clear now what this, and any, storyteller is trying to do – to *displace* the traditional story of the quest (in itself a placebo for origin and for a certain ethics, then). The conceit here is that allegory involves displacement and so one should strictly be able to defer a direct address to the ethical through the infinite delay of the allegorical story. And so one would be heard to recite an athetical story. As one of our voices advocated writing(-living), this one

Anti-Oedipa 101

advocates living(-writing). But on the other hand, whether the moral of the story is explicit or not, something one could only call the 'tone' is always already moralistic – just plain moralistic, not athetically so. This 'tone' is, most likely, no mysterious or charismatic 'gift' but in fact an effect (a potentially poisonous one always) of the institutional and political position of the storyteller, the one who cannot but seduce with his or her stories.[27] The storyteller is the site of a certain power, then, and that power is one which clearly has moral-ethical dimensions. Ipso facto, then, and particularly with the model of the parable in mind, it is self-annulling to use allegory as a form of expression of the athetical – bearing in mind that very little if any of the current chapter has been able to evade narrative discourse. We will try then to pick up from where the 'voices' so far have left off, realising that in building on them we are incorporating them, their self-defeating structures and ideas, and also acknowledging accordingly that some pure athesis is now going to be virtually impossible short of leaving a blank, coming to a stop and moving on to a(nother) point.

Parallel to the story you have just heard, there is another. It invokes the necessary intertwining (or -twinning) of ethics with signification, mentioned earlier. It speaks not so much of an individual's quest for meaning in the form of an origin, as of the different paths borrowed by meaning itself. Our times (the ones apparently in need of an ethics) are surely ones in which we have come more and more to think about language and how it signifies, 'the ways in which it means'. Ours is, if anything, the age of the signifier. Before we began to think about the signifier, in its modern sense, before perhaps the work of de Saussure, words and other bits and pieces of language were thought to mean something by being attached to non-linguistic things, to cats and dogs, but also to love, happiness, anger and so forth. Rather in the way that a label is attached to a parcel, or a postage stamp to a letter.[28] These days, of course, and this is perhaps part of the supposed 'need' for ethical firm ground, we can collect just the labels or the stamps without that to which they were attached having much importance. This 'being attached' which was once, however, so crucial gave us the doctrine of the proper, of 'unum nomen unum nominatum' (one name to each thing named). Once you have the idea that signifiers, particular signifiers, never shift their meaning because they are attached in this way, you begin to believe that each has a universal, once-for-all meaning. So this former age was the age of the universal signifier – as if it were hard currency, fixed to some kind of gold standard, and when you cashed in your signifier, you always got the same thing (object, image) in exchange for it.

Now there has been something of an end to this. We have come to accept the sliding around of meaning – the fact that words and other linguistic paraphernalia are not fixed to a central meaning. We've come off the semiotic gold standard. The currency of signification is floating in a basket of related currencies. And here we can see why, for example, the word 'meaning' itself is used in different ways, taking in 'linguistic meaning', 'significance' (in the sense of 'the meaning of life'), 'intending', 'leading to' (x means y) ... and so on. It floats around like a metaphor for, or an instance of, the problem of meaning generally and its instability in our age. We might therefore talk about the old and the new signifier on the model of the Old and New Penny. The new one involves a lot more play. Its value is by no means fixed. But we have not yet learned – like many people who introduce new currencies – to find our way with this new signifier. We keep trying to attach it to the value of the old. We keep making translations.

So a certain kind of relativism has extended to, or perhaps even derived from, our conceptions of language – and the old, universal, signifier is now very much out of date (and, therefore, sought after? a relic? an antique?) – for all the new, playful, signifier keeps on being referred back to that shadow. (And the very act of referring, in this case, is a technique hanging over from our ways of utilising the old currency.) Again we seem to be faced with a choice between fixed origins and the abyss of unreason. But here too it need not be so. The mistake, it seems to us, is of the order of other mistakes dealt with here. It involves actively looking for some quality called 'the meaning' and then either finding that quality fixed or finding it hopelessly free. In place of this, we can think of meaning as other than 'the meaning' – as an activity, like bathing and so forth. Then it would be as futile to ask 'What is the meaning of a word?' as it is to ask 'What is the bathing of a person?' One can no longer expect a request for meaning (semiotic or ethical, for example) to be 'cashed in'. All one gets instead is refusal.

Perhaps this means, then, refusing the whole problematic of *Lot 49*: a̶/b̶, and notice how we have no way of putting the mark of erasure under erasure, except by intensifying it. The alternative would be some sort of graphic silence, the blank of an unwritten page which nevertheless (how?) expressed the whole problematic we have developed here. But that would run the risk of a type of mysticism, even though the resistance advocated here is certainly not to be confused with a resistance to materiality. So the problem of the athetical cannot but remain as a question – how to end the labyrinth of reading and still read? How to refuse to cop the lot?

Notes

1. R. Barthes, *A Lover's Discourse: Fragments* (London: Cape, 1979), p. 145.
2. See, for example, the following papers: J. M. Krafft, '"And how far-fallen?"': puritan themes in *Gravity's Rainbow*', *Critique: Studies in Modern Fiction*, 18, 3 (1977), pp. 55–73; S. Sanders, 'Pynchon's paranoid history', in G. Levine and D. Leverenz (eds), *Mindful Pleasures: Essays on Thomas Pynchon* (Boston: Little Brown, 1976), pp. 139–59; and M. Smith and K. Tölöyan, 'The new jeremiad: *Gravity's Rainbow*', in R. Pearce (ed.), *Critical Essays on Thomas Pynchon* (Boston: G. K. Hall, 1981), pp. 169–86.
3. M. Hite, *Ideas of Order in the Novels of Thomas Pynchon* (Columbus: Ohio State University Press, 1983).
4. T. Moore, *The Style of Connectedness: 'Gravity's Rainbow' and Thomas Pynchon* (Columbia: University of Missouri Press, 1987). A. Kolodny and D. J. Peters, 'Pynchon's *The Crying of Lot 49*: the novel as subversive experience', *Modern Fiction Studies*, 19, Spring (1973) pp. 79–87.
5. A. J. Friedman and M. Pütz, 'Science as metaphor: Thomas Pynchon and *Gravity's Rainbow*, in Pearce, pp. 69–81. For a further discussion, see L. W. Ozier, 'Antipointsman/antimexico: some mathematical imagery in *Gravity's Rainbow*', *Critique: Studies in Modern Fiction*, 16, 2 (1974), pp. 73–90.
6. Six important articles focusing directly on moral questions in *Lot 49* – and which would be at the centre of the debate on moral dualisms which the present chapter wishes to deconstruct – are: M. Hite, 'Purity as parody in *The Crying of Lot 49*' in her *Ideas of Order*, pp. 67–93; Kolodny and Peters, 'Subversive experience'; E. Mendelson, 'The sacred, the profane, and *The Crying of Lot 49*', in E. Mendelson (ed.), *Pynchon: A Collection of Critical Essays* (Englewood Cliffs: Prentice-Hall, 1978), pp. 112–46; J. W. Slade, 'Thomas Pynchon; postindustrial humanist', *Technology and Culture*, 23 (1982), pp. 53–72; C. R. Stimpson, 'Pre-apocalyptic atavism: Thomas Pynchon's early fiction' in Levine and Leverenz, pp. 31–47; and M. Putz, 'Thomas Pynchon: history, self, and the narrative discourse' in M. Pütz, *The Story of Identity: American Fiction of the Sixties* (Stuttgart: Metzlersche Verlagsbuchhandlung, 1979), pp. 130–57.
7. Thomas Pynchon, *The Crying of Lot 49* (New York/London: Bantam

Books/Jonathan Cape, 1967). All subsequent bracketed page references are to this edition. Other editions of Pynchon texts referred to are: *Gravity's Rainbow* (New York/London: Viking/Cape, 1973); and *V.* (New York/London: Bantam/Cape, 1964).

8. Hite (*Ideas of Order*) comes close to this realisation when part of her argument for 'including middles' involves treating Pynchon's fictions as 'decentralised' (p. 25). What she doesn't point out is that 'centre' and 'middle' can be synonymous, or not. In fact, she relies on 'centre' being coterminous with 'order' or 'ordering principle', à la Derrida. Centring, therefore, excludes middles and decentring (re)includes them.

9. The distinction between 'because' and 'in order to' motives originates in the work of A. Schütz. See his *Collected Papers, Vol. 1* (The Hague: Martinus Nijhoff, 1962), pp. 69–72.

10. G. Bateson, *Steps to an Ecology of Mind* (London: Paladin, 1973). R. D. Laing and A. Esterson, *Sanity, Madness and the Family, Vol 1: Families of Schizophrenics* (London: Tavistock, 1964).

11. This logical point is missed in Moore's (earlier, Kolodny and Peters') transformation of the digital 'either/or' into the analogic 'and/both'. See notes above for full references.

12. The 'redemptive sailor solution' to moral dilemmas is expanded by Plater to cover the other two novels. As well as Oedipa's sailor with the dts, he points to the sailor Mehemet's message to Stencil in *V.*: 'the only change is toward death ... Early and late we are in decay' (p. 433); and to Pig Bodine's gift to the almost non-existent Slothrop: Dillinger's blood-soaked shirt and the words '... what we need isn't right reasons, but just that *grace*. The physical grace to keep it working' (p. 741). See W. M. Plater, *The Grim Phoenix: Reconstructing Thomas Pynchon* (Bloomington: Indiana University Press, 1978), pp. 3, 48, 52, 230–1. The positive valuation of the Demon can be found in a number of articles including that by Friedman and Pütz. They see the Demon as a conceptual point where 'the two patterns [of order and entropy] merge' (p. 69). A similar point is made in A. Mangel, 'Maxwell's demon, entropy, information: *The Crying of Lot 49*', in Levine and Leverenz, pp. 87–100.

13. These phrases are from our previous chapter, PLS RECORD BOOK BID.

14. Examples would be the 'encyclopaedic' readings of *Rainbow* which argue that Pynchon uses copious amounts of factual knowledge for a variety of literary and metaphysical purposes – splitting the seriousness into an arc of literary play. This reading of the rainbow, we owe to Ann Campbell (personal communication). The 'encyclopaedic' tradition is currently occupied by: the introduction to C. Clerc (ed.), *Approaches to 'Gravity's Rainbow'* (Columbus: Ohio State University Press, 1983); E. Mendelson, 'Gravity's encyclopedia', in Levine and Leverenz, pp. 161–95; D. Cowart, *Thomas Pynchon: The Art of Allusion* (Carbondale: Southern Illinois University Press, 1980); J. O. Stark, *Pynchon's Fictions: Thomas Pynchon and the Literature of Information* (Athens: Ohio University Press, 1980); S. Weisenburger, 'The end of

history?: Thomas Pynchon and the uses of the past', in Pearce, pp. 140–56; Smith and Tölöyan, 'The new jeremiad'. These readings relate to the moral in that they hold the encyclopaedic narrative to be that which 'displays the limits and possibilities of action within [our] culture' (E. Mendelson, 'Rainbow corner', *Times Literary Supplement*, 13 June 1975, p. 666.) BOOK BID's difference lies in the fact that, unlike some of the above-mentioned pieces, it invoked not so much an infinitely expanding bandwidth for the 'possibilities of action' as an infinite series of interfacings, connections, or flip-flops. This is largely because BOOK BID was constrained within the more rigidly prescribed parameters of the binary. Our chapter *'Gravity's Rainbow* and the post-rhetorical' addresses more clearly this idea of 'looseness' between binary oppositions.

15. J. Derrida, 'Limited inc.: a b c...', *Glyph*, 2 (1978), pp. 162–254. J. L. Austin, 'Three ways of spilling ink', in his *Philosophical Papers*, 2nd edition (Oxford: Clarendon Press, 1970), pp. 272–87.

16. Certain of the voices or writing positions in this chapter are redeveloped in A. McHoul, 'Labyrinths: writing radical hermeneutics and the post-ethical', *Philosophy Today*, 31 (1987), pp. 211–22.

17. This argument is close to that of Wittgenstein in *Zettel* (Oxford: Blackwell, 1967), §693. It also owes much to the position taken by M. Deitch in his unpublished paper 'Wittgenstein and Derrida: no contest'.

18. See J. Derrida, *Signéponge/Signsponge*, trans. R. Rand (New York: Columbia University Press, 1984). The connections between the '(s)ponge' signature, teaching (pedagogy) and erasure are made by Gregory Ulmer in *Applied Grammatology* (Baltimore: The Johns Hopkins University Press, 1985), pp. 19–20.

19. C. Péguy, *Notre jeunesse*, in his *Oeuvres complètes 1873–1914, Tome IV* (Paris: Editions de la nouvelle revue française, 1916) pp. 39–254. (Also – Geneva: Slatkine Reprints, 1974.)

20. Various writers on Pynchon and science who focus on uses of scientific metaphors assume that the fictions adopt an untheorised and undercritical stance toward science. See: J. O. Stark, 'The arts and sciences of Thomas Pynchon', *Hollins Critic*, 12, 4 (1975), pp. 1–13; Friedman and Pütz, 'Science as metaphor'; A. J. Friedman, 'Science and technology', in Clerc, pp. 69–102; and D. Simberloff, 'Entropy, information and life: biophysics in the novels of Thomas Pynchon', *Perspectives in Biology and Medicine*, 21 (1978), pp. 617–25. However, the continual failures and atrocities of science are to be found there also: a thoroughgoing distaste for the positivistic excesses of science on someone or something's part.

21. On *Les Fins de l'homme: à partir du travail de Jacques Derrida*, and his 'No apocalypse...' and their relations to *Gravity's Rainbow*, see 'Fall out', Chapter 8 below.

22. Much current Pynchon scholarship has begun to take to task the supposed 'nihilism' and 'existential uneasiness' of some earlier readings of Pynchon's work – such as Henkle's accusation of 'moral decay' – and carried over into readings of *Gravity's Rainbow*. See:

23. R. B. Henkle, 'Pynchon's tapestries on the western wall', *Modern Fiction Studies*, 17, 2 (1971), pp. 207–20. The first quoted term is Clerc's from *Approaches*, the second Lasch's in C. Lasch, *The Minimal Self: Psychic Survival in Troubled Times* (London: Picador, 1985), p. 163. The introduction to Clerc's book tries to rally a case for *Rainbow* as a novel which 'often masks itself as antinovelistic, antiliterary, and, by an even greater deceptiveness, antihumanistic' (p. 10). For good or ill, this recent wave of reading Pynchon for a positive morality and metaphysics, which Moore calls 'redemptiveness', only returns criticism to the antithesis of nihilism – a sort of jovial, liberal (or yuppie) discourse on 'community'. The present chapter tries to imagine a space outside both forms of this problematic.

23. 'Game' is used here as a way of glossing Derrida's concept of 'play' along with Wittgenstein's concept of 'language game'. See J. Derrida, 'Structure, sign and play in the discourse of the human sciences', in his *Writing and Difference* (Chicago: University of Chicago Press, 1978), pp. 278–93; and L. Wittgenstein, *Philosophical Investigations* (Oxford: Blackwell, 1968). An important recent rethinking of the concept for literary scholarship is to be found in A. Freadman, 'Untitled (on genre)', *Cultural Studies*, 2, 1 (1988), pp. 67–99.

24. The argument is made by among others M. Foucault in 'What is an author?' in his *Language, Counter-memory, Practice* (Oxford: Blackwell, 1977), pp. 113–38. For Foucault, literature emerges at the moment when language becomes aware of itself as signification. Quilligan's idea of allegory attempts, with mixed success, to play with this notion of doubling. (See M. Quilligan, '["Thomas Pynchon and the language of allegory"]', in Pearce, pp. 187–212.) Although Foucault locates the moment of the doubling of language in literature as being in the nineteenth century, this does not preclude retrospective reading. For details, see A. McHoul, 'Sociology and literature: the voice of fact and the writing of fiction', to appear in *The Australian and New Zealand Journal of Sociology*.

25. Cf. the comparisons between The Paranoids and The Beatles and between *Lot 49* and *Help* (1965) in particular. For studies of paranoia and its inverse in Pynchon, see particularly M. Siegel, *Pynchon: Creative Paranoia in 'Gravity's Rainbow'* (Port Washington: Kennikat Press, 1978); T. Tanner, *Thomas Pynchon* (London: Methuen, 1982); Friedman and Pütz, 'Science as metaphor'; Krafft, 'And how far fallen'; L. Mackey, 'Paranoia, Pynchon, and preterition', *Sub-Stance*, 30 (1981), pp. 16–30; and S. Sanders, 'Pynchon's paranoid history', in Levine and Leverenz, pp. 139–59. The modern-day quest is, of course, typically of a much diminished degree of difficulty by comparison with its mediaeval counterpart; opening up a space for Joycean fun and games. So much so that Plater refers to the Pynchonian quest not even as a 'journey' but as a 'tour', noting along the way, the explicit and implicit Baedeker references. See Plater, *The Grim Phoenix*, pp. 64–134. It's rather a pity after all Plater's sleuthing that Pynchon says he 'transferred' the lot straight from Baedeker, in the 'Introduction' to *Slow Learner*.

26. See note 10 above.
27. R. Chambers, *Story and Situation: Narrative Seduction and the Power of Fiction* (Minneapolis: Manchester University Press & Minnesota University Press, 1984).
28. The history of theories of language and meaning is no more clearly and critically available than in M. Foucault's *The Order of Things* (London: Tavistock, 1970).

4
Telegrammatology

Still an important question then for the reading of *Lot 49*: how to refuse (to cop) the lot? Reading the secondary literature on Pynchon – for example that cited in the notes to the previous chapter – it is easy to notice that the same text fragments are quoted time after time. There is almost a canon of such fragments. Excluded middles being 'bad shit' (136) is a case in point (and of course we have not failed to use it either). The 'direct, epileptic Word' (87) is another. The 'hieroglyphic streets' (136) are a third. But the list is longer.

It is almost as if the critics read the critics and circulated the texts among them that way, rather than looking for new fodder in the 'original(s)'. Thus they generate a whole secondary mode of reading, itself a secret postal system. Or there could be another account: if there is a 'standard reading' (the conceit of our previous discussion), it would be supported by the same 'evidence' again and again, whether the notorious dualisms were read as moral choices, dilemmas, or as dialectically resolved or, worse, transcended.

We might therefore ask what the criteria are for the selection of quoted material in literary (here, Pynchon) studies? Traditionally they are probably based around a notion of support for an argument or thesis. But since the thesis is woven out of a selective reading of the text anyway, the selection of the quotes and the thesis they support must be mutually constitutive. In Popper's terms, the use of this kind of evidence for a theory would give the theory a very low degree of falsifiability. In *Lot 49*'s terms, matching particular letters (bits of literature) with particular destinations (of the metaphysical variety) is known as 'sorting'. Maxwell's Demon is supposed to achieve this in some mystical effortless way – so that the matches come out smoothly on the surface. Oedipa knows better – to re-cite one of our own selective favourites:

> 'Sorting isn't work?' Oedipa said. 'Tell them down at the post office, you'll find yourself in a mailbag headed for Fairbanks, Alaska, without even a FRAGILE sticker going for you'. (62)

How could this sorting, this conspiracy-to-succeed between the letter of the text and the critical argument be subverted – such that other textual possibilities might arise, such that criticism might discover something that it didn't set out to find in the first place?[1]

A clue here is that telegrams are not sorted, at least not in the same way as letters. They have direct delivery, though subject still, of course, to any number of relays and delays. Whoever pays the price of the telegram does so by the word and so may well pay the price, also, of truncation and lost coherence. On this model, suppose we were to take our text-bits first with no extra- or intra-textual semantic destinations 'in mind'. This would mean taking the text as, primarily, a material signifier. For example, we could cut out, collect and send, say, those parts of a text which held the same material, structural or formal positions. This would constitute a new form of 'identification' with the text.[2] What then could we mean by the same position? *Lot 49*, for a start, is made up of six chapters. Each chapter has to start and finish. It has to start and finish with particular units: words, sentences, paragraphs.... So, in a purely structural way, we could take the first sentence of each chapter. Interestingly, when we do this, we get a not-too-bad summary of the plot:

> One summer afternoon Mrs Oedipa Maas came home from a Tupperware party whose hostess had put perhaps too much kirsch in the fondue to find that she, Oedipa, had been named executor, or she supposed executrix, of the estate of one Pierce Inverarity, a California real estate mogul who had once lost two million dollars in his spare time but still had assets numerous and tangled enough to make the job of sorting it all out more than honorary. She left Kinneret, then, with no idea she was moving towards anything new. Things then did not delay in turning curious. Though she saw Mike Fallopian again, and did trace the text of *The Courier's Tragedy* a certain distance, these follow-ups were no more disquieting than other revelations which now seemed to come crowding in exponentially, as if the more she collected the more would come to her, until everything she saw, smelled, dreamed, remembered, would somehow come to be woven into The Tristero. Though her next move should have been to contact Randolph Driblette again, she decided instead to drive up to Berkeley. When she got back to Echo Courts, she found Miles, Dean, Serge and Leonard

arranged around and on the diving board at the end of the swimming pool with their instruments, so composed and motionless that some photographer, hidden from Oedipa, might have been shooting them for an album illustration.

Doubtless, a range of literary-critical remarks could be made at this point, perhaps as cogent as the 'standard reading' and certainly as comprehensive. The critic could, for example, turn to the geographical patterns of contact Oedipa makes; map her journey – as one may map Slothrop's arc-journey through the Zone. Most of the major moves are here, in the formally selected text. So are many of the main characters, with some important exceptions – though, again, they could be brought in with a few skilful moves and connections. Or else, reading the passage in terms of themes, one could point to: alcohol, wills, money, town-city shifts, the build-up of clues, the pointlessness of them despite their temptation as jig-saw material, the textuality of *The Courier's Tragedy* and therefore the relations between Oedipa's and the critics' searches for interpretations, the mathematical nature of the enterprise, the 60s/Beatles connections, the hidden narratorial hand in the shape of the photographer, the inter-textual connections with cinema and so on. And so on. But if our previous discussion has left any mark, if it had any point at all, the point would be not to do that but to refuse and to show how plainly it *could* be done from these structurally culled and essentially random bits.

Equally, we could turn to the final lines of each chapter. Doing so, we get a very different text – one might even say the 'other side' of the lot. And here the sentences are arranged a little differently:

- If the tower is everywhere and the knight of deliverance no proof against its magic, what else?
- After a while she said, 'I will'. And she did.
- She got in and rode with him for two miles before realizing that the whimsies of night-time reception were bringing them KCUF down from Kinneret, and that the disc jockey talking was her husband, Mucho.
- As if the dead really do persist, even in a bottle of wine.
- But by then it was too late to make any difference.
- Oedipa settled back, to await the crying of lot 49.

By any account, this is a markedly different text from the first. If the first was – even using a difficult test for narrative such as

Prince's[3] – an astonishingly narrativistic text, this one is much less so. It uses fewer declarative, propositional utterances. It kicks off, for example, with an interrogative, moves on to reported speech, invokes a plot-tangential coincidence, makes a gnomic remark, becomes resigned and finally, reports an event, but an ultimate one. The tone now is poetic – metaphysical even. Unlike with the first-line text, the themes do not have to be extracted by implication from narrated events – they are there (for all their vagueness) as plain as day.

If the first text seemed to be from a nineteenth-century novel of the 'objectivist', event-reportage, type; this second seems to be more likely an extract from the postmodern philosophical novel, the novel of ellipsis and existential crisis. Here the critic would have to say something like this:

> Unlike the romantic heroine, Oedipa cannot escape from the tower. She, only by fiat, random and impulsive choice, is able to bring her words (I will) and her deeds (She did) together. Only the 'whimsies' bring her into touch with those closest to her in any 'official' capacity (her next of kin, her husband, Mucho). And the line about the dead may well refer back, diegetically, to Mucho whom she discovers changed, almost to the point of disintegration:[4]
>
>> They are stripping away from me ... one by one, my men. My shrink, pursued by Israelis, has gone mad; my husband on LSD, gropes like a child further and further into the rooms and endless rooms of the elaborate candy house of himself and away, hopelessly away, from what has passed, I was hoping forever, for love; my one extra-marital fella has eloped with a depraved 15-year-old; my best guide back to the Trystero has taken a Brody. Where am I? (114)
>
> The dead may persist, in a bottle of wine, too, given Oepida's glimpse of escape in the dt/DT's. And, of course, death will always mean that it's too late to make a difference. Its meaninglessness cuts across all difference. And so on, to the point of waiting for the crying.

But it's always just too paranoid, or too aimless: either to search for textual patterns *or* to recommend, as do the Reader's Liberation

Movement,[5] an endlessly free play of interpretation. The point is that it's not hard to do. It falls out quite easily in the case of these two 'faked' passages. But the point would be, after all of this, *not* to do it. Not to put one's hand into the traps. Instead, it might be better to switch to other genres of text: critically, by now, the telegram and the grammatology.

The discourse of the telegram, such as the one sent to record the book bid at the crying of the Lot, has one notorious feature. While it is primed for accuracy and economy, as we have noted, what is overlooked is that these two aspects can cancel each other out; the telegram is liable to be *erratic*. For example, 'PLS RECORD BOOB BID' is quite an easy thing to have written; and, furthermore, it is self-referentially tied to a main theme of the discussion to follow; a boob, that is, being an error. One should ask next, if Derrida were indeed to have sent the telegram,[6] what would that telegram have looked like? Or: how best could Derrida's work be enfolded into that of Pynchon? – which, for the sake of this exercise, we're taking to be the same question. 'Telegram' may mean the excursus or projection on writing (*tel*, distant; *gramma*, that which is written). And so *Of Grammatology* could itself be a species of telegram being, as it is, an excursus on writing.[7] That might be sufficient to send us looking for error-messages in the text of *Of Grammatology*, read now as telegrammatology.

But there is a second prompting of that strategy, namely that these telegrammatological deliberations so far have considered *methods* of text selection as well as problems of (refusing) *analysis*. To this extent the matter of literary theory has remained in the background. Literary theory, too, has its canon and since Derrida's proper name or names have cropped up here already, we could easily expect an 'application' of his 'theory' to '*Lot 49*', something which the BOOK BID discussion both did and didn't do. But what we seek to pursue here is the idea of reversing the 'subject' and 'object' of theory within a typical arrangement like an application, in order to ask a different question: how could Derrida as 'fiction' be read from the position of Pynchon as 'theory'?

While the former (fiction) is relatively unproblematic given Derrida's concept of 'writing in general', the latter (theory) is not so clear cut. Derrida has consistently tested the borders between literary criticism and its object, by challenging the criteria by which the one circumscribes the other (for example, criteria of authorial intention, thematic unity, discursive coherence), by dividing the material space of commentary as in 'Tympan' or *Glas*, by writing a theoretical fiction or autobiographical theory such as 'Envois', or by disseminating his signature throughout a number of critical texts.⁸ What then might Pynchon's 'theory' be? A telegrammatological observation, in response, would be that *Lot 49* and the rest of the Pynchon oeuvre appear to be relatively perfect (*teleios*, perfect, complete) in material terms; that is as typographical objects. There are possible exceptions. Friedman and Pütz find mistakes in the German proper nouns in *Gravity's Rainbow*, and while they refer to them as 'printer's errors' they are more likely 'language slips', to use their terms which neatly sidestep the theoretical issues of authorship and responsibility.⁹ Additionally, Simmon finds cinécharacter Rotwang's name spelled 'wrongly' in *Gravity's Rainbow*, though this assumes that the 'same' character is being invoked in the fictional list on page 580 of *Rainbow*.¹⁰ This is not a safe assumption for a Pynchon text and the Rotwang case is probably yet another red-herring (or cod) when it comes to questions of determinacy in the 'big novel'.

Lastly, as far as it is possible to tell, the only material error in *Lot 49*, is on page 89 of the Penguin edition¹¹ where a non-speech passage ('They'd never heard it that way...'), is marked as beginning, like speech, with a quote-mark, with a point that looks like this: '. And for the telegrammatologist the error is, if nothing else, at least a *punctum* in Barthes' sense – a point to be noticed, a point which, like Rotwang, sticks out.¹² Moreover, a very good argument could be made to that effect that, in *Lot 49*, it's actually a misprint which serves as Oedipa's first clue, sending her on her errant errand, tracking down what eventually turns out to be, or not to be, the Tristero. That misprint, too, is self-referential. It takes the form of a franking slogan on an airmail envelope, 'put on by the government'. Metzger, typically, doesn't see any heavy import in this mere rhetorical slip when errors of a higher order are possible:¹³

> ... REPORT ALL OBSCENE MAIL TO YOUR POTSMASTER...
>
> 'So they make misprints,' Metzger said, 'let them. As long as they're careful about not pressing the wrong button, you know?' (30)

Bortz, however, sees a tighter connection between the typographical and Realpolitik. Discussing *The Courier's Tragedy*, Bortz suggests that a pornographically corrupted text of the play, contrary to Oedipa's expectations, may actually have suited dominant Puritan (formalist?) purposes: 'What better way to damn it eternally than to change the actual words', he says, 'Remember that Puritans were utterly devoted, like literary critics, to the Word' (117).

So the point (*punctum*) might be that of grammatological (destin)errancy in the senses of both 'deviation' and 'wandering'. Or it might – *vis-à-vis* the Penguin edition's error – be the problem of removing points, unnecessary speech-marks, and so deconstructing the privilege which speech seems to hold (They'd never heard it *that* way...). Or it might be a matter of iteration and how it functions. For the speech-marks are also quote-marks which are, in turn, etymologically connected with 'errancy' as follows: *err-* root of *errant*, in the sense of roaming in quest of adventure, arises from a confusion of *errare* (Latin, to wander) – hence 'err' and 'error' – with the Latin/Romanic *iterare* (from *iter*, a 'journey'; *iterum* = 'again'), which yields 'iterate' in the sense of citation and quotation.[14] Or, again, the point might be the selection and sorting of bits of text for criticism and commentary and how that should be approached. Let us, then, try to collapse these several questions, for it seems they can all be taken as a related, telegrammatological, problem. We can approach this by starting with a grammatological error; in fact with Grammatological error itself, with the errors to be found in the text of *OG*, an English text bearing the names of Derrida and Spivak among others. If error – and as we saw earlier, errancy – are very much part of Pynchon's 'theory', it is also true that the question of error-in-general is one of the 'themes' of *OG*. Here again we are reverting to telegrammatological devices, for the extent to which Derrida's enterprise aims at the *correction* of errors in thinking, is a large and open question, although it would be fair to say that there is often something akin to an identification of *lapsus* involved. But let us make plain that we do not hold any store by the notion of fault or intentionality-in-general in the present discussion of 'error' and we should perhaps refrain from using that term in favour of 'errancy'. Indeed we should be happy to refer to something as general as 'otherness' if the term were less awkward, for we wish also to promote an 'other' reading of Pynchon which marks itself off from, while not being a simple correction of, those readings which, in spite of their careful sorting of textual detail, presume to know where a mistake begins and ends, where it is sent from and addressed to.[15] In *Lot 49* (and even more so in *Gravity's Rainbow*) persons can err, go astray, get lost, like letters without specific destination – even though what they are lost 'from' or 'by' is unclear, undiscloseable. Error/errancy could, in this way, be read as a double theoretical concept like *différance* itself – glossing, as it does, a difference (from the 'proper' form) and a de*fer*ral (errancy as wandering puts off arrival at a destination or a destiny, err ... er ... that is, it hesitates).

Working this way, biding one's time, one could begin to account for what kind of *bid* it is that the Mysterious Bidder makes at the end of *Lot 49*. That is: just as we can provide a reading of *Lot 49* by systematically selecting, for example, its openings and closings, so we could be bidden to provide a reading of *OG* by pulling from it the textual errors 'committed' there.

But how 'systematic' are errors – in the sense that beginnings and endings appear as systematic? One does not usually think of typographical errors being systematic in those terms. On the contrary, so the story goes, they are aleatory, for the most part, unforeseen. According to the story, an author or a proofreader would, we assume, want to remove an error once it was discovered. That would be, we think, the 'normal' procedure: excision and replacement. This is why, when we find typos (to give them their less proper name), we assume them to be readers' discoveries, to have been undiscovered previous to a reading, to have slipped through the net undetected. That is why they are *puncta*, why they stick out like red cods. But why should we believe the story? Certainly it's a story we have held behind our readings for so long – but for what good reason do we give it credence?

Working against that story perhaps typos could, once they had turned up by random or happenstance processes, slips of the finger, *lapsus* of various kinds, and so on, then be left to lie – as it were – to assume their own existence. In this textual space, they would lie outside the domain of intention and also outside its opposite. They would be both and neither intended and/or unintended. They would rob intentionality of its grip on our studies and our readings. To that extent, the typographical error, so constructed, would be the very substance (*under-standing*) of a grammatological reading.

For just as Derrida complains that supposed errors of writing are usually arrived at by comparing writing – wrongly – with speech, showing it to be posterior to speech ('They'd never heard it that way' ...), we can now begin to revalorise the typing or printing error as the very mark of the independence of writing – rightly – from speech. This might then lead us to an instanciation of the grammatological project rather than, say, another re-counting of it à la *Positions*.[16] This would be the grammatology that instanciates, that comes more-or-less instantly, from a distance. Hence the following telegrammatology, reading *OG* as follows:

> The first error (though we must assume there are errors in the collection of these errors and so this may not be the first), setting the pattern for a good deal of errors in the alphabetical chain 'r, s, t', substitutes an 's' for an 'n': a south perhaps for a north. And according to the Rousseau ruse so elaborate and elaborated in *OG* itself (216–29), the south is the place of speech, of the free voice and spirit, the place of passion; while the north – on this highly Eurocentric view – is the place of darkness, cold and need. This is held to be true even if 'the north amounts to the south of the south' (218). This 's', however, works in the text of *OG* to shift '... the question of Being *in* general' to '... the question of Being *is* general' (xiv: 19, italics added).[17] The error amounts to an opening up, to letting in a certain amount of light. A noun, 'Being-in-general' turns to a sentence expressing a proposition – if we might add some hyphens and make some indecent propositions. That is, interestingly enough, the concept of Being *is* generalised in the n → s move. While 'Being-in-general' certainly expresses generality, the idea that Being is general expresses a much more radical form of the generalisation of Being. The point here, then, is that the error is reflexive. The error *instanciates* the very thing that the error-free utterance could only *express*. The errors show what the error-free utterance could only say. To this extent – and here is the point of our argument, touched off by Freud's treatment of *lapsus* and *actes manqués* as condensations and displacements[18] – error does not negate or 'set wrong' necessarily. It can also and, on numerous occasions in *OG* does, bolster, improve, swell, make excessive, illustrate ... and the rest. The errored text can sometimes *write* more than the non-errored text can say. As Wittgenstein says the *inexact* expression can be precisely what is needed in a given situation.[19] Error, then, shows that writing has priority over speaking – in a certain sense, and what this certain sense is is also shown in the errors, as we shall see. And that, after all, is a point (purpose, *punctum*) of *OG*.

A favourite error for Derrivak is the dropping of 's' from 'Nietzsche', the notorious conglomerate of typographical symbols which sounds to the ear like a sneeze and which contains near its centre a nicely inverted 's/z'. Hence we have 's'-less versions of 'Nietzsche's theory of metaphoricity' (xxvii: 13) and 'Nietzsche's *The Twilight of the Idols*' (xxxv: 30). To drop the 's', to point to it by its absence, is to put on the agenda the *voiceless* member of the s/z pair (and we may note that 't' is also the voiceless member of the t/d pair, recalling Pynchon's dt's). While there are indeed other voiced/unvoiced pairs then, s/z is surely the most famous for its Barthesian/Saussurian history and, given that 's' takes the unvoiced position, we could readily adopt it as the sign of writing itself.

Writing is thereby connected, on the one hand, with metaphoricity and, on the other, with error (cf. the Nietz(s)che examples above). Error again? Why so? Because a second dropped 's' occurs in reference to a section of *The Twilight of the Idols* called 'How the "True World" Ultimately Became a Fable: the History of An Error' (xxxv: 30). Error abounds here – in the spelling of Nietzsche's name, in the title of the chapter, and in the fact that, as Spida notes, it was Heidegger who overlooked something from this chapter on error. He overlooked the phrase: 'it *becomes a woman*'. Writing may arise in error, in the slip, the *lapsus* itself and, as such, give rise to the metaphorical, the substitution of one sign for another. But such a shift by writing represents something of an omission, an overlooking of precisely this: itself, its history, its own location in metaphor and error. To write metaphorically, for example, is to locate a domain within writing called 'the metaphorical'. And that is to forget that *all* writing is metaphorical and substitutive. The *later* substitution (for example, the reference to poetic metaphor and other 'rhetorical devices') makes it look as if some purely literal substance (writing) were being played with in a special way. And so 'real' writing becomes unduly literalised. But this way of constructing the opposition between literal and metaphorical overrides the earlier and more general substitution which writing itself is identical with. To point to this is to point past the rhetorical in its conventional sense, to point to a writing which must, then, always be both pre- and post-rhetorical. It must absent itself from the rhetorical in order to give rise to it.

An interesting counter-balance to the dropping of Nietzsche's 's' is its underlining in another case. Viz.: '...Derrida never discusses 'sous rature' at any great length' (lxxx: 30). While foreign words can be either italicised or put into 6's and 9's, as here, it seems peculiar that just one letter should get the italic treatment here; especially as it is the 's' that has come to be associated with the absence of voice and the presence of writing. Derrida never 'discusses' the 'sous rature', the idea that writing is always writing under erasure, that it is continually being lifted off the face of the page even as it is imprinted. How could he 'discuss' it when writing, by virtue of the 'sous rature', cannot do 'discussion' in any recognisable sense? Then it is also that 's' which is italicised – the very letter which is voiceless and which is unpronounced when one speaks the word 'sous' (as /su/) and so which doubly marks writing off from speech. The sign of writing, 's', must therefore stand also for the continually erasable, for that which disappears. To invoke the idea of a shopsign (such as the pawnbroker's balls), Derrida's concept of writing must always appear under *its* shopsign which is the 's':

SOUS
SON
S

We can continue these comments related to italicisation-in-error by referring to another example. On page xviii (line 37) of the Translator's Preface there is a phrase which reads: '... what Lévi-Strauss calls *bricolage in La pensée sauvage*'. Because it falls between the foreign and/or technical term and the book title (itself both foreign and technical), the 'in' gets caught up in the italicisation. An italic falls between two Francophones, recalling a common Latin origin and posing the question of the connection between the italic and the grammatological.

The 'italic', apart from being a term which can perfectly well refer, typo-paradoxically, to the ancient Italian, to the Roman, also means simply a form of typesetting, instanciated here by 'in'. And it is an *in-stance* of relatively pure italicisation; for the italicisation is not being used for anything like stressing or entitling as it routinely is when set apart from the roman. The italicisation of 'in', because it is done here in what we are calling 'error', points to italicisation itself, as such, in its own right, *per se, sui generis*. Then we must only remember that the italic is so called not because Aldus Manutius, who introduced the sloping print, was himself Italian but because he first used the typeface for a whole text, an edition of Virgil published in 1501 and dedicated to Italy itself.

The italic, then, begins life not as a way of marking quotations or additions – which it later became (a task we now reserve for quote-marks and square brackets respectively) – nor as a way of stressing or adding point (as it is today, though we suspect that error may do something similar), nor as a way of marking titles or foreign words – but as a uniform and homogeneous printface. It only mutates into its differentiated uses by virtue of a noticing; the noticing of its high degree of visual difference from straight-standing roman print.

What the relatively pure italicisation of 'in' does, then, is to indicate the move between uniformity and difference in general as a very mark of writing itself. The uniform italic becomes the differentiated italic. Its meaning moves from being based in its attachment to a fixed origin – its dedication to Italy – to being based on a system of differentiation, namely italic/roman. And this shows that meaning can only be generated *in the first place*, regardless of origins, by the grammatological shift of *différance* – a term which we must now italicise to mark, in this case, its transplantation and its meaning.

A second group of errors concerns the letter 'r'. The inversion of 'or' occurs a number of times in the text. On page 53 (line 33), in a quotation from Saussure: '... this is confirmed by the o*r*thographic systems, the speech of deaf mutes, etc.'. On page xxxii, line 28 there is reference to '... the voice of f*r*ogetfulness'. In another quotation from Saussure's *Cours*, Derrida writes of the fact that 'the written f*r*om prevents our seeing this' (37: 32, italics added to all three examples). As far as this last case is concerned, we can say that a distinction arises between the written-from and, presumably, the written-to: the origin and destination of writing – a dialectic which only receives full treatment in the later work of Derrida ('Envois'). What is put on the agenda, as 'form' becomes 'from', is that our traditional obsession with origin and centre gets in the way of our consideration of the destination of writing and the much overlooked fact that destinations are by no means unproblematic in themselves. As we attempted to say in our BOOK BID, Oedipa's problem is as much one of adestination as it is of origin. Hence, the written-from prevents our seeing the written-to and its problems.

An obvious remark to be made about all three inversions of

'or', is that they occur in the context of references to speech or the voice, not a particularly surprising discovery given the subject of OG. But this is highlighted by yet another 'r'-error occurring much later in the text: 'The self-presence of the voice and of the hea*r*ing-oneself speak conceals the very thing that visible space allows to be placed before us' (240: 21, italic added). In a previous line on the same page (240: 16), there is the new concept of 'the hearing-oneself-speak', replete with *two* hyphens and with a very definite 'r'. By putting together the idea of inversion established by the above-mentioned *o*ral errors, and the misspelling of 'hearing', we can read the error ('era') in the ear as the alterity within the speech/hearing system which the written form reveals and so find a further gloss on the problematic OG elaborates.

Let us move finally to the 't'-errors. The first instance is where Derrivak/Spida substitutes 'mediating' for 'meditating': 'It is worth mediating upon the entire passage' (xxvi: 33). We can note here that the dropped 't' shifts us from the psychological or even metaphysical domain of meditation to the quite material domain of mediation. Mediation points to the fact that writing does not 'communicate' in this sense: that a message does not purely and simply arrive at its destination or point of reception without undergoing some change, some mediation. Writing, try as it might, cannot be ultimately and completely *im*mediate, without mediation, try as *we* might to psychologise it. The best writing will ever manage to be is relatively fast, a telegrammatology in fact. And so the 't' omission or substitution points to the necessary processes of omission and substitution themselves.

Still in terms of 't'-errors, on page 204 (line 7) the italicisation slips over into a place it should not go, just as above we saw that it could slip from foreign word to title and take in an 'in' where it ought not. The passage refers to '... those passages in the *Essay that* deal with the sign, art, and imitation'. And further, on page 143 (line 32), a 't' is inserted in the place of an 'f' so that we get: 'And it differance as the project of the mastery of the entity should be understood with reference to the sense of being'. Yet perhaps this last example is actually a failure of punctuation and the passage should read appositionally: 'And it, differance, should be understood...'. We can never really resolve the matter of which error is involved here. Which error is error? And if an error is *in* error does that make it any less (or more) an error? Obviously the simple logic of a double minus giving a plus is no longer in operation: for when we underline the 't' or the 'T' we get a figure not unlike the plus-or-minus sign. The error, then, also self-refers here, there being an essential difference involved in the reading of the error itself and that difference engenders its meaning.

A dropped 't' occurs in another instance where we read: '... there is no need to inuit the object *I* in order to understand the word I...' (liii: 19, stress and final ellipsis in original translation). Let us leave aside for now the possible error by which the final 'I' ought perhaps to have been shown in quotation marks, being a mention rather than a use of that word and turn to the matter of the dropped 't'. In this case it works to reinforce, to re-enact the fact, stated in the sentence, that there is 'no need' to intuit. Intuition is, as it were, placed in double brackets: one set formed by the sentence saying 'no need' and the other set formed by the deformation of the term itself. One, that is, simply *knows* the distinction between words and objects (*I* and the word 'I') by virtue of living in a certain form of life, as Wittgenstein says/shows.[20] It is something which comes to one by virtue of one's material existence, not by virtue of one's reflection or meditation on the matter. It is mediated by the form of life. The whole concept of intuition, in this domain, is deformed. But, quite paradoxically, we arrive at this deformation by a deformation of the *word* 'intuit'! The paradox sets up an abyss: if the typography is correct then we can infer things from words (*from* 'in(t)uition' *to* intuition *by* intuition) while, if the strictly referential meaning of the sentence is correct, then we cannot do so (infer relations between I and 'I'). If it is, it isn't; and if it isn't, it is. Gödel, it may be remembered, also discovered that the typographical aspects of mathematical notation could lead to paradoxes – ones potentially damning for any supposedly perfect TNT (typographical number theory). In fact, he showed that no mathematical system could ever be complete in the sense of eliminating theorems at once necessary to the system and contradictory of it.[21] In place of completeness, of perfect communication then, the abyss – one which leaves us with, in the place of simple intuition, only an 'i' and a 'nuit' – the very 'I' which is in dispute and the long dark night of the abyss itself.

This very partial[22] list of errors is sufficient for us to make our point, perhaps excessively so, for the sort of exegesis we have been practising here risks mistaking error for a truth whereas it has been our intention to demonstrate a kind of reading of refusal, one which opts neither for the randomness of free play nor for the predetermined approach of a rigid thematics. But our practice has brought us to this paradox, which is a paradox of writing itself: any utterance, any mark provides some sort of pose or thesis to the extent that it occurs within materiality, but since it doesn't occur in isolation or endowed with transcendental meaning, it also represents a difference which relativises its pose, inscribes it as difference. Be it as supposedly insignificant as a typographical error, it cannot but make sense, and that within the whole context of sense-making operations in general.

Thus we did not pretend to effect above the simple sort of data-listing that we attempted for the subject of writing in *Gravity's Rainbow*, knowing full well that that exercise is never simple nor free of commentary and exegesis. A taxonomy of errors here would have had to choose, for instance, how much surrounding text to include, what order to place the data in, whether to include errors of translation, of fact, and so on. All of which presumes to know what an error is before undertaking the exercise, whereas it is our contention, in conformity with which we did our reading, that we cannot know what error is and how it is to be distinguished from what we call 'errancy'. As we saw above, a letter mis-placed ('it differance' for 'if differance') may be explained with a little punctuation; so another instance of the problematic error could be when that very term 'differance' (with an 'a') is first used in the text of *OG*. When it first crops up (60: 14), one could well read it as a typographical error and not as a difference which carries meaning.

The question of error then is indistinguishable from the question of how writing has meaning and our reading sought therefore to be just that, a reading of a writing constituted by differance. A reading which inevitably becomes a rewriting. So to return to the paradox stated above: if any mark is always already a writing, then the only possible criticism or commentary is in terms of a rewriting. The present summary or metadiscourse is no more or less a rewriting than the exegesis of our error analysis. The task which befalls an athetic reading therefore, is to explore rather than to ignore the terms of that paradox.

Thus the concept of error and the possibility of commentary on it, as Freud so successfully saw, can lead us into a space outside authorial intention (origin, authenticity) and randomness (the problem of destination), a space of meaning which lies elsewhere. To call this the 'unconscious' would be a gross error – a matter of taking the Freudian metaphor far too far. It effectively points elsewhere – this self-referential error system – it points to a way of writing, to a rhetoric outside or behind or elsewhere than the usual space reserved for rhetoric. If rhetoric involves eloquence, rules and persuasion, then the errant counter-practice establishes itself as inelegant, as a breach of rule which still has meaning and as a means of dissuading us of the writer's power. Accordingly it should perhaps be called the 'unrhetorical' or an athetical rhetoric.

To that end we began with the idea of ends – beginnings and ends of chapters – in our 'Anti-Oedipa' chapter, to introduce the possibility of a reading posed between random and organised textual material. Now we have modified that idea with the notion of *puncta* – salient points which do not rely on a 'natural' or 'given' organisation of the text, but which inscribe themselves in terms of a capacity for surprise. And since the *puncta* we took were errors, like stray threads or faults within the uniform syntactic and grammatical weave of the text, they offered a particular and unusual articulation of inside and outside that text. To the extent that they occurred 'within' the text, they reinforced, by highlighting, its patterns. To the extent that they were not of the 'same' material, they could be extracted from it and brought to bear, for instance, on a text by Pynchon, on questions of selection and sorting of textual data, on its thematics of the misprint, on the problematics it raises for the relations between text and theory.

One might read our readings of errors as exaggerated, as saying no matter what, but they are designed to function precisely in terms of the relations elaborated by Derrida in OG:

> ... the reading must always aim at a certain relationship, unperceived by the writer, between what he commands and what he does not command of the patterns of the language he uses.
>
> This relationship is not a certain quantitative distribution of shadow and light, of weakness and force, but a signifying structure that critical reading should *produce*. (158)

There is no natural, obvious, or automatic reading for the marks that constitute errors, unless it be in terms of a correction which effaces and disavows them as marks of writing. What we read in them is an oblique exposition of the grammatological project, one entirely uncontrolled by the programmed elaboration of ideas within *OG*, but nevertheless existing as instanciations of certain of those ideas. Thus we read, albeit in a different form, what is explicitly there in the text. But by the same token we read what is not there, what the laws of orthography, syntax and logic – to which we must submit in order to comprehend those ideas – disavow, ignore, consider insignificant. We read what is not there to the extent that it escapes those laws.

We read thus something between chance and program, a refusal of and resistance to both; we read, between *r*andomness and *t*hematics, a s*t*ring of let*tr*s errored and errant within writing. We read fi*r*s*t* (although we didn't in fact, let us further subject our text to alteration by submitting to the rigours of alphabetic order that we have both respected and subverted throughout, and take our cue again from Barthes[23]) a misplacing and inversion of the 'r' as the written error that transforms an ear representing the primacy of speech and hearing.

The argument against that primacy and priority might be called the first argument of *OG*. We read *s*econd the letter 's' as sign of writing, as the voiceless side of an s/z pair, or the signature of grammatology's erasure.[24] It is the downward slash of the pen, running with and against the grain of writing, running right to left, then left to right, then back again, following the path of the plough which Derrida gives as the model of writing/tracing, but in the very opposite directions to those described by the voiced 'z'. We read *t*hird the letter 't'. It added nothing that was not already explicited in the preceding examples, but whereas the 's' gave a sign, the 't' provides a post, a post-mark perhaps, of the double grammatological impulse. For the 't' in its singularity, as the mark of a point which is also an intersection or parting of the ways and a sign of deviation, is always already plural. It is always already plural, again, in its form, by virtue of the two strokes which constitute it at the same time as they cancel each other. But it is also plural by virtue of its position; for by following the 's' it becomes post(-)s (hence also *postAL* and, for a Francophone, *posteD*), the point at which, all along, several names have been seeking their intersection within a common piece of writing. So we name ourselves, inscribe and rewrite the names of various fathers,[25] performing a fundamental act of signification divided in its origin.

We offer a token of our theoretical position so far, a token which comes only as an attempt, a bid, a tender submission even.

We want to answer an inquirer who insisted that we name the Parts, draw together the threads of our athetical theory and locate it in an historical context of 'theoretical developments'. Yet – and this is as much an answer as a refusal to answer – the theory, if such it is, is one which refuses definiteness or centredness as much in the domain of the semiotic and the rhetorical as in the domain of the moral-ethical and the metaphysical. It is a theory which might be said to insist, if it is capable of insisting at all, on the 'arhetorical' – periphrasis notwithstanding. So, lest we seem to subscribe to a well-posed ethics of institutional discursive practices, we reply by naming as we have already, tele(ana)grammatically.

Until a moment in the text close to the present one, theory has inhabited these telegrammatologies in a non-specific way. Like 'the plot' (*V.*), the Tristero (*Lot 49*) and 'Them' (*Gravity's Rainbow*), it has made itself felt throughout but, at every attempt at specificity it has become diffuse, threatened to make itself vanish. The theory has shed its light on a number of objects, both moral and rhetorical – but to ask for specificity is like asking for a prism or lens to examine that light. To return to the terms of our previous chapter, once the light passed through it, it is refracted; its parallel lines split into an infinitely widening band and, between the band's expanding extremities, there is only an arc or rainbow. The theory, if it is a theory of refusal, does not collapse when one demands that it be expressed in positive theses – instead it broadens and expands. The trouble (or beauty) of it is not that positive theses are not available; it is that they are all too available, abyssally available. A token selection:

– To read with this theory means reading everything as if it were a telegram: short, to the point, specific, practical, ingrained in the material of life, its utterances physically pasted across the torn-off page, fresh from the teleprinter, the traces of its production left bare. The father is Brecht.

– Telegrammatology transforms anytext into a telegram by refusing to select, quote, cite or iterate according to a metaphysics of presence. Instead, it cuts the text into telegrammic snippets – beginnings, ends, errors – whatever *puncta* may arise: whatever may give pleasure or fear. The fathers are Breton, Barthes, Burroughs and Bowie.

– Error, as we have seen, is just one element – but it has a particular near-centrality. It lives in the middle of the theory between the proliferating margin and the unspeakable centre. Positive error cancels the quest for a monolithic centre. It crosses. Error construed positively can be read as, in relation to or across (a) signature, a cross. The fathers are Freud and Derrida.

– Since these theoretical positive theses tend to inhabit a theoretical middle which is neither a centre nor a margin, their metatheory is one of reincluded middles. Not a logical positivism but an illogical negativism – where the negation should be read as a definite (positive?) refusal rather than, say, hopelessness. The father is Pynchon.

'... there ought to be a punch line to it, but there isn't'.[26]

Notes

1. An obvious cross-reference here would be the type of chance cross-fertilisation and dissemination provided for in Derrida's *Glas*. Just as the organising principle of that text has its own logic which is germane to the argument, so ours follows a different logic – a 'postal' rather than a botanical one. See J. Derrida, *Glas*, trans. J. P. Leavey and R. Rand (Lincoln: University of Nebraska Press, 1986).
2. Here we are alluding to Barthes' argument that the unloved lover, for example, 'identifies' with anyone of the same ilk regardless of other differences. See R. Barthes, *A Lover's Discourse: Fragments* (London: Cape, 1979), p. 129. The identification is no longer psychological or subjective but structural: 'The subject painfully identifies himself with some person (or character) who occupies the same position as himself in the amorous structure'.
3. See G. Prince, *Narratology: The Form and Functioning of Narrative* (Berlin: Mouton, 1982).
4. As often happens, more text has to be dragged into the fray once the process of critical interpretation is under way.
5. The term is Eagleton's. He means phenomenology, hermeneutics, reception-aesthetics and related transgressions of economic determinism. For all that, his fictional reconstruction of 'the consumers' revolution' as a macro-political movement is not without its occasional Pynchonesque humour. It appears just prior to his other satire, the 'Ballad of English Literature' (to the tune of 'Land of Hope and Glory'). See T. Eagleton, 'The revolt of the reader', in his *Against the Grain: Essays 1975–1985* (London: Verso, 1986), pp. 181–4.
6. This assumes that Derrida is a candidate for the Mysterious Bidder, though it may be Genghis Cohen. He does apologise to Oedipa for showing up, after all. Yet it must be admitted that this could be an

apology merely for showing up and not for being 'He'. Nevertheless, a note of caution should be sounded about reading the text such that it's *definite* we don't know who 'He' is. But if it is Jacques, one could also speculate over the identity of the one called 'Loren Passerine'. Again, beginnings and ends furnish a clue, as do syllables. Such speculation is, let it be noted, something of a department within the Pynchon criticism industry. Witness Cowart's identifications of Orson Welles as the Kenosha Kid, Werner von Braun as Blicero, etc. See D. Cowart, *Thomas Pynchon: The Art of Allusion* (Carbondale: Southern Illinois University Press, 1980).

7. J. Derrida, *Of Grammatology*, trans. G.C. Spivak (Baltimore: The Johns Hopkins University Press, 1976). Henceforth: OG. References given in brackets in the text are to pages and *lines* of this edition of the translation. This translation is taken to be a single text rather than a text with another text in the form of a translator's introduction. The collective subject held responsible is called 'Spivak/ Derrida', sometimes 'Spivak', 'Derrida', 'Derrivak' or 'Spida' for short, although a number of other proper names could be added to this agglutinated name, including those of publishers, printers, editors, proofreaders and so on. By means of these devices we telegrammatise issues of authorship and the original/translation relation, which will receive further treatment in the discussion following.

8. *Glas* is referenced in note 1, above. 'Tympan' appears in J. Derrida, *Margins of Philosophy*, trans. A. Bass (Chicago: Chicago University Press, 1982, pp. *ix–xxix*. *Envois* is a major segment of J. Derrida, *The Post Card*, trans. A. Bass (Chicago: University of Chicago Press, 1987).

9. A. J. Friedman and M. Pütz, 'Science as metaphor: Thomas Pynchon and *Gravity's Rainbow*', in R. Pearce (ed.), *Critical Essays on Thomas Pynchon* (Boston: G.K. Hall, 1981), pp. 69–81.

10. S. Simmon, 'Beyond the theatre of war: *Gravity's Rainbow* as film', in Pearce, pp. 124–39; see page 135. Another (just) possible typographical error is pointed out by Morgan. He or she writes a 'sic' after Pynchon's chemical term 'polyimide' on page 576 of *Rainbow*, presumably thinking it should have been, as elsewhere in the novel, 'polyamide'. But whatever mysterious power it is that produces typos is not on Morgan's side because his or her own published version changes the internal chemistry of the word to 'polymide' [sic] [sic]. See page 89, S. Morgan, '*Gravity's Rainbow*: what's the big idea?' in Pearce, pp. 82–98. The page reference is to the 1973 Cape/ Viking edition of *Gravity's Rainbow*.

11. There is also an error on the blurb of that edition and directly relayed into the endpapers of all the British Picador editions of Pynchon. 'Genghis Cohen', it reports, 'likes his sex with the news on'. In fact telesexuality is the penchant of Nefastis not Cohen, the latter being one of the most disputed characters in Pynchon, after the *New York Times Book Review* debate with Romain Gary over ownership of the name (*NYTBR*,12 June 1966, p. 35; 17 July 1966, p. 22). Gary himself, it turns out – 21 years after his initial letter, and

in the same publication – was a very successful novelist both under his own name and in the person of Émile Ajar, a fact which only surfaced after 'their' suicide. No doubt there will be Pynchonian speculations following this; especially since it's, again, the *NYTBR* which published the latest piece of prose under the signature of Pynchon, including the following note with its splendidly ambiguous use of the continuous perfect: 'Thomas Pynchon, author of "Gravity's Rainbow," has been working on another novel'. See J. C. Oates, 'Success and the pseudonymous writer: turning over a new self', *New York Times Book Review*, 6 December 1987, p. 12 and T.R. Pynchon, 'The heart's eternal vow', *New York Times Book Review*, 10 April 1988, pp. 1, 47, 49.

12. R. Barthes, *Camera Lucida* (New York: Hill & Wang, 1981).
13. One of the few critics to notice the misprint is Hite, though she doesn't make much of it. See M. Hite, *Ideas of Order in the Novels of Thomas Pynchon* (Columbus: Ohio State University Press, 1983), p. 74. And on the topic of misprints, Hite carefully notes (p. 107) how the 'R' in 'rocket' gets capitalised and then suggests that the person responsible is called 'Punchon'.
14. Derrida holds that *iter* is itself derived from the Sanscrit word for 'other' (*itara*), thus evoking 'the logic which links repetition to alterity'. *Margins of Philosophy*, p. 315.
15. Again the list of secondary Pynchon material could be lengthy, perhaps as lengthy as our Bibliography. However some instances are more punctual than others. Clerc, for example, writes wonderfully definite (and *arrant*) nonsense about a 'Pynchon' who 'gets inside his characters as much as, if not sometimes more so than, other novelists', who is 'a put-inner . . . rather than a take-outer'. It is apparently he who speaks (who 'playfully inserts' such things as 'oh me I'm hopeless, born a joker never change') on page 122 of *Gravity's Rainbow*. And more. See the Introduction to C. Clerc (ed.), *Approaches to Gravity's Rainbow* (Columbus: Ohio State University Press, 1983), pp. 12, 17.
16. J. Derrida, *Positions*, trans. A. Bass (Chicago: University of Chicago Press, 1981).
17. From this point on, where typographical errors are concerned, both page and line numbers for *OG* are given. See note 7 above.
18. S. Freud, *The Psychopathology of Everyday Life* (Harmondsworth: Penguin, 1975).
19. L. Wittgenstein, *Philosophical Investigations* (Oxford: Blackwell, 1968) pp. 4le–43e.
20. Wittgenstein, *Investigations*, p. 8e and *passim*.
21. For an accessible guide to Gödel, see D. Hofstadter, *Gödel, Escher, Bach: An Eternal Golden Braid* (Harmondsworth: Penguin, 1980). The hard stuff is K. Gödel, 'Some metamathematical results on completeness and consistency, on formally undecidable propositions of *Principia Mathematica* and related systems I', in J. van Heijenoort (ed.), *Frege and Gödel: Two Fundamental Texts in Mathematical Logic* (London: Oxford University Press, 1970), pp. 83–108; or K. Gödel,

On Formally Undecidable Propositions of 'Principia Mathematica' and Related Systems, trans. B. Meltzer (New York: Basic Books, 1962).

22. Other examples not discussed are as follows. Even without analysis, the thematic consistency of the errors is exciting:

xxxvii, 24–25: **a possessive pronoun with a feminine object** [Not a typo, but a reference to the French word *sa* which is in fact an adjective].

lvi, 33: **"Kinship systems", like "phonemic systems", are built by the mind on the level of unconscious thought.** [In a quote from Lévi-Strauss' *Structural Anthropology*; the third pair of double quotes is printed like '69' rather than '66'. This occurs on page 1–vi].

37, 16: **There is an orginary violence of writing** [originary].

38, 16: **That typranny is at bottom the mastery of the body over the soul** ['p' inserted into 'tyranny', re. Rousseau's view of 'the tyranny of writing'].

62, 21: **the meaning of differance in general would be more accsessible** [insertion of 's' into 'accessible'].

62, 40: **concept or opeartion, motor or sensory** [transposition of 'r' and 'a'].

78, 9: **the world turned into a terrestial paradise** ['r' is dropped from 'terrestrial' in a quote from Descartes].

150, 9: **Jean-Jacque's life behind his work** [apostrophe misplaced].

172, 5: **Its full title says it well: Essay on the Origin of Languages, which treats of Melody and Musical Imitation.** [italics dropped on 'and'].

174, 41: **the violenec [*l'inactivité*] of love of self** [transposition of 'e' and 'c', in a quote from Rousseau].

206, 13: **"Imitation has its roots in our perpetual desire to transport ourselves outside ourselves (ibid.).** [close-quote mark is missing in quote from Rousseau].

210, 11: **the** *Examen des deux principes avancés par M. Rameau dans sa brochure intitulé* **"Erreurs sur la musique", dans l'Encyclopédie" (1755).** [extra close-quote mark at end].

213, 5: **What is this second principle It is in nature as well as the first.** [absence of punctuation after 'principle'].

215, 1: **the first grammarians subordinated their art to music** [transposition of 'i' and 'd', in a quote from Rousseau].

259, 8: **The passage from the state of the nature to the state of language and society** [addition of 'the'].

301, 41: **the soverign people** ['e' is dropped].

304, 5: **In its writing, the visible signifier, has always already begun to seperate itself from speech** ['separate' mis-spelled].

309, 14: **on the basic of my writings** ['basis' → 'basic', in a quote from Rousseau].

23. Barthes, *Lover's Discourse*, p. 8.

24. What we are here calling the 'signature of grammatology' is to be compared and contrasted with the question of the signature of the author that we shall take up in a later discussion. For if the author signs a text (of theory) with the anagrammatical mark (both

inscription and dissemination) of the proper name, so we suggest that a theory here named grammatology (or 'grammatology') inscribes its proper name in the ideas we have come to associate with it, and disseminates that name in typographical errancy. Thus also, the motto or ensign of 'sous son s' complements a 'derrière-le-dos' sometimes read as the name of Derrida. See Derrida's *Glas* and *Envois* and the discussion of autobiography as autography in G. Ulmer, *Applied Grammatology* (Baltimore: The Johns Hopkins University Press, 1985), pp. 132–6.

25. While the act of 'naming the father' has a long history, its most immediate father, in this case, was John Hartley. His list of fathers includes at least one mother; and we are ashamed not to be able to match. See J. Hartley, *Videology* (London, Methuen, forthcoming). By way of coincidence, perhaps, Alice Jardine names the section of her book which deals with Pynchon, 'I can get along without you mother'. This is analysed more fully in 'A V', Chapter 7 below. See A. Jardine, *Gynesis: Configurations of Woman and Modernity* (Ithaca: Cornell University Press, 1985), pp. 247–52.

26. *Gravity's Rainbow*, p. 738.

5
Almost But Not Quite Me . . .

There should be, by now, no problems with beginning autobiographically.[1] The first person is, after all, only another mode of address. It slips as easily or as hardly from the pen as any other person. And that, too, is where we begin, with the idea of a person or two flowing from the pen, from the grammatological creation of the person – first or third.

When he was growing up in Britain or New Zealand, there were a good deal of new American things around – exciting things like Coca-Cola, 45rpm records, rock'n'roll. All that revived residue of the Second World War. But chief among these in its Americanness was not the Superman comic or the baseball jacket – it was chewing gum. And with each packet of flat American gum, so unlike the cubed colonial English stuff, came something to think on – a free gift. A dead giveaway. And the free gift was, most often, a transfer.

A transfer. The transfer could be made to work perfectly with a little practice. Lay the coloured side of the paper against the skin and wet thoroughly with spit, or with a wet face-cloth. Allow to dry just enough – not too much – and peel it away. To leave behind a perfect trace. This was not a reproduction, a *mere* tracing from a comic, it was *the* picture text. When you used a transfer, the picture came off on your arm for the first time. This was the wholeness of the picture – if, that is, you could make it all transfer. Nothing was lost, no translation. A perfect transfer of meaning from *a* to *b*; from the paper to me, the corporeal person, in the shape of my arm.

We were, then, transfer junkies. We dyed our arms in colours like the tattoos our grandfathers wore. And nothing has been quite the same since. Until very recently.

Until recently, the copying has meant loss in every case. We were told in school that the poet's intention would never quite come through in the poem – that we must do the best we could. The TV reception was never quite like 'being at the real thing'.

Copy a cassette tape on to another tape and there's loss – drop out. As Pynchon puts it, the 50s and 60s were times of the dropout.[2] Our hunger was for the authenticity of the transfer itself. And now, perhaps, the computer seems better than anything, so far, to give us that kind of copying. The paradigm of original vs. copy is coming undone. We copy our text files on to disk and from disk to disk. We disseminate the copies on disk where they are again copied on to new disks, both hard and soft – and by and large nothing is lost. Almost but not quite all cases provide identicals. Fifty, a hundred generations on, the text may remain exactly the same. Here is the promise of no dropout. This is at least close to the perfect transfer we have been hankering after. Though to be sure, no one would yet be confident enough to say that accidents never happen. We want: no loss, no difference. Only transfer – sameness. It is this we associate with authenticity and originality: the perfect copy. This is the myth of 'our generation of writers'.

As Barthes puts it: myths do not need to be falsehoods in order to be mythical still.[3] The computer *is* able to transfer perfect text copies. It gives repeated examples of success even if it, too, can never completely guarantee against adestination. In the same way, returning to Barthes, French wine *is* good, the Citroën DS *is* sleek, and so on. Myth is myth because its 'speech' is 'depoliticised'. And this is precisely the situation of our myth of transfer. It is a myth which we have sought to trace through the 'Introduction' to Pynchon's *Slow Learner*. Again he must be autobiographical, first person, singular . . .

I had not read the 'Introduction' for over a year. It had first arrived in a decent (but not perfect) photocopy from the USA. But I knew its theme: the 'Pynchon' of the present berates the apprentice 'Pynchon' of the late 50s and early 60s for his youthful prosaic ungainliness. This much I remembered – and particularly the line about the present Mr P. not taking his former self out for a beer or lending him money. On that basis I began to see how this severance between the former and the present could mark a *difference* (or indeed a deferral) around which the 'meaning' of the 'Introduction' could be seen to emerge. But the obvious problem then would be: what of the relation of the supposedly 'present' Mr P? What of this person or figure or character and its relation to, or by, a reading? The problematising of the former Mr P. was of such fascination that it almost eclipsed the harder problem of the speaking- or writing-position of the 'present' one.

This present author/narrator/character (or what?) seemed to elide the very difference or deferral of meaning itself – to be co-present to (or with) the reader, *in* the reading. It looked more like perfect transfer than imperfect difference. Thinking about this and brushing up on my Derrida, Lacan, etc., I came across an article by John Forrester in *Economy & Society* – of which more later.[4] Suffice to say that the article reminded me of the Freudian angle on transfer and transference. More on this, too, below.

All this is of little wonder, except that when I did come to read the 'Introduction' through once again, and more carefully, I found not only the expected reference to one of the Early Stories' narrator as 'almost but not quite me' – close to the start of the piece – but also a very unexpected way of referring to 'literary theft' (alias intertextuality) as 'a strategy of *transfer*' – and this quite close to the end of the 'Introduction'.

It is, then, with these textual boundary markers, these quotations,
as brackets around what we write, that we start our case for the 'present' Pynchon as theory of meaning.

■ ■ ■ ■ ■ ■

Although we shall have to narrow down the options later, the 'Introduction' to *Slow Learner* could first be approached via an odd mixture of several questions: what is it (preface, story, autobiography)? who writes, or is written (author, narrator, character)? and by what function of writing does it work, what theory of meaning? Untangling these is no easy task, and one which should perhaps not be attempted. Instead, it might be more satisfactory to tangle the threads even more: to argue that the questions are all one question – that what is Introduced is a person, a first person who, as author (at least) *is* a theory of meaning.

For many readers the problem is simple. Someone called 'Thomas Pynchon' whose name has appeared on a number of stories and either two or three novels depending on how you count, and is supposed to have had another on the boil since 1973, has not been exactly forthcoming about his biographical bits and pieces. In fact, the standard texts on these works, in place of the obligatory author biography and tracing of lineage and influence, tend to have thin chapters retelling a well-known litany of apparent cover-ups: school and Navy records accidentally destroyed by fire, pictures missing, friends and teachers suddenly out of memory. In place of this: the modals – the 'might have beens', the speculations, the odd glimpses of some Pynchon person.

This makes it all very easy, then, for the 'Introduction' to be read in the way Jonathan Raban did in the *Sunday Times*:[5]

> Pynchon in person . . . is famously insubstantial. The 'About the Author' end-papers of his books are conspicuously blank. In *Slow Learner* he breaks cover for the first time with a remarkably openhanded portrait of the writer as a young man. Here is the sustained pleasure of watching a clever and talented young man struggling to find a style of his own. From such a reticent man it is a weirdly generous book. (From the blurb to Picador edition of *Slow Learner*)

Raban does not think for a moment that the 'Introduction' may be a fiction. Yet surely the one he calls 'The Gargantua of modern fiction' would be able to produce a simple fiction of the 'writer as a young man'? And particularly when the 'Introduction' tells us of a story-writer who managed to fake his way to fame with such spurious knowledge as a cobbled-together theory of entropy which, he tells us, fooled 'even the normally unhoodwinkable Donald Barthelme' (12). If the 'Introduction' tells us anything, it tells us that, whatever Pynchon is, he, she or it is a phoney by his, her or its own standards. That is again: if we believe it.

A straightforward consequence of all this is: that we're not going to get anywhere with the problem(s) of the 'Introduction' at all if we hang our solution around matters of belief or faith, matters of truth or falsehood, matters of sincerity or insincerity. The psychological does not enter into this business at all – unless we assume that there is some constant someone 'on the other end'. A psychological theory of authorship and meaning gets us nowhere for it assumes that the question of who or what writes is already answered.

We need then to reconsider what this 'Introduction' means after something which could be called 'decades of silence from Pynchon on the topic of Pynchon'. What it must mean, if recourse to psychology is illegitimate, is that this 'event', this supposed 'breaking cover' (which may be just another covering up), is no different from any other textual event or occasion. Its problems are the problems of all the others. Tempting as it may be, we ought perhaps to resist reading the 'Introduction' as the key to the stories which follow it. And, by way of one last confession, it is now necessary to say that we would find such a reading very difficult, not having read those stories at the time of writing this! Bear with us, then, if for the moment we use the heuristic of calling the 'Introduction' itself a story in the collection. This helps to fend off its easiest reading.

■ ■ ■ ■ ■ ■ ■

The location of Pynchon – if 'I' is indeed he, or if 'he' is indeed anyone or anything at all worth mentioning – could be addressed through the general problematisation of 'the author' available in a number of (roughly) poststructuralist theories of the same. Those theories, for all their divergence, point to the category of 'author' being that which, in modern times, has been the most central of the principles for ordering texts, particularly those of a 'literary' kind. Indeed, the categorisation of a text or texts *as* literary has turned primarily around the question of authorship. The texts marked 'James Joyce' are literary, one suspects, because they are so marked while, for the same reason, those marked 'Internal Revenue Service' are not.

Accordingly, for many readers, the return of a text to a unique authorial origin, to a subject or person, is its main mark of authenticity. Moreover, an association with some particular person allows a text such further categorisations as: literature, bureaucratic report, biography, personal letter, washing-machine instructions, etc. Author, as a category, is a very powerful device – this much can be agreed upon, if one accepts the central claim of a text like Foucault's 'What is an author?'[6]

However, as Williamson has pointed out, some recent theories of authorship appear – to Williamson's mind wrongly – to have taken the theory of author-as-category to mean something quite different.[7] Barthes, for example, in his equally seminal essay, 'The death of the author' has argued that we should now consider the author-as-person to be 'dead', to be no longer the unproblematic, automatic or default basis for our categorisation and understanding of texts.[8] Texts, argues Barthes, *ought* no longer to be traced to a subjective origin, 'in the mind' of some actual historical or biographical personage. Instead, they should be considered to have 'no other origin than language itself, language which ceaselessly calls into question all origins'.[9]

But perhaps, after all, this is not too dissimilar to Foucault's claim. Foucault is addressing an 'author function' or principle which has been used in common sense, literary criticism and a variety of other fields as a means of understanding and categorising texts, while Barthes is arguing on a much less descriptive (or positivistic?) terrain for a *change* in our dominant mode of address. No doubt, it is wishful thinking to assume that author-psychology readings are a thing of the past. The author, in this sense, is quite alive and well and living in university English Departments, to name only one site. But Barthes' argument still holds: the return to the authorial origin is limiting, politically motivated, conservative and unnecessarily psychological. Equally the Foucault paper, for all its analytic interests, does not exactly *support* authorialist readings: though it does suggest that we make that function our topic rather than our unexplicated resource in literary studies. He is pointing to a new topic, to the discursive practice of the 'author function', rather than to 'author' as creative fountainhead. But his political alignment to that topic is not as openly on display as Barthes'.

Barthes shares much of the theory but is less equivocal on the question of stance. He suggests that, if origins we must have, then language or discourse could well suffice, providing – importantly – that we consider language as calling 'into question all origins'.[10] This is why we think it mistaken of Williamson to write off Barthes' position as one which 'retains the principle of an origin, transferring it from the subject to language as system or process'. And it is certainly going too far to say, further, that 'a phenomenological concept of the subject is thus retained in the Barthesian enterprise'.[11] Unlike Foucault's critical practice which effectively leaves the critic parasitic upon traditional categories and uses of 'author', Barthes has at least suggested means of intervention into the dominant authorial discourse and possible forms of alternative practice. Indeed, as Williamson says: 'the author is maintained as a principle of understanding art, by institutional practices of criticism, literary history, biography, review and so on'[12] – without this retention, even Foucauldian analysis could not proceed as it does for it would have no object. For Barthes, however, it (the author) ought not to be so maintained. Barthes' analysis is not in the domain of fact but of value. His project is not to understand the author function except insofar as understanding is an essential prerequisite for change.

Putting it another way, we could perhaps read Barthes'

announcement of the 'death' of the author as an instance of Foucault's author-function operating in the battle-zone between traditional criticism and poststructuralist theory. The author's 'replacement' by language and language's constant reminder of the questionability of all origins could then be seen as a strategy in that battle. A Foucauldian analysis of the strategy is critical, but to rest content with it only defers the problem of which side one should take. And, faced with the problem(s) of the 'Introduction' to *Slow Learner*, it seems that sides must be taken.

■ ■ ■ ■ ■ ■ ■

But there is another possible version of these 'sides' and strategies for their 'taking', one which inhabits the margins of all of our deliberations on 'Pynchon and authorship', here and in other chapters. To that extent it begs to be explicited, even though, as we shall see, the *Slow Learner* 'Introduction' itself could barely be said to concur with it in the matter of authorship. The differences between this third, Derridean, 'side' and what we would shudder to call 'Pynchon's theory of authorship', however, help us to see what the latter might be and thus take us to the crux of the interpretive problem posed in the present chapter. At the same time, it shows, contrary to at least one possible reading of our work so far, that the Pynchon and Derrida books are not always matched. Sometimes we even suspect they could be cooked, for example.

This third theory of author or author-effects comes by way of the Derridean notion of *signature*. Here we might say, the Barthesian author-as-language is modified to accommodate Derrida's argument that language is always already written, such that the author becomes author-as-writing. The signature is obviously the mark of such authorship and although it 'is not inconsistent with th[e] death or omission of the author',[13] it does not reduce to an unproblematic removal of authorial effects from the discussion of the text. On the contrary, and hence its attraction here, the signature might be seen as a reinscription of the author in terms of a rewriting of the notion; but such a reinscription in no way allows for recourse to an author as origin or controlling intention behind a text. Derrida is, after all and above all, credited with having effected a most thorough deconstruction of such ideas. In this sense, the signature model informs and encompasses the sides of the debate we have looked at so far. In this sense it should be thought of as a theory through which one can read or write other theories: Barthes', Foucault's and 'Pynchon's among them.

The question of the signature arises as the first term of the title of the well-known text 'Signature event context',[14] where the point is made that the signature is, like any utterance, divided. It simply cannot be constituted as singular event but functions in terms of its iterability:[15]

> In order to function, that is, in order to be legible, a signature must have a repeatable, iterable, imitable form: it must be able to detach itself from the present and singular intention of its production. It is its sameness which, in altering its identity and singularity, divides the seal.

Thus the signature repeats, in its difference, that whole list of Derridean 'concepts' like differance, mark, supplement, writing, in its deconstruction of the singularising impulse of Western thinking. At the same time, as is made clear in later texts, particularly *Glas* and *Signsponge*, the signature functions most specifically in terms of author-effect – as a deconstruction of the singularising effect of the author. This repetition-in-difference puts before us precisely a way of addressing the problem of the 'Introduction' which could be reexpressed as follows: how to read the apparently well-anchored singularity and 'authoredness' of this bio-experiential writing while, at the same time, knowing full well that effects of repetition are in play, knowing full well that such repetition must always involve an incomplete transference, a structurally necessary adestination? This notion of signature raises such a problematic and informs our reading of the 'Introduction': but it is by no means identical with that latter text's own theory of authorship and meaning, as we now go on to say.

For, according to Derrida, the signature admits its own singularity – the event which allows one to write cheques and so on – even as it denies it by means of iterability – the event which allows someone else to forge your cheque. Indeed, for Derrida, a model of the signing instance is the traveller's cheque which always requires countersigning. This means that the signature cannot of itself, as a singular instance, guarantee authenticity or authorisation. Instead it automatically calls for a doubling of itself or even the opening of the possibility of a different signature. Pynchon, as the first page of

Slow Learner makes clear, is not averse to reading his early stories like returned cheques – but why are they cancelled? Have they been passed or returned after bouncing? Surely the signature hasn't failed? Or what? But we are ahead of ourselves now. Still, in terms of authors writing texts of literature, the Derridean idea of the signature, unlike the position of the 'Introduction' as we read it, admits the peculiarities, even the uniqueness, of an author's production – her style, her themes and so on – but *insists* that those effects will always necessarily be read outside of the context of their production. By contrast the 'Introduction', in at least one sense, wants to head off the alterity of contexts, to 'justify' and excuse the early Pynchon stories by an authentic recapture of an originary context. And this is the case even though or especially because that privileged origin is sordid, even though or especially because the current writer is wary of 'stepping down the street to have a beer and talk over old times' (3) with the same/different person who was the 'original author'. For Derrida, by complete contrast, there is no contradiction between the two positions; there is a sameness, an identity, which nevertheless functions as a difference:[16]

> The drama that activates and constructs every signature is this insistent, unwearying, potentially infinite repetition of something that remains, every time, irreplaceable.

So far then, this gives us a signature divided into two: i) an act of monumentality or authentification, ii) idiomatic effects dependent on but not restricted to the signatory. Derrida, however, adds a third type of signature which allows for readings that, for want of a better term, we could call 'anagrammatical'. This evokes the way Latin poets placed their names within their poems in a way which both fascinated and threatened Saussure. Here the signature stands for the play of writing within the text – whether deliberately or unintentionally matters little – for the data never reads out in the same way or the same order as it was punched (or *pinched*) in. What is embraced within the idea is that range of textual effects whereby the supposed inside (for example, words and ideas) articulates with the supposed outside (for example, history or author). The matter becomes clearer if we consider the visual arts, where the signature consistently appears to display its problematic status on the edge of the work, not sure whether it is inside or out.

Sometimes the signature is incorporated into the motifs of the work – Gauguin's woodcuts being but one example. At other times, in photography for instance, it appears 'separately' as the title, or on the frame which become therefore to some extent synonymous with the signature. Following this, the signature as reading practice – and we mean particularly our own reading practice, the conceit that we can somehow 'narrate' the 'Introduction''s indigenous theory of authorship and meaning – therefore positions itself against both biographical or psychological criticisms, which seek meaning on the outside, and formalist or structuralist criticisms, which claim to remain on the inside.[17]

Hence the problematic we are addressing to the 'Introduction' – one which is, to repeat, by no means its own preferred strategy – is not 'Who writes?' (to which Barthes answers 'language' and which Foucault considers irrelevant); nor is it the formalist question of the relation between sign and meaning (which must remain at a pre-critical stage on the problem of author); it is, more simply, and retaining Barthes' question under Derrida's erasure and rewriting: 'What signs and countersigns?' – with all of the doubling that this admits and requires. Moreover, instead of demanding an answer from the 'Introduction', we instead prefer simply to put this question up against its own theoretical strategy which, it may be remembered, the text itself calls explicitly 'a strategy of transfer' (21).

■ ■ ■ ■ ■ ■ ■

So let us assume that, whatever options we take up, the issue here is quite other than one of tracing the 'real' biographical origins of Pynchon. Instead, following either Barthes or Derrida, the problem of 'What signs?' would initially be a discursive/signatory one: how to arrange the 'voices', or more strictly 'writing positions' – and finally the writing in general – of the text? Let us make another start on this. There appears to be a now-narrator addressing a possibly fictional then-author – and, as we know, authors can be characters. The 'I' which never calls itself 'Thomas Pynchon' (why should it – *pace* Herbert Stencil) does double duty – shuffling back and forth from now-narrator to then-author/character. It can say '. . . I can remember, these stories were written between 1958 and 1964' (3), but also '. . . I put on horn-rimmed sunglasses at night' (8), where this latter 'I' is also the 'him' of:

... if I were to run into him today, how comfortable would I feel about lending him money, or for that matter even stepping down the street to have a beer and talk over old times? (3)

It can be objected that: surely one talks of oneself this way – this is the mode after all of autobiography. Indeed it *is* that mode and, moreover, the now-narrator attempts with arguable success to put as much moral and literary distance between himself and this then-author as possible. It should always be clear from the tense and the active/passive switching who is speaking or writing. The two signatures should be different. But are they?

For example, there's this: 'Because the story has been anthologised a couple-three times, people think I know more about the subject of entropy than I really do' (12). Who is it, now, that 'knows'? Narrator or character? Or are we to suspect an elision? And: why has the *anthologisation* meant people think that one or both of them know more than he does or they do? Likewise: what 'old times' could the two discuss? One of them's 'old times' are the other's present times. Put simply: we do not know whether to read this as genuine biography (where 'I' slides easily from past to present verbs) or as fictional prose (where the 'I' is much more problematic).

What seems to be falling out from these initial inquiries is the following: every time we attempt to address the question of signature, of 'Pynchon', 'author', 'I', the writing or speaking position, and so on, we come up against a decision as to the *theory of meaning* we are prepared to entertain. On the traditional model, the question of author is solved instantly, without a second thought, by invoking a psychological theory of meaning: roughly the concoction of meaning 'in the mind', its transmission via the text, its reception 'in the mind' of the reader and so on, with 'author' and 'reader' considered as conscious beings and the text as something like inert material – a book, for example. Even on this primitive theory, author emerges only via an underlying (though rarely explicated) theory of meaning. One can suspect that the same must be true, for example, of Barthes' 'discursive' theory with 'author' or its inverted equivalents relying on a Saussurian differentiation of linguistic opposites.[18] In the case of the 'Introduction' this could be: I-now vs. I-then. Without wishing to labour the point further, then, it would be reasonable to conclude that the category of author can be treated in terms of a theory or theories of meaning. The traditional step in searching for a text's meaning has been to turn to its authorship. Following Barthes and Derrida, we must now say that this concept of authorship itself is always only a proxy for a theory of meaning. The author-search has, for too long perhaps, deferred the more basic textual problematic we pose here.

■ ■ ■ ■ ■ ■ ■

By way of illustration, we could consider how author-as-theory-of-meaning emerges at two familiar sites: the biography and the scientific research report. The first instance must include *auto*biography. And here the fact of a separate genre for first person life-stories is illuminating. The first person is so thoroughly embedded as the means of addressing the self that it is possible to use it to collect some, otherwise very diverse, texts. The philosophical use of 'I', for example in phenomenological writings, is easily elided with a quite different use in autobiography. That is, we can easily make deliberately poetic readings of passages such as:[19]

> I hold on to the familiar image I have of you. I take it for granted that you are as I have known you before. Until further notice I hold invariant that segment of my stock of knowledge which concerns you and which I have built up in face-to-face situations, that is, until I receive information to the contrary.

Further elisions could be made, for example with the uses of 'I' in 'fictional' autobiography (Robinson Crusoe); in 'fictional historical' autobiography (Henry VIII); or in cases where an even more problematic field of persons arises (Alice B. Toklas).[20] For all this, the autobiography contains a particular and relatively unique assumption: namely that the meaning of the text is the preservation or conservation of (some) oneself, or at least features of oneself across spatial and historical gaps. This is presumably why authors' prefaces to fictional works often deny the autobiographical qualities that readers have traditionally been trained to find there. The novel ought not to preserve the self, as such: it is supposed to preserve for eternity only one's imaginative capacities, the projection of oneself into another, the creation of personalities in imagination, and so on.

On the other hand, the science report's theory of its own meaning is such that it would efface its authorship. It does so by a convention: namely that third-person, largely passive, forms of writing delete all traces of narration, with that deletion equated with the removal of authorship. And this is all the more significant for a discourse in which one's name on the title-page is essential – and one, moreover, where any practitioner knows that names on title-pages are no guarantee that the individuals referred to had anything to do with the writing or with the scientific 'research' it describes. Moreover, the relations between 'text' and 'research' are connected with and just as problematic as those between 'text' and 'author':[21]

> from the moment a piece of research concerns the text ... the research itself becomes text, production: to it, any 'result' is literally *im-pertinent*. 'Research' is then the name which prudently, under the constraint of certain social conditions, we give to the activity of writing.... [W]hatever [research] searches for, it must not forget its nature as language – and it is this which renders finally inevitable an encounter with writing. In writing, the enunciation deludes the enounced by the effect of the language which produces it.

Science writing attempts to depersonalise itself, to present truth, to speak the very language of nature itself while, at the same time, existing much more than it knows for what it says about its status as text and its authorship. One's authorship (rather than, say, one's 'ideas') in science bring plaudits up to and including Nobel Prizes. And these can be secured not only through research and writing up but also through the feudal sponsorship system of science called 'supervision'. This contradiction, however, is only one facet of a more general problem for theories of textual meaning.

The problem, highlighted by comparing biographical with scientific modes of address, has to do with the position of truth and its guarantees. Biography guarantees truth through appeals to singular experiences. Hence Pynchon writes:

> 'The Small Rain' was my first published story. A friend who'd been away in the army the same two years I'd been in the navy supplied the details. The hurricane really happened, and my friend's Signal Corps detachment had the mission described in the story. (4)

While scientific reportage also requires appeals to (be it noted: potentially collective) experience, the criterion of truth is whether the report is made in conformity with the *self-evident* truths of the particular science in question. Where biography's meaning derives from an appeal to highly singular specifics, science texts derive meaning from the fit of observations into an abstract scheme, or so the story goes. Science and biography: for all their points of contact, these may contain as opposite a pair of ethno-theories of meaning and truth as we can presently muster. The comparison shows clearly the point earlier associated with Derrida's signature model: that even instances of a genre such as autobiography which turns upon the singular and the unique does so within a structure of repetition and imitability, if only because 'singularity' can be as much an institutional truth criterion as the more belabouredly 'public' criteria of science.

■ ■ ■ ■ ■ ■ ■

In connection with our formulation of 'author'-as-theory-of-meaning, then: does the 'Introduction' offer a particular variant of this biographical theory (or institution) of meaning? If so: what is it precisely? As far as precision and certainty go, an object called 'the text's theory of meaning' is probably not on the map at all. That is, it is open to interpretation – to exactly the same degree as the stories it, in its turn, 'interprets'. So we should expect to find a corresponding plurality of authors or readings of authorship. Under what conditions do such readings get made? To take the simplest case: we are very strongly compelled towards a particular reading, *if* we take into account the long period of silence on Pynchon's part, its atypicality in literary circles (contrast: Norman Mailer's *Advertisements for Myself*[22]) and the massive temptation to read the 'Introduction' as the breaking of this silence. This cuts off many of the possible readings of authorship available. It constrains us to read the 'Introduction' as an author-biography with some form of privileged insight into the (other) stories of *Slow Learner*. Such a reading might seem to guarantee that privilege – but what in turn guarantees the reading? To some extent this is arbitrary – we could just as well begin another way where the breaking of cover (or the vow of silence) made no difference to our reading. We could read the 'Introduction' as but another story. Then our problematic could be: how do the various first persons, the several 'I's of the text, conceive their own textual positions?

Working this way, something becomes very evident right away: the basic assumption of structuralist linguistics (that meaning arises out of difference) is not one which is much shared by the 'Introduction'. Its theory of meaning appears to be quite distinct from this Saussurian faith. The 'Introduction' asks for a separation between itself and the stories that follow. They, the stories, are *deferred* in their historical action. They exist in the space of a dialectic between reading (now) and narration (then). One has to wait for history to catch up. There is, with the stories, according to the 'Introduction''s reading, an historical mediation which guarantees their difference. They are not marked as 'present'. In fact, their historical marking is a matter of some detailed chronicling. For example: 'I wrote "Entropy" in '58 or '59 – when I talk about '57 in the story as "back then" I am being almost sarcastic'. (14) *This* is how to read the stories, according to the 'Introduction': with a retrospective knowledge to fill the *differential* between then and now. If this is the space of the stories, how does the 'Introduction' situate itself?

This is another story. The 'Introduction' would have us believe that it arrives all of a sudden; that it comes at once, *im*-mediately. It does not gather its meaning from difference but from sameness, identity with itself, from immediate presence, from the 'true voice' of a collapsed author/narrator calling itself 'I' and using the present tense. This present 'Pynchon' (though the 'I' does not call itself that) is meaningful by virtue of its differentiation from the old 'Pynchon'. The old one exists in the dimension of past/present difference while the new one exists in that of a present/present sameness. The difference between the old and the new Pynchon is the difference between same and difference – between immediacy and deferral. This means that the Pynchon of the present-tense 'I' must declare itself to be on the side of sameness – to hold a theory of meaning which is other than that based on difference. The 'I' argues that: all *that* is past, but this present narration, is now. All and only *that* stuff of the 50s and 60s, has the problem of deferral attached to it. It always did. But this, present, speech (and it is very much the prose of speech) is free of such problems. It reaches over into the ear of the reader and deposits there, intact, the moment's immediate text, the intimate whisper of now. The 'Introduction', in its various ways, is, then, now, very logocentric.

At least it wants to be. But can it be? – given that its presence is itself predicated on the text's difference from a number of other things, including the stories following it. Doesn't this in some way tie it to the very stories which it practically disavows? That is: isn't the divide which the 'Introduction' tries to create between speech (itself) and writing (the stories) a false one? The problem with all of this seems to be not so much the difference/identity play of the 'Introduction' – how could things be otherwise given the Derridean notion of signature? Rather the problem may be that the text of the 'Introduction' does not seem to realise this. On the contrary, it denies it. For the notion of signature would seem to undermine its self-understanding as relatively pure presence. And if the text does not realise this, we have to ask ourselves just what it does realise. Here, at last, we have to come back to the question of transference.

The separation we want to set up shortly is one between meaning as difference and meaning as transference. But in order to do this, and to show that the 'Introduction' stands quite firmly on the side of the latter, it is important to deal with a concept over which the two theories centrally disagree: the concept of *identity*. This is important in another sense, because introductions classically involve identifications. We introduce ourselves to one another, after all, by giving our names, our IDs. An introduction says that this is who I am – or this is who another person is: 'Meet Mr NN, he's the man I've been telling you about . . .' and so on. The very idea of an introduction, including the case in hand, marks a disclosure of identity. Which one? In the case of *Slow Learner* the only name is that on the cover. (The very cover that has, perhaps, been broken?) We assume we're being introduced to a 'Thomas Pynchon', according to the conventions of covering signatures.

But, on the other hand, there's another meaning of 'identity' which has less to do with covers and conversations and more to do with abstract conceptions of what's what. We use 'identity', that is, not simply to address the question of who someone is but also to address questions of sameness: x is identical to y, and so on. So when we're talking about a topic like 'Pynchon's identity', we could either be taken to mean his personal identity or to be referring to the thing that Pynchon is identical with, or equal to, in this more abstract sense. The 'Introduction' itself always appears to be trying to pass off the Pynchon who writes as identical with the one we read. It tries, in *this* sense of identity, to collapse the

Almost but not quite me ...

moment of writing and the moment of reading, to make them identical. If *that* Pynchon, or one of 'his' narrators, was 'almost but not quite me', well then *this* one must be 'exactly me'. Again, the present text refuses deferral. Its theory of meaning/authorship is precisely one which effaces that very problem. It makes the problem look as if it goes away, by forging an identity between the one who writes and the one whom we read. And it's this propensity for making an apparently exact copy that we called earlier in this chapter, the myth of transfer. The 'Introduction"s theory of meaning turns on transference, on the making of perfect copies, on immediacy, on complete identity of the original with the copy.

■ ■ ■ ■ ■ ■ ■

'Transference' is, perhaps, particularly suitable as a theory of meaning for a text which is avowedly autobiographical and almost confessional. It certainly does a deal of apologising, of begging for forgiveness while at the same time asking that the one who is forgiven be taken as distinct from the one who now speaks and makes a perfect transfer. That old one, that one in the past who was also the young one, is associated with all sorts of crimes: of 'an unacceptable level of racist, sexist and proto-Fascist talk' (11) – and one wonders what an acceptable level would be; of failure to see the real effects of 'money and power' (12); of inventing the effect of knowledgeability without anything to back it up ('people think I know more about the subject of entropy than I really do'); of stealing from other sources without acknowledgment:

> Could I, even as I laid down cash for it at the cash register, have been subconsciously planning to loot this faded red volume for the contents of a story? ... Could Willy Sutton rob a safe? (17);

of every literary and moral crime under the sun; of being, in short, 'a smart-assed jerk who didn't know any better, and I apologise for it' (12) is what. The present Pynchon apologises for the past one. This new one exculpates himself from all these crimes, admitting only a small misdemeanour:

> ...chase scenes, for which I remain a dedicated sucker – it is one piece of puerility I am unable to let go of. May Road Runner cartoons never vanish from the video waves, is my attitude. (19)

So this text has a peculiar confessional mode – one where the symptoms of moral and literary transgressions are offered up as those of *someone else*. And so we come, inevitably, upon our first Freudian sense of 'transference' (*Übertragung*): the transfer of symptoms of feelings 'on to a contemporary object ... which applied, and still unconsciously apply, to an infantile object'[23], where the classic instance of such a contemporary object is that most immediately available in the analytic confession, the analyst him- or herself. Alternative destinations can be other patients, family members and so on – even famous personages. Or: one can take on another's transferred symptoms to oneself. Pynchon's 'Introduction' appears to want to transfer – in this sense – *in reverse*, to offload all problems on to a past self so that the present self is cleansed and, in turn, *transferred* into the reading space in pristine form. A double transfer: blame backwards, resultant purity forwards.

However there is a second meaning of the same term (*Übertragung*) in Freud: the transference of a repressed wish. Here an idea or feeling moves from one place to another, as it were, to use a common metaphor, 'within' the same patient – though, as we shall see, the concepts of 'within/without' and 'patient/text' can easily slip around; and so the term 'transfer/ence' becomes subject to the very slippage and play that it describes.

But to continue: this second general sense of 'transference' is the one most often used in the *Interpretation of Dreams*. It glosses the process by which an unconscious idea, not being able to get direct access to the preconscious, exercises 'an effect there by establishing a connection with an idea which already belongs to the preconscious'.[24] In semiotic terms it would be said that the (preconscious) signifier is used for the (repressed) signified, given, as we know from semiotics and psychoanalysis, that signifieds and unconscious repressed ideas cannot be 'expressed' as such in their own right.

In the case of the first meaning, an historical dimension is in play – the dimension of the very past and present 'selves' that Pynchon's 'Introduction' inhabits – one very much the analyst of the other. And although the Pynchon of the 50s is hardly 'infantile' in the strict sense (despite confessing to a lasting 'puerility'), he is often characterised that way by the analyst/narrator of the 'Introduction'. The two meanings of 'transference' in Freud could then be read together to suggest a single general process operating simultaneously in two distinct planes: roughly a synchronic (unconscious → preconscious) and a diachronic (infantile → contemporary) plane. Transference thus does double duty, bringing together as it does the apparently contradictory problematics of hiding or covering up and of disclosure or bringing to presence.

A paradigm case would be that of Ernest Jones, Freud's alter ego, as Brome, his biographer, calls him.[25] As Brome makes clear, Jones was almost but not quite Freud – a deferred Freud who wished to become more than that; to completely close the gap between himself and the powerful other; to have a new identity; to become equal to someone else. This is very like the anxiety of the 'Introduction' where Pynchon-present (especially as author not of the stories but of the novels) wants to become identical with some mythically pure Pynchon, created in the imagination of the reader. Thereby, the old Pynchon has to be seen to take the weight of the negativities upon him. This kind of triangulation (Pynchon-present, Pynchon-of-old, reader) is typical of cases of transference. As Forrester writes:[26]

> Jones has an affair with Loe's nurse Lina, which comes as a tremendous shock to Loe, while Lina then produces pelvic pains dramatically akin to Loe's symptoms – the nicest case of transference, Freud said, he had ever seen.

'Transference' can therefore mean something more than and different from the simpler idea of transfer with which we started, transfer in the sense of making perfect copies. It is not (only) this simple, mythic (albeit widespread) theory of meaning, predicated on sameness and on the arrival of the text at its destination, whole and unsullied. It must now imply that by virtue of and within any case of transference, meaning must slip around from place to place, text to text, person to person in quite unpredictable ways. It suggests, unlike strict theories of difference, that some unprespecifiable element will pass from, for example, origin to destination. Moreover: it suggests a semiotic of local power, by which degrees of antagonism in social relations can be constructed and by which persons can be organised with respect to one another or, to put it more simply: put in their 'correct' place. An example follows. 'It is a lover who speaks...'.

My lover absconds with another. This lover of hers should then be suffering the pains which I suffer by virtue of my lover's actions.

It is he who should be punished, not me. Who, after all, is the transgressor? He knows this. He takes on my symptoms of grief, anguish and pain. He calls me up to tell me about them. He shows me his writings and paintings, his sculpted faces wracked with the pain of grief. He wants to assure me that he suffers these things. By contrast, my face is happy; it seems to bask in the heat of some new found love, akin to his – which is mine. I read the break as a welcome relief. I am symptomatically happy and fulfilled – in exact proportion to the gap which he has made in my life. I talk to him of the burdens he has taken on, of their difficulties. We part from our meeting, our show-down, with him crying. There is no dishonesty in this. We have swapped identities. It is an exact economy. A primitive one which we all know. It involves switching the polarities of our real identities, sufferings and happinesses. Only an absolutely exact change of polarity is possible. Nothing less.

Here transference involves a switching of polarities: and in the case of the 'Introduction', the polarity of difference is switched to that of transference itself. Something, some symptom passes from one patient to another. Some sameness, identity, 'gets through'. It moves from author to reader; the text or some symptom of it, reaches its destination intact. Something, though we can never be sure what, passes. To pass is to transfer – to look whole and unsullied at the other end. But – and this is now crucial if we are to avoid a mythically pure notion of transfer – to pass is also to fake. And so we must be aware of the faking that stands behind every transference, of the essentially fictitious nature of all writing – of the fact that it *is not* what it purports to represent, whether an experience or an experiment. A mythically pure transfer would ideally elide the signifier and the signified; while transference would insist only that some element or symptom of the signified *pass over*, exactly, on to the side of the signifier. Transference is a theory of meaning which risks *looking like*, resembling realism (or pure transfer): and it is precisely its aspect as *resemblance* that is important and not any understanding it may have of itself as realism pure and simple.

■ ■ ■ ■ ■ ■ ■

If the standard theory of meaning as difference can be represented as follows:

a/b

where we take the two sides to be any relevant pair of opposites (signifier/signified, origin/destination, etc.), then the theory of meaning as transference would be represented thus:

a ⋅−→ b

The slash of difference marks a boundary, an infinite deferral, a barrier, an eternal incompleteness of meaning. One side, even though it may manage it partially, never *ultimately* reaches over to the other. But the slash is oblique. It is only *complete* leakage that it prevents. Partial leakage, partial sameness and identity, are things we often overlook on this model. The dot-and-arrow of transference, however, go towards but never reach the opposite extreme. This symbol is not one of division but represents some *particle* of *a* breaking free and joining *b* – where the particle *may*, but only in the ideal, be the whole of *a* itself. At least something gets through. The theories, then, are not strict opposites. They allow for each other as minimal cases. They represent tendencies rather than positions anyone might actually occupy. Of course meaning must involve sameness, as the case of the signature reminds us. There must be some recognition, familiarity or repetition for it to work. For example, the structure of the sentence can remain stable while its 'fillers' change from word to word. Difference always implies transference and vice versa. So we cannot easily put the barrier (slash) of difference between difference and transference:

*(a/b) / (a ⋅−→ b)

Nor can we simply assume that difference transfers, partly or wholly, into transference as such:

*(a/b) ⋅−→ (a ⋅−→ b)

If, however, a theory of meaning were to permit either of the two formulations immediately above, it would be bound to treat them as identical since any distinction, of whatever kind, *between* difference and transference would have been cancelled by this point. The two would collapse:

*((a/b) / (a ⋅−→ b)) = ((a/b) ⋅−→ (a ⋅−→ b))

This imaginary theorisation suggests an identity between the sign of difference (the slash) and the sign of transference (dot-arrow). But this must be false except insofar as both *operations* (and in logic operators cannot be used as functions in their own right) allow for each other *as minimal possibilities* only. They are not *completely* identical. They only partially transfer one to the other. The sign of equality needs to be replaced perhaps by the sign of transference (dot-arrow), with that sign considered always and only as a *partial* transfer. The hypothetical formulation would then be:

*((a/b) / (a ·→ b)) ·→ ((a/b) ·→ (a ·→ b))

However, it soon becomes evident that, while it is more satisfactory than any of the previous examples, this form of notation will end in meaninglessness. Clearly we cannot satisfactorily differentiate difference from transference; but neither can we *strictly* transfer either one into the other. The term describing their relation cannot be one of them alone; and neither can it be equality. Their relation is abyssal.

Significantly, however, the dot-arrow symbolism does not itself represent the exact opposite of the slash. It does not represent a necessarily complete identity of *a* and *b*. Its use does not, for example, necessitate a complete identity between, say, intention and reception, origin and destination, or old Pynchon and new – if such a shorthand is allowed. Instead, it means the passing of some symptom or symptoms, whether crucial or not. The symptom is at least noticeable. It's something our attention is drawn to: the *obsession* with chase scenes, the *inability* of the old Pynchon to develop an ear for regional accents, his *lapsing* into sexism and so on. The feature which is transferred (one way or the other) is like a certain element of photographic representation according to Roland Barthes:[27]

> this element ... rises from the scene, shoots out of it like an arrow, and pierces me. A Latin word exists to designate this wound, this prick, this mark made by a pointed instrument: the word suits me all the better in that it also refers to the notion of punctuation, and because the photographs I am speaking of are in effect punctuated, sometimes even speckled with these sensitive points; precisely these marks, these wounds are so many *points.* This ... element ... I shall therefore call *punctum.*

Ideally the punctuation mark of transference (·→) would be so arranged as to show some leaking, of whatever proportions, from *a* to *b*. What is leaked might be called symptom, or *punctum*, but also

Almost but not quite me ...

proxy. What it allows for is the terrible asymmetry that structuralist theories of difference fail to see. For example, if we set up

m/f

as opposites where these stand for gender oppositions, we soon see that the second can be defined as the absence of the first:

f =def ~m

but that the first does not have a reciprocal relation:

m ≠def ~f

That is: there is, in our culture and in many others, a politically dominant modality in which the female is defined as the absence of the male, but not vice versa. The positivity of maleness is not the exact *equal* of the negativity of femaleness. It is naïve to think that such an ideal actually operates yet, though the struggle for its operation is everywhere about us.

The symbolism of transference does not assume a structuralist a priori equality between whatever terms are entered into it. And, more radically, it suggests that complete opposites are never actually encountered, but are the consequences of thinking with ideal systems – of mathematising signifying systems. Transference appears to preserve difference much more than difference allows for transference. If we could use the transference symbol, then, in a way which did not make it look like the (mistaken) annihilation of difference altogether, it would be a very useful and liberating semiotic. The 'Introduction', and this is our central point, does not take us this far. On the contrary. And yet it does open up the space in which it can be thought. It opens up a space between sheer identity and sheer difference: 'a strategy of transfer' (21).

■ ■ ■ ■ ■ ■ ■

But this strategy, for such it is, no longer being merely descriptive, means a good deal of risk. It means, for example, the risk of being accused of theft: the very literary theft which is confessed in the 'Introduction'. If the letter, for example, does partially transfer from a to b, then the question of the remainder which goes astray becomes a matter for investigation. There is always the hint of a crime – the idea that someone or something deliberately intervened to prevent perfect transfer. Or else the opposite of this: getting meaning going in one's stories by the tactic of imitative recognisability (for example, by plundering Karl Baedeker's 1899 Guide to Egypt) – by making some narrative details identical, the same, from place to place, from Baedeker to 'Under the Rose' (though Pynchon doesn't mention the transference from 'Under the Rose' to *V*.) – is to risk the charge of *wholesale* theft; of appropriating that which *was* successfully transferred (rather than the lost remainder, the bits of Baedeker we may never now recover). The two crimes: theft of the remainder and theft of the absent, almost seem to cancel one another. Already we want to call plagiarism 'intertextuality', or else the opposite. And we want to call literary 'oversight' something like 'the impossibility of complete description'. Or else the opposite. There is the crime of an always imperfect authenticity (for example, to 'history'); and the crime of neglecting this, letting it pass, 'distorting'. The situation makes every writing a crime. The two crimes, at this time, do not yet cancel one another. There is (as Althusser used to say, and he should know) no innocent writing.

■ ■ ■ ■ ■ ■ ■

There is a still further way we can write this problematic of transference. We have already seen, that is, how transference poses itself as a third relation outside the dialectic of identity and difference and that it in fact operates on the first of these terms in a way that reminds us of the ambiguity of 'identity'. But in fact, what is true of identity must be true also of its opposite, non-identity. Non-identity can be a concept referring to the self, or else it can be a semantic concept referring to structures of signification. And non-identity is, of course, nothing other than difference. So, in this sense, transference is not merely a third term to *add* to identity and difference. It doesn't simply stand to one side (*or* in between those terms): it radically alters our conception of the opposition between them. It changes the meaning of that oppositionality.

Hence the metaphysical and the semantic meanings of 'non/identity' suggest two different kinds of meaning, or two uses of the word 'meaning'. The first would be a metaphysical conception of meaning ('the meaning of life') and the second semantic one ('the meaning of a word'). While the standard identity/difference opposition suggests that we should keep these two senses of 'meaning' separate (for instance, as signified and signifier), the problematic of an adestinational transference suggests a relation between them – a relation which was already hinted at in the form of the relation between the concepts of author and meaning – namely: that one's identity, one's selfhood is *written* into being, thereby putting a conception of meaning-as-writing essentially prior to a consideration of authorship. In this field, transference implies the importance of *some* degree of sameness in the face of absolute difference. Hence one's identity (the meaning of one's life) cannot emerge from a pure play of difference, even *as* it is written. It always contains the grain of the immediate, of the non-deferred. There is always at least a residuum of presence.

However, transference does not fool itself that the meaning, the message, or whatever, passes across the abyss without any kind of loss whatsoever; from sender to receiver without change. A destinational transference (unlike transfer simpliciter), as the term implies, always allows both for the possibility that some things will never reach their destination, and for the possibility that, nevertheless, some things do or can. And as with uncertainty in particle physics, we can never be sure, in advance, just which particle(s) this will pertain to. To go on to say that because it is always possible that any given particle will *not* reach its destination, then one must give up on destination altogether is as pointless as the suggestion that we must cherish destination as the *sine qua non* of meaning, assuming that wherever the text arrives it was 'meant' to be there. In semantics the teleological and the anti-teleological are equally untenable.

Instead, transference poses a difference between semantic and metaphysical forms of non/identity around which a theory of meaning may form. By contrast, difference-theory locates *its* central distinction in the opposition between identity and non-identity (both in the semantic sense). We could, therefore, represent difference and transference on a single grid:

	T	
metaphysics	R	*semantics*
	A	
	N	
identity	S	non-identity
	F	
	E	DIFFERENCE
	R	
non-identity	E	identity
	N	
	C	
	E	

So effectively, the theory of transference makes a very different cut from that of difference, and it also makes that cut in a different direction. All this can be said much more simply, as follows: (1) the self is written into being, but *some* element of self must already be available for this to occur; (2) the play of difference which creates the self in writing, contains some trace of identity; (3) the metaphysical self is the product of a purely semantic process, yet that process is never utterly free of the metaphysics of presence.

Is this a return to a theory of meaning as consciousness? A phenomenology? Essentially no: or else it is a post-phenomenology. If meaning entails consciousness, this entailment is trivial. The conscious self is only one construction of the metaphysics of identity. It is indeed – like psychological theories of authorship – a prevalent and powerful one – but this does not mean that consciousness should be considered such a criterion of selfhood that it must go wherever self goes.

All that transference requires is that something is sent from being *a* to being *b* (in both senses of 'being'): it is transferred. This something that is sent is perhaps in toto a different something from what arrives. For example: we can see an analogy between the symptoms of two sufferers, where the analogy implies that *something* is the same, say, the form or the structure of the symptom if not its content. The thing that arrives may even be an absence. Not getting a letter can be a positivity: a definite meaning. That somebody 'didn't even write' can be crucial, as Godard's contribution to the film-collection *Paris vu par* makes clear.

In the case of Pynchon, we can see how acute this potential contradiction is when we realise that the 'Introduction' itself locates the meaning of the subsequent stories in transference-as-intertextuality (theft, plagiarism) as a means of *refusing* to face up to the meaning of the text(s) as autobiographic transfer. The intertextual transference defers the autobiographical: and yet at the same time the very text of the 'Introduction' is itself in the mode of autobiography. What is denied is manifestly present – *that* is what makes this 'personal' declaration so novel:

> Why I adopted such a strategy of transfer is no longer clear to me. Displacing my personal experience off into other environments went back at least as far as 'The Small Rain'. Part of this was an unkind impatience with fiction I felt then to be 'too autobiographical'. Somewhere I had come up with the notion

that one's personal life had nothing to do with fiction, when the truth, as everyone knows, is nearly the direct opposite. (21)

Nearly, but not quite, the direct opposite. This 'not quite' is the crack of transference. This 'Introduction', this most recent of Pynchon's fictions makes it quite clear that autobiography has much to do with fiction: it is fiction (if not vice versa); one's life is always already a fictional construct regardless of how it is written. Regardless of how it is written, it is written: it is available only in its tellability. And the 'Introduction' is a central piece of autobiographical fiction. It is in this light that we can understand what has been glossed as Pynchon's silence about himself, and perhaps why that silence is fabulous. For in one sense, there has been no silence. Pynchon only ever wrote autobiography.

■ ■ ■ ■ ■ ■ ■

The 'Introduction' offers us a quite distinct literature from the usual fare marked with a 'Pynchon' tag – and a new and troublesome theory of literature, to some extent, to go along with it. It is certainly the case that belletristic criticism, up to and including Leavis, held a theory based on a simplistic notion of transfer. But this was an ideally pure transfer which might go better under the title of 'transmission'. Interestingly enough the same faith in transmission is still upheld by technicist theories of meaning of the 'information processing' (sender/receiver) variety.[28] But the 'Introduction''s theory speaks to an uncertain and unpredictable, at best partial, transfer, subject to the vicissitudes of contextuality and play. It is, however, equally distinct from strictly structuralist (and formalist) difference theories. For these latter tend to eschew all transference, by and large, assuming it to necessitate complete transfer. The 'Introduction' asks us not to throw out the transference baby with the total-identity bathwater. The theory is almost but not quite lit. crit. At the same time, and particularly since it is far from embracing the signature model, it's equally almost but not quite grammatological.

One might express the difference between transference- and difference-theories thus:

$$\frac{d}{t}$$

where the 't' is strictly voiceless for all that it seems to be on the side of speech and presence. The difference between them may only be occasionally important, but one of those occasions would appear to be the advent of 'Pynchon's Autobiography'. It begins with the small rain...

■ ■ ■ ■ ■ ■ ■

coming back like a cancelled or bounced cheque:

> You may already know what a blow to the ego it can be to have to read over anything you wrote 20 years ago, even cancelled checks. My first reaction, rereading these stories, was *oh my god*, accompanied by physical symptoms we shouldn't dwell upon. (3)

Something of a blow to the ego, an embarrassment nobody, not even a bank wants to keep hanging around. It leaves us with the quandary of what to do with it, problems of publication (does my wife know I spent this much?), of reading (checking the cheque against one's monthly statement), of archiving (should I keep it for the taxman?). The similarity between the stories Pynchon wrote 20 years ago and a cancelled cheque goes further than the frivolity here, and hence his reaction. The author's problem in the 'Introduction' to *Slow Learner* is that he both does and doesn't recognise the signature as his own. Those stories he has signed like a cheque and the chequered career of 'bad ear', 'puerility', racism, sexism and proto-Fascism, short-changing, overwriting, theft, bad habits and dumb theories bouncing around here, have all been debited to his account. Now he'd prefer not to countersign them, so he uses the space in front of their publication like the 60 days they give you to question the transactions made in your account. He sets the record straight by means of confession, self-criticism, of both apology and *apologia*. Now what he writes will not be marked by the same bad ear, puerility, racism, sexism and so on. It was almost but not quite me who wrote that back then.

The 'Introduction' to *Slow Learner* mentions almost all of Pynchon's published fiction. Apart from the stories published in the volume itself, *V.* is referred to as a novel 'I had published' (22), and *Lot 49* gets panned on the same page. On the other hand 'Mortality and Mercy in Vienna'[29] gets left out at one end of his production and *Gravity's Rainbow* at the other. The problem then is: does he also sign for these others here; and, if we were to find puerility, racism or sexism in those texts – more pertinently the latter in view of his organicist notion of the author's development (in spite of the 'up-and-down shape of my learning curve' (22)) – who should we imagine to have been their author?

So we come to asking again, as we did from the start, who is this first person transferred to the present of the pages written in introduction to a lot of fiction? Can we expect to find his identity formed through the different writing selves that are scattered throughout this short text? And the answer obviously is that there is no answer to that sort of paradox, since the writing self, as soon as it writes, be that operation as simple as the signing of a cheque, ruins its own identity and becomes forever an author of fictions only. In this sense the author is not simply dead, but his condition remains always in doubt. 'In a stable condition' may at the limit describe the dead, but then there is further instability: decomposition.

Of all the faults the author chides himself for, there is one which stands out, particularly once it is a question of establishing an identity. There is one fault that is marked by the sort of physicality that might allow positive identification, a distinguishing mark or characteristic that would set this author apart, placing him in the company of the Van Goghs and the kidnapped Gettys of this or that world. It is his 'bad ear'. It is the first fault mentioned and the idea returns on the last pages – 'I was also beginning to shut up and listen to the American voices around me' (22). Indeed, in the final lines, the question of writing, or education in writing, returns to that of the ear in the context of 'a bunch of old guys sitting round playing rock'n'roll' (23). One might reasonably assume that the first mistake of trying 'to show off my ear before I had one' (5) continues to haunt the writer of the 'Introduction'.

Now this might feasibly help narrow the search for the mysterious Thomas Pynchon, but the real question here is whether one Thomas can recognise himself any more than another. As we remember one story, he never was too hot on recognition, never gave credence to what he heard, had to see to believe. It all came back to him, and his first reaction was, just like here, *'oh my God'*. But we are getting ahead, at least an ear ahead, of ourselves. The confusion between author and narrator, the difficulty in recognising the difference, or wanting to almost but not quite annul the difference, has led on the introducer's own admission, to acts of bad faith in the stories themselves. There is a doubt in respect of recognition which generalises to confusion among stories. Yet, to return to what we just said, one thing stands out as distinguishing mark, namely this bad ear. At the beginning and the end then, is the matter of a mutilated body, the event of someone showing off an organ that wasn't his own and doubt about both the fact and victim of a mutilation. At the beginning and the end there were always at least two, maybe more, stories when it came to a question of authorship. There was he who was that he was, supreme creator, and then a later version of the same, but full of holes; then a later version still, completely reconstituted. This is the story the introducer tries to put out, and there are many disciples of that story who will attest to its verity. But then there is the story of one who doubts, a complicated story in itself which, in view of how it turns out, is probably yet another version of the same old one. Be that as it may, in between, in the space opened by what the story calls doubt, the story that goes by that name, there is something completely different. The Pynchon-narrator-introducer who almost but not quite signs the text in question here, divides it as he signs it, is countersigned by a recidivist *doubting T*homas whose initials provide the signature for a whole range of fictions – not the least being *Gravity's Rainbow* – that continue to be our focus here.

Notes

1. We are grateful to participants at the Murdoch University 'Moving the Boundaries' seminar who commented on an earlier solo performance of 'Almost but not quite me . . .' and, in particular, to John Frow whose insistence on a distinction between the several Freudian conceptions of transference and a cruder view of transfer as 'packing things in a pantechnicon and removing them from place to place' remains only partially satisfied in the present version. Unfortunately, John did literally pack his things into a pantechnicon and remove them and himself before the discussions got any further. We miss him.
2. *Slow Learner: Early Stories* (Boston: Little Brown, 1984), p. 8. Subsequent page references, shown in parentheses, are to this edition which has the same pagination as the British clothbound edition by Jonathan Cape.

3. R. Barthes, *Mythologies* (London: Paladin, 1973).
4. J. Forrester, 'Who is in analysis with whom? Freud, Lacan, Derrida', *Economy and Society*, 13 (1984), pp. 153–77.
5. If this were true, it would have posed a particular problem for the editors at Penguin Books who, it seems, *must* include an 'About the Author' before each title page. The only one to our knowledge who has 'escaped' is J.D. Salinger, a giant of obscurity by Pynchon's standards. The Penguin editions of *V.* and *Lot 49* from 1974 manage to find quite a deal to say about TRP. We quote from the latter:

    Thomas Pynchon was born in Long Island in 1937. He served in the navy for a short time and then entered Cornell University, from which he graduated in 1958. After living in Greenwich Village he moved to Seattle and then to Mexico. His novel V [sic] which was published in 1963 (and is also available in Penguins) earned Pynchon an international reputation as a novelist. His other publications include a number of uncollected short stories. Thomas Pynchon's latest book is *Gravity's Rainbow* (1973).

6. M. Foucault, 'What is an author?' in his *Language, Counter-memory and Practice*, trans. D. Bouchard (Oxford: Blackwell, 1977), pp. 113–38.
7. D. Williamson, *Authorship and Criticism*, Occasional Paper 7 (Sydney: Local Consumption Publications, 1985).
8. R. Barthes, 'The death of the author', in *Image-Music-Text*, trans. S. Heath (London: Fontana, 1977), pp. 142–8.
9. Barthes, 'Death', p. 146.
10. Barthes, 'Death', p. 146.
11. Williamson, p. 13. See also our paper 'The late(r) Barthes: constituting fragmenting subjects', *Boundary 2*, 14 (1986), pp. 261–78.
12. Williamson, p. 13.
13. J. Derrida, *Signéponge/Signsponge*, trans. R. Rand (New York: Columbia University Press, 1984), p. 22.
14. J. Derrida, *Margins of Philosophy*, trans. A. Bass (Chicago: University of Chicago Press, 1982), pp. 307–30.
15. *Margins*, pp. 328–9.
16. *Signsponge*, p. 20.
17. *Signsponge*, p. 22.
18. F. de Saussure, *Course in General Linguistics* (London: Fontana, 1974).
19. A. Schütz, *Collected Papers Vol. 1: Studies in Social Theory* (The Hague: Martinus Nijhoff, 1964), p. 39.
20. Fictional autobiographies would seem to provide critical marginal cases for the examination of theories of meaning and author in fiction. The ones referred to here are: G. Stein, *The Autobiography of Alice B. Toklas* (London: Bodley Head, 1933); D. Defoe, *The life & strange and surprising adventures of Robinson Crusoe of York, mariner,: who lived eight and twenty years all alone in an un-inhabited island . . ./ written by himself* (Oxford: Blackwell/Shakespeare Head Press, 1927); M. George, *The Autobiography of Henry VIII* (London: Macmillan,

1987). How fiction is constructed in each case is quite different. Pynchon's 'Introduction' could be compared with all three. Other contenders would be those instances of autobiography which are not done, for the most part, in the first person and act more as *comptes rendus* or historical summaries of academic disciplines, artistic movements or rock bands ('The Autobiography of Supertramp' being an interesting theft in point). See: F. R. Moulten and J. J. Schifferes (eds), *The Autobiography of Science* (London: J. Murray, 1963); M. Jean (ed.), *The Autobiography of Surrealism* (New York: Viking Press, 1980). In the first of these texts, we found the following passage which is not without its relevance to the present case:

> But what is the life of a literary or scientific man, and where are we to find the history of it? In his works. Newton and Euler are their own best biographers (Henry Hunter, Preface to *The Letters of Euler* (London, 1802)).

21. R. Barthes, 'Writers, intellectuals, teachers' in *Image-Music-Text*, trans. S. Heath (London: Fontana, 1977), pp. 190–215. Whether language produces writing or vice versa is, by this stage, a moot point: either way his argument re science writing still holds.
22. N. Mailer, *Advertisements for Myself* (London: Deutsch, 1961).
23. S. Freud, *The Interpretation of Dreams* (Harmondsworth: Pelican, 1976), p. 716; see also p. 289.
24. Freud, p. 716.
25. V. Brome, *Ernest Jones: Freud's Alter Ego* (London: Caliban, 1982).
26. Forrester, p. 157.
27. R. Barthes, *Camera Lucida: Reflections on Photography*, trans. R. Howard (New York: Hill and Wang, 1981), pp. 26–7.
28. Cf. A. McHoul, 'Announcing: a contribution to the critique of information processing models of human communication', *Human Studies*, 6 (1983), pp. 279–94.
29. 'Mortality and mercy in Vienna', *Epoch*, 9, Spring (1959), pp. 195–213.

6

"Die Welt ist alles was der Fall ist"
(Wittgenstein, Weissmann, Pynchon)

"Le signe est toujours le signe de la chute" (Derrida)[1]

V. / 'V.' / *V.*?

The text, *V.*, does not use the signifier, 'V.' to represent a character, V., in the way that *Robinson Crusoe* uses the signifier, 'Robinson Crusoe', to represent a character, Robinson Crusoe. Something has changed in/as the novel – almost imperceptibly – in the space of the texts between, texts which we call 'history'. For a start, V. is always absent, hinted at, forced into a shadowy (non-)existence in the way Bowie mimes out a glass cage which is not 'there'. V.: she/it is pure signifier – the (as we used to say) conscious pure effect of signification.

In another sense V. (not 'V.') is *the* signifier. The signified of the novel is absent. The signified of the novel might have been V. But V. is absent, as signified, and so is transformed into pure signifier. If we were to admit to a signified, we should have to say that the signifier-in-general is the signified of *V.*. The text is about signification in a world where the transcendental signified is absent. So the opposition, 'V.' v. V., is broken down, levelled to a single plain of signification. Character (Hamlet) and name ('Hamlet') are fused; for V. exists only as a name, as the effect of naming.

But weren't we also taught another fallacy greater than the confusion of use and mention? Wasn't the gross sin of the English Department to confuse Hamlet and *Hamlet*? So then V. exists as nothing more than the ensemble of V.s and 'V.'s – which are also identical with each other. The text is the ensemble of material graphemes + signifiers. For V. is no thing, *res*, object. With the absence of the transcendental signified and the materiality of the signifier, there arrives the graphematic text. Character, name, text: they are fused (melted + wired for explosion). So where can the critic/reader take hold – if they dare? Where the critic/reader has always taken hold: in the *repetition* of the text-thing-name which is the signifier.

V is:

> an asymmetric V to the east where it's dark and there are no more bars (2) / Section v of chapter 1 (27) / '...V-Note, McClintic Sphere. Paola Maijstral.' Nothing but proper nouns (40) / Not who, but what: what is she (43) / the sentences on V. suddenly acquired a light of their own (44) / The V.-jigsaw (44) / ...

Herbert Stencil (the copy, the trace, the one who signifies V. and so is – in another sense – the signifi*er*): V. is his own hunted object. Just like the search for truth, the absent 'real', the 'beyond talk', the 'beyond signification' that signification points to – Stencil's search is pointless. Nothing is pointed to. There is no point – except *the* point, the full-stop which always follows V. Mercilessly and with great typographical pains, that stop is almost always there – following, shadowing. Beyond V. there is the stop, the closure, the end (as both finality and goal). But that can never be reached – for we never penetrate beyond the limits of signification. Stencil is doomed to copy, to trace, to ceaselessly iterate the signifier 'V.' For beyond the repetition of that signifier there is no real closure. The point of it all is a/to stop. And to stop is the most difficult thing because for Stencil that can never happen until the limits of the signifier are somehow magically transgressed. V. is

> half TV (of which Fergus the man was becoming an extension) (45) / Veronica (=true image), the sewer rat whom the mad priest made a sister / V., a future saint – depending on which story you listened to (110) / . .

The stories are always multiple. There is no 'how it was/is'. Rumour, text, dossier, signification and counter-signification circulate, play across and upon each other *as* (can we say) the(?) text. For there is no longer any 'the text' – only multiple repetitions of V., of 'V.', of V. and of . . . There is only

> talking, talking, talking, nothing but MG-words, inanimate-words he couldn't really talk back at. (18)

The text that cannot be talked back at – where turns cannot be taken to talk – *writing*. Writing, like that of Fausto Maijstral – V.'s ultimate writer, her literal confessor. Fausto, the magisterial author whose texts are fragmented, blown up, blown to the wind. Fausto, in his eternal confessional, writes:

> The writing itself even constitutes another rejection, another 'character' added to the past. (286)

That character we write, us, in our confessions; that signifier-made-man that we so often mistook for a man-made-signifier, forces us to ask 'why do we confess?' We confess precisely to *make* ourselves: to repeat a discourse without which we would not be 'selves', let alone ourselves. Power does not have us confess to 'find out' about us, to police us, but to ensure we are *produced* in certain ways from the beginning – if there is a beginning. To control the discourse of confession (the priest, the critic, the judge . . .) is to control the very construction of subjects.

> The word is, in . . . fact, meaningless, based as it is on the false assumption that identity is single, soul continuous. (287)

V. promises confluence, a coming together, an identity, a point where there is sameness. But if we move *up* the V, there is only divergence, absence of identity, absence of character. So all the 'characters' are caught in the yo-yoing up and down the V between identity and absence: Kurt Mondaugen, the engineer-poet with one eye to the world and one eye on the moon – the one who knows the wise-man, Wittgenstein, also the engineer-poet whose text is present-as-logic and absent-as-mysticism. And Profane, Winsome, Paola, Ploy . . . : they are all wo/men of letters. They are caught too in this spread of signification that V. casts like Medusa from the

JAMES COOK UNIVERSITY OF NORTH QUEENSLAND

POSTAL ADDRESS:
Post Office,
James Cook University, Q. 4811.
AUSTRALIA.

TELEPHONE:
Townsville (077) 81 4111

TELEX:
AA47009

29 DEC 1981

Dear Wills,

29 Dec and I am at work (minus air-conditioning, $40^{\circ}+$), doing something on V because we said we would write something on it. I am collecting all sorts of interesting bits from the text which can be put together such that V. reads as a text on 'the sign'. If you have a copy, note how the full stop is used in 'V.' when it's the subject of Stencil's search that's in question and how the stop is dropped at other times. The title has a stop in it also (please amend above accordingly). I've collected every instance of the use of 'V' and of 'V.' as well as all the V-words, all references to language, word, texts...., and all cases of Saussurian 'oppositionality' (two complementary halves, etc) of which there are many. This is all I've written so far:

V. only exists as the effect of 'V.' (the Sr, chain of Srs in the, or as the, text $V_{\bullet}$). $V_{\bullet}$ is identical with the repetition/iteration and placing of that chain. The novel, $V_{\bullet}$, is a novel about the sign. 'V.' is the Sr of the sign. ~~xxxxxxxxxxxxxxxxxxxxxxxxxxxxxxx~~ Where $V_{\bullet}$ is one Sd of the sign, the sign itself is the other Sd of $V_{\bullet}$ The relation of 'V.' to $V_{\bullet}$ is the metaphor for the sign in $V_{\bullet}$ and that working through in $V_{\bullet}$ shows the sign to be only ~~with~~ Sr, but that Sr in the act of signifying and so producing — continually — a continually absent (because always in production) Sd - i.e., $V_{\bullet\bullet}$

absence
of
Sd.

I also want to point to the absence of identity in $V_{\bullet}$ (Rainbow would be better here, where Slothrop just fades out — becomes an odd mention every 100 pages or so at the end; still this is also there in $V_{\bullet\bullet}$.)

Overall: Stencil's search is (along with the other searches in the novel) for the Sd — the material, corporeal entity outside discourse. Course he's not going to find it. See how everyone hunts things in $V_{\bullet}$ See how everyone 'talks proper nouns'.

--*-*-*-*-*-*-*-*-*-*-*-*-*-*-

? ←

Hope all is well with you and Mme Wills. I am sending a cartoon I did specially for you to remind you of Oz francophilia. All your stuff is well under the house — no major rain as yet. I don't think the wines (esp. reds) like that position ⑧ we may have to drink them quickly when you get back! Tom took your bike for a ride last week. He said it needed it. I've been turning it over religiously so all is not bad.

We got our pussy-chatte. Not the Burmese we wanted but a cross between a Persian grey and a grey alley-cat. She is very sweet and kitteny right now but growing all the time. We call her 'V.', because she had a pinch in her tail.

Much love from all of us to both of you,

Alec

[Freud: "valley is a common female symbol in dreams." (Int. Dr.)]

Med. to the USA in the form of tentacles. Naming, naming, naming... and nothing else. V. is

> V. and a conspiracy (141) / She's yielded him only the poor skeleton of a dossier. Most of what he has is inference. He doesn't know who she is, nor what she is. He's trying to find out (140) / Stencil's words seemed to fall insubstantial (140) / ...

Stencil talks of (that is, stencils) Stencil in the 3rd person – he, the trace, traces the copy that he is – that third person. Stencil is he. And V. is she?

> Truthfully he didn't know what sex V. might be, nor even what genus and species. (210)

Stencil is the trace and V. (at least half) machine. But she/machine is only the effect of talking heads and moving styluses, a conspiracy, a plot/narrative. He's trying to find out what there is of V. outside of V.-text. Of course there is nothing – only the dossier, this history, his story of V., the totality of just more V.-text. Nothing but noting.

> versions of history (209) / his V-structure (209) / the ultimate Plot Which Has No Name (210) / Fausto V (298) / God v. Caesar (301) / ...

Just when the structure looks like a system, a thing, a confluence, a shape, then it lapses back into an arbitrary piece of graphics – just a shape, a stamp, an imprint. The most important thing in the world (Crusoe's 'other'), the motor of history, the key to it all: and then it just turns out to be another signifier. The plot which has no name becomes nothing more *than* a name. We think, through the word we can find the world – then it turns – and it turns out that the word is all that is the world that is all that is the case. The word is the *case*:

> the boards and back of a book, the tray in which the compositor has his types before him, that which falls or happens [*der Fall*], an instance of disease, an odd character, the grammatical relation of a noun, pronoun or adjective to another word ... the nominative being imagined as a vertical line, and the oblique cases in various stages of falling.... (*Chambers*)

V.: the symbol for potential difference (electrical). 'This word flip was weird' (272)/'This word "flip" was weird': which is correct?

> He had found out from this sound man about a two-triode circuit called a flip-flop, which when it was turned on could be one of two ways, depending on which tube was conducting and which was cut off: set or reset, flip or flop. (273)

Which is *correct*? Use/mention. V./'V.' Flip/flop. A matter of life/ death?

> He tried to tell himself meeting V. and dying were separate and unconnected (362) / V. in Spain, V. on Crete; V. crippled in Corfu (364) / his mental age roughly five. V. had fled (364) / V. by this time was a remarkably scattered concept (364) / . . .

V. is all over. V. is all over the wor(l)d. V. is death (when it is all over). Virginia, Victoria, vicious, Vheissu, Vera, venery, Vogelsang, Venus, vectors. . . V. is all about. V. is what it is all about. Eternal condemnation to the signifier. Like

> a gentle lady plant pathologist, originally from the Isle of Man, who had the distinction of being the only Manx monoglot in the world and consequently spoke to no one. (395)

> Stencil sketched the entire history of V. that night and strengthened a long suspicion. That it did add up only to the recurrence of an initial and a few dead objects. (419)

Not an end, an initial. So now we can free that initial of its delimiting typography – the quotation and its marks, the citation and (as Derrida is yet to say) its 'entre guillemets' – and so speak only of

■ ■ ■ ■ ■ ■ ■

Fall, m. -(e)s/-ë: fall, accident, plunge, downfall, decline, ruin, decay, collapse, overthrow, drop, lapse, slump, depression, surrender, death, cadence, case, instance, example, matter, situation, event, circumstance, eventuality, occurrence, outcome, occasion, case (jur.), case (med.), case (ling.) (*Cassell/ Harrap/Langenscheidt*).

Every sign, linguistic or non-linguistic, spoken or written . . ., as a small or large unity, can be *cited*, put between quotation marks; thereby it can break with every given context, and engender infinitely new contexts in an absolutely nonsaturable fashion.[2]

One V would be the transcendental signified regulating the difference between the animate and the inanimate, accident and intention. V would be the impossibility of such a transcendental signified. To begin with the search for V would be indistinguishable from the differences and deferrals which compose *her*. But more than this, the dualities animate and inanimate, intention and accident, would pre-empt the possibility of their own resolution in that their transcendental signified, V, would have to be either intention or accident, either animate or inanimate. These dualities do not allow of a neutral term, they are absolutely binary. Hence their intersections, their Vs, are catastrophic, they are tropes of the fall. V is the figure of the fall. Any instance of her is her downfall, and inevitably involves a *situation*.

For when we say that these dualities are absolutely binary, that they do not allow of a neutral term, we do not mean that their difference is irreducible, unless it is. We mean rather that for them to be absolutely binary, their difference would have to be irreducible and thus regulated by a transcendental signified. There would thus have to be a V outside of both the animate and the inanimate, outside of both intention and accident. V can only be posited as that impossibility, and every instance of V becomes a case of the fall, displaying the catastrophe that any V-event must imply, being the occurrence of her own impossibility.

The problem of difference is also one of priority. That is to say that the problem is immediately posed by the event, any event, itself. The slightest displacement or derivation, even repetition, institutes the structure within which difference has the possibility of occurring. Repetition, copy and stencil are not then reinforcements of the same without being the marks of difference. Once again only a transcendental principle can regulate the matter of priority. Some point in the chain which can obscure the fact of its belonging to the chain well enough or long enough, by virtue of some system of privilege, to appear to have brought the chain into operation. In espionage parlance all such links are known as sources. There is no doubt that V is the source of the hermeneutic *V.*; there is no doubt that if V, then *V. V.* is the articulation of such a proposition. It merely instances the possibility of the sign. But by doing so it implies both the necessity of its structure, that of the supplement, and hence the impossibility of its completion, outside of V.

Just as Stencil would seem to posit the necessity of V in order to resolve the oppositions accident/intention, inanimate/animate, it is as reasonable to maintain that in order to sustain the oppositions, V is inscribed as a necessity. For as long as V is absent, there is no absolute priority.

> Who is to say whether I'm here so the people can read the meters or whether the radiation in me is because they have to measure. Which way does it go? (267)

Whereas the geographical and human loci for the occurrence of V remain plural and imprecise – Vheissu, Valetta, Victoria, Veronica

– the body remains the most common instance of the materiality of this signifier, and the most frequented site for the differences inanimate/animate, and accident/intention. Either the body is synthetic to a small or large extent – Bongo-Shaftsbury's arm, Esther's nose, Godolphin's face, the Bad Priest – or the body is partial, part to a larger machine – yoyoing, the fetish. Thus the body is designed so as to correct its own accidents, the accidents of its *original* design which show design and accident to share the same structure. Thus the animate comes to be riven by and riveted to the inanimate, for once it is capable of waste it is composed of decay, and once it is capable of the extrapolations of (call it) desire, it is never-more intact, its context never-more enclosed.

■ ■ ■ ■ ■ ■ ■

Benny Profane's humanist whinge, the fear of a creeping inanimate, relies on the history of the body being determined teleologically, and on the possibility of repressing the contradiction which such a notion implies. In Profane's view of things there is a system of degeneracy which is consistent with the passing of linear time. From the switch on Bongo-Shaftsbury's arm, to the murder of 60 000 Hereros, to SHROUD's reference to the similarity between concentration camp corpses and car bodies piled up in a wrecker's yard, there runs a straight line with reference to which the differential increase in the inanimate can be plotted, like a V on its side. Back at the beginning, in this view of things, there would have been only the animate, and presumably, pure intention. For this view is repeated by Maijstral, Itague, and Stencil. The problem would then be, of course (and this is Profane's problem and Stencil's problem), to explain how the inanimate and accident come about. Stencil's plotting of the chronology of V-events assumes that the odd, off-chance occurrences of her bits and pieces, her random incidences, once plotted, will lead back to a single controlled event. How randomness could have issued from that single intention, leaving Stencil with an apparently infinite series of possibilities, that is Stencil's dilemma.

The writing of V is a deconstruction of both the teleological system which informs Profane's gripe with the inanimate and that which informs Stencil's search for V. Teleology becomes not so much a matter of the end as it does a matter of the origin, the initial. As if to problematise the notion of an origin untouched by

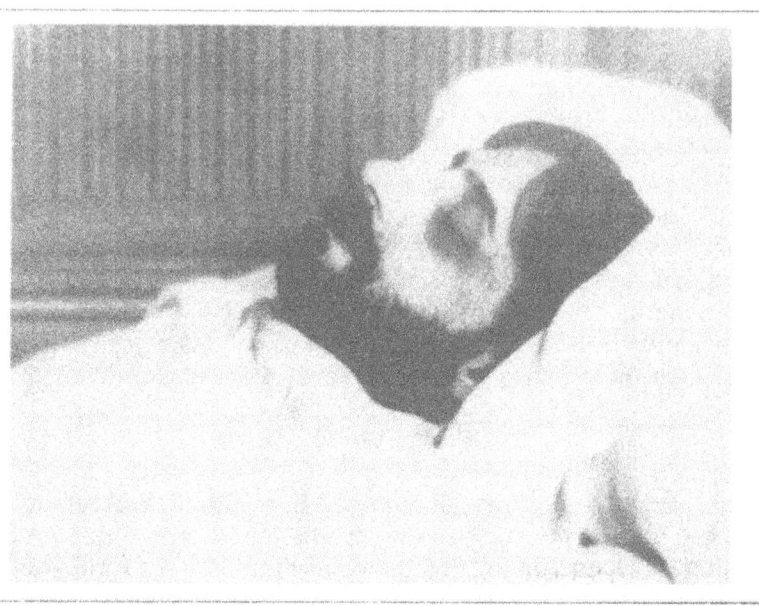

8/1/82

MARCEL PROUST, 1922
PHOTOGRAPH BY MAN RAY

Dear,
Here's Proust recovering from too many madeleines. Derrida is in jail in Prague. Thanks for the cartoon, I got halfway thru' a reading of V. again en route but airplanes get to be very situational. I agree about the sign and should in that respect be able to make something out of "absolute difference" + "the conspiracy/randomness thing.
  Off to Bombay soon + soon after we might drink some at Henri together, if any remainder. Love to Ruth, "Willy Chitlin—

Alec + Ruth McHoul
27 Evans Street
Belgian Gardens,
Townsville QLD.
AUSTRALIE.

the differences which now comprise its history, Profane is left with a schlemihl principle which he must convince himself to be pure animate, but which functions remarkably like a machine. And Stencil is left with traces of a V which he must convince himself to be the century's, if not history's controlling principle, but which adds up to an accident of catastrophic proportions, and still remains capable of being added to.

■ ■ ■ ■ ■ ■ ■

What keeps the animate alive, keeps it from being inanimate, is the source. For the inanimate, as SHROUD is quick enough to point out, is simply discontinued animate. Ideally the animate is discontinued only long enough to return to the animate. Like the partridge droppings in Slab's pear-tree, it will fall inanimate through space only long enough to reach the ground and fertilise the tree. But as Profane discovers in the sewer, on Alligator Patrol, it doesn't quite work that way. Under the street, under the inanimate city, closer to where the real earth throbs, Profane discovers that the space of circulation of waste is vast and long enough for all sorts of unnatural excesses to be introduced. To begin with it had all been contained within the natural order – children were given alligators as pets, animate toys. In no time at all, somewhere within the spaces of that natural order there arrived a state of affairs where

> an old man had killed and boiled a catechumen, had committed sodomy with a rat, had discussed a rodent nunhood with V. (110)

In the event, V had to be there somewhere. In any event V, the event itself, *there* as a condition of possibility of its own disaster. Within this same waste space the possibility of Stencil happening to tangle with the inanimateness of a bullet from Profane's gun. In the New York sewer. Within the structure of Profane's animate order.

■ ■ ■ ■ ■ ■ ■

Rachel Owlglass makes a V-connection with Benny Profane through her relationship with Esther, and hence Schoenmaker and Godolphin. She also has, to Profane's mind, an improper relationship with the inanimateness of her MG. It is in this connection that the problematic of the sexual is most raised and so implicated in the problematic of the in/animate. When Rachel first nearly runs him over, she is possibly as inanimate as the car she is driving. Then he catches her in flagrant *auto*-affection,

> her throat open to the summer constellations . . . he saw her left hand snake out all pale to fondle the gearshift. (20)

So there is little wonder that the eventual description of their sexual intercourse is a peculiar combination of the biological and the mechanical.

> Ready at the slightest pressure surge in the blood lines, endocrine imbalance, quickening of the nerves at the love-breeding zones to pivot into some covenant with Profane the schlemihl . . . one hand moved to automatic. (336)

We've all heard it said, sex without love (read between women and men with souls) is purely mechanical. But that isn't exactly the point here. Any form of coupling be it covenant or intumescence, will seem to fall within the structure of the prosthetic. If the supplement is possible, then the supplement of another nature is possible, and nature is no longer simple nature. Sex where Benny Profane is concerned, demands the addition of one nature to another. Thus it is necessarily anxiety-producing for him who fears contamination by the inanimate. Sex, procreation, demands accident and chance, as Maijstral will note, implying a line of things further along which he would not go (292). Profane's defence is supposed to be his schlemihlhood. But as Rachel points out, once even a flabby clumsy soul is amplified into a Universal Principle (359) –

> A schlemihl is a schlemihl (134) –

it merely assumes the function of a tautology. And tautologies work like clockwork. There are no surprises.

The uneasy coupling of one body with another, the articulateness of the body and the world, whether it be Profane on the street,

> looking for something to make the fact of his own disassembly plausible as that of any machine (30);

or his erection taking a punt on an employment agency, or Mrs Buffo's suck hour, not to mention the whole range of operation, surgery and prosthesis: these make for a system wherein animate is forever attached to inanimate.[3]

> It is at work everywhere, functioning smoothly at times, at other times in fits and starts. It breathes, it heats, it eats. It shits and fucks.

As well read, then, Schoenmaker's seduction of Esther. Not just in the context of relationships of power and seduction, the combined effect of being supine, taking Nembutal, and having things inserted into one's nostrils. But also in terms of the automatism of sex.

> She was sexually turned on, was all: as if Schoenmaker had located and flipped a secret switch or clitoris somewhere inside her nasal cavity. A cavity is a cavity after all. (96)

A connection is a connection, once a connection is possible. And the possibilities are limitless, as Mélanie discovers, for she dies as a result of it. But her death is caused not simply by an erect and inanimate pole (in any event erect animate poles have been known to cause death as Mondaugen would confirm), not simply as a result of the connection of the animate and the inanimate, but rather by a bad connection, a wrong connection. The machine breaks down in her case because a part is missing.

So Esther gets a nose-job from Schoenmaker, with Trench in attendance, then she gets another sort of job from Schoenmaker, with Trench still looking on, from behind the curtains, in the wings. As if there were the rehearsal and the real thing, subtraction of a piece of the body in one case, addition of a piece of someone else's in the other, it matters little in that any number of possibilities are allowed for just within the space of a repetition. Esther's nos: that says it all.

> No meaning yes ... No ... Different ... No ... Again ... No. (97)

Once nos can be repeated there is no saying whether the nos are simply repeats, differences, or contraries. And if no cannot even be preserved from yes (the truth-tables overturned), what hope for the sanctity of the animate?

Neil McGarver

JAMES COOK UNIVERSITY OF NORTH QUEENSLAND

POSTAL ADDRESS: Post Office, James Cook University, Q. 4811, AUSTRALIA.
TELEPHONE: Townsville (077) 81 4111
TELEX: AA47009

<u>Language</u>   v. / <u>V</u>

'The sr.' as the sd. of <u>V</u>

Do that by working through oppositions

Dentist / Psych. ⟷ Animate / Inanim. (Fetish)
+ nose job
Conspiracy / Randomness   SR
                              (Humanist complaint?)

) Confessor   Fantasy / reality
man - machine ?
         Yo-yo   place / people
                           v
                         Name
                    Difference / identity
~~Matrey~~   Names as homonyms?

<u>sign posts</u>

Not only is there something particularly precious about Eigenvalue's showcase teeth (either of their own right or by right of some possible connection with V) but there is also something special about teeth themselves, and hence Eigenvalue's introduction to Psychodontia. In the tooth there is a particular concentration of both essential matter and excrement. A casing of synthetic material surrounds a central nerve. So much so that the nerve can be fully extracted as an alternative to prosthetics.

> The pulp is soft and laced with little blood vessels and nerves. The enamel, mostly calcium, is inanimate. (139)

Without repeating the obvious concerning decay and rot, it remains that teeth bring out both the permissible and the sinister in the matter of prosthesis. False teeth fulfil not only the same function as real teeth, but they also look the same. They are the proof that the animate could live with the inanimate, that it does of necessity, all along. When the Bad Priest's teeth are removed she is said to be 'past speech' (322). How can something so removeable be so essential to natural speech? How could Psychodontia, a mouth full of paraphernalia, be a talking cure?

Eigenvalue points to a similarity between psychiatry and dentistry in terms of their relationship to confession.

> Back around the turn of the century, psychoanalysis had usurped from the priesthood the role of the father-confessor. Now, it seemed, the analyst in his turn was about to be deposed by, of all people, the dentist. (138)

Exactly in what sense Eigenvalue doesn't really explain. He merely goes on to mention the structure of the tooth with respect to the inanimate, as just mentioned, and then goes on to say that cavities occur for good reason.

> But even if there are several per tooth, there's no conscious organisation there against the life of the pulp, no conspiracy. Yet we have men like Stencil, who must go about grouping the world's random caries into cabals. (139)

Thus on the one hand Eigenvalue's teeth (which are not his teeth) attract a Stencil who wishes to extract information to an Eigenvalue who wishes to diagnose Stencil's situation. But on the other hand Eigenvalue's teeth (which may or may not be V's teeth, and not just one particular set of teeth but teeth in general as Eigenvalue considers them in relation to things around them) bring together the matter of the animate/inanimate and the matter of intention/ accident or conspiracy/randomness, and that within the context of confession. For confession – as Profane's reference to the covenant in connection with sex with Rachel suggests – is another form of coupling. The mechanics of confession involves extraction, transferral, transmutation, trade-off, discard, discount. All of which occurs, need it be repeated, within the simple structure of a repetition.

Confession requires the repetition of real life as anecdote. It is supposed to guarantee that the space of sense which it opens up, is restricted to the closed circle between penitent's mouth and confessor's ear. But we all know how much extra to that has occurred, fallen, within the enclosure of the confessional. Almost anything one can imagine. The confessional readily becomes the site of any number of excesses, exaggerations, misinterpretations, the simple excess of the monologue itself – what is one doing talking to someone else when one is really only talking to oneself, since actually talking is what counts most, bringing oneself to say it, to hear the sound of one's own voice, but knowing that someone else is eavesdropping? What is interesting about the confessional is the fact that its paradoxes have a concrete structure. To begin with, for half of Christendom the very institution is an unnecessary supplement. But even within it there is the further concrete structure of the wall or curtain which separates penitent and confessor. The possible fall of one's words through the event of the circulation of their meaning is marked by the curtain, written on the wall. The curtain of the confessional marks the rupture in language. It hangs like a shroud over whatever one says, since one has no idea what exactly is going to happen to what one says. The confessional curtain is at one and the same time the threat of nonabsolution, and the trace, even flimsy and fetish-like, of potential difference (V) in one's speech. Thus the space of the confessional, as Fausto Maijstral more than suggests, is the space of writing. The difference in language which is always there. Without writing, that difference doesn't leave its mark. There remains no trace of it. But wherever a trace is left, memory, repetition, text, language is no longer coherent. Its event is also its possible collapse.

Consider once more Benny Profane (unconfessed?), in any case V-connected to Fausto through Paola from the beginning, back in the sewer, trying his best to preserve intact, safe from alligators, the smooth functioning of the disposal of waste from the animate. He is in pursuit, knows he is straying, veers to the left, lands in Fairing's parish. Here what drapes within the structure of confession has gone right off the wall:

> Profane had moved across the frontier. (108)

Henceforth there is little hope of purity. Not even, especially not, in the writing.

> The stories, by the time Profane heard them, were pretty much apocryphal and more fantasy than the record itself warranted. At no point in the twenty or so years the legend had been handed on did it occur to anyone to question the old priest's sanity. It is this way with sewer stories. They just are. Truth or falsity don't apply. (108)

When Profane first comes across V, he discovers what *V.* is all about. Anecdote, fantasy, apocrypha, sewer stories. No context can contain it. One stumbles from one thing to the next, in pursuit of whatever.

This is how the text works, within the structure of prosthesis. Anything will fit the purpose in the extreme. Like Godolphin's cheekbone:

> It's worth a fortune. Before they melted it down it was one of a set of pastoral figurines, eighteenth century – nymphs, shepherdesses – looted from a château.... (88)

Why shouldn't it still be worth a fortune when any conglomeration of signs amounts to the awkwardness of a graft, and the work of art, the text, having no origin, cannot be destined for any final form which fulfils it?

■ ■ ■ ■ ■ ■ ■

When it comes to Fausto's confessions, to his writing, the creeping inanimate theory reveals its contradictions quite clearly. He mentions discontinuity early in the piece:

> The present Fausto can look nowhere but back on the separate stages of his own history. No continuity, no logic. (310)

He himself numbers at least four, discontinuous even if consecutive. The only thing which is common to all four Faustos is writing. Fausto I of the generation of '37, Fausto II of the journals and poems, Fausto III of the indecipherable entries, and Fausto IV of the confession. (And Fausto V, still unwritten.) To say that writing is a problem of context is in one sense to confirm what Fausto's story would seek to demonstrate: that the practice of writing is tied closely to the events which constitute its conditions of possibility, which give rise to it. But to say that writing is a problem of context is also to exploit, to the fullest extent, the concept of dissemination. Fausto's writing is from start to finish in pieces. Even in the confessional, the word breaks up immediately it is spoken. Fausto's writing has certain breaks, written into it. But those breaks number many more than the four he has inscribed. How else could someone called Stencil light upon a single reference, part of a vague recollection, already second or third hand, and make of it the central sense to the story? Unless all writing operated that way. Fausto's confessions tell both of a V who falls to pieces, comes apart, and of writing, like *V.*, which does likewise.

■ ■ ■ ■ ■ ■ ■

Stencil wishes to discover whether V simply turns up at every earth-shattering event, or whether she is the actual cause of that event; whether she is real woman or simply clockwork. To make such a judgement, he has to know a lot about V and the more he discovers the more trouble he has deciding what is relevant. The problem of V, as Stencil perceives it, the problem of accident and intention, is also therefore a problem of context. The problem V is first raised in the context of writing. V first occurs to Stencil as a note in a diary, already read and glossed over. He last mentions her in another note left to Maijstral. She has by this time fallen to pieces. All Stencil is following by this time is spare parts. One may well ask why he continues to look for her when it is clear that she has been completely dismantled. But obviously the search can only become more of an obsession when she is in bits and pieces. Stencil's activity grows in intensity in inverse proportion to V's unity. If V is the end of Stencil's search, then *V.* is about there being no end to it.

■ ■ ■ ■ ■ ■ ■

A stencil allows for repetition, reproduction if you insist. But, as we have insisted, it is within that same structure that difference occurs. Stencilisation, which describes the construction of *V.*, allows for a variety of relationships between pieces of the text. These pieces are mostly related, or introduced, in terms of a progressive, if incomplete, composite of Stencil's encounters with V. We refer simply to those chapters which do not refer to the present time of the narrative. The Alexandria episode relates a Foreign Office encounter with V presumably constructed from Stencil père's journals; similarly the Florence episode which occurs in the context of Stencil's conversation with Eigenvalue. Mondaugen's story, although Stencilised, is recounted by the man himself, and the confessions of Fausto Maijstral already exist as written text. The Epilogue is allowed as third person, eye-of-God narrative by even the strictest literary convention. Which leaves 'V. in love', as pure invention of Stencil's, at least until we learn that Stencil has it from Porcépic and police records. The episode is in any case introduced with minimal textual support.

'So what year is it.'
'It is 1913,' said Stencil.
'Why not,' said Profane. (368)

And indeed.

■ ■ ■ ■ ■ ■ ■

'V. in love' recounts a fatal accident, or was it intention? 'V. in love' recounts the story of the Fetish, the fetish. f/v? The fetish is the deferral of an absence. One does not have to believe Freud or even Lacan to accept that. For a fetishised object replaces the sexual object on the one hand, and introduces the possibility of transfer, ad infinitum, on the other. One does not have to insist about castration in order to accept the fetish within the framework of the supplement, both replacing and adding to. Mélanie is V's fetish – already supplemented to the tune of a silent 'e', making **une** *fétiche* where the dictionary prefers the masculine. Mélanie brings a number of things together, animate and inanimate, but mostly she extends the prosthetics of the body outside the frame of the body. A body of parts, replaceable parts, suggested many times already in *V.* and with respect to V herself, is now complemented by a body which becomes part of a larger machine. And hence the shift in context from a problem which seems directly connected to the inanimate, and would be solved within its own terms, to the larger problem of Stencil's, which raises the whole conspiracy/randomness debate. By this we mean that as long as it is simply a matter of more or less synthetic bodies, of clockwork bodies in the extreme, then the problem of accident and intention remains restricted by the contours of the body. A question of a body with or without a soul, with or without an animate source. But the fetish is another matter. The fetish allows the body to become a shift in (a) gear. Once Mélanie dances with automata, cannot exist without her mirror, becomes V's fetish, becomes Stencil's V's fetish, Stencil's obsession, there is no stopping it. The obsession, intense intention, is inseparable from pure accident.

■ ■ ■ ■ ■ ■ ■

If the continuity of V's decadence were to have been preserved, or (re-)constructed in *V.*, then there would have been an *automatic* (reading of) Victoria Wren that

> was being gradually replaced by V.; something entirely different, for which the young century had as yet no name. (386)

It would then be correct to assume an alternative: either she existed as part in a larger scheme which a number of theories of human behaviour – Freudian, behaviourist, etc. – provided for, in which she would be no more than

> a purely determined organism, an automaton, constructed, only quaintly, of human flesh. (386)

Either that or she would become by choice an inanimate object of desire. These are the alternatives Stencil outlines once V is in love. Either animate within a conspiratorial intention, or by her own intention inanimate. That is how Stencil reads V, as a continuity producing a puzzling alternative, a Victoria Wren gradually being replaced by V,

> a falling-away from what is human. (380)

V is a puzzle. V, V., or *V.* must at least be the possibility of constructing a complete picture from a number of pieces. But V is never a completed picture, never even gets into proper order. For V is a problem with the idea that a continuity can produce difference, a spanner in its works. How can humanity fall away into non-humanity, continuously? How can Victoria Wren, as intact notion (for V, as attempt at her reconstruction, has to assume her to have been somewhere somehow intact) come to be replaced by something that is not Victoria Wren but V? How can something called Stencil, called Profane, called all the other characters and all the other events, come to be grafted on to an intact Victoria Wren, or an intact original V? If V, then how *V.*?

V is the transcendental signified which *V.* deconstructs, in the writing, so that there is henceforth none. V is the necessity and impossibility of such a notion. For otherwise we are left with what we started with, a source which is always already inscribed with its own difference, and which cannot therefore be a source, which cannot but be difference, trace, writing, text. This decadence which V is said to become, is quite simply the event, the sign itself. Every case of V is a case of the fall. The case of V is the catastrophe of a world which cannot sustain absolute difference outside of a transcendental signified and the ruin of sense and meaning which is so implied. Every event involves enough difference to include its own downfall. V is the sign of such a divergence. The hope of retracing each of its vectors to a point of original divergence, or convergence, means stretching it a bit. A part. Apart. Many parts. To the point where only a thread, a slim chance, the most insignificant trace, can hold it together. A thread of a weave of a text of a V.

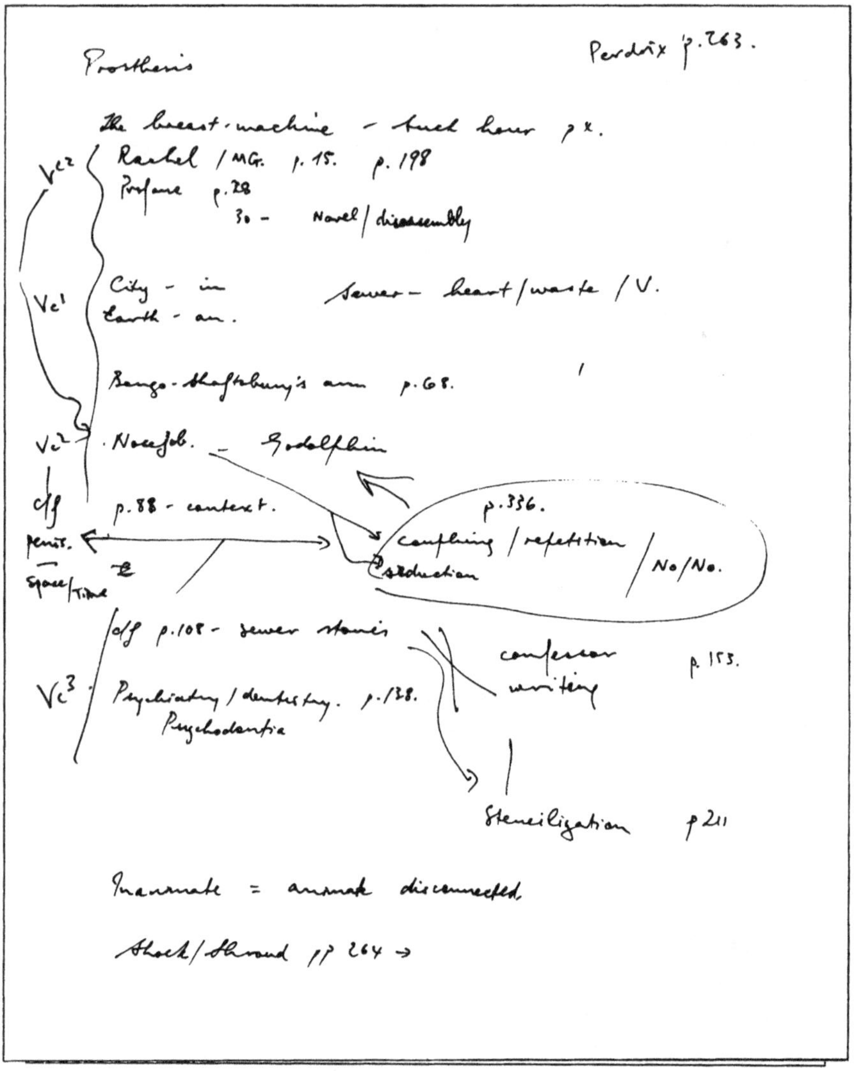

[Handwritten notes, approximate transcription:]

Prosthesis   Perdrix p. 263.

　　　　The breast-machine — bad hour p. x.
Vc² { Rachel / MG. p. 15.   p. 198
　　　 Profane p. 28
　　　　　　30 — Novel / disassembly

Vc¹ { City — in　　　sewer — heart / waste / V.
　　　 earth — an.

　　　Bongo-Shaftesbury's arm   p. 68.

Vc² } · Nosejob. — Godolphin
d/g   p. 88 — context.　　　　　p. 336.
penis ←————————→ Coupling / repetition / No/No.
Space/Time　　　　　　seduction

　　　 d/g p. 108 — sewer stories
Vc³ { Psychiatry / dentistry. p. 138.   confessor   p. 153.
　　　 Psychodontia　　　　　　writing

　　　　　　　　　　　　　　　Stencilization   p. 211

Inanimate = animate disconnected.

Shock / Shroud pp. 264 →

Notes

1. The quotations making up the V of the title have the following sources. The one on the left is spoken by Weissmann and translated by Mondaugen in Pynchon's *V*. (pp. 258–9). Mondaugen claims to have 'heard that somewhere before'. The 'somewhere' is possibly the opening proposition of Wittgenstein's *Tractatus*. See L. Wittgenstein, *Tractatus Logico-Philosophicus* (London: Routledge and Kegan Paul, 1961), p. 6. However, Mondaugen would have had to have been very quick off the mark to recognise the proposition as Wittgenstein's. Mondaugen hears it in 1922, the year after the first publication of the *Tractatus* in the *Annalen der Naturphilosophie*. So, stuck in the middle of Deutsch-Südwestafrika, Mondaugen would most likely have required a postal subscription. Interestingly enough, Wittgenstein himself, as late as November 1921, only thought of the *Tractatus* as 'in press'. See the correspondence in L. Wittgenstein, *Letters to C. K. Ogden*, ed., trans. G. H. von Wright (Oxford/London: Blackwell/Routledge and Kegan Paul, 1973). This and other quotations, shown in parentheses throughout the chapter, are from the New York, Bantam Books edition of *V.*, 1964. The second title quotation is from J. Derrida, *De la Grammatologie* (Paris: Éditions de Minuit, 1967), p. 401. Plater makes quite a deal out of the world being all that is the case, reading that proposition as committing both 'Pynchon' and 'Wittgenstein' to a theory of 'closed systems'. The current chapter works directly against the grain of that reading. See: W.M. Plater, *The Grim Phoenix: Reconstructing Thomas Pynchon* (Bloomington: Indiana University Press, 1978), pp. 2–63.
2. J. Derrida, *Margins of Philosophy*, trans. A. Bass (Chicago: University of Chicago Press, 1982) p. 320.
3. G. Deleuze and F. Guattari, *Anti-Oedipus*, trans. H. R. Lane, R. Hurley and M. Seem (Minneapolis: University of Minnesota Press, 1986), p. 1.

7

Between the two, there is both confusion *and* distinction ('exquisite confusion'), hymen, the dance of the penna, the flight of the Idea ... a 'hesitation' turning into writing. In folding it back upon itself, the text thus *parts* (with) reference, spreads it like

A V

(Jacques Derrida, *Dissemination*[1])

And so again a V, a spreading of pages, a bookmatching, thus: Godolphin, in the novel *V.*, in the fictional city of Florence, unable to go to the Consul-General, must make his confession in the street to a rather bad priest, as it turns out, in the form of passing Englishwoman, VW, Victoria Wren. But fearing her connection with the press, he prefaces his confession as follows:

'This isn't for general dissemination ... and it may be wrong. Who am I to know my own motives....' (154)[2]

With a preface like this in place, it must be confessed that here, in 'A V', among other things, we rely on a prior reading of a passing figure or figures who, at least in part, at least as enigmatically as V. it- or herself, could be called 'woman' (or perhaps 'women'). Though what *that* is (or those are) is an essentially problematic issue to be treated here also. In treating the figures of 'woman', a W, a doubling of V, in this text – woman having been so unclear in our earlier discussions as to be all but absent – we hope to resituate while reaffirming our earlier reading of *V*. We are spurred on from the start by a V as fold of the hymen, a two-fold fold which becomes also the points of a pen, and so of writing, and of writing-woman in particular. Also, in a more risky or scary sense still, writing on the body of woman. Derrida, as we have only just read, has it that the text, under such readings, 'spreads [reference] like a V', but he goes on from there, '... like a V, a gap that pivots on its point, a dancer, a flower, or Idea'. This reading-writing might be called, then, not only 'grammatological' but also 'gynetic'.[3]

Earlier, we read V. as absent transcendental signified, V as the case of its impossibility, *V.* as its deconstruction. We read that we don't 'know what sex V. might be, nor even what genus and species' (210), that it is 'a remarkably scattered concept' (364). How to put the pieces together, how to put pieces together in general, is the only and permanent problem of reading. Mallarmé's *Mimique* and Plato's *Philebus* are examples from Derrida's *Dissemination*, a hymen of writing torn by the pen between them, hymen here called a V among other things.

At least some of the time, or in some way, the V. of Pynchon's *V.* is a number of women – Victoria Wren, the one in love with Mélanie, Veronica Manganese. And while V. certainly becomes generalised, 'scattered', the leap to reading it as 'woman' in general is a great and textually unwarranted one. V. is just as much not a woman but a place called Vheissu; 'as if the place were ... a dark woman tattooed from head to toes', a woman 'you would be in love with' (156). Here 'woman' ceases to be what a 'V' might, at the limit, symbolise and '*a* woman' becomes the *aistheton* or *explanans* of the V-place itself. There is a changing of places, a transfer, albeit a cryptic one, *à rébus* perhaps.

Those two concerns, that of how one text treats (of) another, and that of what 'woman' might be if not any number of specific women, are raised anew in recent feminist discussions; for example in *Gynesis* by Alice Jardine and *Alice Doesn't* by Teresa de Lauretis.[4] The books' subtitles provide more explicit perspectives: *Configurations of Woman and Modernity* for the first, and *Feminism, Semiotics, Cinema* for the second.

Whereas *Alice Doesn't* doesn't specifically refer to *V.* Alice (Jardine) does. Whereas Alice (Jardine) doesn't specifically refer to Alice (as in Wonderland), *Alice Doesn't* does. Lewis Carroll's *Alice*, in spite of the fact that Alice is 'hardly a feminist heroine' becomes for de Lauretis 'a parable suggesting ... the adventure of critical feminism' (AD, 2).

« « *Beginning here a series of asides to 'A V' – resisting the relegation of the footnote – marks of putting A V aside, hence the chevrons. While, of course, never escaping the text that contains them, they grasp for a kind of parergonality and, if they ever leaked out altogether, would stand as a weak kind of signature.* 'A V' is, then, too, spread, split, beginning here where we should not quickly gloss over the fact that de Lauretis also points to Carroll's *'erotic interest in the seven-year-old girl for whom the book was written'* (AD, 2) as evidence of her suspicions about the figure of *the* character, Alice, in relation to feminism. We should note in particular the kind of transfer de Lauretis is suggesting. While this whole question needs a fuller treatment, it is important also to mention that Pynchon's fictions are replete with many an episode of much less obscured paedophilia (of the man-girl type) and that the Pynchon industry, by and large, has seen fit to valorise this aspect of his writing. The bookmatching project, in this case, might want to make connections between, for example, de Lauretis taking Foucault to task for neglecting feminist critiques of masculine perversions (AD, 94) and, for another example, Siegel's positive reading of Slothrop fucking children such as Bianca in Gravity's Rainbow *('perhaps the only time he is really moved emotionally during sex')* – though Siegel is by no means alone in this lack of critical distance.[5] » »

By contrast with AD's *Alice*, on the other hand, Pynchon's *V.* is for Jardine 'a perfect example of the thematization rather than constitution of gynesis' (AJ, 247). And by 'gynesis' she means:

> the putting into discourse of 'woman' as that *process* diagnosed in France as intrinsic to the condition of modernity; indeed, the valorization of the feminine, woman, and her obligatory, that is, historical connotations, as somehow intrinsic to new and necessary modes of thinking, writing, speaking. The object produced by this process is neither a person nor a thing, but a horizon, that toward which the process is tending: a *gynema.* This *gynema* is a reading effect, a woman-in-effect that is never stable and has no identity. (AJ, 25)

In some ways, there could be no clearer statement than this of what our previous chapter on *V.* wanted to express, aided by or hampered with, as the case may be, a problematic of writing barely up to the task. The question is: what regulates or defines the articulations that are put into effect in these texts? This is the question of the composition of V., the relations of *V.*, V., and 'V'; the question finally of how any discourse engages the texts it reads.

« « *Let us name our favoured contender for this principle: 'differAnce', as Ulmer writes it, with a big A, sitting as he says, like a pyramid, after Derrida's own excursus on the A as pyramid, following Hegel.*[6] *The pyramid is the site of cryptographic investigation par excellence, of scripts severed from logos, from the tongue: 'The a ... is not heard; it remains silent, secret, and discreet, like a tomb'. And just as Derrida shifts the E of differEnce to an A in this manner, so AJ shifts the idealist-feminist belief in a gEnesis by fiat of a new woman to a less decisive gYnesis. This E – Y shift of gYnesis, which we identify with the shift to differAnce, also works through our pEnchant for pYnchon, making us such AVid readers of these texts.* » »

Thus the question of a V., our question here of 'A V', is a matter of how *Gynesis* (AJ, after its author), and *Alice Doesn't* (AD, after its title, and this contrivance of acronymisation whereby the author's name is favoured there and the title's name here, has its own logic, explicitation of which we shall hold in reserve), treat a corpus of texts by male authors as exemplary in their development of notions of woman. For AJ and AD claim above all to be discourses about woman, yet in order to elaborate those discourses they resort to reading. Not, one supposes, that there was ever any other possibility. So in AD:

> Each essay may be seen as an eccentric reading, a confrontation with theoretical discourses and expressive practices (cinema, language, narrative, imaging) which construct and effect a certain representation of 'woman.' By 'woman' I mean a fictional construct, a distillate from diverse but congruent discourses dominant in Western cultures (critical and scientific, literary or juridical discourses), which works as both their vanishing point and their specific condition of existence. (AD, 5)

The main thrust of AD is in terms of a critique of existing representations of 'woman' which fall back on and affect the everyday lives and living conditions of 'women':

> By *women*, on the other hand, I will mean the real historical beings who cannot as yet be defined outside of those discursive formations, but whose material existence is nonetheless certain, and the very condition of this book. The relation between women as historical subjects and the notion of woman as it is

produced by hegemonic discourses is neither a direct relation of identity, a one-to-one correspondence, nor a relation of simple implication. Like all other relations expressed in language, it is an arbitrary and symbolic one, that is to say, culturally set up. The manner and the effects of that set-up are what the book intends to explore. And since one of the rhetorical strategies is questioning the terms in which the relationship between *women* and *woman* has been cast, the two terms will be kept distinct. (AD, 5–6)

A very complex problematic is exposed and, not so obviously, denied a solution here. Its elements are impossible to disengage properly, as AD maintains. There are (hegemonic) discourses from which 'woman' is distilled as an effect. And there are also real historical 'women', presumably prior to 'woman', that is prior to the discourses which produce the effect of 'woman'. Yet those 'women' 'cannot be defined outside' discourse, not yet (although there is no suggestion as to what this projection or promise might look forward to). Three levels of discourse then – 'woman' as textual effect, AD's apparently privileged analytic discourse(s), and historical women – and within such a system how could the relation between woman and women ever be anything but mediated through the discursive level, through the arbitrary and symbolic operations of language? Yet given that, what is the logic that determines that the two will be kept apart? If their relations are cast according to linguistic conditions, within discursive formations, and hence determined by hegemonic forces within those formations, does it for all that lie within the logic of such a system to argue for their being kept apart? Similarly, does the fact that the correspondence between the two is not one-to-one nor simply one of implication allow the arbitrary distinction being put into place here? It would seem on the other hand that AD's move is one of resistance, but of a type of resistance which contradicts the rationality of the argument hitherto established, and so which puts itself outside of itself. It is a resistance which takes a certain liberty with the logic of the possibility of transgression dominating the discussion, exceeding that logic in order to borrow a strategic advantage for itself alone. There is a type of rupture in the field of difference at the same time as difference is being posited. If one were to call this a fold, a logic of the hymen or V, would that be going too fast?[7]

« « AJ invites a counter-move for masculine writers, one which we could envisage taking up: 'we might ask why Derrida did not operate a complete reversal – on the testicles, for example, as perfect parergon of any male text' (AJ, 191). For us, a critical irony of the testes is that their main function is to retain sperm for later use. They are no more than temporary ink-wells, holding pens. Granted they are among the conditions of possibility of, but in themselves they are equally withholders of, jouissance. Sperms, it will be remembered, carry only half of the normal complement of genetic information and so are, strictly, foreign bodies inside the body. They would be rejected if special cells inside the testes did not continually supply them with the missing, female, half of the code. Those cells are often called 'nurse' or 'mother' cells. And now we see the peculiarity of calling the move from hymen to testicles 'a complete reversal'. While the two represent vulnerability, weak points easily attacked, the fear of loss in each case is quite distinct. The castration fear is the boy-child's own fear while the tearing of the hymen is the obsession of the parent, particularly the father. Nothing is completely reversed. » »

The argument of AJ seems at first to be very similar to that of AD, but what for the latter seems represented as only a threat, that is an increasing fictionalisation of woman which becomes a more refined distillate of hegemonic discourse, is for the former not only a risk but also a promise and celebration, the way to *gynesis*:

> within this ever-increasing inflation of quotation marks around the word 'woman,' women as thinking, writing subjects are placed in the position of constantly wondering whether it is a question of women or woman.... To refuse 'woman' or the 'feminine' as cultural and libidinal constructions (as in 'men's femininity') is, ironically, to return to metaphysical – anatomical – definitions of sexual identity. To accept a metaphorization, a semiosis of woman, on the other hand, means risking once again the absence of women as subjects in the struggles of modernity. (AJ, 36–7)

Once having argued that 'if man and woman exist, they do so only within the symbolic ... determined by language and by the political' (47), AJ doesn't see any advantage in contradicting that argument in practice by reverting to an arbitrarily separate category of 'real historical women'. AJ prefers instead to explore the most radical formulations and problematisations of the symbolic, and of woman within those formulations, in order to evoke the 'promise and fear ... at the heart of gynesis' (AJ, 73), 'the putting into discourse of "woman" or the "feminine" as problematic' (AJ, 236). Where both AJ and AD are equally and clearly dissatisfied with the woman produced in phallocentric representations, AD would seek to 'correct' that representation of woman by reference to women as they (somehow) *are* in spite of such representations, while AJ would 'redefine' woman by reference to a series of radical recent attempts to recast *representation* itself.

That there are at least two (related as well as distinct) feminisms at work in these differences between AJ and AD is obvious enough. By 'at work' we mean to indicate the way in which the two feminisms are complexly bound up in both texts; we do not mean to say that AD and AJ clearly and unproblematically side with one or the other. However both acknowledge this difference (within feminism) and characterise it as a difference between the Anglo-American and French (AJ,15–22; AD,186), one more empirical, more pragmatic, the other more theoretical. Concerning the terms of address of the two books, there is also the distinction to be made between semiotics and poststructuralism, for whereas both of those currents are seen as arriving from France and Europe, the latter is a more recent arrival, one still more clearly marked by its transatlanticism. For AJ however, the difference in play here is important. It is read as a difference between more conservative and more radical feminisms:

> It is too easy to put gynesis down to 'idealism' as somehow opposed to feminism, a true 'materialism.' As long as we do not explore the boundaries of and possible common spaces between modernity and feminism; as long as we do not recognize new kinds of artificial, symbolic constructions of the subject, representation, and (especially) experience, we will be engaging in what are ultimately conservative and dated polemics, not radical theory and practice. (AJ,155)

If one were also, again, to call this divergence between feminisms a V-effect, here before the event of a more detailed analysis, where would that take us?

> « « *It might take us to a point where our 'A V' looks like an 'up yours!' sign in the face of feminism – which we hope it is not, though we (like*

Godolphin re his motives) can never be sure how our signs will arrive, or at what destinations. So in a more than purely precious sense: we do not know what we are writing. How could we then pretend to be able to see 'inside' feminism(s), to speak for them? There is considerable risk, then, in what we write here. The very worst we could hope for would be to be read as giving advice, or cultivating our Jardine at the expense of an always necessary and 'more pragmatic' feminism. » »

The analysis we have already partly embarked on centres on a series of texts, or names representing texts, which come under the spotlight in AJ and AD; Calvino, Abish, Foucault, Derrida, Roeg, Pynchon. And through discussion of how AJ and AD, as 'master' texts, relate to their chosen subtexts, we might be able to elaborate a concept of difference, at least textual difference, in a couple of feminisms. And this might in turn shed new light on the distinction between 'woman' and 'women' as well as that between a radical and a conservative feminism.

Both books introduce early on texts which seem to read as allegories. For AD, the text is Calvino's *Invisible Cities* and, for AJ, Abish's 'Crossing the Great Void'.[8] Zobeide is Calvino's city in which men dream they see a naked woman running, dream of pursuing and losing her, and so build a city like the one in the dreams, only rearranging spaces and walls so she will be unable to escape again. AD reads as follows:

> The city is a text which tells the story of male desire by performing the absence of woman and by producing woman as text, as pure representation.... Like cinema, the city of Zobeide is an imaginary signifier, a practice of language, a continuous movement of representations built from a dream of woman, built to keep woman captive. (AD, 13, 14)

Zobeide thus remains within definable rhetorical relations, as metaphor or allegory of cinema, as representation of male desire and occlusion or exclusion of woman (other than through fixed representations of her), who is nevertheless posited as object of that desire. Throughout the chapter Zobeide continues to be evoked as being *like*, as being the aistheton for, various things – cinematic theory (AD, 17–18), Lévi-Strauss' structuralism (21), Lacan's psychoanalysis (21), Metz' analyses of identification (29), questions of signification, representation, and subject processes –

returning us to cinematic theory in general (31). And the metaphoric narrative develops, finally, such that the analyst, the feminist film theorist, is herself walking, not running, through the city, presumably clothed and not naked, performing the contradiction of existing within the dominant institutions of discourse (those which rely on but exclude woman), while at the same time resisting them. By consenting first to play a man's game, that is by feigning to fill the space man provides for her in his desire, the feminist theorist seeks to alter her experience of that space and thus challenge the designs of male desire.

> « « *De-signs of de-sires. The masters de-sign, refuse to sign, or cross out their signings in order to hide behind anonymity in their schemes, their designs. Calvino simply refers to 'men of various nations', their only unity being 'an identical dream', the fleeing woman. While feminism actively seeks the meaning of (this) 'woman', patriarchy already knows too well the meaning of 'man' and so erases it at every step. Derrida's re-writing of the semiotic term 'sign' as a verb which thus invokes, provokes and problematises the signature as network of textual designs and desires, could accordingly be called a* gynetic *sign practice. In that the signature is one linguistic event par excellence which cannot be spoken but only written, we are reminded again of the bar which ties Derrida's deconstruction of the logocentric and the feminist critique of phallocentrism.*[9] » »

Thus Zobeide – and Godolphin's invisible city could be read identically, especially the Vheissu he narrates/confesses to VW (151–7) – functions as more than simple allegory. There is a double operation of likeness and dissimilarity at work here. While in one breath AD posits Zobeide as that which is like cinema, in the next:

> I chose this text as a pre-text, a subterfuge, a lure, and an expedient.... The story of Zobeide therefore is a pretext to dramatize and to perform on my part the contradiction of feminist discourse itself: what does it mean to speak, to write, to make films *as* a woman? (AD, 14)

As AD would have it, in spite of or as well as the comparisons made between Zobeide and cinema and cinematic theory, the story of Zobeide comes now to be a new story of the woman within it – as a lure, as a dramatisation of a contradiction. What the shift from text-as-allegory to text-as-pretext does is throw textual relations into an abyssal structure. Such is the practice of pretextualisation. It allows for an allegory to be an allegory of two things at the same time, one involving a simple one-to-one correspondence – between Zobeide and cinema – the other masquerading as such, but allowing the woman within the allegory to deny its allegorical status. The allegorical status of Zobeide allowed it to be compared to cinema, to a cinema formed by phallocentric discursive formations; but once allegory is replaced by pretext the former allegory cannot hold. It becomes a whole other question, that of a radicalisation of textual operations held to be the basis for elaboration of the relation discussed above, that between women and woman:

> a critical feminist reading of the text, of all the texts of culture ... changes the representation into a performance which exceeds the text. For women to enact the contradiction is to demonstrate the non-coincidence of woman and women. To perform the terms of the production of woman as text, as image, is to resist identification with that image. (AD, 36)

What is perhaps not as explicit as it could be here is the idea that the women, one of whom has, it seems, just enacted the contradiction and performed the text of Calvino, exists not historically, as flesh and blood, at least not for these readers, but rather as reading, enactment and/or performance, and so remains within the discursive formations which, as she admits, she could not exist outside of. Despite the overall theory focused on 'real' historical women, then, AD nevertheless seems to admit a space for textual relations[10] – yet those relations do not lead to a subsequent retheorisation which would inevitably make the category of the 'real' more problematic.

Like Calvino's *Invisible Cities* in AD, Abish's 'Crossing the Great Void' encloses a chapter of AJ. Here the allegorical relation is made explicit:

> But rather than pursue an interpretation at this point, let this almost plot-summary stand simply as an allegory ... [for] ... *Gynesis*: a new kind of writing on the woman's body, a map of new spaces yet to be explored, with 'woman' supplying the only directions, the only images, upon which Postmodern Man feels he can rely. (AJ, 52)

For the story tells of a certain Zachary who is looking for his father, last seen in the Great North African Desert, and who is offered the help of a woman named Track who claims she has a map of the region tattooed on her back. There is thus a remarkable similarity between the stories of Zobeide and Zachary – in the first case a city built from the search for fleeing woman; in the second a search through a desert with a woman as guide. But more than that, in each case the woman is not so much the object of the search (or not just that, more in one case than the other), as the metonymic signifier of the search itself. In Zobeide the paths she takes become the streets of the city; in the Great Void the tracks are written upon her body. Hence the question asked of the text by the feminist critic or theorist is the same:

> Among all the pathways, roads, tracks, and spaces in Abish's short story, all crisscrossing their ways through false images, illusions, and misconnections, which direction might or should the feminist critic take? (AJ, 51)

Can a feminist writer take the part of a woman who exists only as the object of man's desire, can she inhabit the city of his dreams; can she on the other hand identify with a woman who has gained for herself the power to show the way, as in Abish (rather than creating the way out of fear as she flees, as in Calvino), when this has been at the expense of the integrity of her body? But there is an important difference in the stories which returns us to the initial difference between these two feminisms.

Zobeide is the city of man's representations; woman is asked to bear those representations. The feminist in AD does not perform that role as asked or expected and so hopes to force change in how those representations operate. The woman in the 'Great Void', on the other hand, brings a variety of choices to a man whose system is already in crisis – the map tattooed on Track's back becomes in the event a labyrinth of different feminisms and different postmodern problematisations of representation – among which a feminist choice is to be made. In the terms of AJ's discussion, the map is primarily the inscription of various male theorists' (Lacan, Deleuze, Derrida) interrogations of the problematic, but it is not insisted here that what is involved is a straightforward exploitation of the female body. That idea does have some currency at various points in the discussion, and we shall return to it. But there is the suggestion that the process has involved the collusion or collaboration of women theorists' (Kristeva, Cixous, Irigaray) inquiries also.

Thus what separates AJ from AD is the latter's desire to 'correct' representation by undermining (by fiat) the phallocentric hegemony within it, contrasting with the former's desire to profit as much as possible from rewritings of the whole field of representation and their apparent recourse to figures of woman for this purpose, in the hope and with the risk that what will emerge will be a new 'woman-in-effect'. (AJ, 25)

At this point it is necessary to attenuate our obvious preferences in this 'debate', preferences which ultimately have to do with getting a critical purchase on a novel (*V.*) whose gender politics is, by the standards of *any* feminism one might care to name, to say the very least, dubious. So if we keep returning to that difference between AJ and AD as feminisms, it is because they are both alike in seeking the failure or the success of representations of woman within *texts* and, in terms of their approach to those texts, they are much more difficult to tell apart than we have allowed up to now.

They both adopt very loose forms of allegorical resemblance and give themselves the possibility of departing from the terms of the allegory in order to read the text in, for want of a much better word, more 'deconstructive' ways. This movement or turn does not appear to be a problem for AJ, committed to a radical concept of textuality, and to the attendant notion of body, for its *gynema* is a conceptual projection that can only be articulated through textual material – 'a reading effect ... that is never stable and has no identity' (AJ, 25). It may become a problem if at some point the feminine references within the problematic lose their specificity, entangling woman 'in her own apocalypse' (AJ, 155). On the other hand, it appears as an obvious problem for AD, committed to the idea of 'real historical' women, inevitably inscribed within discursive practices but arbitrarily separated from them for the purposes of analysis and resistance.

The matter emerges as a problem in another discussion in AD, one involving a reading of the Nicolas Roeg film *Bad Timing*, and in the process referring to the work of Foucault. According to the Introduction:

> My analysis will start from certain notions contained in the writings of Michel Foucault which have become increasingly

influential in film theory, and engage them from a feminist critical position. The reading is again eccentric: it argues both with and against Foucault's concepts.... (AD, 9)

While it is not so clear in the discussion of *Bad Timing* to what extent the argument is with, in the sense of in favour of, Foucault, there is a marked change of tone once the argument is against. AD seems from the start to adopt a sort of ironic distance with respect to Foucault's ideas, noting that there is growing interest in them as a means of analysis of the 'practical field' – genres, techniques, audiences, distribution, spectatorship – in which cinematic discourse is deployed; and drawing on his concepts of power and resistance to argue, with caution, for a micro-analytics of cinema, and the possibility of resistance in immediate and local power relations (AD, 85–7). But, it is noted:

> Were one to adopt, and to adapt, Foucault's method of historical analysis to cinema ... one would have to abandon the idea of cinema as a self-contained system, semiotic or economic, imaginary or visionary. (AD, 85)

The danger lies therefore in what a redefining of the conceptual field might lead to in terms of certain cherished concepts within that field, given that 'no phenomenon or event [is left] outside the reach of [the] discursive order' (AD, 87). And the argument proceeds again along the lines of a problem of differentiation, sexual, symbolic, mythical, patriarchal, ideological, cultural:

> He speaks as if these plebeian masses were sexually or otherwise undifferentiated, as if these 'common people' were untouched by 'abstract' ideas, unencumbered by symbolic processes, mythical production, patriarchal structures – in short, as if they were immune to ideology, which is to say, outside of culture. (AD, 94)

This position relies on a notion of difference for which the paradigm is sexual difference, a notion of absolute difference relying on male and female as trancendental signifiers. Yet such a feminism is also caught in the paradox caused by recognising such a system to have allowed the institutionalisation of a phallocentric power structure. Thus for AD, it is repeated time and time again, 'a woman (or a man) is not an undivided identity, a stable unity of "consciousness", but the term of a shifting series of ideological positions' (AD, 14). This feminism does call for a redefining of the notion of difference, but it finds Foucault's series of shifting configurations to be going too far, and perhaps in the wrong direction.

> « « *One cannot have both a master-discourse of m/f relations governing all other possible sets of relations and, at the same time, MF's highly eventalised, local-specific (almost non-) reading of historical change, emergence and disjunction. It is equally contradictory for AD to accept MF's general reading strategies while he, for example, uses those strategies to read as over-policed, 'inconsequential bucolic pleasures' what she reads as sanctioned 'rape and sexual extortion performed on little girls' (AD, 94). If the general Foucauldian strategy can lead to such opposite analyses, what else is there to guarantee AD's reading over MF's?*[11] » »

The paradox returns in AD's reading of *Bad Timing*. This is a film in which a woman, Milena, falls victim to the malpractice, professional and sexual, of her doctor lover, Alex, and as a result bears the scar of a tracheotomy. The message is finally that the type of resistance woman resorts to, or the very fact of her resistance within a given micropolitical instance, becomes inscribed upon her body. Gender is reasserted through physicality: she is made to wear her sexuality on her throat. But according to AD's analysis, the scar is not the mark of a gendered sexuality so much as it marks the difference between terms of a contradiction:

> This resistance, the film suggests, is not located within the terms of the productive apparati of power/knowledge ... but neither is it located outside of those practices and discourses which constitute the given social world. It is, quite simply, difference .... Milena ... is neither bound by the rules and institutions of power/knowledge nor 'free' of them, and *this* contradiction is what the scar signifies: her passion and her silence, her experience of difference, her history – past, present – inscribed and displayed in her sexed body ... in contradiction, in excess of those dialectical oppositions. (AD, 95–6)

The position on difference here, if not directly comparable to Foucault's supposed 'undifferentiation', seems nevertheless to be closer to what can be loosely called a poststructuralist position. It would be easy to dismiss as a contradiction this 'resistance' which is also 'a mark ... of subjection' (AD,95) not produced within the power/knowledge apparati and not located outside of social practice and discourse. Such a resistance would seem to have everything to do with power and knowledge. Both within the terms of the narrative – Milena is operated upon and scarred but saved precisely because of the bad timing which is the film's major diegetic function and the crux of the relationship between Alex (the lover) and Netusil (the detective); and within the terms of the film's thematics – the violence done to the body can surely be read here as standing for the hermeneutic impulse, implicating medicine and psychoanalysis as policing institutions, making Milena victim of a will to possess and know in more ways than one but always within relations of power. But the importance of such a feminist position on difference is its acknowledgement of difference precisely as a *contradiction*, and as an excess of dialectical oppositions, as the mark of a relation rather than of a separation or distinction. Thus something of the scar's resistance is its resistance to a dialectical view of difference. But what else would seem to underwrite AD's reading of the scar here is its 'primary' inscription within texuality, and within narrative relations, thus directing the discussion and the analysis; and also its use as a mark of 'marking'; for it is the very characteristics of the mark, trace, or *restance*, which pertain to every written mark, that are being used here to describe this excessive and contradictory difference, dare we say *differance*. Though it is said that 'the scar is a sign of radical difference ... absolute negativity' (AD, 95), the chapter's title and subsequent discussion frame it as a 'now' which is also a 'nowhere', a negativity which functions as borders (AD, 101). Once again, however, AD's analysis explicitly evokes that *absolute* difference whose model is sexual difference, and *that* concept of difference is continually undermined by the formulations the argument borrows. There is, as it were, a constant but unconscious, untheorised erasure of the concept as it comes to be written in the text of AD. Thus in conclusion:

> What the filmic image of the scar inscribes is the figure of an irreducible difference, of that which is elided, left out, not represented or representable. (AD, 101)

On the contrary, as in the 'now'/'nowhere' formulation, there is representation here, that of a mark; it may well be the mark of the elided, the unrepresented or unrepresentable, but it is inscribed at least as mark, not so much of irreducible difference but of difference reducible precisely to effects of marking, of writing.

> « « *How to theorise this constant return to writing? What will operates here? As if writing were always threatening to become some new centre. For us it is rather that the monotony of this return, the uniformity of writing, its flatness, always defers a centre. So one might think: uniformity and flatness, writing as a desert; and then we would be Calvino's 'men of various nations' imagining, within it, 'woman'. One who always gets away. One who refuses to be stalled by the re-arranged spaces and walls of our textual city. That might be the reproach. Let us repeat, then, that a return to writing should not reduce the movement of feminism, that it can always escape, work like writing as an excess, that what we call 'writing' and 'feminism' will, both collectively and separately, always spread like a V.* » »

The whole of AJ's discussion is, on the other hand, informed by Derrida's writing such as our references to difference and differance have just evoked. He and Deleuze are said to be the two philosophers privileged in the study (AJ, 127), yet it is probably the name and text of Derrida which return more than any other. Although there is some discomfort about the prominence given to his ideas, the assumption seems to be, for AJ, that any discussion of 'strategies of genderization' or 'sedimentation of gender categories' (AJ, 188) in the context of the problematisation of representation, cannot but refer to Derrida if it is to stand a chance of engendering gynesis. And so it must also concentrate on 'hymen', 'invagination' and the 'woman' of Nietzsche and of philosophy, as prime examples of a discourse which borrows from the female and the feminine in order to deconstruct the apparatuses of phallogocentrism. Thus Derrida is far from being the brief mention in AJ that Foucault is in AD, where close attention is not given to the latter's texts, in spite of the close reading that AD makes of *Bad Timing*. On the contrary in AJ, expository readings of Derrida's texts form the basis of much discussion, and there is more than a token attempt to respond to the intricacies and double gestures of those texts in like kind. And whatever objection there might be, as we shall shortly discuss, it is not directed at the undecidability or non-differentiation of sexual difference. Derrida's hymen, which AD would no doubt read as an extreme provocation, is described by AJ with no discernible shift in tone:

> The hymen is the locus of the abolition of the difference between difference and nondifference.... Under Derrida's pen, the hymen .... becomes the father-less, always feminine paradigm of undecidability ... There is no question of woman here, 'but a metaphor' [*Dissemination*, 242] designating that which dances across the secure territories of truth, unsettling them. (AJ, 190–1)

The problem, when it arises, is rather what room is 'left here for our feminist questions?' (AJ, 191); whether this is a

> new ruse of reason, a kind of 'seducing' of feminist discourse ... a new kind of desire on the part of (Modern) Man to occupy all positions at once ... a new version of an old male fantasy: that of escaping the laws of the fathers through the independent and at the same time dependent female ... a way of depersonalizing sexual identity while maintaining the amorous relationship through women? (AJ, 207)

These are left as mostly rhetorical, unanswered questions, except for the tautological statement that 'what turns feminist criticisms will take at the angles of these questions – and others – will depend on how we respond to contemporary thought – a thought where woman *is* the angle' (AJ, 207). In other words how feminisms will respond will depend on how they will respond. Yet we should perhaps not read this only as tautology, just as we did not read AD's central contradiction as contradiction alone but also as a problematisation of absolute difference. We should read it instead as a deferral of the questions, for they are unanswerable except within a simple logic, the logic of phallogocentrism whose mastery AJ has been content to see Derrida deconstruct. For the questions finally cannot be answered in terms of 'ruses', 'desires', 'fantasies' – Derrida's strategies are surely all of those – but in terms of their effects and the readings performed upon them by feminist readers such as AJ. And as long as such readings seek to engage their object productively – and it would only be the most reductive reading which could not be said to do that, something like a reading which is a complete refusal to read – then Derrida's sedimentary genderisation becomes part of the ruses, desires, and fantasies of feminism.[12]

It nevertheless remains the case that we have turned AJ (and the 'unspoken' text of AD) back at AD. Why, we ask, could the work of Foucault not undergo the sort of 'pretextualisation' previously performed on Calvino, via the same kind of reading which inscribed its resistance and so became a reading of transformation? While it is not to be denied that strategies of resistance may borrow differing degrees of opposition, tending here towards a measure of sympathy, there towards an outright refusal, what is not clear is the logic which informs such positioning, and such a question seems to return us to our point of departure. Feminism and feminisms are rightly preoccupied with positions and positionings. For such a preoccupation, the need for shifting strategies, has brought them to the possibility of treating texts in a variety of ways which do not respect authorial intention, the text's integrity, its teleology, but seek to engage reader and text in a dynamic relation. But what those, or these, feminisms do not always realise fully, is the extent to which, once begun, such an enterprise becomes an interminable struggle, a continuous effort of negotiation of the text's border, like a pirouette upon a hymen; that in talking and writing about texts, and perhaps within feminisms themselves, the only question is how this fits with that. A question, still, of difference.

Yet such a question about such an enterprise, as perhaps AJ's final question for Derrida does realise, obeys a logic of tautology that needs to be bent to an economy, even a dance, of differance. And the model proposed here is that of a V, if not yet, or ever, of 'A V'. A V which must be made to exceed Stencil's simple quest, for everything he learns about it up to its uncertain sex, genus, and species, and beyond, through its Veronicas and Victorias, rats and prosthetic Bad Priests, Valettas and Vheissus, belies the singularity of the *telos* he seems to insist on ascribing to it. This much we have been through already elsewhere and concluded that V is the sign of divergence constituted by originary difference. Thus in V, or V., inasmuch as she be a woman, there plays the hymen of that difference.

Let us look more closely at the logic of *V.* as, in AJ's words, a 'thematization ... of gynesis'. After discussing Vheissu as 'one of the most important V functions' (AJ, 248), suggesting that *V. is U.*

(you) and thus beside the point in this quest for an eternally absent 'other', AJ concludes:

> So perhaps if V. is not Vheissu (which is you), perhaps she is nothing more than an image, a concept, 'like a woman': 'half of something there are usually two sides to' (*V.*,10). (AJ, 249)

> « « The reading of Vheissu as 'V is you' is also noted by Leverenz, though he doesn't make the further transformation to 'U'. Levine prefers to read it as the Sartrean vécu, lived experience, something familiar, other than other. Hite, to whom we owe this collection of Vheissian versions, states confidently that 'it is a pun – "Wie heisst du?," "What is your name?"'[13] All of these sound equally plausible and fishy to us and we refuse to be collaborators, unless it be to read AJ's U/V function in the light of the importance of colour in Vheissu, how it represents the country's only depth, like living in 'a madman's kaleidoscope' (155). » »

Yet, having astutely explicited this U/V function, AJ, committed nonetheless to an elaboration of woman as concept, is thereafter content to return to *V.*'s readings of V. as primarily a series of *women*, concluding with the story of the Bad Priest. And while it is true that this prosthetic woman describes a 'body-without-organs ... the pure female desiring machine' (AJ, 252), to limit V. to a female body is to revert to the sometimes contradictory logic of AD, for V. continues to be as much site (and even when she is a body – a body after all which comes apart even down to its essential sexuality), as much a series of places, as a series of genderised forms. We have a woman Bad Priest who comes to pieces and is dispersed by the children who flee with their treasures (like, perhaps, the woman of Zobeide dispersed through the streets of the city); and a place akin to both lost horizon and polar waste whose practices are seen by a bewildered Godolphin as a tattooed woman (equally like, perhaps, Track's back map to an oasis for a misguided Zachary):

> '... their music, poetry, laws and ceremonies come no closer. They are skin too. Like the skin of a tattooed savage. I often put it that way to myself – like a woman. I hope I don't offend.' (155)

Vheissu as other V. must continue to resonate, especially in connection with the Bad Priest, for she/it displays strikingly similar characteristics, especially the violence of competing forces expressed for the Bad Priest as a decomposition, but which in Vheissu is a feature of its composition:

> Vheissu is hardly a restful place. There's barbarity, insurrection, internecine feud. (155)

Yet that violence also has the positivity of constant change, playing upon a signifying surface which is the sole medium of meaning, for here there is surface without depth, skin without soul:

> Everything changes. No sequence of colors is the same from day to day. As if you lived inside a madman's kaleidoscope. Even your dreams become flooded with colors, with shapes no Occidental ever saw. ... They are, they are Vheissu, its raiment, perhaps its skin ... beneath her skin ... Nothing. (154–5,188)

The tattooed woman's skin, the erotic scar, becomes the site of that violence and that change, and of phallogocentric man Godolphin's last g(r)asp at a will to mastery and truth:

> soon that skin, the gaudy godawful riot of pattern and color, would begin to get between you and whatever it was in her you thought you loved ... it would get so bad that you would begin praying to whatever god you knew of to send some leprosy to her. ... To flay that tattooing to a heap of red, purple and green debris, leave the veins and ligaments raw and quivering and open at last to your eyes and your touch. I'm sorry. (156)

Godolphin has his epiphany, as one might expect, starving and freezing in the Antarctic cold:

> The skin which had wrinkled through my nightmares was all there had ever been. Vheissu itself, a gaudy dream ... a dream of annihilation. (190)

Vheissu then rejoins woman not just by virtue of her tattoo but also in terms of her entanglement within her own apocalypse, and inscribes herself as site of emerging *gynema*. The difference between such a Vheissu and a V. initial to a yet-to-be-ascribed historical name, could perhaps be that between AJ's 'woman' as concept and AD's 'real historical' women. That is the case as long as V. reduces to the Veronicas and Victorias that haunt generations of Stencil.

Our point here is this. Just as *V.* and V. recount (the failure of) a somewhat less than postmodern conceptualisation of woman as truth at the same time as they thematise gynesis, even a gynetic feminism will manifest an originary divergence between itself and its others. That is, it will become to some extent the battle ground of its own becoming. And so it is with the differences between AD and AJ, coming and going between each other, between their positions and their lapses, the one practising a radicalised notion of text here, and a reductive process of reading there; the other risking entanglement in its own apocalypse here, and the stasis of a pleonastic questioning there. Between feminisms, between allegory and pretext, and between woman and women the divergence that is all V.

A V, we said earlier, that is not, yet, 'A V'; cannot be, at least until the end, and then only in deference to certain institutional forms. Our 'A V', thus far and thus limited, borrows a discursive tone and form of analysis which posits a series of texts – especially AD and AJ – as knowable objects, whose central sense, if not truth, is attainable by means of familiar rhetorical ploys of comparison, exposition, *sous-entendre*, and so on.

So it turns out that 'A V''s AJ and AD occupy a rhetorical position hardly much different after all from AD's 'real historical' women. Alec and David, by means of 'A V', turn out in deed to resemble AD, in allegorical if not pretextual terms. By contrast, in a former 'V' (Chapter 7) we tried to develop what we can now confess to being a pretextual approach to *V.*, and in so doing to elaborate a V perhaps more closely resembling AJ's woman than AD's empirical women. But that distinction between this 'A V' as discourse or 'analysis' and the earlier 'V'-chapter as writing is only summary, and both come and go to some extent between the two modes of what Derrida refers to as a 'double science'. Similarly AJ almost always maintains a 'discursive', even analytic, tone in elaborating gynetic woman, so that the distinction between AJ and AD can appear as one not so much of approach as of object. However AJ's woman is far from being merely the *correction* of a false representation of AD's 'real historical' women. It/she is a projection, absent as a knowable object from the text. It/she remains, as it were, to become – in forms obeying the processes of new representations; merely sketched in profile within the critiques of phallogocentric representation undertaken by the male philosophers under discussion. So always, discourse-that-would-be-writing exists for the most part as projection, experiment, surprise.

Hence 'A V', borrowing from the profile or projection of AJ and the pretextualisation of AD to let initial letters do the work of writing in an article dominated by discourse; in order to outline whatever difference between the two as effects of signature and ruination of inside/outside distinctions, practices of invagination which bring us back to what is here being called play of hymen.

« « *In AJ there exists a profile of familiarity with a certain Derrida, one we can call a Jacques – hence aD or aJ – the one which risks itself as signifier of a grammatological enterprise intent on undermining the authority of the proper name. In AD, where the single word 'Derrida' appears once (AD, 164) as a pretext for a footnote sending the reader to Spivak (AD, 212), there is no real engagement, let alone the marriage of convenience of AJ, just that orphan practice of pretextualisation, a token Derrida before the name or the letter.* » »

'A V' compares also two sides of a particular medium of modernity, what for Gregory Ulmer will usher in the 'open pedagogy' that is grammatology's most obvious and important application.[14] In these terms a reductive view of AD is tempting. On that reading AD, in contrast to AJ, becomes the audio-track of a standard narrative film in spite of calls for 'a continued and sustained work with and against narrative' (AD, 156); for its voice serves to complement the bodies of its central 'real historical' women, to fix them as preexisting objects of knowledge, in spite once again of the acknowledged, but we think contradictory, fact that such women exist only within discourse. By the same AV-reduction, AJ on the other hand becomes a visual track, like Vheissu, the experiments in representation it analyses 'flooded with colors, with shapes no Occidental ever saw'. We approach and avoid such a reductive reading, not wishing to invoke an Authorised Version, absolutely not of feminism(s) generally, and not even of the two particular feminist texts in question.

However, 'A V' does not pretend to hide its own sympathies, finds finally that the positionings of (at least two) feminisms, whether they acknowledge this or not, put into effect a play of differance that must always exceed any notion of absolute difference based on the sexual. A play of differance not reducible to the sexual but articulated through the hymen as figure of undecidability. 'A V' seeks to demonstrate that undecidability in an indefinite article, a 'V' whose hymen comes about, now, as an effect of an inversion. Standing in contrast to a 'V' already mentioned, 'A V' makes explicit the hymenal bar and the marriage to V which means its disappearance. Without that hymen, A and V would revert to being inverted terms within a simple opposition. But such a graphic of absolute difference is outside the scope of the writing instruments here in use, which leaves us now with the promised 'A V'.

■ ■ ■ ■ ■ ■ ■

« « *Projection:* « « « « « «   **A** *the ascending rocket, Gottfried depending on the always undecidable hymen effect within it.* **V** *the fall of the same. As with all projections, we can only wait to see how it falls out.*

Notes

1. J. Derrida, *Dissemination*, trans. B. Johnson (Chicago: University of Chicago Press, 1981), p. 239.
2. References to *V.* are to the Bantam Books edition (New York, 1964) and are given in parentheses in the text.
3. A. Jardine, *Gynesis: Configurations of Woman and Modernity* (Ithaca: Cornell University Press, 1985). Subsequent references are in the text and employ the abbreviation 'AJ'.
4. T. de Lauretis, *Alice Doesn't: Feminism, Semiotics, Cinema* (Bloomington: Indiana University Press, 1984). Subsequent references are in the text and employ the abbreviation 'AD'.
5. M.R. Siegel, *Pynchon: Creative Paranoia in Gravity's Rainbow* (Port Washington: Kennikat Press, 1978), p. 53. For Clerc 'the author's sympathy for children comes through so genuinely' in the case of Ilse and Bianca. See his *Approaches to 'Gravity's Rainbow'* (Columbus: Ohio State University Press, 1983), p. 19.
6. G. Ulmer, *Applied Grammatology: Post(e)-pedagogy from Jacques Derrida to Joseph Beuys* (Baltimore: The Johns Hopkins University Press, 1985), p. 17. J. Derrida, 'Differance', in his *Speech and Phenomena, and Other Essays on Husserl's Theory of Signs*, trans. D.B. Allison (Evanston: Northwestern University Press, 1973), p. 132.

7. In mathematics, one of the ways of managing a sudden transgression or *Aufhebung* from one part of a system (to a second part not usually abutting the first) is through a 'fold' in the fabric of the system, a doubling-back. This is sometimes called a 'catastrophe'. In the present case it is more of a cata-trope, a downward figure, a V.
8. I. Calvino, *Invisible Cities*, trans. W. Weaver (New York/London: Harcourt Brace Jovanovich/Secker & Warburg, 1974), p. 39. Originally: *Le città invisibili* (Turin: Einaudi, 1972). W. Abish, 'Crossing the great void', in *In the Future Perfect* (New York: New Directions, 1977).
9. On this see E. Grosz, 'Derrida, Irigaray and deconstruction', in J. Borghino et al. (eds), *Leftwright*, Intervention 20 (Sydney: Intervention Publications, 1986), pp. 71–81.
10. We cannot follow all the aspects of AD's unelaborated notions of textuality here. Many remain by implication within the notions of woman/women as discursive effect. Perhaps the most explicit statement made is surprisingly 'deconstructive' in approach (or is it a throwback to Althusser?), approving 'symptomatic' readings which seek out 'the invisible subtext made of the gaps and excess in the narrative or visual texture of a film' (p. 57). Yet, once again, what seems to be advocated is a corrective reading that will replace the missing woman with a satisfactory representation of her.
11. M. Foucault, *The History of Sexuality, Volume 1: An Introduction*, trans. R. Hurley (New York: Vintage, 1980), p. 32.
12. AJ's identification of the 'ruse of reason' with the strategies of modern man (or men) always risks marginalising feminism, reproducing it as a discourse of unreason and thus of desire and fantasy *at the expense of*, for example, rationality and analysis. This perhaps shows how difficult a course both AD and AJ are embarked on, writing 'scholarly' texts against the 'ruse of reason'. The problem could be recast as that of the marginality of feminism though that would come as hardly any surprise or threat. The de-marginalisation, the making 'proper' and 'scholarly' of feminist discourse – which AD, AJ and also the present text risk in their different ways – might, in fact, turn out to be no more than an incorporation, a pacification of

> that doodle in the margins: feminism. In the scenario as it now stands feminism appears as a character only in the most cryptic sense, that is, as a graphic mark. How is that mark transformed into a proper name . . . ? How is it written, from the margins, into the body of the text? It might be said that feminism is written in . . . not as a character but as a body of knowledge. Let's call that body of knowledge 'Feminist Theory'. As marginalia feminism is not, however, a disciplined body. It is the activity of writing that constitutes a disciplining process – the transformation of a political movement into an academic discipline. Paradoxically it can be argued that this very process – the writing in of Feminist Theory, the disciplining of feminism – constitutes, at the level of institutional politics, a writing out of feminism.

From L. Stern, 'High noon in the valley of the dolls or the character of feminism', *Australian Journal of Cultural Studies*, Special Issue on Literature and Popular Culture (1987), pp. 106–18. This quotation, p. 109.

13. M. Hite, *Ideas of Order in the Novels of Thomas Pynchon* (Columbus: Ohio State University Press, 1983), pp. 54, 161. The Levine and Leverenz readings appear in the former's 'Risking the moment: anarchy and possibility in Pynchon's fiction' in G. Levine and D. Leverenz (eds), *Mindful Pleasures: Essays on Thomas Pynchon* (Boston: Little Brown, 1976), p. 136, n4.
14. Ulmer, pp. 304–7. We find Ulmer to be a little optimistic here.

8
Fall out

Nuclear war, so Derrida tells us, and we see no reason, not quite yet, to dispute it, though if we were to live underground in Nevada, Mururoa, or a handful of other warm places on the globe, then we might be persuaded otherwise; nuclear war 'has not taken place: one can only talk and write about it ... some might call it a fable, then, a pure invention: in the sense in which it is said that a myth, an image, a fiction, a utopia, a rhetorical figure, a fantasy, a phantasm, are inventions'.[1] So we begin with our own nuclear fable, or, you might say, our limited nuclear engagement.

Before us, perhaps just before the end of the world, in the course of writing this chapter, two books: *Gravity's Rainbow* by Thomas Pynchon and *Les Fins de l'homme: à partir du travail de Jacques Derrida*.[2] Each of these books has its ending in a kind of affirmation of community, which is also a dispersal. In the latter case: 'Silence. C'est la fin, *the end*.... On applaudit. On sort' (695). In the former an invitation to a singalong as the rocket 'reaches its last unmeasurable gap above the roof.... Follow the bouncing ball.... Now everybody – ' (760). We try to imagine the *very* end, after that, after those endings, and in order to do so we have to imagine that it is still not quite the end, not the very unimaginable end upon which all this is posited.

So the hero of our present fable, a combined persona, manages to escape, to home for some, to a nuclear free zone in the South Pacific, on the beach waiting for the winter cloud eating dog food straight out of the can like Mad Max, with those same two books for company. Why? Their weight, length, compactness, any number of utopian or fantasmatic reasons, but it's true it could have been *Glas* or *Ulysses*, even the Bible. But they are in fact (that is, in fable) those ones before us, so if it were to happen to either of *us*, just now as we write, they would be the most convenient to grab. But getting back to the story: on the beach somebody big comes along sooner or later and doesn't want to share our hero's dog food. He has to think fast, make a choice between one of two projectiles as a first strike. But the dilemma is this: not simply which book to sacrifice first, which would make the better projectile, guessing weight against potential Kg/cm^2 in his bicep, length of trajectory, speed on impact and so on – that is enough of a problem in itself. No, the real dilemma is here: the one to choose *not* to throw – would it be because he wanted to keep it as a still better missile in reserve, or would it be because he considered it to be the better choice as reading matter after the aggressor was dispatched, with nothing else to do but wait and read until the very very end? And in any case, would the choice be the same or not, even assuming he had solved that initial dilemma? (And we think if Pynchon were telling this story he would have his hero throw either book, say 'Here, read this' and, as the adversary got engrossed, the hero would clobber him with the other one.) In other words, can a choice be made, here, close to the end, between the book as missile and the book as an object of reading? That is the core question, the nuclear question facing us here.

Which brings us back to the protonuclear question: why *these* two books before us as we write this chapter? We have already referred to a possible comparison between their parting words, but on closer examination we would be forced to admit that there we were exaggerating the extent of our arsenal. *Les Fins de l'homme* is not really before us here for the sake of all of its 695 pages, although given our fable that is an important consideration, but rather because it contains the original delivery of the paper 'Of an apocalyptic tone recently adopted in philosophy'.[3] It is that much slimmer volume, and the (already cited) 'Apocalypse' paper from *Diacritics* that form the corpus brought to bear on, and perhaps risking being sacrificed for, *Gravity's Rainbow*. Once again, fiction and theory. But which? It's unclear. An unclear fall-out.

So let us return to the question of the end of 'Of an apocalyptic tone' which would be more to the point than the end of *Les Fins de l'homme* as a basis of comparison with *Gravity's Rainbow*, except of course for the fact that there is much to recommend, from the point of view of a Gottfried for instance, the title of the full volume of the Cerisy conference. Here it is:

> The end approaches. Now there is no more time to tell the truth on the apocalypse. But what are we doing, you will still insist, to what ends do we want to come, when we come to tell you, here and now, let's go, 'come', the apocalypse, it's finished, that's all, I tell you this, that's what happens, that's what comes. (AT, 95)

Fall out 213

Again then, an exhortation to join in some sort of affirmation, some sort of song, or at least a refrain of the end; and at the same time a suspended dismissal, and we think the comparison with *Gravity's Rainbow* holds. The *QED* here being that both texts in question treat in some form or another of the eschatological.

Yet that does not resolve our nuclear question, that of the *rapprochement*, *détente* or whatever between these two texts. For since literature 'produces its referent as a fictive or fabulous referent, which in itself is dependent on the possibility of archivizing' (NA, 26–7), and to the extent that nuclear war implies the total destruction of literature as archive, then 'nuclear war is the only possible referent of any discourse and any experience that would share their condition with that of literature ... the absolute referent, the horizon and condition of all the others' (NA, 28). That does not mean that the only possible comparison, structural or otherwise, between two pieces of 'literature' is in terms of nuclear war in particular, or eschatology in general, but that the only *final* comparison, after all else and thus preceding all else, is on those terms. Or more precisely, that before or beyond all else, at least in terms of this hypothesis, writing can only ever be *about* nuclear war as total destruction. That idea is expressed in a different, but finally widened context in 'Of an apocalyptic tone':

> as soon as we no longer know very well who speaks or who writes (who addresses what to whom), the text becomes apocalyptic ... wouldn't the apocalyptic be a transcendental condition of all discourse, of all experience itself, of every mark or every trace? (AT, 87, translation modified)

Thus the sort of comparison we have given so far is rendered somewhat pleonastic, since it merely marks the inevitable eschatology of 'literature', the apocalypse of every mark. The texts before us now require further detailed analysis, development of a relationship as allies or adversaries if they, and hence this chapter, are to reply to the nuclear question. But, and we agree this may only be a ruse, such an advanced step (*pas*) cannot be advanced here, has to be refused (*pas*),[4] deferred, for it is beyond the scope of this chapter which would be content were it able, here at the end, to properly formulate its central or nuclear question. Remember there are two of them in current circulation: (a) is a choice to be made between book as missile and book as object of reading? and

(b) why these two books here before us now? – that is *GR/Fins*, or is it *GR/AT, NA*, for there is already fission here. We suspect (a) and (b) are something of the same question, since if books are to be treated as missiles, these particular two would be bound, together, to be prime candidates – and not only because of the momentum they could produce once launched by a nuclear survivor on a beach, or by a nuclear reader before a wordprocessor.

We can hear the objection that this chapter hardly seems to know where it is headed, that it seems to be avoiding the very issue it explicitly set as its object, namely how to read a book that is also a missile, or what special significance can be attributed to relating *Gravity's Rainbow* to some of Derrida's references to the apocalypse or to the nuclear age, outside of a common eschatological structure that we have heard pervades literature in general. To be quite honest, it is something of a chance, an accident, fall-out from a similar question raised earlier, which becomes here further radicalised, namely what are the operations of comparative literature in the nuclear age, if all literature has a common absolute or transcendental referent and that referent implies the end of literary reference, how does one text fit into another? That question was previously posed in bookmatching *The Crying of Lot 49* and *The Post Card* in Chapter 2.

But this chapter hardly knows where it is headed to the extent that every message is similarly defined, divided in its address and destination. That was the basis, stated above from 'Of an apocalyptic tone', developed from Derrida's 'Le Facteur de la vérité' and 'Envois',[5] for the constitution of every mark as apocalyptic. Which doesn't mean of course that, by 'consciously' seeking not to know where it is headed, it will be any more or less divided, but a certain type of division may become more explicit. And division is particularly the mark of the nuclear missile as we wait for it now, minutely programmed and accurately addressed, yet failing to arrive – not just because it hasn't been sent or because of some starwars fantasy that will intercept it before it falls, but simply because its arrival will be the end, an event far exceeding, monstrously so, the simple idea of arrival.

From that point of view we could further develop relations between our two texts in question, our two missiles in trajectory. *Gravity's Rainbow* radically divides the event of fiction, of character and narrative, so that for instance, it is impossible to tell with any certainty, among many other things, how the final pages relate to the structure of the novel, whether this is the firing of the 00000 with Gottfried inside enshrouded in lace and Imipolex G, Blicero's 'final madness', as the logical description seems to indicate, and then whether 'real' or 'imagined' since Blicero by this time may only be a myth (of course the event could also refer to an occurrence prior to its position within the narrative sequence since linear consecution was never a prime concern of this novel, and then, Blicero may only ever have been a myth); whether it refers to the firing of the reconstituted 00001 by the Schwarzkommando, or, as many critics assume, a nuclear missile indeed falling on the Orpheus Theatre in LA sometime around 1973.[6] Furthermore, even presuming we could answer those queries, any number of other questions could be raised concerning the 'descent' of the final paragraphs. Then *Gravity's Rainbow* also radically divides rhetorical operations, or at least 'Euclidean' rhetorical operations, allowing detour past any recall, as parable and parabola, for instance, are overwritten by the rocket trajectory to create a new material rhetorical space or order.[7] Finally, although we doubt the list ends here, *Gravity's Rainbow* radically divides generic categories so that the book can be viewed as a film as easily as it can be read as a novel, so that the unwieldiness and obscenity that so disturbed a Pulitzer prize jury was as much as anything else anxiety at the idea of just where this text might go, having so seriously exceeded the constituted bounds of 'literature'.[8]

The divided address of 'Of an apocalyptic tone' is concentrated, or summarised, in the event of 'viens'[9] as affirmative tone perverting the original sense of philosophy as Kant would have it defined (AT, 66–70), exceeding 'philosophical, pedagogical, or didactic demonstration' (AT, 93, trans. modified). 'Viens' similarly represents a problematic of *rhetoric* ('it submits with difficulty to the rhetoric required by the present scene'); of *narratology* ('"Come" no more lets itself be stopped and interpellated by ... a logic of the event'); and of *genre* ('a *récit*, already [of *d*errida *j*acques], a recitative and a song') (AT, 93, trans. modified).

All that makes for a somewhat explosive combination. 'Viens' risks the mystagogic, creation of cliques, priests and rituals, overtones of the oracular, such as Kant denounced (AT, 75–6); yet it is also inscribed within a program of 'lucid vigilance' (AT, 88) once one refers to the apocalypse as revelation and to the words of John; it risks obscurantism while seeking to clarify the constitution of the event (AT, 93), it risks a tone of authoritative convocation while seeking to function as invitation. Thus the adoption of an apocalyptic tone, the marking of the utterance with its constitutive apocalyptic structure, does nothing to avoid the problematic of rhetorical strategies that determined the whole exercise; on the contrary it relaunches that problematic with differentially increased urgency:

> Literature and literary criticism cannot speak of anything else ... they can only multiply their strategic manoeuvres in order to assimilate that wholly unassimilable other.... Capable of speaking only of that, literature cannot help but speak of other things as well, and invent strategies for speaking of other things, for putting off the encounter with the wholly other.... (NA, 28)

The strategic problem concentrated in the nuclear question concerns above all speed. One must remain 'critically vigilant', not rush into thinking the question of speed is a new one, yet remaining aware that in doing so one risks becoming a 'suicidal sleepwalker', or 'domesticating the terror' (NA, 21). Hence one must learn to go both fast and slow.

Similarly, the possibility that, by virtue of their varied rhetorical positionings, or posturings, or interventions, the texts before us remain poised to strike at any number of targets within a given discursive field, especially that where technology or philosophy borders literature – none of this allows us to return home and sleep safe in our literary critical or theoretical beds, secure in the knowledge that we are protected by an umbrella of dissuasive firepower. That begs rather than answers the nuclear question. The very reason for the emergence of what is being called 'nuclear criticism' resides in the notion that – besides the fact of its being a structure common to every trace, the apocalypse is too important a thing to be left in the hands of a fringe of experts or lunatics – it also inevitably, and therefore by obligation, concerns all writing that treats of 'information and communication, structures of language ... of codes and graphic decoding' (NA, 23).

Thus inasmuch as the nuclear question underwrites this text also, it raises for it, more explicitly and urgently than ever before, the matter of its own strategic choices:

> we are representatives of humanity and of the incompetent humanities which have to think through as rigorously as possible

the problem of competence, given that the stakes of the nuclear question are those of humanity, of the humanities.... In our techno-scientifico-militaro-diplomatic incompetence, we may consider ourselves, however, as competent as others to deal with a phenomenon whose essential feature is that of being *fabulously textual*.... In the undecidable and at the moment of a decision that has no common ground with any other, we have to reinvent invention or conceive of another 'pragmatics'. (NA, 22, 23)

From this point of view we can return for a final time to the nuclear sub-question: why these two texts (now that it has been established that there are at least three) before us now? And we ask, as ever, with a mind to realigning competences, or at least to locating and testing out the frontiers between competences. That is, we insist that a work of fiction can be deployed in a theoretical field as something other than an example or instance but rather as an intervention; and that a work of theory can equally be invested with a tone that redefines its habitual reliance on a limpid prose and a single address. When a scientifico-militaro-political apparatus gives itself the competence of total destruction which reaches well outside the scientific, military, and political domains, then it is time, if not quite too late, to reassess the resources of our own domain, its external and internal boundaries, to chance a crossover or two, to throw texts together in ways which also disperse or disseminate them, to give apocalypse a chance, even just to let our own discourse be informed by notions of fission, of trajectory, of strategic deployment, and indeed of various degrees and kinds of disarmament.

The possibility, threat, or fantasy of nuclear war is thus something of an *événement-limite* (in the sense in which the French term *date-limite* means a deadline) for the history of literature, an extreme case of the event. And this is so both because it threatens the literary archive with destruction and because it emphasises the divided nature of the event:

> Hence we meet again the necessity and impossibility of thinking the event, the coming or venue of a first time which would also be a last time. (NA, 30)

Nuclear war – total nuclear war – is, once again, that which occurs without happening, since it requires that we treat it as though it were *about* to happen, on the threshold. That is the very logic of dissuasion. And nuclear war is that which, should it occur or arrive, would negate its very purpose, that of winning or surviving or protecting. It is, we are told, a last resort, a fall-back position. But it is the event itself which falls back upon itself in odd reversal. It is quite simply, that which is the case, that which befalls (us), that whose event(uality) is a case of catastrophe, a fall of language and literature towards the end. That which falls.

... *Brennschluss* ...

The screaming that comes across the sky is, for Prentice and others, not the precursor but the event itself. If you hear the V2 coming it means it has already come, already exploded and you have survived it. Nothing extraordinary about that, it travels faster than the speed of sound. What about Slothrop's hardons then? They precede the falling of the rockets; his sexual conquests form a Poisson distribution that matches the bombs' targets, and some begin to wonder if his hormones don't form part of the missile's guidance system.[10] If they are right, whether or not it is Jamf's Pavlovian experiments with Imipolex-G gone awry, it means that not only is he the perfect operative to seek out the Rocket in the Zone, but as a personal note, the chances of there being a direct hit on his skull, of his being the rocket's very own fall guy, must be greater than for anybody else.

Given the paradox or nonsense that that represents in Aristotelian logic or in a physics of cause and effect, being reminded also that we are here within the structures of the fabulous and of the textual, not knowing where those structures exactly begin or end, or even what order they arrive in, the rocket's paradox and Slothrop's dilemma may best be (re)represented as tricks or turns of syntax. Tricks or turns of a syntax of what falls. We can be slightly more precise. Since the event, rendered of course in language by the verbal functions, is here divided, what might more faithfully represent the tricks or turns occurring in these cases, is the operation of the *preposition*, especially in terms of how, in English at least, it breaks from its noun phrase to come and modify the verb and so disturb the strictures of formal prose, capable finally of being the cata-*strophe* itself, that which falls at the end. Falls in, falls out, falls for, falls back..., the list is long if not endless and although other species and generations are waiting to arm themselves we don't seek to abuse the reader until she falls asleep, nor the speech police of whom one always risks falling afoul. We shall keep to the first two simple cases just cited, one of which of course spreads over all the rest like an ominous cloud, a return of the expressed, coming to settle and infect us all, some slowly, some more quickly, we won't go into all the attendant problems either, you've been thoroughly warned about them and we gave no illusions at least not since the title of this very chapter.

Allow us just one little aside that we promise will bring us back if not to earth then to ground zero. One of the few prepositions that is not used nor even mentioned with the verb 'fall' is *with*. Instead it is interpolated in Latinate form in the word that has come to be unleashed with fury upon the American (among other) academic scene(s) to distinguish it from a pure negativity and to better render a German word. We're talking about, always have been more or less, 'de*con*struction' ('The hypothesis of this total destruction watches over deconstruction, it guides its footsteps'. [NA, 27]).

If one were to give credence or credit to a current discourse on deconstruction, or Derridean deconstruction, the soft or the hard, there would be those who came to it or had it come to them; those who fell to it and those who fell over, or into it; and now, those who have fallen out of, or out with, it. Read Jeffrey Mehlman, presumably as one of those 'who came to deconstruction at a time when it had to be engaged against the expectations (and wishes) of one's teachers', on 'the era of its academic respectability'.[11] The importance of Derrida is not what it used to be; it is not as important for some, not in the same way as previously, because it has become too important in general. The French, we are continually told, never took him too seriously after the seventies,[12] but we suspect there must be another type of adulation at work which assumes that his current reputation in France is the signifier of the real importance of his ideas.

The tone of such a discourse is not particularly new, clear, or nuclear. It is an invasion rather than an explosion that is assumed to have taken place, the establishment of a new dominance and the dominance of a new establishment. But it is an invasion as pervasion which is evoked and so there is a phenomenon of fall-out, though in the two senses we have just suggested – some get the sickness while others renounce the cause. And one would not have to look too far to find a tone of apocalypse in the implied distinction between a preterite and an elect, those whose foreheads bear the Name of the Father and those inscribed with the mark of the Beast; there lurk sacrificial lambs and plagues and deaths of firstborn and more.

For the apocalypse is also a rerun of the passover and, as that feast suggests, initiated in the context of captivity, established as yearly ritual, and promised as final solution, there is nothing new to it. There is nothing new or nothing wrong in a continual redeployment and redefinition of discursive and theoretical positions, it takes place with or without explicit declarations to that effect. It is a function of the nuclear and of the apocalyptic as the jockeying which occurs once the end is in view, or whenever an end is in view:

> the end approaches, but the apocalypse is long-lived. . . . It [the task of demystification] is interminable, because no-one can exhaust the over-determinations and the indeterminations of apocalyptic stratagems. And above all because the ethico-political motif or motivation of those stratagems is never reducible to something simple. (AT 89, trans. modified)

The mistake is not that positions have changed and need to be corrected, for such a task – and we are involved in it at this instant – is an important and necessary form of analysis. The mistake is precisely to think it is ever over, a mistake which reduces the analysis to something simple, to the idea that there is now only adulation where there was once suspicion or hostility, to a series of rote or command words, or to a policing of discursive formations. The fact that there is a Derrida and a deconstruction that has arrived in the academy is a sure sign, for any close reader of Derrida, that he or it has also not arrived, cannot arrive in the singular sense that fellows-in fallen out seem to be all too eager to assume. The field of deconstruction like any field in the nuclear age is open to a whole series of deployments only some of whose positions have been defined or occupied, and indeed Mehlman would conclude by positioning his text in such a field, seeking to provoke and thereby raise the stakes in order to save deconstruction from itself.[13]

The type of response we are promoting here is more wary of the strategies that revert to military logistics with their attendant regimentation, like orders to fall into line, curb the body discursive, restrain the textual impulses, not that there aren't always laws to be endlessly negotiated, not that there is free space out there, it is more like the Zone Slothrop finds himself in with determined and ruthless opposing forces, vigilantes and prophets around every corner, and although one final analogy beckons for Slothrop last appears in the narrative first degree looking at a cryptic headline and a picture of Hiroshima before becoming a 'scattering ... among the Humility, among the gray and preterite souls ... adrift in the hostile light of the sky' (742), falling out all over the Zone, that is not where we want to come to, not yet, it would be too soon and analogy does not recover or contain the textual engagements being promoted here, so it is not the fall-out of the aftermath then but that marring of synchronies to be practised now as a pre-positioning within the nuclear age and the apocalyptic perspective, a resistance which is not reducible to a simple opposition like a falling out of personalities, more akin instead to a manipulation of syntax at the limits of taste, legitimacy and propriety, falling out of step and all but out of bounds with interventions upon the institutionalised academic forms, here and there, never escaping risks of impotence or recuperation but shifting each time the stance and the centre of gravity so one falls falls falls and dances as it falls.

■ ■ ■ ■ ■ ■ ■

We have not through all this forgotten our nuclear umbrella question. What marks the nuclear question and all the apocalypse asks in coming, is an answer still falling after the end.

Notes

1. J. Derrida, 'No apocalypse, not now: full speed ahead, seven missiles, seven missives', *Diacritics*, 14, 2 (1984), pp. 20–31. This quote p. 23. Henceforth 'NA', with page number given in parentheses in the text.
2. J.-L. Nancy and P. Lacoue-Labarthe (eds), *Les Fins de l'homme: à partir du travail de Jacques Derrida: Colloque de Cerisy 23 juillet – 2 août 1980* (Paris: Galilée, 1981). *Gravity's Rainbow* (New York/London: Viking Press/Cape, 1973).
3. J. Derrida, 'Of an apocalyptic tone recently adopted in philosophy', trans. J. P. Leavey, *Semeia*, 23 (1982), pp. 63–97. Henceforth 'AT' with further page references given in parentheses in the text. The

4. translation appears reprinted and modified in *Oxford Literary Review*, 6, 2 (1984), pp. 3–37. The *Semeia* version translates the paper as it was delivered at Cerisy (in *Les Fins de l'homme*, pp. 445–79); the *OLR* version takes account of the book form, *D'un ton apocalyptique adopté naguère en philosophie* (Paris: Galilée, 1983).
4. This egregious pun is a travesty of a much more important, identical, pun made by Derrida. See 'Pas' in his *Parages* (Paris: Galilée, 1986), pp. 19–116.
5. Both of these are to be found in J. Derrida, *The Post Card*, trans. A. Bass (Chicago: University of Chicago Press, 1987).
6. This reading of the final page is so common in Pynchon criticism that it almost passes without notice, as an authoritative reading. See, for a most explicit example, E. Mendelson, 'Gravity's encyclopedia', in G. Levine and D. Leverenz (eds), *Mindful Pleasures: Essays on Thomas Pynchon* (Boston: Little Brown, 1976), pp. 161–95 – especially pages 194–5. The other, less frequent, alternative is the much safer one of refusing a definite and positive thesis. Molly Hite, for example, takes the latter track, quoting the rocket as 'poised above the heads of "us"'. See M. Hite, *Ideas of Order in the Novels of Thomas Pynchon* (Columbus: Ohio State University Press, 1983), p. 97.
7. See Chapter 1 in this volume.
8. To be exact, they called it 'unreadable', 'turgid' and 'overwritten'. See Hite, *Ideas of Order*, p. 132. She is quoting from the article 'Newsmakers', *Newsweek*, 20 May 1974.
9. Derrida's use of this word, taken from the recurring invocation of *The Apocalypse of St John* (and also from Blanchot) relies more on resonance than precision, as the following discussion shows. It is an invitation to, or promise of an *event* without the sense of closure which the event implies. Thus for Derrida it works as a type of impossible philosopheme, similar to the *coup de don* of *Spurs* or Heidegger's gift of being. See J. Derrida, *Spurs/Eperons: Nietzsche's Styles*, trans. B. Harlow (Chicago: University of Chicago Press, 1979), pp. 108–19. In relation to Blanchot, see J. Derrida, 'Living on / borderlines', trans. J. Hulbert, in H. Bloom *et al.* (eds), *Deconstruction and Criticism* (New York: Seabury, 1979), pp. 75–175; and 'Pas' referred to in note 4 above.
10. *Gravity's Rainbow*, pp. 84–6.
11. J. Mehlman, 'Writing and deference: the politics of literary adulation', *Representations*, 15 (1986), pp. 1–14. This quote, pp. 1–2. Gregory Ulmer, on the other hand, reads the term 'deconstruction' as covering only a small part of a larger Derridean territory and cites Derrida to the effect that he used or uses the word 'for the sake of rapid convenience, though it is a word I have never liked and one whose fortune has disagreeably surprised me'. Accordingly, Ulmer prefers to pit the term 'grammatology' (as 'Writing') somewhat against and/or in complementary relation to 'deconstruction'. This is refreshing and accurate after such influential writers as Culler have used the latter term almost synonymously with everything 'after structuralism'. Derrida has taken a number of opportunities to

distance himself from the word but a recently published article concerning the translation of the word into Japanese has him explaining the complexity of its sense in very explicit terms. See J. Derrida, 'Lettre à un ami japonais', in *Pysché* (Paris: Galilée, 1987), pp. 387–93; C. V. McDonald (ed.), *The Ear of the Other* (New York: Schocken Books, 1985); G. Ulmer, *Applied Grammatology: Post(e)-pedagogy from Jacques Derrida to Joseph Beuys* (Baltimore: The Johns Hopkins University Press, 1985), p. x; J. Culler, *On Deconstruction: Theory and Criticism after Structuralism* (Ithaca: Cornell University Press, 1982). The Derrida quote is from 'The time of a thesis', in A. Montefiore (ed.), *Philosophy in France Today* (Cambridge: Cambridge University Press, 1983), p. 44.
12. Mehlman, 'Writing and deference', p. 8.
13. Mehlman, 'Writing and deference', p. 14.

Bibliography

The Bibliography contains all works referred to in the preceding chapters as well as a small number of others on and around Pynchon's writing which have been important – either positively or negatively – for our analyses. However, it is not a comprehensive bibliography, either of Pynchon scholarship or contemporary literary theory. Those interested in the former should turn to the journal *Pynchon Notes* which contains a continually updating list. Unfortunately we know of no parallel for CLT.

■ ■ ■ ■ ■ ■ ■

Abernethy, P. L. 'Entropy in Pynchon's *The Crying of Lot 49*', *Critique: Studies in Modern Fiction*, 14, 2 (1972), pp. 18–33.
Abish, W. *In the Future Perfect* (New York: New Directions, 1977).
Ames, S. 'Pynchon and visible language: écriture', *International Fiction Review*, 4 (1977), pp. 170–3.
Austin, J. L. 'Three ways of spilling ink', in his *Philosophical Papers*, 2nd edition (Oxford: Clarendon Press, 1970), pp. 272–87.
Barbour, J. 'Oedipa and the Scottish Demon', in T. Threadgold (ed.), *SASSC Working Papers, Vol. 2* (Sydney: Sydney Association for Studies in Society and Culture, 1988), pp. 55–63.
Barthes, R. *Elements of Semiology* (London: Cape, 1967).
Barthes, R. *Mythologies* (London: Paladin, 1973).
Barthes, R. *S/Z* (London: Cape, 1975).
Barthes, R. *The Pleasure of the Text*, trans. R. Miller (London: Cape, 1976).
Barthes, R. 'The death of the author', in *Image-Music-Text*, trans. S. Heath (London: Fontana, 1977), pp. 142–8.
Barthes, R. 'Writers, intellectuals, teachers', in *Image-Music-Text*, trans. S. Heath (London: Fontana, 1977), pp. 190–215.
Barthes, R. *A Lover's Discourse: Fragments* (London: Cape, 1979).
Barthes, R. *Camera Lucida: Reflections on Photography*, trans. R. Howard (New York: Hill and Wang, 1981).
Barthes, R. 'Towards a structural analysis of narrative', in S. Sontag (ed.), *A Barthes Reader* (London: Cape, 1982), pp. 251–95.
Bateson, G. *Steps to an Ecology of Mind* (London: Paladin, 1973).
Bennett, D. 'Parody, postmodernism, and the politics of reading', *Critical Quarterly*, 27, 4 (1985), pp. 27–43.
Berressem, H. 'Godolphin-Goodolphin-Goodol'phin-Goodol'Pyn-Goodol'Pym: a question of integration', *Pynchon Notes*, 10, October (1982), pp. 3–17.
Bloom, H. (ed.), *Thomas Pynchon* (New York: Chelsea House, 1986).
Bloom, H. (ed.), *Thomas Pynchon's 'Gravity's Rainbow'* (New York: Chelsea House, 1986).
Brome, V. *Ernest Jones: Freud's Alter Ego* (London: Caliban, 1982).

Calvino, I. *Invisible Cities*, trans. W. Weaver (New York/London: Harcourt Brace Jovanovich/Secker & Warburg, 1974). =*Le città invisibili* (Turin: Einaudi, 1972).

Chambers, R. *Story and Situation: Narrative Seduction and the Power of Fiction* (Minneapolis: Manchester University Press and Minnesota University Press, 1984).

Clark, B. L. and C. Fuoroli, 'A review of major Pynchon criticism', in R. Pearce (ed.), *Critical Essays on Thomas Pynchon* (Boston: G.K. Hall, 1981), pp. 230–54.

Clerc, C. (ed.), *Approaches to 'Gravity's Rainbow'* (Columbus: Ohio State University Press, 1983).

Clerc, C. 'Film in *Gravity's Rainbow*', in C. Clerc (ed.), *Approaches to 'Gravity's Rainbow'* (Columbus: Ohio State University Press, 1983), pp. 103–51.

Clifford, J. and G. Marcus (eds), *Writing Culture: The Poetics and Politics of Ethnography* (Berkeley: University of California Press, 1986).

Cooper, P. L. *Signs and Symptoms: Thomas Pynchon and the Contemporary World* (Berkeley: University of California Press, 1983).

Cowart, D. *Thomas Pynchon: The Art of Allusion* (Carbondale: Southern Illinois University Press, 1980).

Culler, J. *On Deconstruction: Theory and Criticism after Structuralism* (Ithaca: Cornell University Press, 1982).

Defoe, D. *The life & strange and surprising adventures of Robinson Crusoe of York, mariner,: who lived eight and twenty years all alone in an uninhabited island.../written by himself* (Oxford: Blackwell/Shakespeare Head Press, 1927).

Deitch, M. 'Wittgenstein and Derrida: no contest', unpublished paper.

de Lauretis, T. *Alice Doesn't: Feminism, Semiotics, Cinema* (Bloomington: Indiana University Press, 1984).

Deleuze, G. and F. Guattari, *Anti-Oedipus*, trans. H. R. Lane, R. Hurley and M. Seem (Minneapolis: University of Minnesota Press, 1986).

DeLillo, D. *White Noise* (New York: Viking/Penguin, 1984).

de Man, P. *Allegories of Reading: Figural Language in Rousseau, Nietzsche, Rilke, and Proust* (New Haven: Yale University Press, 1979).

Derrida, J. *Speech and Phenomena, and Other Essays on Husserl's Theory of Signs*, trans. D. B. Allison (Evanston: Northwestern University Press, 1973).

Derrida, J. *Of Grammatology*, trans. G. C. Spivak (Baltimore: The Johns Hopkins University Press, 1976). =*De la Grammatologie* (Paris: Éditions de Minuit, 1967).

Derrida, J. 'Signature event context', *Glyph*, 1 (1977), pp. 172–97.

Derrida, J. 'Limited inc.: abc...', *Glyph*, 2 (1978), pp. 162–254.

Derrida, J. *Writing and Difference*, trans. A. Bass (Chicago: University of Chicago Press, 1978).

Derrida, J. *Spurs/Eperons: Nietzsche's Styles*, trans. B. Harlow (Chicago: University of Chicago Press, 1979).

Derrida, J. 'Living on / borderlines', trans. J. Hulbert, in H. Bloom *et al.* (eds), *Deconstruction and Criticism* (New York: Seabury, 1979), pp. 75–175.

Derrida, J. *Positions*, trans. A. Bass (Chicago: University of Chicago Press, 1981).
Derrida, J. *Dissemination*, trans. B. Johnson (Chicago: University of Chicago Press, 1981). =*La dissémination* (Paris: Seuil, 1972).
Derrida, J. *Margins of Philosophy*, trans. A. Bass (Chicago: University of Chicago Press, 1982). =*Marges de la philosophie* (Paris: Minuit, 1972).
Derrida, J. 'Of an apocalyptic tone recently adopted in philosophy', trans. J. P. Leavey, *Semeia*, 23 (1982), pp. 63–97. =*D'un ton apocalyptique adopté naguère en philosophie* (Paris: Galilée, 1983).
Derrida, J. 'The time of a thesis: punctuations', in A. Montefiore (ed.), *Philosophy in France Today* (Cambridge: Cambridge University Press, 1983), pp. 34–50.
Derrida, J. *Signéponge/Signsponge*, trans. R. Rand (New York: Columbia University Press, 1984).
Derrida, J. 'No apocalypse, not now: full speed ahead, seven missiles, seven missives', *Diacritics*, 14, 2 (1984), pp. 20–31.
Derrida, J. *Glas*, trans. J.P. Leavey and R. Rand (Lincoln: University of Nebraska Press, 1986). =*Glas* (Paris: Galilée, 1974).
Derrida, J. *Parages* (Paris: Galilée, 1986).
Derrida, J. *The Post Card*, trans. A. Bass (Chicago: University of Chicago Press, 1987). =*La Carte postale, de Socrate à Freud et au-delà* (Paris: Flammarion, 1980).
Derrida, J. 'Lettre à un ami japonais', in his *Pysché* (Paris: Galilée, 1987), pp. 387–93.
de Saussure, F. *Course in General Linguistics* (London: Fontana, 1974).
Eagleton, T. 'The revolt of the reader', in his *Against the Grain: Essays 1975–1985* (London: Verso, 1986), pp. 181–4.
Forrester, J. 'Who is in analysis with whom? Freud, Lacan, Derrida', *Economy and Society*, 13 (1984), pp. 153–77.
Foucault, M. *The Order of Things* (London: Tavistock, 1970).
Foucault, M. 'Orders of discourse', *Social Science Information*, 10, 2 (1971), pp. 7–30.
Foucault, M. 'What is an author?' in his *Language, Counter-memory, Practice*, trans. D. Bouchard (Oxford: Blackwell, 1977), pp. 113–38.
Foucault, M. *The History of Sexuality, Volume 1: An Introduction*, trans. R. Hurley (New York: Vintage, 1980).
Fowler, D. '*A Reader's Guide to 'Gravity's Rainbow'* (Ann Arbor: Ardis Publishers, 1980).
Freadman, A. 'Untitled (on genre)', *Cultural Studies*, 2, 1 (1988), pp. 67–99.
Freud, S. *The Psychopathology of Everyday Life* (Harmondsworth: Penguin 1975).
Freud, S. *The Interpretation of Dreams* (Harmondsworth, Pelican, 1976).
Friedman, A. J. and M. Pütz, 'Science as metaphor: Thomas Pynchon and *Gravity's Rainbow*', in R. Pearce (ed.), *Critical Essays on Thomas Pynchon* (Boston: G. K. Hall, 1981), pp. 69–81.
Fussell, P. 'The ritual of military memory', in H. Bloom (ed.), *Thomas Pynchon's 'Gravity's Rainbow'* (New York: Chelsea House, 1986), pp. 21–8.
Gary, R. 'Genghis Cohn', *New York Times Book Review*, 12 June 1966, p. 35.
Genet, J. *The Thief's Journal* (Harmondsworth: Penguin, 1967).

Genette, G. *Figures I* (Paris: Seuil, 1966).
Genette, G. *Narrative Discourse* (Oxford: Blackwell, 1980).
George, M. *The Autobiography of Henry VIII* (London: Macmillan, 1987).
Gödel, K. *On Formally Undecidable Propositions of 'Principia Mathematica' and Related Systems*, trans. B. Meltzer (New York: Basic Books, 1962).
Gödel, K. 'Some metamathematical results on completeness and consistency, on formally undecidable propositions of *Principia Mathematica* and related systems I', in J. van Heijenoort (ed.), *Frege and Gödel: Two Fundamental Texts in Mathematical Logic* (London: Oxford University Press, 1970), pp. 83–108.
Grosz, E. 'Derrida, Irigaray and deconstruction', in J. Borghino *et al.* (eds), *Leftwright*, Intervention 20 (Sydney: Intervention Publications, 1986), pp. 71–81.
Hartley, J. *Videology* (London, Methuen, forthcoming).
Hartman, G. *The Fate of Reading and Other Essays* (Chicago: University of Chicago Press, 1975).
Henkle, R. B. 'Pynchon's tapestries on the western wall', *Modern Fiction Studies*, 17, 2 (1971), pp. 207–20.
Hipkiss, R. A. *The American Absurd: Pynchon, Vonnegut, and Barth* (Port Washington: National University Publications/Associated Faculty Press, 1984).
Hite, M. *Ideas of Order in the Novels of Thomas Pynchon* (Columbus: Ohio State University Press, 1983).
Hofstadter, D. *Gödel, Escher, Bach: An Eternal Golden Braid* (Harmondsworth: Penguin, 1980).
Hume, K. *Pynchon's Mythography: An Approach to 'Gravity's Rainbow'* (Carbondale: Southern Illinois University Press, 1987).
Hunter, H. Preface to *The Letters of Euler* (London, 1802).
Ickstadt, H. (ed.), *Ordnung und Entropie: Zum Romanwerk von Thomas Pynchon* (Hamburg: Rowalt, 1981).
Jakobson, R. 'Linguistics and poetics', in his *Selected Writings Vol. III* (The Hague: Mouton, 1981), pp. 18–51.
Jardine, A. *Gynesis: Configurations of Woman and Modernity* (Ithaca: Cornell University Press, 1985).
Jean, M. (ed.), *The Autobiography of Surrealism* (New York: Viking Press, 1980).
Kaufman, M. 'Brünnhilde and the chemists: women in *Gravity's Rainbow*', in G. Levine and D. Leverenz (eds), *Mindful Pleasures: Essays on Thomas Pynchon* (Boston: Little Brown, 1976), pp. 197–227.
Kermode, F. 'The use of codes', in S. Chatman (ed.), *Approaches to Poetics* (New York: Columbia University Press, 1973), pp. 51–79.
Kolodny, A. and D. J. Peters, 'Pynchon's *The Crying of Lot 49*: the novel as subversive experience', *Modern Fiction Studies*, 19, Spring (1973), pp. 79–87.
Krafft, J. M. ' "And how far-fallen?": Puritan themes in *Gravity's Rainbow*', *Critique: Studies in Modern Fiction*, 18, 3 (1977), pp. 55–73.
Laing, R. D. and A. Esterson, *Sanity, Madness and the Family, Vol 1: Families of Schizophrenics* (London: Tavistock, 1964).
Lakoff, R. 'Remarks on this and that', in M. W. Galy *et al.* (eds), *Papers from the Tenth Regional Meeting of the Chicago Linguistic Society* (Chicago: Chicago Linguistic Society, 1979), pp. 345–56.

Lasch, C. *The Minimal Self: Psychic Survival in Troubled Times* (London: Picador, 1985), pp. 154–62.
Leverenz, D. 'On trying to read *Gravity's Rainbow*', in G. Levine and D. Leverenz (eds), *Mindful Pleasures: Essays on Thomas Pynchon* (Boston: Little Brown, 1976), pp. 229–49.
Levine, G. and D. Leverenz (eds), *Mindful Pleasures: Essays on Thomas Pynchon* (Boston: Little Brown, 1976).
Lhamon, W. T. 'Pentecost, promiscuity, and Pynchon's *V.*: from the Scaffold to the Impulsive', in G. Levine and D. Leverenz (eds), *Mindful Pleasures: Essays on Thomas Pynchon* (Boston: Little Brown, 1976), pp. 69–86.
MacAdam, A. 'Pynchon as satirist: to write, to mean', *Yale Review*, 67 (1975), pp. 555–66.
Mackey, D. A. *The Rainbow Quest of Thomas Pynchon* (San Bernardino: Borges Press, 1980).
Mackey, L. 'Paranoia, Pynchon, and preterition', *SubStance*, 30 (1981), pp. 16–30.
Mailer, N. *Advertisements for Myself* (London: Deutsch, 1961).
Mangel, A. 'Maxwell's demon, entropy, information: *The Crying of Lot 49*', in G. Levine and D. Leverenz (eds), *Mindful Pleasures: Essays on Thomas Pynchon* (Boston: Little Brown, 1976), pp. 87–100.
McConnell, F. D. *Four Postwar American Novelists: Bellow, Mailer, Barth and Pynchon* (Chicago: University of Chicago Press, 1978).
McDonald, C. V. (ed.), *The Ear of the Other* (New York: Schocken Books, 1985).
McHale, B. 'Modernist reading, postmodern text: the case of *Gravity's Rainbow*', *Poetics Today*, 1, 1/2 (1979), pp. 85–110.
McHale, B. *Postmodern Fiction* (New York: Methuen, 1987).
McHoul, A. 'Announcing: a contribution to the critique of information processing models of human communication', *Human Studies*, 6 (1983) pp. 279–94.
McHoul, A. *Wittgenstein On Certainty and the Problem of Rule in Social Science* (Toronto: Toronto Semiotic Circle, 1986).
McHoul, A. 'Labyrinths: writing radical hermeneutics and the post-ethical', *Philosophy Today*, 31 (1987), pp. 211–22.
McHoul, A. 'Sociology and literature: the voice of fact and the writing of fiction', to appear in *The Australian and New Zealand Journal of Sociology*.
McHoul, A. and D. Wills, 'The late(r) Barthes: constituting fragmenting subjects', *Boundary 2*, 14 (1986), pp. 261–78.
Mehlman, J. 'Writing and deference: the politics of literary adulation', *Representations*, 15 (1986), pp. 1–14.
Mendelson, E. 'Rainbow corner', *Times Literary Supplement*, 13 June 1975, p. 666.
Mendelson, E. 'Gravity's encyclopedia', in G. Levine and D. Leverenz (eds), *Mindful Pleasures: Essays on Thomas Pynchon* (Boston: Little Brown, 1976), pp. 161–95.
Mendelson, E. (ed.), *Pynchon: A Collection of Critical Essays* (Englewood Cliffs: Prentice-Hall, 1978).
Mendelson, E. 'Introduction', in E. Mendelson (ed.), *Pynchon: A Collection of Critical Essays* (Englewood Cliffs: Prentice-Hall, 1978), pp. 1–15.

Moore, T. *The Style of Connectedness: 'Gravity's Rainbow' and Thomas Pynchon* (Columbia: University of Missouri Press, 1987).
Morgan, S. 'Gravity's Rainbow: what's the big idea?', in R. Pearce (ed.), *Critical Essays on Thomas Pynchon* (Boston: G. K. Hall, 1981), pp. 82–98.
Moulten, R. R. and J. J. Schifferes (eds), *The Autobiography of Science* (London: J. Murray, 1963).
Nancy, J.-L. and P. Lacoue-Labarthe (eds), *Les Fins de l'homme: à partir du travail de Jacques Derrida: Colloque de Cerisy 23 juillet - 2 août 1980* (Paris: Galilée, 1981).
Newman, R. D. *Understanding Thomas Pynchon* (Columbia: University of South Carolina Press, 1986).
Nicholson, C. E. and R. W. Stevenson, *Notes on Pynchon's 'The Crying of Lot 49'* (Beirut: Longman/York Press, 1981).
Oates, J. C. 'Success and the pseudonymous writer: turning over a new self', *New York Times Book Review*, 6 December 1987, p. 12.
Ozier, L. W. 'Antipointsman/antimexico: some mathematical imagery in Gravity's Rainbow', *Critique: Studies in Modern Fiction*, 16, 2 (1974), pp. 73–90.
Pearce, R. (ed.), *Critical Essays on Thomas Pynchon* (Boston: G. K. Hall, 1981).
Péguy, C. *Notre jeunesse*, in his *Oeuvres complètes 1873–1914, Tome IV* (Paris: Éditions de la Nouvelle revue française, 1916), pp. 39–254.
Petillon, P.-Y. 'Thomas Pynchon et l'espace aléatoire', *Critique*, 379, December (1978), pp. 1107–42.
Petillon, P.-Y. 'American graffiti: S = k log W', *Critique*, 462, November (1985), pp. 1090–1105.
Plater, W. M. *The Grim Phoenix: Reconstructing Thomas Pynchon* (Bloomington: Indiana University Press, 1978).
Poirier, R. 'The politics of self-parody', *Partisan Review*, 35, 3 (1968), pp. 339–53.
Prince, G. *Narratology: The Form and Functioning of Narrative* (Berlin: Mouton, 1982).
Pütz, M. 'Thomas Pynchon: history, self, and the narrative discourse', in M. Pütz, *The Story of Identity: American Fiction of the Sixties* (Stuttgart: Metzlersche Verlagsbuchhandlung, 1979), pp. 130–57.
Pynchon, T. 'Mortality and mercy in Vienna', *Epoch*, 9, Spring (1959), pp. 195–213.
Pynchon, T. *V.* (New York/London: Bantam Books/Jonathan Cape, 1964). First published by Lippincott (Philadelphia), March 1963.
Pynchon, T. 'Pros and Cohns', *New York Times Book Review*, 17 July 1966, pp. 22, 24.
Pynchon, T. *The Crying of Lot 49* (New York/London: Bantam Books/Jonathan Cape, 1967). First published by Lippincott (Philadelphia), March 1966.
Pynchon, T. *Gravity's Rainbow* (New York/London: Viking/Jonathan Cape, 1973). First published in this edition.
Pynchon, T. 'Introduction', in R. Fariña, *Been Down So Long It Looks Like Up To Me* (New York: Penguin, 1983), pp. v–xiv.
Pynchon, T. *Slow Learner: Early Stories* (Boston/London: Little Brown/Jonathan Cape, 1984). First published in this edition.

Pynchon, T. 'The heart's eternal vow', *New York Times Book Review*, 10 April 1988, pp. 1, 47, 49.
Quilligan, M. *The Language of Allegory: Defining the Genre* (Ithaca: Cornell University Press, 1979).
Quilligan, M. '["Thomas Pynchon and the language of allegory"]', in R. Pearce (ed.), *Critical Essays on Thomas Pynchon* (Boston: G.K. Hall, 1981), pp. 187–212.
Richardson, R. O. 'The absurd animate in Thomas Pynchon's *V.*', *Studies in the Twentieth Century*, 9 (1972), pp. 35–58.
Robbe-Grillet, A. *Jealousy* (=*La Jalousie*) (London: Calder, 1965).
Sanders, S. 'Pynchon's paranoid history', in G. Levine and D. Leverenz (eds), *Mindful Pleasures: Essays on Thomas Pynchon* (Boston: Little Brown, 1976), pp. 139–59.
Schaub, T. *Pynchon: The Voice of Ambiguity* (Urbana: University of Illinois Press, 1980.)
Schaub, T. 'Where have we been, where are we headed? A retrospective view of Pynchon criticism', *Pynchon Notes*, 7, October (1983), pp. 5–21.
Schütz, A. *Collected Papers, Vol. 1: Studies in Social Theory* (The Hague: Martinus Nijhoff, 1962).
Searle, J. R. 'Re-iterating the differences: a reply to Derrida', *Glyph*, 1 (1977), pp. 198–208.
Seed, D. 'Order in Thomas Pynchon's "Entropy"', *Journal of Narrative Technique*, 11 (1981), pp. 135–53.
Seidel, M. 'The satiric plots of *Gravity's Rainbow*', in E. Mendelson (ed.), *Pynchon: A Collection of Critical Essays* (Englewood Cliffs: Prentice-Hall, 1978), pp. 193–212.
Siegel, J. 'Who is Thomas Pynchon ... and why did he take off with my wife?', *Playboy*, March (1977), p. 97.
Siegel, M. *Pynchon: Creative Paranoia in 'Gravity's Rainbow'* (Port Washington: Kennikat Press, 1978).
Silverman, D. and B. Torode, *The Material Word: Some Theories of Language and its Limits* (London: Routledge & Kegan Paul, 1980).
Simberloff, D. 'Entropy, information and life: biophysics in the novels of Thomas Pynchon', *Perspectives in Biology and Medicine*, 21 (1978), pp. 617–25.
Simmon, S. '*Gravity's Rainbow* described', *Critique: Studies in Modern Fiction*, 16, 2 (1974), pp. 54–67.
Simmon, S. 'Beyond the theatre of war: *Gravity's Rainbow* as film', in R. Pearce (ed.), *Critical Essays on Thomas Pynchon* (Boston: G. K. Hall, 1981), pp. 124–39.
Slade, J. W. *Thomas Pynchon* (New York: Warner Communications, 1974).
Slade, J. W. 'Thomas Pynchon: postindustrial humanist', *Technology and Culture*, 23 (1982), pp. 53–72.
Smith, M. and K. Tölöyan, 'The new jeremiad: *Gravity's Rainbow*', in R. Pearce (ed.), *Critical Essays on Thomas Pynchon* (Boston: G. K. Hall, 1981), pp. 169–86.
Solberg, S. M. 'On comparing apples and oranges: James Joyce and Thomas Pynchon', *Comparative Literature Studies*, 26, March (1979), pp. 33–40.

Stark, J. O. *Pynchon's Fictions: Thomas Pynchon and the Literature of Information* (Athens: Ohio University Press, 1980).
Stein, G. *The Autobiography of Alice B. Toklas* (London: Bodley Head, 1933).
Stern, L. 'High noon in the valley of the dolls or the character of feminism', *Australian Journal of Cultural Studies*, Special Issue on Literature and Popular Culture (1987), pp. 106–18.
Stimpson, C. R. 'Pre-apocalyptic atavism: Thomas Pynchon's early fiction', in G. Levine and D. Leverenz (eds), *Mindful Pleasures: Essays on Thomas Pynchon* (Boston: Little Brown, 1976), pp. 31–47.
Tanner, T. 'V. and V-2', in E. Mendelson (ed.), *Pynchon: A Collection of Critical Essays* (Englewood Cliffs: Prentice-Hall, 1978), pp. 47–55.
Tanner, T. *Thomas Pynchon* (London: Methuen, 1982).
Tölöyan, K. 'War as background in *Gravity's Rainbow*', in C. Clerc (ed.), *Approaches to 'Gravity's Rainbow'* (Columbus: Ohio State University Press, 1983), pp. 31–67.
Ulmer, G. *Applied Grammatology: Post(e)-pedagogy from Jacques Derrida to Joseph Beuys* (Baltimore: The Johns Hopkins University Press, 1985).
Walsh, T. P. and C. Northouse, *John Barth, Jerzy Kosinski and Thomas Pynchon: A Reference Guide* (Boston: G.K. Hall, 1977).
Weisenburger, S. C. 'The end of history?: Thomas Pynchon and the uses of the past', in R. Pearce (ed.), *Critical Essays on Thomas Pynchon* (Boston: G. K. Hall, 1981), pp. 140–56.
Weisenburger, S. C. *A 'Gravity's Rainbow' Companion: Sources and Contexts for Pynchon's Novel* (Athens: University of Georgia Press, 1988).
Werner, C. H. 'Recognizing reality, realizing responsibility' in H. Bloom (ed.), *Thomas Pynchon* (New York: Chelsea House, 1986), pp. 191–202; also in the other Bloom volume, pp. 85–96.
Williamson, D. *Authorship and Criticism*, Occasional Paper 7 (Sydney: Local Consumption Publications, 1985).
Wills, D. 'Post/Card/Match/Book/*Envois*/Derrida', *SubStance*, 43 (1984), pp. 19–38.
Wills, D. 'Prosthesis: an introduction to textual artifice', *Southern Review*, 17, 1 (1984), pp. 59–67.
Wills, D. 'Post(e(s)', in E. Grosz *et al.* (eds), *Futur*Fall: Excursions into Postmodernity* (Sydney: Power Institute Publications, 1986).
Winston, M. 'The quest for Pynchon', *Twentieth Century Literature*, 21, 3 (1975), pp. 278–87.
Wittgenstein, L. *Tractatus Logico-Philosophicus* (London: Routledge & Kegan Paul, 1961).
Wittgenstein, L. *Zettel* (Oxford: Blackwell, 1967).
Wittgenstein, L. *Philosophical Investigations* (Oxford: Blackwell, 1968).
Wittgenstein, L. *Letters to C. K. Ogden*, ed. trans. G. H. von Wright (Oxford/London: Blackwell/Routledge and Kegan Paul, 1973).
Wolfley, L. C. 'Repression's rainbow: the presence of Norman O. Brown in Pynchon's big novel', *PMLA*, 92 (1978), pp. 873–9. Reprinted in Pearce, pp. 99–123.
Young, D. R. 'Acoustic guitar construction', in T. Wheeler (ed.), *The Guitar Book* (New York: Harper & Row, 1974), pp. 46–53.

Index

Abish, Walter
  'Crossing the Great Void', 193, 195–6, 204
active/passive, 141
address, 68, 70, 114–15
adestination, 11, 54, 68, 71*ff*, 81
  under question, 150
aleatoriness, 115
allegory, 15–16, 58, 99–101, 195
  departure from, 197
  v. pretext, 206
alphabet, 16–17, 124
Althusser, Louis, 154
anagram, 139
analogy, *see* parody/analogy/satire
animate/inanimate, 55, 61, 68
  and accident/intention, 168*ff*
apocalypse, 17, 73, 197, 211–21
athetical, the, 90*ff*
author(ship)
  biography, 133
  death of (Barthes), 5, 135–7
  as function (Foucault), 136–7
  pre-critical concept of, 2, 6, 16, 37, 112
  as signature (Derrida), 137–40
  speculations on Pynchon, 2–3, 133*ff*
autobiography, 131–60

bad ear, 159, 160
Baedeker, Karl, 9, 154
bar, *see* hymen
Barthelme, Donald, 134
Barthes, Roland, 2, 5, 9, 15, 51, 56, 57, 86, 113, 117, 124, 125, 132, 141–2
  on authorship, 135–7
  on photography, 152
Bateson, Gregory, 90–1, 100
Beatles, the, 100, 110
because- and in-order-to motives (Schutz), 90
Bennett, David, 56–7

binary oppositions/dualities, 3, 17, 37, 67, 75, 81, 86, 88, 169
  avoidance of, 91–2
  flip-flop, 61, 82, 89, 92, 168
  v. spacing, 10, 52*ff*
  yo-yo, 94, 165, 171
  see under individual binaries
Bloom, Harold, 14–15
  on Byron the Bulb, 15
body-without-organs (Deleuze and Guattari), 204
both/and, *see* either/or
book-missile, 211–12
bookmatching, 11–13, 186, 188, 214
Bowie, David, 125, 163
Brecht, Bertolt, 23, 125
Breton, André, 125
bricolage, 8
Brome, Vincent, 149
Burroughs, William, 125
Byron the Bulb, *see* Bloom, Harold

Calvino, Italo
  Invisible Cities, 193–7, 203, 204
Carroll, Lewis, 188
  see also paedophilia
catastrophe, 218
cause *v.* probability, 87
characterological readings, 33
chaos, *see* order
cheque/ (signing/bouncing), 138–9, 158–9
  see also signature
cinema, 38–45, 53, 110, 194
  see also Roeg
  see also projection
citationality, 9, 32, 52, 74, 114, 168
Cixous, Hélène, 13, 197
Clerc, Charles, 4, 6, 38
closure, 13
comparative literature, 83
  see also bookmatching
concept(ual) objects, 58
  see also material typonymy

233

confession, 165, 178, 186
  and writing, 179–80
connotation and metalanguage, 57
consciousness, 49, 199
conspiracy theories, 51
  and randomness, 177–8
contemporary literary theory (CLT), 2*ff*, 112
copy *v*. original, 131–2, 147, 170
  see also stencil(isation)
correspondence theories, 11
Courier's Tragedy, The, 68–70, 84, 110, 113–14
Cowart, David, 38, 47
Crying of Lot 49, The, 67–84, 86–103, 108–26
  chapter beginnings and endings of, 109–11
  as moral/ethical dilemma, 88, 97–9
  as quest/allegory, 99–100
  re sameness and difference, 96–7
  as the search for origin, 92–4
  standardised reading of, 111
cryptography, 189
cybernetics, *see* humanism

de Lauretis, Teresa
  Alice Doesn't, 187*ff*
deferral, 13, 57–8, 68, 75, 95–6, 145, 149, 169
  and absence, 181
  see also difference/differance
degree–zero, 23, 38
Derrida, Jacques
  'Of an Apocalyptic Tone', 211*ff*
  critique of Searle, 53, 74
  Dissemination, 186, 202
  double science, 206
  'Double Session', 17
  'Envois', 68*ff*, 113, 119, 214
  'Facteur de la vérité, Le', 214
  as fiction, 112
  Fins de l'homme, Les, 211*ff*
  Glas, 5, 113, 138, 211
  Of Grammatology, 112*ff*
  'Limited inc . . .', 92
  'No Apocalypse', 211*ff*
  on nuclear war, 211*ff*
  at Oxford, 73
  Positions, 116
  reception in France, 219
  on signature, 137–40
  'Signature Event Context', 138
  Signsponge, 138
  Speech and Phenomena, 13
  'Tympan', 113
desire, masculine, 194
desire machine, 175, 204
destination, *see* origin
destinerrance, 90, 114
  see also adestination, error
diachronic/synchronic, 149
difference/differance, 8, 10, 68, 79, 115, 119, 132, 189
  in feminism, 199–201, 203
  and sameness/identity, 96–7, 132, 145, 165
  sexual, 198, 208
digital, the, 75–82
disarmament, 217
dissemination, 14, 80, 113, 132, 186
dissolution/solution, 62
double science, 206
double-bind, 89, 91
dropout, 132
dualities, *see* binary oppositions
DT's/*dt* (*delirium tremens*/time differential), 78*ff*, 92, 111, 157

either/or *v*. both/and, 75, 90*ff*
elect *v*. preterite, 3, 86, 220
empirical readings
  indeterminacy of, 48–9
encyclopaedic criticism, 3
entropy, 76, 80
  entropy-based criticism, 3, 33, 37, 50
'Entropy', 145
epistemology, 5
erasure, 13, 57, 62, 75, 117, 124
error
  etymology of the term, 114
  as found in *Of Grammatology*, 116–21
  and meaning, 122
  systems/taxonomy of, 115
  textual, 112*ff*

ethics, *see* moral/ethical
événement-limite, 217
eventialisation (Foucault), 199
excluded middle, 55, 61, 75, 88, 90–1, 108
exegetical drive, 1
existentialism, 98
  vécu, 204

Fall, der, 163, 167, 168
fall, 170, 178, 183, 208
  final(?), 221
  prepositional possibilities, 218–19
  see also apocalypse
falsifiability (Popper), 108
fantasy *v.* the 'real', 38–48
feminism(s), 187*ff*
Forrester, John, 133
fortida, 71
Foucault, Michel, 13, 188, 193, 197–200, 203
  on author-function, 136–7
Freud, Sigmund, 15, 71, 72, 83, 126
  fetish, 181
  fortida, 71
  Interpretation of Dreams, The, 148
  on slips, 116, 122
  on transference, 133, 148–9
Friedman, Alan, 87

game, 98
  see also play
Gauguin, Paul, 140
gender, 71, 153
  politics, 196–7
Genette, Gérard, 56
genre, 215
goals, 95
Godard, Jean-Luc, 156
Gödel, Kurt, 121
graft, 179
Grail, the, 99
grammatology, 7, 112, 116*ff*, 157, 187, 207
  see also telegrammatology
Gravity's Rainbow, 23–63, 211–21
  alternative reading of Slothrop, 48

characterological reading, 24–31
and cinema, 38–45, 53
and Derrida on apocalypse, 211–21
linguistic marks in, 33–7
gynesis, 187*ff*

Hartman, Geoffrey, 13
hebephrenia, *see* paranoia
Hegel, G.F.W., 189
hegemony, 190–1
Heidegger, Martin, 71, 72, 83
hermeneutic bind, 68
historical criticism, 3
Hite, Molly, 6, 13, 86, 204
human subjectivity, 62
  v. other theories of the self, 156
  phenomenological subject, 136
  see also consciousness
humanism, 14, 17, 51, 98, 171
  and post-humanism/cybernetics, 81
  and technologism, 62
hymen, 186, 190–1, 203, 207
  as bar in '**A V**', 208
  Derrida's, 201
  of difference, 203
  Jardine's, 202

ID, 146, 159
identity, 146*ff*
  v. non-identity, 154
  see also difference/differance
inanimate, *see* animate
ink, 84, 191
intertextuality/plagiarism, 38, 154
invagination, 201, 207
Irigaray, Luce, 197
italicisation, 118*ff*
iterability/iteration, 138
  connection with error, 114
  see also citationality

Jakobson, Roman, 56
Jardine, Alice
  Gynesis, 187*ff*
John the Baptist, 215
Jones, Ernest, 149
jouissance, 191

Joyce, James, 2
   see also Ulysses

Kant, Immanuel, 215
Kermode, Frank, 5, 6, 15
Kolodny, Annette, 86
Kristeva, Julia, 13, 197

labyrinths, 92*ff*
Lacan, Jacques, 71, 74, 133, 181, 193
Laing, R.D., 90
lapsus, *see* error
leakage, 151
Leverenz, David, 23, 51, 204
Lévi-Strauss, Claude, 8, 193
Levine, George, 204
literary criticism
   on Pynchon, 1*ff*
Lodge, David, 56
logocentrism, 5–7, 17, 37, 79, 81, 145, 194
   see also presence, voice
lover, the, 70*ff*, 74, 149–50

Mailer, Norman, 144
Mallarmé, Stéphane, 187
Manutius, Aldus, 118
mapping, 60, 71
material grapheme, 164
material typonymy, 6, 53*ff*
   examples of, 60–1
mathematics, 97, 110
Maxwell, James Clerk, 76–7, 92, 97, 108
McHale, Brian, 5–6, 15, 45–6, 49–52, 57, 60
meaning, theories of, 141
   'author' as, 144
   diagram of, 155
   difference as, 155–6
   metaphysical *v.* semantic, 155
   transference as, 147
Mehlman, Jeffrey, 219
Mendelson, Edward, 47
mention *v.* use, 52, 168
metacommunications, 91
metafiction/parody, 57, 62, 80
metalepsis, 16

metaphoric *v.* literal, 61, 77–9
   science metaphors, 87
metaphysical reductionism, 86
Metz, Christian, 193
mise en abyme, 50, 57–9, 73, 79
misprint, *see* error
monster *v.* treasure, 94, 100
Moore, Thomas, 2, 86
moral/ethical, 14, 17, 37, 50, 87*ff*
   and signifying practice, 89
   see also semio-ethics
'Mortality and Mercy in Vienna', 158
mystique/politique, 96–7
myth, 132
naming the father, 73, 125–6, 220
narrative voice, 3, 6–7, 37, 46–7, 53
narratology, 215
Nietzsche, Friedrich, 9, 58, 201
nuclear war, 211–21
   effect on 'deconstructive' criticism, 219–21
   as textual construction, 216–17

ontology, 4, 5
open pedagogy, 207
order *v.* chaos, 3, 86
orders of discourse, 50
origin/destination, 90
   and centre, 93
   see also adestination
original, *see* copy

paedophilia, 188
   masculine perversions, 188
parable/parabola, 58–60
parergon, 191
paradigmatic series/syntagmatic chain, 56
paranoia/hebephrenia, 3, 59, 61, 68, 87, 100, 111
parergon, 191
Paris, Matthew, 73
parody/analogy/satire, 58–9
parody/metafiction, 57, 62, 80
passive/active, 141
passover, 220
Péguy, Charles, 96
Peters, Daniel, 86

phallocentrism, 194, 197, 198, 207
  see also hegemony
phallogocentrism, 201–2, 205–7
pharmakon, 58
phenomenological writing, 142
Plater, William, 13
Plato/plato, 72ff, 83, 187
  see also pS/PS
plagiarism/intertextuality, 38, 154
play v. seriousness, 9, 92
ploughing, 78–9
poetic function, 56
Poirier, Richard, 57
politique/mystique, 96–7
Popper, Karl, 108
'post hoc ergo propter hoc' fallacy, 56
post-phenomenology, 156
post-rhetorical, the, 6, 17, 50, 54ff, 67, 117
  see also material typonymy
post/posting/postal/postage, 54, 67–84, 108
postage stamp/postmark, 72–3, 83, 101, 124
postcard, 70
postmodernism, 5, 38, 48, 54, 56, 80, 93, 98, 111, 206
poststructuralism, 3, 5, 12, 54, 57, 135, 137, 192, 200
potential difference (V), 178
power
  and knowledge, 200
  and resistance, 149, 165, 197, 200, 203, 221
presence, 4, 7, 12, 13, 145–6, 155
preterite, see elect
pretext(ualisation), 195, 203, 206
  see also allegory
Prince, Gerald, 111
probability v. cause, 87
projection (cinema/prediction), 208
proper name, 207
prosthesis, 76ff, 80–1, 92, 174, 179, 182, 204
Proust, Marcel, 55, 172
pS/PS (plato-Socrates/postscript), 83
psychodontia, 177–8

punctum/puncta, 91, 113ff
  in Barthes, 152
Pütz, Manfred, 87
pyramid, 189

quest, 99–100
Quilligan, Maureen 14–17
quotational frequency
  of passages in Pynchon, 108

Raban, Jonathan, 134
rainbow, see spectrum
Readers' Liberation Movement (Eagleton), 111–12
'real', the, see fantasy
recto/verso, 54
repetition, 164–5, 178
  see also citationality
restance, see trace
resistance, see power
rhetoric, 'Euclidean', 215
Robbe-Grillet, Alain
  La Jalousie, 55–6
Robinson Crusoe, 163
Roeg, Nicolas
  Bad Timing, 193, 197, 199ff
Rousseau, Jean-Jacques, 9

Sanders, Scott, 50–1
Sartre, Jean-Paul
  vécu, 204
satire, see parody/analogy/satire
Saussure, Ferdinand de, 101, 117, 139, 141, 145
scar, 200–1, 205
Schlemihl(hood), 173–4
Schutz, Alfred
  on motives, 90
  see also phenomenological writing
scientific writing, 143–4
scientifico-militaro-political apparatus
  and literature, 217
Searle, John, 53, 74
seduction, and storytelling, 101, 175
semantics, see meaning
semio-ethics, 90, 125
seriousness, see play

sexual(ity), 173–5
Siegel, Mark, 23
signature, 113, 124, 126, 188, 194
   as theory of 'authorship', 137–40
signifier/signified, 50–1, 79, 88, 90, 148–50, 163–4
   absolute/transcendental signified, 6, 89, 164, 169–70, 183, 187, 198, 214
   and ethics, 89–90
   materiality of signifier, 171
   pure signifier, 163
   signification, as currency, 102
Simmon, Scott, 38, 113
slips, see error
Slow Learner, 'Introduction' to, 131–60
'Small Rain', The, 143, 156
Socrates, 72*ff*, 83
   see also pS/PS
solution/dissolution, 62
sorting, 68, 76, 108, 114
spacing, 12*ff*
   see also binary oppositions
spectrum/rainbow, 92
speech *v.* writing, 4, 17, 115, 118
   see also logocentrism
Spivak, Gayatri, 116*ff*, 207
standard reading, 86, 108
stencil(isation), 167, 181
storytelling, 99
   see also seduction
structuralist linguistics, 145
   see also Saussure
stylistics/technicism, 52
subject/object, of theory, 112
substance *v.* rhetoric, see material typonymy
supplement, 58, 170
synchronic/diachronic, 149
syntagmatic chain/paradigmatic series, 56

Tanner, Tony, 5, 6, 15, 49, 61
technicism/stylistics, 52
telegram, discourse of, 112
telegrammatology, 108–26
   outlined schematically, 125–6

teleology, 171
   see also origin/destination
testicles, 191
thematic readings, 33
Tolkien, J.R.R., 99
trace/*restance*, 167, 173, 179, 183, 200
   see also differance, writing
transfer(ence), 131–60, 182
   distinction from difference, 151
   formally analysed, 150–2
   rebus, 187
   as theory of meaning, 147
transferential interface, 77–8
transmission theory, 157
treasure *v.* monster, 94, 100
Troyes, Chrétien de, 99
typographical number theory (TNT), 121
typography, 5, 33–7
   see also error
typonymy, see material typonymy

Ulmer, Gregory, 12, 15, 58, 189, 207
Ulysses, 55, 211
'Under the Rose', 154
'unum nomen unum nominatum' doctrine of, 101
use *v.* mention, 52, 168

V., 163–83, 186–208
   episodes in past, 181–2
vector, 183
verso/recto, 54
Vheissu, re 'woman', 204–6
viens, 215*ff*
voice, 6, 7, 10
   in confession, 178
   see also speech *v.* writing

W.A.S.T.E., 78, 83, 90
Weisenburger, Steven, 47
Williamson, Dugald, 135–6
Wittgenstein, Ludwig, 9, 13, 116, 121, 165
woman-in-effect, 188, 197
women, empirical/real historical, 189*ff*, 206–7

'woman'/'women', 186*ff*
  as fiction, 189, 191
  representation of, 191*ff*
wooden leg, *see* prosthesis
writing
  Derridean concept of, 5–7, 10, 68, 75, 112, 137, 165, 178, 201

writing position, 92, 132, 140
writing practice, 1
  see also grammatology

Young, David Russell, 11

zero degree, 23, 38

GPSR Compliance

The European Union's (EU) General Product Safety Regulation (GPSR) is a set of rules that requires consumer products to be safe and our obligations to ensure this.

If you have any concerns about our products, you can contact us on

ProductSafety@springernature.com

In case Publisher is established outside the EU, the EU authorized representative is:

Springer Nature Customer Service Center GmbH
Europaplatz 3
69115 Heidelberg, Germany

www.ingramcontent.com/pod-product-compliance
Lightning Source LLC
Chambersburg PA
CBHW031519100426
42873CB00013B/138